The Unchosen Life
Tori Day

About the author

Tori lives in West Yorkshire with her husband, her grown-up step daughter and her babies, aged five and two.

When she struggled to get pregnant with her first daughter, she found herself reaching for a pen and paper. Her journal became her companion throughout her journey to conceive and eventually formed the basis for her first book, *Warrior*.

Infertility is a subject close to Tori's heart, and she continues to be an active campaigner for better support for those struggling with infertility.

The Unchosen Life explores what comes next for those who don't manage to get pregnant, stay pregnant or have babies. Tori believes infertility should be talked about more and understood more. She hopes that this book may give the many women who don't get the happy ending they long for, something to relate to.

www.toridayblog.wordpress.com
Twitter @toridaywrites
Instagram @toridaywarrior

Copyright © 2021 Tori Day
All rights reserved.

Published by Tori Day 2021
West Yorkshire, United Kingdom

No parts of this publication may be reproduced, stored in a retrieval system, or transmitted in any form or by any means, electronic, mechanical, photocopying, recording, or otherwise, without the prior written permission of the copyright owner.

This book is sold subject to the condition that it shall not, by way of trade or otherwise, be lent, resold, hired out, or otherwise circulated without the publisher's prior consent in any form of binding or cover other than that in which it is published and without a similar condition including this condition being imposed on the subsequent purchaser. Under no circumstances may any part of this book be photocopied for resale.

While every effort has been made to trace the owners of copyright material reproduced herein, the publisher would like to apologise for any omissions and will be pleased to incorporate missing acknowledgements in any further editions.

Chapter 1

January 2018

Clara checked for her passport in her shoulder bag. It was still there. The same place it had been five minutes ago and the same place it would be when she checked it again in five minutes' time. She looked at the departure board again. Bangkok, 16:40, no gate announced yet.

There was a slight tremble in her fingers as she picked up her coffee cup. She was torn between finishing her drink quickly, so she was ready to move as soon as the gate was announced, and making it last so she had something to do with her hands. She fiddled with her phone. No new messages or notifications in the last few minutes. She opened Facebook and was greeted with a photo of her soon-to-be ex-husband, Christopher. He was in a bar with a crowd of people she recognised as his colleagues from work. She closed it down quickly and pondered de-friending him. But then he wouldn't see the photos she'd take on her life-changing trip. Not that she cared about that, really. But, you know. Instead, she opened WhatsApp. *Jess was typing*. The new message appeared with a blue dot.

Jess: Are you nearly there yet? I'm sooo jealous. Don't forget me on your adventures! Love you ooo

Clara smiled. She was nowhere near nearly there yet. She was two hours into her thirty-three-hour trip. Manchester to Heathrow, Heathrow to Bangkok, Bangkok to Sydney, Sydney to Cairns. Not a trip you'd want to do with young kids, she reminded herself, as she watched a family of four walk by. The mum was handing a bag of crisps to a toddler in a pushchair to try and placate her as she squirmed about, pulling at the straps. The dad had a tiny baby strapped to his chest and was effortlessly pulling along a family-sized suitcase. They looked tired, but happy. She imagined the couple later, on a sunny balcony, sharing a bottle of wine while both babies slept peacefully. They'd share stories about the funny things their little one had said that day and congratulate themselves on their happy lives.

Stop it, she scolded herself. She didn't know the first thing about them. Maybe they were looking at her enviously, unburdened by children and all their paraphernalia. She could read her book on the plane, watch a film, snooze when she fancied it, eat her meal with two hands and no interruptions.

Her phone buzzed again.

Mum: I'm proud of you, darling. Text me when you get there. xxx

Clara slid her hand inside her bag again and felt the reassuring shape of her passport. The departure board flashed and updated. Bangkok, gate six. Her stomach lurched and she decided to label the feeling as excitement.

She drained her coffee cup and put on her backpack. This involved placing it on the chair behind her and squatting as she slid her arms through the straps and did up the waist and chest buckles. She straightened up and leaned forward slightly so as not to topple backwards. Perhaps she shouldn't have bought all those guidebooks. She could have bought just the first one she needed and picked the others up along the way. Is that what backpackers did, she wondered? She slung her shoulder-bag across her chest and followed signs to the gate. Backpackers. Yes, she was a thirty-six-year-old backpacker. Not a thirty-six-year-old mum, not a wife – or at least, not for much longer – and not in gainful employment. She was officially a free spirit. Her stomach lurched again. Definitely excitement.

Clara blinked a few times. Her eyes were dry and scratchy from the air-conditioning on the plane. She tried to focus on the romcom on the screen in front of her, but she was restless. She took her headphones out and glanced around.

'I'm going to Brisbane,' the woman next to her announced.

Clara took her in: powdery skin; unnaturally curly, platinum hair; pink lipstick that bled into the lines around her mouth. She smelt of expensive perfume.

'I'm visiting my daughter and my new grandson.' The woman beamed at Clara. 'Haven't met him yet.' She produced a photo from her handbag. Clara didn't have much option but to take it and have a look. There he was. A round-cheeked, blond-haired, blue-eyed boy, grinning at the camera.

'Aww, he's lovely. Congratulations.' She passed the photo back.

'My daughter married an Aussie and moved there. I was devastated, but I'm staying with them for a month and will be able to look after him when they go out, and have him all to myself.'

'That's great.' Clara smiled at her. At what point can I put my headphones back in without being rude, she wondered? The woman was grinning down at the photo. Clara sighed inwardly and asked, 'How old is he?'

'Six months. Do you have any children?'

Clara felt a familiar twist in her gut. 'No.' She took a deep breath. 'I can't have them.'

'Oh, I'm sorry, I didn't mean...' The woman looked down at her hands, clearly embarrassed.

'It's okay. Wasn't meant to be, I suppose.' Clara wondered why she was the one doing the reassuring.

'You never know, dear. You're still young.' The woman put a hand on her arm and nodded sagely. Clara gave a tight smile, then used the opportunity to put her headphones back in and return to the film. Her eyes were no longer dry and scratchy.

The plane bumped down onto the runway in Bangkok, thirty minutes ahead of schedule. Clara connected to the airport Wi-Fi and checked Facebook. No sign of

Christopher in her feed this time. Jess had posted a collage of pictures of the two of them together over the years, with the message: Can't believe my bestie is going away FOR A WHOLE YEAR!! Have an amazing time, Clara. Love you (kissing face). Clara smiled and hastily typed a comment, then scrolled on. A friend from her old work had got a puppy, someone she used to go to school with was running a marathon for charity and someone she met once at a party was very cross about someone else's decision not to vaccinate her children. All caught up, then. She considered an airport selfie with something like #happytravelling or #newlifehereicome, then messaged her mum instead to update her on progress.

The terminal was a hive of activity, people scurrying this way and that, a melting pot of nationalities, Tannoy announcements repeated in different languages, screens blinking and flashing with arrival and departure times. Everything was too loud and too bright. Clara's limbs ached and she longed to climb into her soft king-size bed with Egyptian cotton sheets. She spotted some reclining seats that looked like sun-loungers, facing the floor-to-ceiling window that ran the length of one wall. She plonked herself down on one next to a Thai man with an eye-mask who was snoring softly. She had an hour until boarding before the next leg of the journey started. She set an alarm on her phone and closed her eyes.

The humidity hit her as she stepped out of the airport doors in Cairns. Her hair started to frizz almost instantly. She'd have to get it braided like Monica from *Friends* in *The One Where They go to Barbados*. Sweat had started to bead on her upper lip and she wiped it away with the back of her hand. Looking for the bus stop would be the sensible thing to do – she was on a budget – but the line of taxis was just too tempting. She couldn't face any more delays to arriving at her destination, having a shower and being able to stretch out on a bed. One last tiny leg of her journey, and she'd be there. And it'd be alright. The driver in the taxi at the front of the queue nodded when she gave him the name of the hostel, and she collapsed in the back seat. The air-con was on and the leather was cool against her legs. She breathed a sigh of relief. She'd made it to the other side of the world on her own; she was really doing this.

'Where have you come from, darl'?'

'England.'

'Crikey. Long trip!' He smiled at her in the rearview mirror. He had kind eyes and she had a sudden urge to tell him her whole story.

Instead, she just smiled and said, 'It certainly was.'

Half an hour later, they were pulling up in a busy shopping street, outside a modern-looking building with a mural of a woman and an octopus on the wall. Clara knew from her careful planning that Cairns esplanade and the lagoon were only a few minutes' walk away. It was 4pm here, but her body clock was all mixed up. She thanked the driver and made her way into the brightly coloured reception. Her back ached with the weight of her backpack. She'd never wanted a shower more in her life.

She straightened her top, tucked her hair behind her ears and approached the reception desk. A plump woman with an impressive cleavage greeted her. A strand of the woman's hair was caught in a breeze from the fan on her desk; Clara wanted to tuck it back into the clip it had escaped from.

'Hi, I have a reservation. It's Clara Davis – erm, Ellison.'

The woman tapped away at her screen and frowned. Clara's grip on her backpack tightened and her stomach lurched unpleasantly. Please tell me you have my booking, she urged silently.

'We have a space in a mixed dorm…with use of the communal bathroom…' She clicked her mouse.

'Erm, no. I booked a female-only dorm with an en suite.' Sweat prickled Clara's armpits. She may be a backpacker, but 'communal bathroom' was a step too far on the first stop of the journey.

'Sorry, there's none – Oh wait, there is an empty dorm with an en suite. I could put you in there if you like, but you'd be on your own.'

Clara let go of a breath and released her grip on her backpack strap. 'Yes, please. I'll take it.'

She dragged herself up two flights of stairs, legs aching, back sodden with sweat, and fiddled with the key in the lock. It finally clicked and the door sprang open.

Clara took in her surroundings. A blue plastic-looking floor with a paler blue rug and a lime green wall. It reminded her of one of those trendy conference centres that smelt like coffee and pastries and had words in swirly script on the walls, such as 'thrive', 'learn', 'collaborate', 'grow'. There were no words on the wall here and the metal-framed bunk-beds and the smell of bleach, in place of coffee, brought her bluntly back to where she was. An open window overlooked some shops and the busy street below, bringing in the smell of barbecues. She threw her backpack on the nearest bed and crossed the room to open the door to the bathroom. A shower over a plastic tray, with a shower curtain and a small sink and toilet were crammed into a space about the size of her downstairs loo at home. The shower curtain smelt of damp and there was mildew on the bottom corner.

The mildew was too much. All the angst and self doubt she'd been keeping at bay for the thirty-three hour trip took its claim. She sank to her knees and sobbed. A dormitory to herself had sounded good and now she felt faintly ridiculous. *What am I doing here? In a youth hostel in Australia, by myself?* Still crying and hiccupping, she found her towel and shower gel, stripped off her sweaty clothes and stepped into the tiny shower. Her tears mingled with the water from the weak spray. As she washed off the journey, her sobbing subsided and she started to get a hold of herself. She put a clean T-shirt on and fell asleep on the nearest bed.

Chapter 2

March 2012

'So, I have news,' Clara said, as she settled herself across from Jess in the steam room.

'You got the promotion?' Jess said.

'I did, actually, but that's not what I meant.'

'Oh, well congratulations, anyway. You're doing a bungee jump?'

'What? No, it's not a guessing game. Shall I tell you?'

'Wait. One more guess – you're pregnant?'

'No, but closer.' Clara lifted one thigh at a time off the tiled surface. 'We're going to start trying.'

'Really? I thought you wanted to wait? Hang on, I can't see you through all this steam.' Jess moved across the room and sat next to Clara. Her top lip glistened and beads of sweat had formed on her forehead.

'It was in my plan to wait another year, but Christopher suggested it and straightaway I thought, yes. It feels right, you know?'

'Wow. Well, great. That's exciting.' Jess smiled. 'You'll still come on spa days with me when you have kids though, right? And nights out?'

'Of course I will. Christopher will look after the kids.'

'How many are you going to have?'

'Two, I thought. A girl first, then a boy.'

'You know you don't get to choose? Even you can't plan that, Clar.'

'I can try,' Clara said. 'God, it's hot in here. I might go for a swim to cool off.' Her thighs were slick against the dark blue mosaic tiles and her nostrils burnt when she breathed in through them.

'You should try the plunge pool.'

'I don't know. I might have a heart attack,' Clara said.

'Go on. I will if you will.' Jess knew she couldn't resist a challenge.

'Let's do it,' Clara said.

She had to stay stooped over as she left the steam room as it was too hot to stand up to full height, and trying to do so made her dizzy. She remembered a scene from a *Point Horror* book she'd read as a teenager, where a girl got locked in a steam room. She'd dropped to the floor to breathe in the coolest air, then managed to escape by using the underwire from her bikini to pick the lock. Clara shuddered, despite the heat.

The ice-cold plunge pool was right next to the steam room and it did actually look inviting from her sweaty point of view. It was supposed to cleanse and reinvigorate the body and sharpen the mind. Just about big enough for two people, it had a steel ladder at one side and was deep enough to cover your head.

Jess dipped her toe in. 'You first,' she said.

Clara took a deep breath. She was going to have to go for it. She counted to three and then jumped straight in – no toe test. A thousand tiny needles stabbed at her body and her chest constricted so she couldn't catch her breath.

'Oh…my…God,' she managed. Then, 'Get in here.'

Jess sat on the edge and dangled her feet in. 'Argh, it makes my bones ache.'

'You can't inch in, that's torture. It's called a *plunge* pool for a reason. Now plunge!'

Jess pushed herself off the side and slid in.

'Oh my GOD!' she gasped.

Clara laughed. 'Yep. It's actually not so bad once you get used to it.' The needles had stopped and she did feel strangely invigorated, but not enough to loiter any longer. She climbed up the ladder and Jess followed. Her skin was now goose-fleshed, all sweat beads washed away in the plunge pool for the next people.

'I'm going to do a few lengths before our treatments.' Clara nodded towards the pool.

'Okay, I'll be here.' Jess sat down on a sun-lounger and picked up a magazine from a table. Clara envied her friend's ability to stay slim while eating what she wanted and not doing any exercise. Her long legs were stretched out in front of her, pale skin with a smattering of freckles on her thighs. Her black swimming costume showed off her narrow waist and accentuated her modest cleavage.

Clara pushed herself to swim fast enough to get her heart rate up as she moved up and down the pool. Satisfied they'd decided to start trying – and she'd told Jess, so it was now official – she started calculating dates in her head. She'd taken her last pill two weeks ago, so technically she could get pregnant any time now. If it was this month, the baby would be due in December. *Hmm, do I want a Christmas baby? Maybe we should wait a month. But then, perhaps January isn't the best month for a birthday, either. It's all cold and dark and depressing, with everyone skint and fat after Christmas. Wait two months, then?*

She'd always been conventional. Fitting the mould, rather than breaking it. She'd done reasonably well at school, she was conscientious and the teachers liked her. She'd had a group of close friends, and a satisfying social life. She'd gone on holidays, had boyfriends, suffered some heartaches, which were eased by ice cream, back-to-back episodes of *Friends* and long, tearful phone calls with Jess. The usual stuff for anyone growing up in the '90s. She'd gone to university, enjoyed three years of house-sharing with friends, drinking too much, eating too many takeaways and more mini dramas involving the opposite sex. She'd met Christopher (never Chris), and after graduating, they'd moved to London and started their graduate training programmes, while renting a tiny flat in a less-than-desirable area. It didn't matter; they were 'young professionals' – basically, students with some cash. Jess had lived around the corner and the student lifestyle continued, but now, instead of McDonald's and KFC, it was Café Rouge and Pizza Express. Christopher had popped the question on a weekend mini-break in Copenhagen, in front of the mermaid statue and a group of Japanese tourists. Clara had been embarrassed at the public nature of it, and a bit irritated that he hadn't picked a quieter, more private moment, but overall she'd been delighted and, of course, she'd accepted.

They'd tied the knot and moved back up north, with their graduate traineeships complete, and good jobs and reasonably healthy pay packets secured. All was well. They were happy. They'd settled into their routine of Friday drinks after work, Sunday pub lunches, exotic holidays, friends' hen and stag parties. Things were good. Then, as convention dictates, they'd decided to try for a baby.

'I think we should go for it,' Christopher had said one morning, a few weeks' back, over his toast and jam.

'Hmm?' Clara looked up from her Kindle. 'Go for what?'

'I think we should have a baby.'

She put the Kindle down. 'Have a baby?'

Christopher was smiling at her, waiting for her to say more. As Clara was thinking through all the rational reasons for it being a sensible suggestion, something stirred inside her. *Yes,* she thought, *yes.* She imagined breaking the news she was pregnant to her mum and Jess. She imagined her neat figure with a perfect little bump, the spare room converted to a nursery. She imagined holding her baby, joining the pram brigade in the local coffee shop. She pictured family holidays, splashing about with a toddler in the swimming pool, she and Christopher laughing as their offspring got ice cream all over their face and grinned at them. They could give a child a home full of stability and security, full of love.

I want that.

She beamed at Christopher, blue eyes meeting brown. 'Let's do it.'

Later, over their Caesar salads, Clara told Jess her predicament about due dates, and when to actually start trying, and asked for her thoughts. Jess laughed and suggested Clara draw up a spreadsheet.

'That's actually a good idea,' Clara said.

'No, I was joking! Clar, you can't plan this down to that level of detail. You're going to have to chill and let nature take its course.'

'Right, I can do that. Of course.' Clara wasn't sure who she was trying to convince.

And there it began. The beginning of the end. Given the charmed life she'd led so far, Clara naively assumed this would just happen. The pieces would slot into place, naturally and effortlessly. She'd taken the pill as an effective contraception for the last ten years and it hadn't let her down. So when she stopped, she'd get pregnant, right? Well, wrong actually, as it happened.

Chapter 3

January 2018

Clara jolted awake at the sound of laughter from outside the door. Voices faded into the distance as the happy gathering continued down the hallway. She rubbed her eyes and reached for her phone. It was 8pm, but she hardly registered the time as there was a message from Christopher. She sat up. Without giving herself time to think she slid the screen open.

Christopher: I know we said we weren't going to stay in touch, but I just wanted to say I hope you got there safely. I miss you. x

She set the phone down on the bed and nudged it away with her foot, putting as much distance between herself and the phone as possible. *He misses me?*

She stood up and made her way over to the window. The evening crowd was gearing up, the street outside a mêlée of excitement and high jinx. The smell of barbecues hit her, causing her stomach to growl. She watched a couple, hand in hand, browsing a menu at a restaurant opposite. *He misses me?* She shook her head. A group of friends were laughing and joking, high-fiving and back-slapping their way down the street – the general buzz of people going about their lives and enjoying themselves. *Okay, forget Christopher for now. I can be one of them. I can do that.* She pulled on some shorts, threw her guidebook, phone, purse and lip balm in her shoulder bag and made her way out onto the street.

She crossed over to the restaurant she could see from her room and examined the menu. Lobster bisque, clam chowder, steak tartare. Inside there were tablecloths and couples. Clara edged away. Perhaps she'd grab a sandwich and go sit on a bench, or, even better, the beach. She consulted her guidebook and set off in the general direction of the Coral Sea. Before long she spotted the silver fish on steel poles that she'd seen pictures of, and knew she'd found the lagoon – the swimming pool right by the seafront. She located the source of the barbecue smell; there were groups of people, some sitting cross-legged on the grass, some lying stretched out on their backs, hands behind heads. Picnic blankets were spread out in an array of prints, and burgers and sausages were being placed in bread rolls and passed around.

He misses me? She squashed the thought down, telling herself to carry on. This was 'The Big Trip'. The one where she put her life back together and figured out how to be happy. You know, that one. She kept walking. Past the barbecues. Women and a few men jumped about wearing various shades of Lycra. Their sweaty bodies moved in time to music, hips swinging and right arms lassoing some imaginary thing in the distance. Clara recognised the moves from her own Zumba class. She pasted on a smile when one of the Lycra-clad women caught her eye as she passed, and then made her way round the edge of the pool, past more people enjoying themselves, and onto the beach. Slipped off her flip-flops. The sand felt warm under her feet as she walked towards the sea. She thought of photos she'd seen on Instagram, of people on idyllic beaches jumping up in the air, arms flung wide. Perhaps she could do that too, to show just how much fun she was having. She could post it on Facebook for Christopher to see. That would require someone to take the photo though; it wouldn't work as a selfie. She hastily snapped a picture of herself with the sea and sky in the background. That'd do. The water made her jump as the tide came in and covered her feet. It was cooler than she'd expected, but not unpleasant. She imagined it healing her, taking away the pain of the last six years. As if that's all it took. Unfortunately this wasn't a film; real life doesn't tend to be that neat. The jet lag was giving the whole experience a surreal feeling, as though she wasn't really here. She wasn't settled into her surroundings somehow.

As Clara walked along the shore, she felt self-conscious, dangling her flip-flops from one hand with forced carelessness. Her head throbbed with a nagging headache, and her stomach protested again. Time to head back up the beach and into the shopping streets to find something to eat. She looked guiltily at McDonald's. It was approximately ten years since she'd eaten a McDonald's sober. A few after a night out, maybe, due to lack of other options. It didn't seem right to come halfway round the world and get a Big Mac as her first meal. But: free Wi-Fi. She could get something quickly and catch up on what was happening at home at the same time, then disappear safely back to her room and start her adventures properly tomorrow. She looked from left to right as if someone she knew might appear and scold her, then ducked in the door. She glanced at the message from Christopher and typed out a hasty reply.

Clara: I'm here safely. x

She didn't want to be responsible for him wondering if the plane had crashed or if she'd been kidnapped when she arrived and was now being held hostage somewhere, being fed rice with maggots in. That had happened in a film they'd once seen about an British backpacker in Australia – but that was in the outback, and this was the East Coast. Clara didn't want to encourage regular contact, either. That wouldn't do.

She texted Jess next.

Clara: I'm in Maccy Ds x

Jess: No way. What are you doing there?? o

The 'love' at the end of the message in place of a kiss gave Clara a pang for home and her best friend.

Clara: I was hungry and didn't want to have a sad dine-for-one meal in a restaurant. x

Jess: Behave yourself, nothing sad about enjoying a meal on your own. You're an independent traveller. o

Clara: Well, I'm not enjoying this meal. It tastes like cardboard. Why is it so much better when you're drunk?? I was lured in with the promise of free Wi-Fi but I can't get it to connect, so I can't even post my selfie on the beach to show how strong and independent I am. x

Jess: You are strong and independent. I wouldn't dare do what you're doing. o

Clara: Or wouldn't be stupid enough to take off to the other side of the world by yourself when your marriage has just broken down. x

Jess: Right, enough with the self-pity. You've done the hard bit. Things can only get better now. No more Maccy Ds! ooo

Clara put her phone back in her bag. Jess was right. She knew her better than anyone. It must be the jet lag. She vowed to start enjoying herself properly tomorrow. Things would definitely feel better after a good night's rest.

The next morning Clara woke up having slept ten hours straight. She stretched and rolled onto her back. She was a little groggy, but all together more human. Sitting up in the bottom bunk, being careful not to bang her head on the bed above, she looked around. Empty bunk-beds, quiet. Okay, 'The Big Trip' starts here. It was time to embrace the backpacker experience. The hostel offered breakfast as part of the deal, so she'd embrace that.

The sun had warmed strips of the floor where it came in through the blinds and she could see dust motes in the air. She followed a warm strip to the bathroom, enjoying the feeling on her feet. Today was a new day and she vowed to stay strong and positive. Taking off to the other side of the world just had to be the right decision.

The water in the shower was lukewarm, which wasn't entirely unwelcome in the stuffy bathroom. The smell of damp was less welcome. She dressed quickly and found her way to the breakfast room – a smallish room with a big wooden table in the middle. It was swarming with people. A girl in hot pants, who couldn't be more than nineteen, was buttering toast at one of the counters. Clara took in her tanned, toned thighs, and glanced down self-consciously at her own pale, neglected ones, in her significantly longer shorts. She felt frumpy, like someone's mum. The irony wasn't lost on her. A group of teenagers, or perhaps they were actually in their twenties, moved effortlessly around each other, grabbing bowls and cartons of cereal, slopping milk on the counter. Clara resisted the urge to reach for a cloth and wipe it up.

'Excuse me, do you know where the coffee is?' she asked one of them. He gestured vaguely in the direction of a jar of Nescafé in the corner. *Oh.* She started opening cupboard doors looking for a mug. The first one was empty; the second had one lone mug left in it, but when she pulled it out, she noticed the tide marks inside. She sighed and took it over to the sink, weaving around bodies and apologising as she went. Now, what to eat? There were rice crispies, cornflakes and cheap white bread. She picked up the carton of cornflakes and recommenced the cupboard search for a bowl, moving around people again and trying not to get in the way. None to be found. Her jaw clenched. She needed her coffee and longed for the peace and quiet of her old kitchen, with the coffee machine and clean Orla Kiely crockery all neatly lined up in the cupboard.

There were some dirty bowls in the sink. She could wash one. She eyed the communal table for a space. There was a space at one end, if she squeezed in next to hot-pants girl and brushed away the crumbs on the table, or she could join a group of boys gathered round an iPad, laughing at some video. Defeated, she put down the cornflakes and mug and left.

Twenty minutes later, she was sitting at a café on the seafront, double espresso and eggs Benedict in front of her. So, she'd failed at the backpacker breakfast, but it was hard to care when she could see the sea, drink lovely coffee and eat perfectly cooked eggs.

The first month passed by as Clara worked her way through the list of things to do and see on her travel itinerary. On the surface she was enjoying herself, once she'd adjusted to the lack of structure. It was a stark contrast to her nine-to-five world of meetings and spreadsheets, though not a completely unwelcome one. And yet... while she took in the sights, it was through the eyes of a person she was trying to be. The photos of her riding in a cable-car over the rainforest, posted on Facebook, which had been 'liked' and commented on, created the illusion of a woman having the time of her life. But when Clara swam in the sea, her mind was full of what might have been. On the beach, she sat on her towel and applied suncream to skin which yearned to be touched, then cast about listlessly for something to do. During a trip to Port Douglas she'd had to hide in the toilets in a café, overcome with emotion, when a woman her age and a small child came in and shared a chocolate milkshake. That was her truth. A truth which wasn't shared on Facebook.

After the first couple of days, two Dutch girls had moved into Clara's room, and she had experienced sleeping in a shared dorm. They'd exchanged pleasantries and it was all fairly uneventful. She hadn't told the girls what led her to be there, opting to stick to the role of carefree traveller. Tonight, she was taking the Greyhound bus down to Airlie beach, where she'd explore the Whitsunday Islands and, she'd decided, make a concerted effort to find some friends.

So, Clara was sitting on a hard bench, backpack by her feet, glancing at her watch in the fading light. The bus was an hour late and her bum was numb. Were they always late? Was it coming? She'd checked at least three or four times that she was at the right bus stop, at the right time. There was a boy to her left, wearing a woven fedora hat and strumming a guitar. She had to suppress a smile at the cliché. A girl sat reading a book on a grass bank above the bus stop. Neither of them looked too concerned about the bus being late. Should she interrupt the girl reading or the boy playing his guitar to voice her concerns?

The boy spoke up, solving her dilemma. 'Don't worry, they're sometimes late. It'll be here soon.'

'Oh, thanks. I was starting to wonder.'

A further twenty minutes of restless waiting and watch-checking and the bus appeared around the corner, headlights beaming, reassuring Greyhound logo down the side. After loading her bag into the storage area underneath and having her ticket checked, Clara was safely installed in a window seat with, happily, an empty seat to her left. She did want to make friends, but this was a ten-hour overnight bus journey; she wasn't going to be at her most gregarious.

Chapter 4

February 2014

The first six or so months of trying for a baby were exciting: full of possibility and promise. Having sex for the purpose nature intended, being drawn to the baby aisle in supermarkets, assuming they'd need things from there soon, doing pregnancy tests 'for fun' around the time her period was due, just to see if it had worked. Clara would cover up the test and bring it back into the bedroom for them both to look at together after the allotted three minutes. There'd be a sense of occasion, of possibility and hope. There was a pinch of disappointment on discovering only one line on the stick, but they'd only been trying for a few months. Surely next month would be different? And for now she could have a glass of wine with dinner. So, you know, swings and roundabouts.

They felt like the couples you see on adverts, or in films, all dressed in white (who knows why?) grinning down at a test together. That'd be them next month – or perhaps the month after – but it wouldn't be long. They were fairly confident of that.

Then as the months rolled by, excitement and hope slowly morphed into disappointment, worry and anxiety. They stopped doing tests. Clara couldn't bear to see any more negative results. She'd find out soon enough if she wasn't pregnant; why not let her period arriving give her the answer? That was less cruel than building up to 'test day' and imagining the happy result, planning breaking the news to friends and family and shopping for maternity clothes, only to be disappointed.

A niggling thought had started to surface, the first seed of doubt. 'How to get pregnant' and 'How long does it take to get pregnant?' became Clara's top Google searches.

Ovulation tests and fertility lubricants were suddenly essential bits of kit.

'He refuses to even discuss it,' Clara said to Jess on the phone.

'That's because he's a man and they're all emotionally stunted. The only emotion they can do is anger, otherwise it's head-in-the-sand-pretend-it's-not-happening.'

'That's a bit harsh, not to mention sexist.' Clara could almost feel Jess rolling her eyes down the phone.

'When is the last time you saw him cry? Apart from when his football team lost?'

'He doesn't even like football. You're comparing him to Dave.'

'So never, then?'

'Well, no… but that doesn't mean he's emotionally stunted. He likes to do things his own way. Anyway, I don't know why I'm defending him now. I rang you to rant about him.'

'Go ahead, rant away.'

'Oh, I don't know. Things have changed. We used to be able to talk about anything. Now I feel like I'm annoying him every time I bring it up.'

'He probably doesn't mean to make you feel like that.'

'No, maybe not. I just think we should go to the doctor to rule out any problems, and he thinks I'm being silly. Either that, or he's scared. I don't know, as he won't talk about it, and that's my point.'

'Just make the appointment and tell him he has to go.'

'Well, that's one way to deal with it, but isn't that a little pushy?'

'Clar, you won't get anywhere without being pushy. He needs you to take control.'

Clara suspected again that Jess was talking about Dave, who moved straight out of his mum and dad's and in with her. He was five years younger than Jess and had never quite cut the apron strings. Jess ruled the roost in their house and he wouldn't have it any other way.

'I'll bring it up again when he's in a better mood. He wants a baby too, I know he does.'

Christopher had experienced loss as a child. His older brother, James, had died when he was ten and Christopher was seven. They'd both been in a car accident. Their friend's dad was driving. Christopher had a broken arm and concussion. James hadn't been wearing a seat belt and had died at the scene. It was in the news at the time. His friend's dad wasn't prosecuted as the accident wasn't his fault, but he later had a breakdown and spent time in a mental health facility.

Christopher's parents were never the same. His brother's absence was felt keenly at Christmases, birthdays, anniversaries, and pretty much all the time. A permanent shadow on family life – happy events were never as happy as they should have been.

Christopher didn't like to talk about it, shutting down quickly when his name came up, so Clara stopped bringing it up and they carried on as normal. That's Christopher all over: don't talk about it and it's like it never happened. Except, it's not quite like it never happened. Clara saw the flash of pain cross his face when friends talked about their childhoods and playing with their siblings; she saw the anger beneath the surface in the firm set of his jaw if passengers didn't put their seatbelts on, his quiet but firm insistence before setting off. He never said why; some of his closest friends didn't know. Clara feared he was employing the same tactic now. Don't talk about it and it's not happening.

'We should go to the doctor,' she said to him later that day, as she chopped chorizo for the risotto.

'What for?'

'Because we're not getting pregnant. There might be a reason, something wrong.'

'No, there's nothing wrong.'

'You don't know that.' She tried to avoid touching the chorizo too much; her fingertips were turning orange. She looked up. Christopher was immersed in his laptop. 'Christopher!' she said, exasperated. 'I'm trying to talk to you seriously and you're too busy doing…whatever it is you're doing.'

'I'm looking at a quote for the roof fixing. It could start raining in. There are even more loose slates now.'

Clara took a deep breath. 'Can you do that later? This is important.'

'Let me just do this.'

He didn't look up and the back of her eyes stung in frustration, but she didn't have the energy to push it further. She turned back to her orange fingers, shoulders sagging as she reached for the pack of chicken breasts.

Chapter 5

February 2018

Clara was getting twitchy. The boat set off at ten o'clock and she was still waiting in the office for someone to tell her where to go. She'd arrived at the allotted time, signed various forms and been told someone would be with her shortly to take her to where the boat was docked. No one else seemed to be around, which was adding to her sense of unease. She approached the woman at reception, a young and attractive brunette with very precise eyebrows.

'Excuse me, I'm on the Whitsundays tour setting off at 10am. Should I be going somewhere by now?'

The woman raised her perfect eyebrows. 'Yes! You'll need to get a move on.' She glanced at a tiny watch-face on a silver bangle round her wrist. 'It's about twenty minutes' walk from here.'

Clara's heart beat faster. She'd followed the instructions and been here in plenty of time and now she was being made to rush – which she hated – through no fault of her own. The woman drew a route on a map and handed it to Clara.

'Go now, you'll be fine.'

Exactly twenty minutes later she half-jogged into the harbour and spotted her boat. It was still there. A group of people were sitting on the jetty having some sort of induction talk and she was late.

'Hi, I'm Clara. I'm so sorry I'm late.'

'No worries, come join us. I'm Todd,' the boy giving the induction talk said. Okay, he was a man, just. He was probably about twenty. Definitely no more than twenty-five.

Clara tried to slow her breathing to normal after the half-jog in the heat, while she found a spot to sit down. She looked around the group and was pleased to see she wasn't the oldest. In fact, there was a real mix of people. She scrutinised them, looking for possible friends. Her eyes stopped at a dark-haired woman about her age; she didn't appear to be with anyone and was clutching a guidebook in her lap. A kindred spirit? The two women made eye contact and smiled. Clara thought she seemed happy to see her, too. A potential friendship right there. Her shoulders relaxed a little.

She scanned the rest of the group with interest. There was a man and woman who she guessed from their body language were a couple. They looked to be in their fifties, they were tanned and had that 'comfortable-in-their-own-skin' look about them. The man had white hair and broad shoulders. He gave Clara a warm smile as she arranged herself in her seat and placed her bag between her feet. The woman was wearing a white linen dress, a straw hat and large sunglasses which obscured half her face. Her right leg was crossed towards the man, her foot tapping up and down and occasionally brushing against his calf.

There was a dark-skinned woman with a teenage girl, who Clara assumed was her daughter. They were both sitting cross-legged on the wooden planks of the jetty. The girl was fiddling with the beads at the end of her tight braids. Clara briefly wondered if there was a dad on the scene. She tried to imagine a scenario where she'd have gone on holiday with just her mum as a teenager; and couldn't. Then she moved on to the final party – another group of twenty-somethings, three girls and a boy, sitting on the bench closest to the water. They looked pretty much like the other backpackers she'd come across so far: tanned young faces free of make-up, hair that had clearly been left to dry naturally in the sun, flip-flopped feet, and wrists and ankles adorned with friendship bracelets. They wouldn't have looked out of place in a travel brochure for gap years.

'We'll visit Whitehaven beach this afternoon – the best beach in Australia and maybe even the world,' Todd boasted. 'So, if you want to put your belongings in here, we'll get going.' He was handing out navy blue shoulder bags made of hessian. Clara glanced down at her smaller backpack, having left the big one in storage at the hostel, then at the bag Todd was holding out to her.

'I brought my own bag –'

'Everyone has to fit their stuff in here, so we don't get overloaded with too much weight on board.' He was still holding the bag out. *This would have been useful to know in advance.* Clara took it and tried shoving her backpack inside. A bit was poking out of the top. *That'd do, wouldn't it?* She put it over her shoulder as the dark-haired woman approached.

'All right, I see you're having the same problem as me, so,' she said, in a thick Irish accent. She indicated her own bulging blue bag.

'Yes. They could have warned us there was a limit on what we could bring.' Clara rolled her eyes in a way she hoped said 'I'd like to be your friend'.

'I'm Deirdre.'

'Clara.' She took the offered hand and felt herself relax. Friends it is.

'Go on, ladies, I'll let you off with your bags,' Todd said, ushering them towards the boat.

Clara buried her toes in sand that looked like white powder; it was almost the consistency of sherbet. They'd been warned to be extra careful with phones and cameras, as the sand could get into the mechanism and break them. Todd wasn't kidding about this being the best beach. It was postcard perfect. The cloudless sky was bright blue and the water was almost turquoise – so translucent you could see the marine life in all their technicoloured glory by paddling in up to your knees. It was like being in *Finding Nemo*. The only thing marring the experience was Clara's churning gut. She was grateful to be off the boat temporarily, but still green around the gills. She may as well have taken two

Smarties, for all the good the sea-sickness tablets had done her.

'Ah, it's grand isn't it?' Deirdre sighed next to her.

'Beautiful,' Clara said.

'You're getting some colour back in your cheeks now, so you are.'

'Yes, glad to be on solid ground.'

Deirdre nodded.

'How long have you been travelling?' Clara asked.

'About a month so far. I'm travelling down the East Coast then staying in Sydney.'

'Did you…come with anyone?'

'No, by myself. It was sort of last minute. I split up with my husband last year and I turned forty a few months back and thought, what the hell, you know?'

'Oh, I'm sorry to hear that, but good on you for getting on with it and doing something fun.'

'It's fine. Well, it's not, you know. Bastard had an affair with his secretary. Such a cliché. It's embarrassing, so.'

Clara shook her head grimly. 'Arsehole.'

'True enough.' Deirdre laughed out loud.

There was something about the calmness of the warm air, the smell of salt water and the lapping of the tide which made it feel as though the normal rules of polite conversation with someone you'd just met didn't apply.

'My husband had an affair too,' Clara said.

'No!'

'Yes, we wanted a baby and it didn't happen. We coped in our own ways, I guess.'

'Ah, I'm so sorry. That's really shit.'

'Yes it is.' Clara smiled sadly.

She felt lighter for saying the words out loud and grateful to Deirdre for accepting it as it was. She was so used to platitudes. It was shit.

'When I tell people about not being able to have a baby, I often wish I hadn't. They don't get it and say things like "perhaps it wasn't meant to be" or "you're lucky – you can do what you want when you want", or worse, flippantly offer me their toddler when they're mid-tantrum. It's like they think I'm not entitled to grieve because I can't miss something I never had.'

'You're grieving for the life you imagined and planned for yourself.'

'Yes!'

'I get it.'

'What about you, did you ever –'

'Want kids? Nah…'

They both laughed.

Deirdre wandered down to the shore for a paddle and Clara was left feeling pensive. She sometimes felt as though she was living someone else's life and didn't quite fit. She'd had it all figured out: the husband, the career, and baby was next on the agenda. Now she was living a life she didn't choose and trying to reconcile what she'd thought would happen with what was actually happening.

She also grappled with whether having a baby was definitely what she wanted, or what she'd thought she should want. Society tells girls they should aspire to be mums. Was it programmed into you since the first time you picked up a doll as a little girl? Or did it come later, when you argued with your own mother as a teenager and thought to yourself, I'll do it differently? Is the expectation that you'll become a mother placed on you by society and internalised so you think it's your own idea, or is it something more visceral, innate? The need to reproduce and leave a part of you behind? To have your chance at shaping a life? She could ponder all she liked, but in the end it didn't matter – she just knew she wanted it.

The Rioja was delicious. The sun was setting over the blue horizon, a glorious smell was wafting up from the galley kitchen, and the group were gathered on the deck, talking enthusiastically about the first day of the trip. Clara took a selfie with the sea in the background, which she'd have to upload later. There was no Wi-Fi or even a phone signal on the boat. She wondered what Christopher was doing and whether he still missed her. She hadn't heard from him since the initial exchange, which was definitely a good thing. Definitely. He was probably busy having sex with Sarah, which was fine with her. She was on a boat on the Great Barrier Reef after all, and everyone knows that trumps new-relationship sex. She tuned into the conversation.

'I saw a lionfish,' said Ian, the man with white hair.

'I hope you kept your distance,' said his wife, Simone.

'Yes.' He inclined his head towards her, so their hair touched. 'It was on the bed of the sea, tucked half behind a rock, but I could see it clearly.'

The teenage girl had a card showing the different types of fish you could spot snorkelling or scuba diving. Ian pointed the lionfish out to her.

'Is it dangerous?' she asked. 'It doesn't look it.' Her skin was already a few shades darker after a day in the sun on and off the boat.

'Well, it's unlikely to kill you, but it is venomous, and if you trod on its spikes, you'd definitely know about it.' He winked at her, like a friendly uncle might.

'I saw a load of jellyfish.' Deirdre joined in the conversation. 'They swam right past me, but didn't sting, thank God. They were quite something to look at, you know?'

'They're pretty aren't they? I saw them too; they were bright pink,' said one of the twenty-something girls. *Lauren.* Clara remembered her name as she was speaking. 'One bumped against my hand, but only the squishy part on top, not the tentacles.'

'You didn't freak out at that?' The freckly girl next to her nudged her knee with her own, affectionately.

Plates of steaming food arrived from the kitchen: lamb flatbreads, halloumi skewers with thick chunks of green peppers, couscous and a fresh salad, with the reddest tomatoes Clara had ever seen, were placed in the middle of the table. She took a sip of her wine and enjoyed the feeling of the alcohol entering her bloodstream. Her skin was pleasantly warm from the sun and wind. The wine, and the smell of the food, had calmed her queasy stomach and she was suddenly ravenous. The conversation ambled on, relaxed and easy, as everyone loaded their plates and the boat bobbed about gently on the calm sea. The temperature had dropped to a more comfortable level. Clara joined in the conversation, between mouthfuls of halloumi and couscous, which beat McDonald's, hands down.

'Who's scuba-diving tomorrow?' the freckly girl asked. There were nods and murmurs of assent all round.

'I'm hoping to, but never done it before,' Clara said. 'Have to confess, the thought of it panics me.'

'Ah, you'll be grand,' Deirdre said.

'Hmm, it's just the thought of being too far down to bolt to the surface if the equipment fails.'

'You won't be. It's a trial dive, we'll only go down a few metres,' Simone said.

'Really?' It would look good on Facebook if she could get some photos in scuba gear.

'Yes, it'd be a real shame to miss out. We have a policy of trying everything once.'

'Apart from morris dancing,' Ian said. 'No, seriously, I had a bad accident a few years' back. I'm lucky to be here, so we make the most of life.'

Okay, Clara thought, I need to stop thinking about my Facebook account and Christopher seeing my exciting photos while this man is talking about his near-death experience.

'What happened?' Deirdre asked.

Ian had a mouthful of lamb and gestured to his wife to speak for him.

'He was windsurfing on Lake Garda and the wind took him, tossed him into the rocks like a rag doll. Broke his back in three places and he was underwater for ten minutes.'

'Oh, God.'

The group shuffled in their respective seats, chewing slowed. Simone had everyone's attention.

'I wasn't breathing and my heart stopped,' Ian said. 'I was technically dead. Simone saved my life. She gave me CPR until the air ambulance arrived, despite people telling her to stop. They thought it was too late.'

'Jeez. Makes you think, so,' Deirdre said.

'I wasn't letting him go.'

'She saved my life, then I married her.'

Clara tried to imagine a world where she'd saved Christopher's life. Perhaps he'd had a heart attack from the stress of working too much and she'd called the ambulance. Or something more dramatic, like a skiing accident where he'd had to chew off his own leg and she'd taken off her ski jacket to stem the bleeding. Would a dramatic incident like that have cemented their relationship so they'd never split up? IVF was a pretty dramatic incident and that hadn't cemented them. *Anyway, listen.*

'After three years of physio. You missed that bit,' Simone said.

'Right, so after she brought me back from the brink, the docs told me I'd never walk again. My spinal cord was badly damaged; they said I'd be paralysed from the waist down.'

'Wowsers,' Lauren said. 'You proved them wrong.' She was leaning against the freckly girl who had her arm draped over her shoulders.

'He certainly did.' Simone laced her fingers through his.

'I had four major operations. Then I didn't give up. I wanted my life, as I knew it, back. I walked with a zimmer-frame, then a stick. I proposed to Simone and promised her I'd spend the rest of my life having adventures with her.' Ian freed his fingers and turned in his seat to pull his shirt up and reveal a long, angry red scar along his spine.

Clara was alarmed to feel a lump in her throat. She coughed and took a sip of wine.

'So, it didn't give you a phobia of water then.'

'Fran!' Lauren scolded, sitting up to face the freckly girl. *Ah, that was her name.* Clara tried to remember it. *Freckly Fran – that was handy.*

'No way. Life is for living. I didn't fight that hard to sit at home being careful for the rest of my days.' Ian's eyes crinkled at the edges.

'You know what?' Clara said. 'I'm going to try scuba-diving.' And it wasn't just for the Facebook photos.

'Ah, that's grand.'

'Pleased to hear it,' Ian said, as he used his finger to push the last bit of couscous onto his fork.

Plates were tidied away and thick wedges of bright red watermelon appeared. Clara's mouth watered. Perhaps the trick of beating sea-sickness was a combination of an emotional epiphany and constantly eating.

The next day the wind picked up and, with it, the rocking of the boat. Clara tried to focus on the horizon and breathe deeply. The sea-sickness was back with a vengeance and she was regretting the food and wine from the night before. The tablets made her mouth feel dry and chalky, no matter how much water she drank, and she still felt sick. Todd was showing them the scuba equipment and explaining what would happen. Clara forced herself to look away from the horizon and focus on what he was saying.

'To clean the mask, you spit in it and give the lens a good wipe.' He demonstrated with a healthy dollop of saliva. It was sort of gross and didn't help Clara's delicate disposition. She caught Lauren pulling a face and smiled at her. 'You might need to clear your mask underwater. Once it's on, you raise the bottom half and blow sharply out of your nose to get rid of any water.' Clara fidgeted. *Take it off underwater? That doesn't seem like solid advice.* She decided she'd come to the top to sort it out if it leaked.

'It's easy to do. The important thing is to stay calm. We'll all practise before we dive. I need to see you all do it before you can go down.'

Oh. Oh, well, maybe it'd be easier than it looked. Clara remembered Ian's story from last night. Life was for having adventures, and that sometimes meant stepping outside your comfort zone. And anyway, if she could inject herself with hormones every day, this should be a breeze. So really, she was worrying about nothing.

'Now, come grab a mask and check it for size. It should seal completely against your face. No gaps.'

Damn, this would be the next challenge. Clara cursed her small face; she knew they'd all be too big for her and she'd have a leak problem. She wondered if she could ask for a kid's one. She had to buy the glasses she wore for driving from the teenagers' section at Specsavers, because the adults' ones were way too wide for her face. She stood up and the boat lurched. She grabbed onto a railing and her stomach churned. *Oh, God.* She looked back out to the horizon and took some deep breaths. No, it was no good. Her mouth filled with water. She looked around, frantically. The toilet was all the way down the steep wooden stairs, below deck. No way she'd make it. She dashed to the edge of the boat and her stomach heaved as she vomited over the edge. The sick splattered against the side of the boat. She saw last night's cous-cous as a second wave engulfed her.

'You're at the wrong side!' Todd cried. 'The wind is working against you there.'

Very helpful, Clara thought, as she tried to catch her breath. She didn't look round. After a few minutes of spitting and deep breathing, she slowly edged away from the side of the boat. Deirdre appeared at her side with a tissue and a bottle of water.

'Thank you.' She took them appreciatively. Her hands were trembling. Deirdre led her to the back of the boat.

'Come sit here in the middle and look out. There's less movement here.'

Clara did as she was told. Half an hour later the boat stopped, near the shore, at the scuba spot, and the rocking eased to a gentle sway. Her head ached and her mouth was dry, her stomach, delicate. The rest of the party were donning their masks and attaching themselves to oxygen tanks. Reluctantly, she picked up a mask and, as she'd suspected, it was too big.

'Are they all the same size?' she asked nobody in particular.

'Erm, I think they're different,' Fran replied. 'Here, look inside. This one says M.'

'Oh yes, thanks.' The one Clara had in her hand was an L. She searched for an S, but couldn't find one, so settled on the M, which was still a bit too big. Todd came over and helped her attach an oxygen tank to her back. It was heavy, and she lurched to one side and grabbed hold of the bench. It didn't feel appropriate to ask someone to take a photo; the more pressing need was to regain her balance and composure before walking to the edge of the boat and clambering down the ladder. She'd try to get a photo afterwards. The water was shallow enough to stand up in. It came up to her chest. The group stood in a semi-circle around Todd.

'So, as I showed you on the deck, we're going to take it in turns to duck under the surface, let some water leak into your mask, then clear it. I'll demonstrate. If you all put your masks on and the mouthpiece in, you can breathe normally. Now, on the count of three…'

Clara instinctively held her breath as she bobbed down under the water. It took a few moments to remember she could breathe, but it was as though she'd forgotten how. Okay, relax, she told herself. Just breathe. She did, and it made a sound like Darth Vadar, but she could breathe and she could see. Todd was tilting the bottom half of his mask a few millimetres away from his face to let some water trickle in. He put it back in place and the water was about halfway up his eyes. He tilted it again and blew air out of his nose. He quickly put it back in place and it was clear. Easy. He signalled for everyone to come up to the surface.

'Okay, straightforward enough,' he said. 'Who's first up? Ian?'

Ian nodded and the two of them disappeared under the surface. Two minutes later, they were back, all good.

'Simone, you next?' Same again, no problems. Clara was next, if he was working his way round the semi-circle. She tried to breathe through her queasiness. *I've got this.*

'Clara.'

Oh, crap. She pulled her mask back on and put the mouthpiece, which now tasted of salt, into her mouth. She shuddered. They went under the surface. Todd signalled for her to leak water into her mask. She did, then tried to mimic what he'd done, only the water didn't disappear; more came in and she accidentally inhaled it. She stood up, coughing and spluttering. The salt water was stinging her nose and trickling down her throat. She heaved again at the acrid salty taste at the back of her throat, but managed to keep control through sheer will. Vomiting in the sea in front of these people just couldn't happen.

'Try again?' Todd asked. Clara nodded and they went back down. This time she only got as far as letting water in, before she panicked and stood up.

'Okay, I think maybe you should stick to snorkelling today,' Todd said.

Clara said nothing, a mixture of disappointment and relief rendering her mute. She wanted more than anything to be on steady land. The shore was only metres away. She swam over, waded up onto the beach and sat down on the sand, shedding her oxygen tank. She saw the others perform the task with no issues, then they all disappeared under the water. *Well, that went well,* she thought. *I can add scuba-diving to my list of failures.*

Grateful to be on dry land, she tilted her face to the sun and closed her eyes. This should have been an idyllic moment. She opened her eyes a crack and looked at the blue sky, the heads bobbing up to the surface of the water every now and again, the boat rocking on the waves. *Nope, not the boat rocking.* She quickly refocused her gaze on the steady horizon as a fresh bout of nausea rose.

She dug her heels into the sand and wondered if she should be feeling happier yet. She played a game with herself, imagining her younger self. The one who'd just got married and thought she knew where she was going, seeing herself now, sitting on the sand. Would she think it was exciting, or wonder what on earth happened? Perhaps she'd think this was only part of the picture and Christopher and their kids were off building sandcastles, just out of shot. The familiar yearning threatened to take hold. She rolled onto her stomach, picked up a handful of sand and watched it fall through her fingers as she allowed herself to feel the pain of what might have been. No one was going to call her 'Mum'. She wasn't going to go through childbirth, or feel the world shift as she held a newborn in her arms. She wasn't going to be shouted for in the middle of the night when her child had had a nightmare, or know what it was like not to be the centre of her own universe any more. The pain of it was almost physical.

Clara forced herself to keep breathing, keep trying, keep on keeping on. She patted the sand flat and had a word with herself. *Right now, I am the centre of my own universe.*

With renewed determination, she left the comfort of the steady land and swam back to the rocky boat.

Chapter 6

May 2010

Clara dabbed at her eyes. It was the third time she'd heard the extract from *The Velveteen Rabbit* read at a wedding, but the bit about not being able to be ugly when you're real got her every time. She looked at Jess. She was tilting her head back and blinking her eyes, trying not to smudge her mascara. Even Christopher was smiling indulgently. There was something in the air at weddings, the atmosphere thick with emotion and sentimentality; no one was immune, it seemed. With her and Christopher's wedding looming, Clara couldn't help but imagine herself up there.

'Do you think she'll say "obey"?' she whispered to Jess, over the lump in her throat.

'No way. She's not taking his surname, there's no way she's obeying,' Jess whispered back.

'I think this church is quite progressive, as far as churches go,' Clara said. 'You're probably right.'

Jess narrowed her eyes. She hadn't been comfortable in church since she fell over the toadstool and showed her knickers during her initiation to Brownies, and Tawny Owl had joked that God was watching.

There was the usual nervous shuffling at the 'if anyone knows of any just cause or lawful impediment' part. Clara waited for someone to play the prankster and choose this moment to noisily clear their throat. When it didn't come, the vicar continued and the congregation breathed a collective sigh of relief. After a few sniggers at the groom's middle name (Reginald, after his grandad) they were pronounced husband and wife.

'You may now kiss,' the vicar said.

'See, no "man" and wife or you may now "kiss the bride". Progressive,' Clara said.

Jess nodded, impressed. They stood and scrambled for position to get a good photo as the newlyweds made their way back down the aisle, smartphones aloft, necks craned. Sarah, the bride, smiled at her friends and family as she clutched her new husband's hand. Her cheeks were flushed under her make-up as she faced the various phones, dipping her chin slightly to present her face at the most flattering angle for the photos.

Christopher squeezed Clara's hand and winked. 'Our turn next,' he said.

Clara twisted the diamond ring back and forth with her thumb – a nervous gesture. She couldn't wait to be married, all safe and settled down, but she wasn't sure about the actual wedding day: the being centre of attention and having everything about her scrutinised. She didn't want people commenting on their choice of readings, her dress, their song for the first dance, the meal, how many free drinks their guests got before they had to put their hands in their pockets. But unless they eloped, all that was inevitable. She nodded and returned the hand-squeeze.

The guests were starting to file out of the church.

'Now for the fun bit,' Dave said, rubbing his hands together.

Jess swatted his arm. 'It's all fun.' A look passed between them that made Clara look away, as though she'd intruded. Jess and Dave had been engaged for three years and hadn't booked a wedding date yet. 'We're saving up' was their standard response to queries about their upcoming nuptials, but Clara knew how Dave shut down whenever Jess raised the subject. A year in, she'd stopped raising it and they'd reached stalemate.

'What time's the grub?' Dave asked, changing the subject.

Jess rolled her eyes. 'There are canapés when we arrive at the reception venue and the meal is at four.'

He checked his watch, 'Aww, man, I should have had a bigger breakfast. Oh, well, more room for beer, eh, Christopher?' He patted his belly. Christopher nodded. He wasn't a big drinker and would probably go for an extra long run tomorrow to make up for the calories ingested.

'So, how long do you think it'll be 'til she's preggo?' Jess asked, struggling to eat her mini-Yorkshire pudding with roast beef one-handed as she held her champagne glass in the other. Clara was in a similar predicament. She wiped some gravy off her chin with her wrist and shoved the rest of it in her mouth so she had a hand free.

'Umm,' she said, through her mouthful of Yorkshire pudding, 'she said at the hen do she was coming off the pill straight after their honeymoon.' She swallowed. 'Something about malaria tablets and not being able to take them if you're pregnant, so they were waiting.'

'I bet she's knocked up within a few months.'

'I don't see what the big rush is.'

'So you and Christopher aren't going to start trying as soon as you're married?'

'God, no.' The truth was, Clara wasn't in a rush. She wanted to enjoy being married first and get used to that. A waiter with a tray of goat's cheese tartlets was circling and Clara saw Dave struggling to pick up as many as he could while still holding his beer. In the end, he bent to put his pint between his feet, signalling for the waiter to hang on, then took one in each hand and popped them into his mouth whole, one after the other.

'Dave!' Jess nudged him. 'Leave some for others.'

'What? I only had toast for brekkie, I'm starving.' He was already eyeing up some fish goujons approaching from the left. The smell of the freshly cooked batter made Clara's own stomach rumble and she took one for herself. It left her with greasy fingers and she had nothing to wipe her hand on. Christopher noticed and passed her a clean white handkerchief from his pocket.

'How old are you, man?' Dave was shaking his head, smiling. 'I think my grandad uses handkerchiefs. What's wrong with a tissue, or the back of your pants?'

Christopher floundered, uncomfortable in these sorts of social situations, then recovered. 'Just looking after the missus.'

Clara winced. Not the right thing to say, but she knew he'd reached for the first response he could think of. Luckily, Jess didn't pounce on him for being sexist.

'Ooh, look, the seating plans are over there,' Jess said. 'Come look.' She led Clara off by the hand. The tables were named after places of significance to the happy couple. Clara, Christopher, Jess and Dave were at Yosemite National Park (where Mark had proposed). There was Pizza Express (where they'd had their first date), Paris (their first mini-break) and Clara wasn't sure what had happened on the National Express coach. Probably best not to ask.

'Oh good, we're all together,' Jess was saying. 'Who are Katy and Stephen?'

Clara shrugged. 'Dunno. Oh, hang on, I do know. They're from Mark's work.'

'Wait, is she the one who –?'

'Broke her boyfriend's penis during sex? Yes.'

Jess spurted her champagne. 'Oh my God. My drink totally went up my nose, but it was worth it. That's a great opener around the dinner table. This is Clara, she's an accountant, engaged to Christopher, the investment banker, they're due to get married in a couple of months, and here's Katy. She broke Stephen's penis, but they're still together.'

Clara pulled a face. 'Maybe not. How do you break a penis anyway?'

'I think it was the string that snapped. Apparently it was like a blood bath.'

'Oh, God. Wish I hadn't asked.' She grimaced.

Thankfully, the subject didn't come up over the dinner table and they relaxed into the day, alcohol lowering inhibitions and the chicken in white wine sauce staunching the rumbling tummies. A few more tears were shed during the speeches, especially the groom's, once he got past the clichés about his bride looking beautiful. There was a particularly poignant story about how he'd been searching for the perfect woman, and after many disappointing dates he'd realised she'd been sitting across from him at work the whole time. It stayed the right side of cheesy and had most of the guests reaching for the tissues (or cotton handkerchiefs).

Their first dance was to something by the Goo Goo Dolls. The couple swayed awkwardly, then, with desperate arm gestures, insisted everyone joined them. Dave was one of the first up. A few beers and songs down the line, 'Billie Jean' by Michael Jackson came on. He handed his beer to Jess and started stamping his feet in a rhythmic way to the opening beats. A circle cleared around him, seeing he meant business. It was strangely compelling to watch him shake his hips in time to the music. A man Clara didn't recognise joined him and a crowd gathered around, whooping and clapping to the beat as a full-on dance-off began. Dave was surprisingly agile for someone who spent a lot of time sitting down watching football and drinking lager; the man had moves. Clara was laughing as she clapped along, watching the scene unfold. Jess was shaking her head and tutting in a 'yep-he's-mine-what's-he-like?' sort of way. Christopher looked bemused, but reluctantly clapped too. Dave finished a particularly energetic move, popping his shoulders and raising his knees in a way not dissimilar to some of the moves Clara did at her aerobics class. He held his arms out to the crowd, encouraging applause, then nodded to his opponent.

His opponent accepted the challenge and moved to the centre of the circle, where Dave gave him space to do his stuff. He waited for the beat of the music, then dropped to the floor and started doing the Worm, reminiscent of a 1980s break-dance routine. The crowd went wild and even Dave was clapping and whooping. He accepted defeat after that. The two men shook hands good-naturedly and danced the rest of the song together. The circle around them closed in and the dance floor became a homogenous mass of sweaty bodies and flushed faces.

There was a positive correlation with the amount of alcohol consumed and the amount of people on the dance floor. The night wore on: high heels were abandoned under tables, kids skidded on their knees, women danced in circles and men slung their arms over each other's shoulders, beer slopping onto the floor from their bottles. The wedding was later called a success. Wasn't the groom's speech moving? The bride's dress beautiful? The flower girls so sweet? The band were great, too – got everyone up and dancing. What a great venue. Think they got a good deal because it was a Thursday. How lovely. What a lovely day.

Later, as Clara lay in the double bed in their room at the Travelodge, next to Christopher, it struck her that she was blessed. She had great friends and was ready to marry the love of her life. She thought back to the conversation she'd had with Jess about trying for babies after getting married. It all sounded so *grown-up*, so serious. Weren't they all supposed to achieve first? Properly establish their careers and check off a long list of exciting things to do, like jumping out of planes and scuba-diving? Perhaps she and Christopher could do all those things when they were married. They'd be one of those cool couples that people envied. Kids would come later, when they'd had their fill of excitement and were ready for a change of pace. That decided, she closed her eyes, content with her lot, and her contentment was not solely down to the amount of champagne she'd drunk.

Chapter 7

February 2018

'Fold,' Ian said, placing his cards on the table.

Todd grinned as he laid his cards out for all to see: a flush. He pulled the pile of chips towards him. Clara rolled her eyes; she'd been rooting for Ian. They were back at the hostel after the boat trip, having drinks together, before going their separate ways for the next legs of their trips. Simone put her hand on Ian's shoulder.

'Can't win 'em all,' he said with a shrug.

'Tough luck, mate. I'll get the drinks in.' Todd headed off to the bar.

'What time do you leave on Thursday?' Deirdre asked Clara.

'The Greyhound goes at ten in the morning. Think I arrive at Hervey Bay around midnight.'

'That's a long journey, for sure.'

'Yes, I'm getting used to them now, though, and at least it's not another boat.' Clara adjusted her elbow to avoid a sticky spot on the table. 'Are you still going to try and book on the same Fraser Island tour?'

'Done!' Deirdre held up a screenshot of a booking confirmation on her phone. 'I'll see you there.'

'That's brilliant!'

Deirdre was as glad to have found Clara, as Clara was her. Deirdre had known about her husband's affair for months before confronting him. Shamefully, she'd thought she could pretend it wasn't happening and put it to the back of her mind. It hadn't worked. Every call saying he was working late was like a stab, just under her ribcage. Each time she caught him angling his phone away from her while texting, a little more of her self-respect ebbed away. It'd all come to a head one night when they were supposed to be going to her mum's seventieth birthday party, and he'd said he had a headache and was going to stay home. Deirdre knew. She knew from the way he wouldn't meet her eye, from the slope of his shoulders as he turned to put his mug in the dishwasher while he delivered his excuse. In the office, or anywhere else, was one thing, but bringing her into their house was too much. She couldn't pretend that wasn't happening.

Surprising herself, she'd said, 'Holly coming over, is she?'

His hand stilled on the mug. He kept his eyes on the dishwasher.

'What?'

'Holly, the girl you're shagging. Is she coming over while I'm at my mum's party?'

Her eyes burned into the back of his head. He straightened, closed the dishwasher door. Opened his mouth, closed it again.

'I don't...I didn't –'

'Didn't think I knew? Yeah, shame. I'll stay at my mum and dad's after the party and when I come back tomorrow, I want you to be gone.'

She flounced out of the kitchen. Her hands trembled as she packed a bag. She couldn't believe what she'd done, and now she was going to have to hold it together for the party and make small talk with all the guests.

It was her fortieth birthday the week after, and it'd been a whirlwind of booking flights and searching for jobs in Australia, something she'd thought about previously but her husband wouldn't entertain. Now here she was, picked up and put down somewhere else entirely. Clara could identify with that.

Todd reappeared carrying a tray of shots. Oh, God, Clara thought, sipping her Chenin Blanc. How can I get out of this without seeming rude?

He put the tray on the table and started placing a shot in front of everyone.

'I'm okay, thanks –' Clara started as he got to her.

'We're celebrating my win,' he said, raising an eyebrow as he set it down in front of her. She put a hand to the side of her neck and tried to smile, but it ended up more of a grimace; she hadn't quite gotten over scuba-gate.

'Bottoms up everyone!' Todd downed his shot and slammed the glass upside-down on the table. Clara raised the glass to her lips and took a sip of the potent liquid. It burned her throat. She put it back down. She looked around the table. Most of the group were playing ball. Deirdre had downed hers, as had all the younger members of the party. Simone had made a valiant effort, but her shot glass was still half full. No one said anything, so she quietly left her glass on the table and went back to her wine.

'Waste not, want not,' Todd said, picking up Clara's glass and pouring the rest of the contents down his throat. Oh well, that solves that, she thought. He was swaying slightly as he stood up and started calling over some of his friends from a nearby table. Moments later, a group descended on them and the decibel level rose.

Clara chose that moment to escape to the toilet. In the cubicle, she sat down on the closed lid and got out her phone. She connected to the hostel's Wi-Fi and opened Facebook. Jess and Dave were celebrating their anniversary in a cottage in the Lake District, according to the caption. She scrolled through photos of them in a hot tub, in a bar, heads bent together as they clinked glasses and smiled at the camera, and one of them next to Lake Windermere – a full-length shot, obviously taken by a passer-by. Clara couldn't remember Jess telling her they were going on a mini-break. This is the sort of thing she'd usually know, but then she wasn't usually on the other side of the world. The thought left her unsettled. She continued scrolling and then Christopher's face popped up. And Sarah's. They were walking through some unidentifiable woods. It was Sarah's post, and Christopher was tagged. Sarah had captioned it 'Winter walks with the Mr #nature #love #happydays'.

Clara took a deep breath in and out. Perhaps she should have had that shot, after all. She closed tha app down and put the phone back in her bag. Then she took it out again and opened up the message from Christopher where he'd said he missed her. He'd obviously gotten over missing her pretty quickly. She hastily typed out 'Still miss me, do you?' Her thumb hovered over the send button, then she sighed and deleted it. After a while, resting her head on her hands she became aware of a tentative knock at the door.

'Clara, you in there?'

Deirdre.

'Yeah, I'm just...hang on.'

She ran her hands over her face, then stood up and opened the door.

'Everything okay? Thought you might be sick again.'

'Oh no, not sick...just...'

Deirdre narrowed her eyes in concern. 'Do you want to get out of here?

'Yes, please.'

'Ah, this is better,' Clara said. They were sitting outside a bar on the beachfront, sipping Amaretto Sours.

'What was going on back there?'

'Oh, I stupidly looked at Facebook and pictures of my ex-husband with his current girlfriend. You know, the usual.'

'Ah, that's rough.'

'I should probably block him. I just thought I was past all that. I'm a grown-up, not some teenager checking out boys on Snapchat or whatever it is they do.'

Deirdre gave a snort. 'Love's a kicker, no matter how old you are. Anyway, talking of getting old, I was glad of an excuse to leave that hostel bar if I'm honest. The music was getting too loud back there.'

'Tell me about it. Think I've just about had my fill of Todd anyway. He was a twat.' That may have been the Amaretto Sour talking.

Another snort. 'He wasn't the best scuba instructor,' Deirdre said. 'Don't let it put you off, though. With another instructor you'd probably be grand.'

'Hmm.'

'Come on, this is your Big Trip. You're supposed to be having adventures.'

'Well, maybe if diving didn't involve going on a boat first, and if I could go in straight from the shore.'

'I'm sure you can do that.'

'I don't know. Scuba-diving aside, I'm not sure this is me. I mean it's still my Big Trip, of course it is. I'm not thinking of abandoning it, but maybe adjusting it a bit. I probably need to do something other than bumming around.'

As much as Clara was trying, she was also acutely aware that you shouldn't have to try so hard to enjoy something. Married life, going to work, eating out and seeing friends: having a routine had been something she'd enjoyed. Backpacking with teenagers, as it was turning out, not so much. But an idea was taking hold.

'Adjusting how?'

'I think I need to be with more like-minded people, and I think I'd like to have a purpose. Have some structure.'

Deirdre nodded thoughtfully.

'I don't think backpacking indefinitely is going to work for me.'

'So, you could work?'

'Exactly what I was thinking. I need to do some research.'

'Go for it. But before you sign yourself up for a job, let's enjoy our next adventure. Fraser Island is going to be immense.'

'You're right. Sorry, didn't mean to put a dampener on things. To Fraser Island!'

They clinked glasses.

Clara used the computer in the reception of the hostel later that evening. She started by Googling 'jobs abroad'. Holiday rep, chalet girl, night-club promoter. She wrinkled her nose. *Nope.* She chewed her lip and thought for a while. Then she Googled 'working with kids abroad'. Gap year childcare opportunities, au pair, kids' holiday club rep. On she scrolled. Her finger stilled when she saw 'Teaching English as a Foreign Language'. She clicked the link. Half an hour later she was clutching a handful of print-outs at ten cents a sheet, mind whizzing with new information and possibilities. She picked up her phone. Her mum answered on the second ring.

'Clara! Hello, darling! Michael, it's Clara,' she said, sounding further away. Clara pictured her putting her hand over the mouthpiece as she called her dad. 'How are you love? How's the big adventure? Are you back from your boat trip? How was it?'

'One question at a time, Mum!'

'Sorry, love. How was the boat trip?'

'It was...not that great, actually. I was seasick. But I did make a friend, Deirdre, and we're going to Fraser Island together. But anyway, Mum, I wanted to talk to you about teaching.'

'Teaching?'

'Yeah, I'm thinking about applying for a place on a Teaching English as a Foreign Language course in Singapore. It takes four weeks, then I should be able to get a job there.'

'Sounds great.' She could almost hear her mum smiling down the phone. 'I've always said you'd make a good teacher.'

'I'm not talking about being a teacher permanently. Just for now. Abroad. That's different.'

'You'd still be teaching kids and I think you'd be great at it.'

'Well, thanks. I'm not trying to follow in your footsteps or anything, though.'

'What's wrong with following in your mum's footsteps?'

'Oh no, nothing. Sorry, I didn't mean that the way it came out. I just meant, I wanted to do my own thing.'

'It's okay, love. I know what you meant. Sue's daughter taught English in South Korea. Do you remember Sue from yoga? She has a lazy eye, always wears purple leggings. Anyway, her daughter did it. Loved it. Becky, she's called. Shall I get her number for you? Or you could make friends with her on Facebook. Becky Sherwood.'

'That might be a bit random, Mum. I don't know her.'

'I'll ask Sue first, tee her up.'

'Uh, yeah, okay then. Why not?'

By the time Clara left for Fraser Island, she'd finished pouring over her print-outs and had a conversation with Sue-with-the-purple-leggings' daughter over Facebook messenger. Satisfied it sounded like something that would suit her, she'd completed and sent an application for a course in Singapore. Amazing what a bit of forward planning did for her. She already felt more like herself.

Chapter 8

June 2014

Low sperm count. Low motility. Low ovarian reserve. The words swam around Clara's head. Surely these were someone else's results. She and Christopher were young and healthy. She felt like she was at the end of the long tunnel, the consultant doctor, with her neat bob and trendy glasses, at the far end, talking across a big void.

'You could have a chance of success with ICSI, but it would depend on how you responded to the stimulation, Clara. Donor eggs would give you greater odds.'

Icksey, what is that? It sounded like a pet's name. Clara imagined calling out of her back door, 'Here Icksey, time to come in!' She giggled to herself. Christopher narrowed his eyes at her, irritated – or embarrassed, she wasn't sure.

'Are you okay?' the doctor asked from the other end of the tunnel.

'Sorry, yes…I…You were saying, Icksey.'

'I-C-S-I. It stands for Intracytoplasmic Sperm Injection. It's where we inject the sperm directly into the egg. It improves chances when the male partner has low sperm count or motility. I'm sorry to say that in your case, it's both.'

Christopher was looking down at his hands, silent.

'Well, so, okay, we could try that…' Clara said, her voice unsteady. A beat passed.

'Yes, by all means give it a go.' The doctor was nodding, her bob swishing but staying as neat as ever. 'However, I do have to warn you, with your raised FSH levels, you may not produce enough good quality eggs.'

'FSH?' *Why was this woman speaking in riddles?*

'Follicle Stimulating Hormone. It's responsible for the growth of ovarian follicles, where eggs are produced. Your FSH levels are typical of a woman much older than you.'

Suddenly the tunnel disappeared and Clara was firmly in the room. The bright lights, the vase of flowers, the ticking clock and the clinical smell. It was all real. 'Wait, what? So, basically, you're saying Christopher's sperm are not up to much and neither are my eggs? We'd need to inject his sperm into…*someone else's egg*?'

'There are difficulties on both sides, yes.' The doctor's eyes were kind through her glasses, though she kept an air of professionalism and distance.

'So, what would you say our chances of IVF – of *ICSI* working would be?'

'With your own eggs? I'd say about ten percent.'

A muscle in Christopher's cheek twitched. Clara tried to unhear what she'd just heard. To rewind half an hour and have a completely different conversation with this consultant, with her nice hair and glasses. The clock ticked. The strip lights overhead made a faint buzzing sound. She noticed a beige mark on the knee of her jeans. Tea splashed from when they were in the waiting room. She wet her finger and rubbed at it. It stayed the same. She tried to retreat back to the other side of the tunnel, but she was still in the room. A couple of yellow petals lay on the desk at the side of a vase of flowers. She wanted to pick them up and put them in the bin. She waited for a familiar prickling sensation behind her eyes. There was nothing.

'It's a lot to take in. I suggest you go home and consider your options. Talk it through. If you do decide to go ahead, you'll have some sessions with a counsellor, as a matter of course.'

Christopher was shuffling in his seat, picking up his bag and preparing to stand.

Clara didn't move.

'What would you do?' she asked the consultant, looking her squarely in the eye.

'I'd think it over, carefully. Fertility treatment takes its toll, physically and emotionally. It's not something to be entered into lightly.' Her smile was sympathetic.

'Right, but would you do it? Would you give ICSI a shot?'

'Clara.' Christopher found his voice and laid his hand on her arm. She shook it off and maintained eye contact with the consultant.

'I can't answer that. I'm not in your position and it's a very personal choice. You have to do what's right for you.'

Christopher was standing now and, just like that, all the fight went out of her.

'Okay,' she said. She allowed Christopher to lead her out of the room.

'So, what do you want to do?'

Christopher shrugged. It was a week after their consultation and they were no further on with making any decisions.

'I don't think I can even consider using donor eggs without trying with my own first.' Clara put down her coffee too hard and some of it slopped onto the wooden table. Christopher picked up a napkin and mopped it up.

'Five grand for a ten percent shot at it working. You wouldn't bet on those odds, would you?' he said.

'It's not about the money. It's about knowing we're doing all we can to have a baby.'

'It'll be about the money when we've emptied out our savings and are up to our eyeballs in debt. How far do we go, how long do we keep trying for?'

'Maybe two or three tries with my eggs?'

'Right, so ten to fifteen thousand.'

'Will you stop thinking about the money?!' Clara snapped.

'One of us has to.'

'Do you actually want to have a baby?' Seeing the hurt look on his face, she regretted her words instantly.

'That's not fair, you know I do. I just –'

'I'm sorry.' She reached for his hand across the table.

'I didn't imagine it'd be this way. Doctors and money and injections…'

'I know. It's not how I thought we'd make a baby, either,' she said, more gently. 'But we don't always get to choose. This is the situation we're in, and if we want a chance, these are our options.'

Christopher was quiet.

'I don't want to look back in ten years' time and think if only we'd done this or that. I need to know we're doing everything we can and giving ourselves the best chance. We can always earn more money.'

Christopher raised an eyebrow, but said nothing. Clara fixed her gaze on him, willing him to say something else. When he didn't, she picked up her coffee and looked out of the window, frustrated.

Later that night, after Clara had exhausted herself reading through everything Google could throw up regarding ICSI, IVF and donor eggs, she switched to aimlessly scrolling through her social media feeds instead. She was lying on her stomach on their bed, and Christopher was downstairs watching a documentary about the Industrial Revolution. She flicked through her Instagram feed and paused. There it was, in among the baby photos, sunsets and people's culinary creations: a photo of a negative pregnancy test. Clara blinked and pushed herself up onto her elbow. The post was by a friend of a colleague – someone Clara had once shared a bento box with on a work night out. It was captioned 'Not our turn this time *sad face* #infertilitysucks #ivf #frozentransfer'.

She scrolled though the comments.

So sorry hun, stay strong xxx

It will be your turn soon, hang on in there xx
Lots of love xxxxx

Clara clicked the hashtags and was soon lost in a maze of posts about infertility, going into the minutest of details around people's battles to become pregnant. Photos of people in clinics about to have their embryo transfers, photos of ovulation tests, of people crying, photos of needles arranged into hearts, and couples holding up chalkboards with messages about how many eggs retrieved, how many embryos, and dates of transfer. And strangely, lots of pictures of pineapples. Clara was intrigued. A quick Google search explained that the trying to concieve community had adopted the pineapple as an infertility symbol. Apparently, pineapples are the only fruit that rarely grow from seeds. They often require intervention to produce fruit, as they have to pollinate with a different variety which is unlikely to be growing nearby. Assisted conception for fruit. Who knew?

Clara went down to the kitchen and poured herself a glass of wine. She walked quickly past the living room where Christopher was drinking a coffee – she heard the words 'new manufacturing processes in Europe and the United States' coming from the TV – and hurried back upstairs.

She propped up the pillows, settled down on the bed and placed her wine on the bedside table. Then she picked up her phone and tapped 'new account' in her Instagram app. What should she call it? She chewed her bottom lip as she thought. 'Tryingforababy'? No, too obvious. 'Dreamingofbeingamum'? Too soppy. She twisted to take a sip of her wine, then typed 'Trying2b3'. That'd do. Next, she chose a photo of herself from her camera roll – one in which she wasn't actually recognisable. It was one Christopher had taken when they were on a mini-break to Reykjavik. It showed her from behind, in silhouette, as she inched into the blue lagoon, snow-topped mountains in the background. It was symbolic, maybe. Anyway, it was a nice photo and didn't show her face. She spent the next twenty minutes or so clicking infertility-related hashtags and following people. A few followed back straightaway. She "liked" and commented on a few posts and gained a few more followers. Christopher came into the bedroom and she jumped and put her phone down.

He looked bemused. 'Guilty conscience?'

'What? No, I'm doing research.'

'Did you know coal produces three times more energy than wood, and that the Industrial Revolution started in Britain?'

'Yes, coal mining started properly in the eighteenth century in the UK. I did 'A' level history, but why's that important right now?'

'I've been watching this fascinating documentary.'

'That's great, but I have other things on my mind right now.' Clara tried not to sound snappy.

'Of course, sorry.' He sat down on the bed next to her, picked up her wine and took a sip. 'Do you want to talk about it some more?'

'No, I think I just want to go to sleep.'

'Okay.' He squeezed her hand and got up to get changed into his pyjamas. As soon as he left the room to go and brush his teeth, Clara picked up her phone again. Fifty followers. She found a photo online of a sperm being injected into an egg and posted it with the caption 'ICSI? Any tips or success stories?'

Christopher came back into the room and got into bed. Clara put her phone down again, drained her glass, had some vague thoughts about getting up to brush her teeth, then turned on her side to be the small spoon.

The next morning, Clara had thirty more followers and a couple of replies to her post. One from someone called 'IVFgotthis', telling her ICSI had worked for her, but how sadly her pregnancy ended in miscarriage, and wishing her luck. Another from 'Journeytoconcieve' said 'tips – stay away from Google and keep yourself busy. Let us know how you get on. x'

And just like that, Clara had a new support network. Anonymous women she'd never met, who knew exactly what she was going through.

Chapter 9

February 2018

Clara sniffled and wiped her nose on the back of her hand. She lay sprawled like a starfish in the middle of the double bed at the motel in Hervey Bay. It was raining outside and her back and legs ached from the long bus journey. Her top was damp after the dash from the bus station to the motel, but it was too much effort to change it. She'd put her pyjamas on soon. The room was nothing special, but it was a room for two. Two mugs by the little plastic kettle. Two teaspoons. Two biscuits. She rolled onto her side and looked at the empty half of the bed, tracing the white cotton sheet with her fingertips. This should feel better than the dormitory with its empty bunk-beds, but it was too familiar. Too similar to hotel rooms she'd shared with Christopher over the years. She couldn't help but imagine him here. Then she imagined a travel cot in the corner, the two of them whispering over cups of tea so they didn't wake the child, making plans for the next day, for the rest of their lives. A tear trickled down the side of her face and onto the pillow. She had no plan for after she returned from her travels. Not even a solid plan about *when* she might return. Her stomach fluttered with uneasy butterflies. She pressed her hand against it and tried to recall some of the enthusiasm she'd had when she originally booked the trip.

I'm seizing an opportunity, not moping and wallowing, she said to herself.

She swung her legs over the side of the bed and started the night-time ritual of washing her face and brushing her teeth, in the perfectly adequate en suite, with no mildew. She made a conscious effort not to imagine Christopher brushing his teeth next to her, and she definitely didn't imagine sitting a toddler on her knee to brush their teeth.

Then she crawled between the sheets, exhausted, and fell into a fitful sleep in which she dreamed of scuba-diving and searching through a stack of pregnancy tests, where a second line would appear then disappear in front of her eyes.

Clara gripped Deirdre's hand on impulse as the open-topped four-by-four bumped over sand dunes at a crazy speed. With her other hand she gripped the side of the vehicle, in an attempt to stop herself bouncing out of her seat. Her heart was pounding as sand and trees raced by. The driver, Tom, epitomised the description 'laid back': hair whipping his forehead in the wind, shades covering his eyes, hands firmly on the wheel. She could see the muscles and tendons in his tanned forearms. She hoped to God he knew what he was doing. Eventually they arrived at a clearing and pulled up on the seventy-five-mile beach.

'Everyone okay?' he asked.

'Got kinda wild back there, so it did.' Deirdre forced a laugh, trying to detangle her hair.

'Sure, it's bumpy. Who wants to jump out for a while? Don't recommend a dip though.'

'Are there sharks?' a red-headed, skinny twenty-something asked as he climbed out of the vehicle.

'Sure, mate, hundreds of the beggars. And strong currents too. Not safe.'

The boy's eyes widened as he looked at the innocent-looking waves. The girl he was with – a petite blonde girl with a pretty face – reached for his hand and pulled him back a little, as though he were about to dash off for the water and jump straight in.

Clara took in the view. Beach and sea as far as she could see in either direction. But no sunbathers or paddlers. There were a couple of fishermen dotted about and several more four-by-fours whizzing up and down; then, in the distance, to her surprise she saw a small plane coming into land.

'Oh yeah, this beach is basically the main road on the island and it's used as a landing strip for light aircrafts,' Tom said, following her gaze. 'When you're ready I'll take you up to the Maheno shipwreck, and it'll be a smoother ride there.'

Later that day they were lounging in the champagne pools near the top of the island. No sharks or strong currents in there, just idyllic, warm, blue-green water.

'So, you alright?' Deirdre asked. It was the first moment of calm they'd had since they were reunited at the meeting point for the trip at Hervey Bay.

'Oh, I'm good.' Clara replied. The standard response.

Deirdre didn't say anything, giving her more time.

'Well, I had a wobble when I arrived in the motel room by myself.'

Deirdre nodded.

'I'm fine when I'm busy and with people, like now. It's hard to be sad here.' She gestured at the picture perfect surroundings. 'But it feels like a temporary fix. When I'm on my own and I start thinking….' She trailed off.

'Don't rush yourself to feel "better". it doesn't work like that. Healing can be a slow process. One day you might realise you don't feel as sad, the ache has eased and you're laughing more than you're crying.'

Clara raised her eyebrows. 'Sounds like you're talking from experience.'

'Yeah, well. I –' Deirdre started. 'Jesus, would you look at that?' She was pointing into the distance. Clara squinted and saw a pack of dingoes jostling each other, trying to get at something. There was blood on the sand. A shark had washed up on the shore and they were getting their fill.

'Urgh, well that spoils the mood,' Clara said, although she found herself fascinated and couldn't look away as they brutally tore into the animal with their teeth. It was like a David Attenborough programme with no edits. 'God. Hope they stay away from our tent tonight.'

'It must be safe. Imagine the news if tourists kept getting attacked by dingoes.'

'Yes, hopefully they get plenty to eat, if that's anything to go by.' She nodded towards the gruesome scene.

'Ah, don't worry about that, ladies.' Tom had overheard and was approaching. 'More interested in the wildlife than you. Plus, we'll be fenced in at the campsite, so they can't get to us.'

'That's a relief.' Clara chewed her lip and kept watching, transfixed by the gory show. The shark was resembling a bloody skeleton, like an old-fashioned cartoon, with nearly all the flesh gone. She shuddered. Nature was cruel.

That evening the group sat around a camp-fire inside the fenced campsite. It had grown chilly and Clara had pulled on a grey hoody with her shorts. Her stomach cramped lightly in the way that told her her period would be arriving shortly. She took a moment to realise that she'd stopped tracking her cycle. If she did a quick calculation she could just about work out the timing was right, but there were no charts, no agonising wait for her period's arrival (or hopefully non-arrival). She didn't even have any tampons with her. Hopefully Deirdre could help her out if needed. Her period would be nothing more than a minor irritation, and that was progress.

Her feet were still bare and she wiggled her toes in the sand. The red-haired boy was re-living the dingoes versus shark display from earlier.

'Did you see their teeth, though?'

His girlfriend rolled her eyes indulgently.

Tom smiled in a knowing way. He'd seen it all before, Clara guessed.

'Before the campsites were enclosed in fences, they used to come roaming when people left food out. One time a dingo got inside a tent where two girls were sleeping.' He was feeding the boy's macabre fascination.

'No!' he said. 'What happened?'

'They screamed and it ran off.'

'Oh.' He nodded, but Clara sensed he was disappointed. *Strange boy.*

A party around another camp-fire nearby started singing, and one of them strummed a guitar. Clara glanced at Deirdre and saw she was suppressing a smile, as well. They made eye contact and each broke into a grin. This is proper backpacking, Clara thought. She was enjoying herself for the first time since leaving Manchester. She knew it was because her mindset had changed. This was now a holiday, not an indefinite drifting about, trying to make herself happy. She had the semblance of a plan for the rest of the trip and if all worked out, she'd soon have somewhere more permanent to live and a new challenge to focus on in Singapore. The more she'd thought about it, the more she hoped she was successful in getting a place on the course. Teaching would be good for her. That aside, she had to wonder what Christopher would think if he could see her now, sitting cross-legged on the sand with a group of near strangers, who in this moment felt like close friends. She wondered, but didn't wonder enough to take a photo and post it on Facebook for a reaction. That too, was progress. Clara smiled and listened to the sound of singing and the waves in the background, pierced by the occasional howl of a dingo.

Chapter 10

February 2002

'Try a jalapeño.'

'They're too spicy.' Clara swatted away Christopher's hand as it hovered by her mouth. 'Stop it.' She laughed.

He popped the jalapeño into his own mouth and settled back against the pillows. 'Wimp,' he teased. On impulse she wiped a dollop of mayonnaise on his cheek.

'Hey!' He sat up straight in mock horror, then put his Subway wrapper on the floor and began to tickle her.

'Stop, my sandwich…You're getting mayo on the sheets.' She squirmed away from him. 'You're supposed to be in your lecture anyway. You need to get ready.'

Christopher checked the digital clock on top of the TV, which was showing the afternoon episode of *Neighbours*. 'Sod it. I'll get the notes from Nick.'

Clara rolled her eyes, but giggled as he resumed his tickling. She dropped her sandwich when he stopped tickling and kissed her, momentarily wondering whether it had landed the right way up on the carpet and about the fact her breath probably wasn't the freshest after last night's Bacardi and Cokes and the sneaky cigarettes she sometimes had when drinking. Then all thoughts went out of her mind as his hand travelled up her thigh.

'You know you're my favourite girlfriend,' he said a while later, as they sat propped up against the pillows.

'What? I thought I was your only girlfriend,' she said into his bare chest, tweaking his nipple.

'Ha ha, of course you are. I mean I haven't enjoyed spending time with a girl so much before.'

'Erm, thanks… I think,' she said, a half-smile on her lips.

'You know what I mean. Usually I want to be with my friends, playing pool in the pub, but you're…you…you're different. Fun.'

'Thanks. You're fun too.' She grinned at him.

He reached for the open pack of Haribos on his lap and took out a jelly ring. 'Here, put this on.'

She stretched out the sweet and put it on her thumb.

'No, on your ring finger, left hand.'

'No way. I'm not marrying you and not with a Haribo ring.' She put it in her mouth and chewed, then stuck her tongue out to show him the pieces.

'One day I'll ask you and you'll say yes.' He smiled.

'Ha! You're sure of yourself aren't you?'

'I'm sure of you.'

Chapter 11

March 2018

'I've jumped more than 500 times,' Sam said. 'Don't worry, I'll get you down safely.'

The wooden bench Clara was straddling rumbled underneath her. She was sweating under her bright red jumpsuit, the straps of her harness pressing down uncomfortably on her shoulders. The fields through the window were getting smaller as the plane rose up and up. She took a deep breath and tried to feel reassured by the skydiving instructor's words. She nodded at him. The roar of the plane made it difficult to talk back. Deirdre was sitting on the bench opposite, wearing a matching red jumpsuit. She gave her a thumbs up sign and grinned. Clara returned the gesture. Skydiving would more than make up for the scuba-dive fail.

'Okay, dudes, we're 16,000 feet. Who's up first?'

The door opened on Clara's side of the plane and the duo in front of her began shuffling towards the opening. Her stomach dipped and her palms sweated. *Oh, God.* She was really doing this, then. She watched in horrified fascination as the first pair disappeared through the door with a whoop and a squeal. She was always first in the queue at Alton Towers, but sixty seconds of free-fall was something else.

'Remember, when we get to the door, dangle your legs over the edge and curve your body into a banana shape, backwards. Rest your head on my shoulder and I'll put my hand on your forehead to protect your neck and to stop you head-butting me and knocking me out.' Sam was talking clearly and calmly into her ear as they shuffled along the bench to the opening. Her legs trembled as she tried to move along in time with him.

The open door was in front of her and she was being nudged to the edge. Clara's heart hammered against her ribcage as she followed the instruction and dangled her legs over the edge into nothing but open air. She bit the inside of her cheeks for something to concentrate on, then she did as she was told: arched her back and rested her head against Sam's shoulder. She felt a cool reassuring hand on her forehead, then they were falling forward and somersaulting through the air. The wind whooshed loudly in Clara's ears and she saw the plane race off in front, getting smaller, then the sea, then sky, then sea again, all merging into one. She started laughing, hysterically. Sam had let go of her forehead and made an 'okay' symbol with both of his hands. She returned the signal. She really was okay. Tears were streaming down her cheeks and her mouth was dry from the wind, but she couldn't stop laughing. Then it was like someone pressed a switch and they stopped, suspended in mid-air. The wind died down and they were floating calmly. The parachute had opened, and they could speak to each other easily.

'Okay?' he asked her.

'That was incredible.'

'Want to do some acrobatics?'

'Yes!'

He turned the angle of the parachute so they swooped round in a big loop. Clara took in the beach below. People were sunbathing, children were building sandcastles and, in the sea, huge dark shapes were circling. 'Are they sharks?'

'Yes, plenty of them. They don't usually bother people though; they tend to stay away from the shore.' Clara wasn't convinced and made a mental note not to take a dip later.

Minutes later, the beach was approaching and they were coming into land.

'Lift up your legs, straight out in front.' Clara did as she was told and they landed on the beach with a bump.

'Can we do it again?' she asked, as soon as they were still, the parachute flopped on the sand behind them.

'Sure can. Pretty awesome isn't it?'

'I think it might have been the best thing I've ever done.'

'Clara, thanks for a great jump.' He shook her hand and maintained eye contact. Clara felt he was making a joke she didn't get. Something inside her stirred. She returned his smile and held on to his hand a moment longer than was strictly necessary.

'He likes you.' Deirdre nodded towards Sam as he stood at the bar ordering their drinks.

'No, he's just friendly.' Clara took in his broad shoulders and blond hair. His relaxed demeanour was a sharp contrast to Christopher and all his seriousness. Deirdre gave her a look which said she begged to differ. Sam returned, tray balanced expertly on one hand, and placed four beers on the table. He took the seat opposite Clara.

'Cheers.' He raised his glass and they clinked, all smiles and enthusiasm. 'To jumping out of planes!'

'I'll drink to that.' Deirdre took a long gulp of her beer. Sam met Clara's eye and winked. Her insides flipped pleasantly as she lifted her glass to her lips, holding his gaze.

'You're a much better skydiving instructor than my scuba-diving instructor.'

He raised an eyebrow at her quizzically.

'No, I mean you're better at skydiving instructing than he was at scuba instructing. You're a grown-up, for a start.'

'I'm forty-two. If I'm not a grown-up now, I never will be.' His green eyes crinkled at the edges.

She leaned forward conspiratorially, 'My scuba-diving instructor was about twelve, and he didn't let me do it.'

'Didn't *let* you do it? What do you mean?'

'I couldn't clear the mask under the water and I panicked, but in my defence, I'd recently thrown up.'

'You'd recently *thrown up?*'

'Oh yes, I get sea sick.' She flushed and mentally kicked herself. 'Sorry, that's probably not so attractive.'

'I find sea sickness very attractive.'

She spurted some of her drink onto the table as she laughed. 'You do not!'

'Well no, that'd be weird, but he sounds like a drongo.'

'A *drongo*?'

'Yeah. You know, a galah. A dipstick.'

'Galah. I remember that from *Home and Away*. Alf used to say it. "Flaming galah."'

'Sure, that's it. So, another beer.' He banged his hand on the table, decisively. Clara considered. She was lightheaded. What the hell, she thought. I'm free and single, Christopher certainly didn't waste any time. Deirdre had slipped away to a quieter area of the bar with her own instructor while they'd been talking. Clara found herself nodding and then realised he was already halfway to the bar, anyway. She slid out a mirror from her shoulder bag and wiped underneath her eyes to clear any smudges of mascara. She checked her teeth and brushed a few strands of hair into place, then tucked it safely away as Sam returned with their beers. He slid into the booth next to her instead of reclaiming his seat opposite. His thigh was covered in blond hair and the proximity to her own thigh both excited and unsettled her. She'd only need to move her leg an inch and they'd be touching.

'See that woman over there?' Sam asked.

Clara followed his gaze and saw a woman sitting alone, twirling a straw in her drink. 'Yep.'

'She's been stood up.'

'How do you know?'

'The man she was supposed to meet had an existential crisis, in the shower when he was getting ready, as he discovered his first grey hair on his chest.'

Clara shook her head, smiling.

'Yep, he's currently at home drinking Jack Daniels and crying. He wanted to achieve great things, you see, but he's still working in the same bar he took as a temporary job when he was studying. She's probably better off without him.'

'I'm sure she is,' Clara said. 'What about him?' She nodded towards a man sitting at the bar nursing a glass containing amber liquid and scrolling through his phone.

'Ah, I'm glad you asked. He's scrolling through Tinder trying to find someone who shares his kink.'

'And what's his kink?'

'He likes to combine food and sex. His speciality is spaghetti.'

'Spaghetti?'

'Yes. Or noodles will do. Basically, he likes to tie his partner up with them, then eat them when she uses a safe word. Really gets him going. In fact, he can't get off without some sort of stringy carbohydrate.'

Clara snorted in spite of herself. The man at the bar paused his scrolling and smiled as he took a sip from his drink.

'There you go, he's got a match,' Sam said.

'What, another person with a spaghetti fetish?'

'Yep. I'm sure it's a thing.'

'Okay, what about that couple over there?'

Sam followed her eye-line to a middle-aged couple sitting at a corner table. The man was feeding a beer mat back and forth through his fingers and the woman was staring into space, her drink untouched in front of her.

'She's just told him she has a penchant for outdoor sex, after twenty years of marriage. She wants to drag him down to the beach now and have her way with him right there on the sand. But he's appalled and has just called her a dirty slut. Now neither of them knows how to come back from it.'

Clara laughed out loud. 'You have quite an imagination. But why is everyone thinking about sex? You're obsessed.'

'Of course everyone is thinking about sex. Aren't you?' He turned to face her and his thigh touched hers. The contact caused a flood of warmth through her body and her cheeks flushed.

'I, uh…'

He was looking at her mouth. Her body responded before her mind had chance to catch up. She dropped her gaze to his mouth. It was all the encouragement he needed and his lips were on hers, his hand on her bare thigh under the table. A spark lit in the pit of her stomach. An ember that had lain dormant for a long time was now flickering into life. Emboldened by the alcohol, she put her fingers in his hair and pulled him closer. His tongue found hers and the flame spread downwards.

'My place is not far from here,' he said, pulling away briefly, his eyes searching hers. Her answering smile said it all. He took her hand and led her out of the bar. His place really wasn't far. A modern apartment over a surf shop with a white tiled floor, a black leather settee and oak coffee table. It had a view of the sea. The door closed behind them and he pulled her close. His body was firm and strong against her softer, more yielding one. His mouth found hers and her tongue explored him. He tasted like beer and excitement. She ran her hands over his toned body, and then slipped them under his T-shirt. His skin was warm and taut; soft hairs started on his chest and followed a trail down to the top of his shorts. She paused there and looked at him. His eyes were heavy with lust. He pulled his T-shirt over his head and she breathed in the smell of him, suncream and the faint tang of fresh sweat causing her body to throb in anticipation. Her skin hummed as his fingers found their way under her T-shirt. He expertly unclasped her bra and she gasped as he found her nipple. She grappled with her top and bra to get them off and then they were in a pile on the floor. Their mouths found each other hungrily, bare flesh against bare flesh. As one, without saying anything, they moved over to the leather sofa and he fell on top of her. In one swift move, he pulled at her shorts and knickers, sliding them down her legs and dropping them on the floor.

'Do you have a condom?' she murmured into the skin of his neck, gasping as his fingers found the place she most wanted them. He started circling his finger and she cried out in pleasure, arching her back, pushing herself against him. He kissed her breast, then briefly left her trembling and wanting on the settee while he went into the bathroom. He came back holding a foil square and a few moments later she was lost in primal pleasure, the only thing existing was their bodies, their desire.

Clara washed her hands in Sam's bathroom and wished she'd brought her clothes with her. She was stark naked and had no choice but to walk back out boldly and retrieve her garments from the various places they'd been slung. She opened the door slowly and poked her head out. Sam was laying on the settee, unselfconsciously, one arm flung back over his head, the other over his stomach, penis flaccid, resting on his leg.

'Hi,' he said. 'Come over here.'

She opened the door and made a conscious effort not to cover herself with her hands as she walked back to him. She retrieved her knickers as she stepped over the post-sex detritus and slipped them on before sitting back down on the settee. He sat up and kissed her shoulder.

'That was pretty awesome.'

She smiled and picked up a cushion to cover her breasts.

'So, how long are you around for?' he asked, picking up his shorts from the floor and sliding back into them.

'Not long. Headed to Sydney next, then I'm hoping to go to Singapore to do a TEFL training course.'

'To do a what?'

'Oh, sorry, Teaching English as a Foreign Language.'

'Sounds neat. Are you a teacher in the UK?'

'No, I'm an accountant.'

'That's impressive.'

'It's okay. I mean, it paid the mortgage.'

'So, probably a bit late to ask this,' he gestured at their state of undress, 'but I'm assuming no husband or boyfriend back home?'

'We split up.'

'I'm sorry to hear that. Well obviously, I'm not that sorry.'

She laughed.

'What happened?'

She hesitated and he sensed her reluctance.

'Sorry, you don't have to answer.'

She retrieved her bra from the back of the settee and turned away from him while she did up the fastening at her waist then twisted it round and back into place.

'No, it's okay. He…we wanted a baby and it didn't happen, things sort of just…fell apart.'

'Ah, kids. I got a whole bunch. They're overrated.'

Silence.

'Oh no, I didn't mean….Sorry, I keep saying the wrong thing.'

'It's okay,' she said. But it wasn't. The post-sex glow was fading and being replaced with an uncomfortable feeling. Her mouth was dry, her head fuzzy with the start of a hangover as the effects of the alcohol wore off. 'Actually, I think I should go,' she said, standing up and pulling on her shorts and T-shirt.

'Oh strewth, me and my big mouth. Don't go.' He put his hand on her wrist, but she pulled it away.

'Sorry, I...just...I should probably check Deirdre is okay. Thanks for...a great time though.' She headed out the door before he could see her eyes threatening to spill tears.

'I can't believe he said that.' Deirdre's eyes were wide.

'He did, but I think he was just trying to make light of the situation. Only it didn't work.' Clara uncrossed her legs and slid her hands under her thighs to stop them sticking to the leather seat on the train. 'I'm a bit freaked out that I had sex with someone other than Christopher. I mean, it's been a while.'

'Will you keep in touch?'

'I doubt it.' Clara rolled her eyes. 'Hardly looking for romance, am I?'

'A holiday fling?'

'A very short one. It was fun, though.' She couldn't contain her smile.

'Look at you! You so needed that lay.'

'Maybe.' She looked down at her knees. 'Yeah, I guess I did.'

'Good for you, so.'

'I still can't believe it happened. I blame the skydive. It was the adrenaline, got me all out of sorts. It should come with a warning.'

'What – "Be Careful: Doing a skydive may lead to sex with the instructor"?'

Clara laughed. 'Yes! I wouldn't have slept with someone I'd just met without all that excitement first. And the beer; that might be to blame, too.'

'Ah, relax. You had a good time didn't you?'

'Yes.' Clara couldn't help grinning. 'Until after, anyway, when I remembered my heartbreak.' Clara paused. 'Oh God, that sounded so self-pitying didn't it?'

'A little, but I'll let you off. I'm just glad you had some fun.'

'I bet he sleeps with all his skydiving students.'

'Maybe so. Sounds like he knew what he was doing, anyway.'

'He did. I can't remember the last time I had sex like that. Trying for a baby for so long really kills any passion.'

'I can imagine.'

'It was like being a horny teenager again. Apart from we're both adults so knew what we were doing.' She allowed herself a moment to enjoy the recollection, then brought herself back to the present. 'Anyway, what about your instructor? James, was it?'

'Ah, nothing like that. He was a nice enough bloke, but pretty sure he was gay. Not that I was interested, anyway, so.'

Clara nodded. 'So, what shall we do when we get to Sydney?'

'Let's get settled into our hotel, then see how we feel.'

'Do you feel like we're cheating by getting the train and staying in a hotel?'

'Cheating, how?' Deirdre asked.

'Well, I was supposed to be backpacking on a budget, roughing it, having adventures and finding happiness and all that.'

'Behave yourself, would you?' She swatted her with her train ticket. 'How's the application going?'

'It's all done. Submitted. I should hear if I've been accepted any day, now.'

Deirdre nodded and sat back in her seat, satisfied.

Clara regarded her new friend. She was going to miss her. This would be their last week together before they parted company. And Clara would be thrown into the unknown yet again. She watched the Gold Coast whizz by through the window and tried to focus on the here and now.

The train was considerably faster than the Greyhound and, before too long, they were settling into their new home for the next week.

'We actually have a wardrobe,' Clara said. 'I'm going to unpack and hang things up, then hide my backpack under my bed.'

'Me too. It'll be nice not to live out of a bag and wear crumpled clothes...and, oh look, there's an iron and ironing board in here!' Deirdre held the creaky wardrobe door open.

'Ooh, we can iron! Get the kettle on and let's have a cup of tea to celebrate.'

'God, we're exciting, aren't we? What would Todd think if he could see us now?'

'He'd think we're old and boring. It's one thing backpacking straight from uni, but when you've got used to your home comforts over the years, you feel it more. Anyway, who cares what Todd would think?'

'Hear hear,' said Deirdre, as they clinked tea-cups. 'Now, where shall we explore first? It's got to be the Opera House and Harbour Bridge.'

'Yep, got to be. They should be about twenty minutes' walk away,' Clara said, reaching for her guidebook.

Chapter 12

March 2015

'Hello, I'm Caroline.'

Caroline the counsellor, Clara thought. She had brown bushy hair, shot through with grey, which she was trying to contain in a clip at the crown of her head. Her complexion was doughy. A double chin gave way to a jowly neck which hung over an ill-fitting flowery blouse. Her green pleated skirt bulged over her hips, so that the pleats didn't hang properly, and her tights sagged where her feet disappeared inside her sensible rubber-soled shoes. Her appearance was the antithesis to the consultant's, with the latter's sharp hairstyle and expensive-looking glasses. Perhaps the look was designed to put her clients at ease, Clara wondered.

'I'm Clara,' she said, aware that Caroline was waiting for her to say something.

'Hello, Clara. It's lovely to meet you.' She smiled and Clara found herself relaxing a little. 'So, we offer this service to all our clients undergoing fertility treatments. It's a safe space for you to talk about how you're feeling. One thing you should know is I'm unshockable. You can say whatever you like. In fact, this only works if you're completely honest.'

'Okay.' Clara nodded.

Silence. She was doing that thing that counsellors did, where they stayed quiet until you felt you had to fill it by spilling out your innermost feelings. Clara still didn't say anything.

'Perhaps you could tell me a bit about yourself.'

'Okay. I'm married to Christopher. We've been trying for a baby and it hasn't worked, which is why I'm here. I'm an accountant and he's an investment banker.'

'An accountant. Do you enjoy your job?'

Clara shrugged. 'I like that I can organise what I'm doing and I know when something's right or wrong. I like to control the numbers.'

Caroline noted something down on her pad.

'And I like to help people, my clients. That bit's satisfying.'

Clara looked around the room. A painting of a red-and-white-striped deckchair on a beach hung on the far wall. Bright yellow sand and blue sky. Perhaps it was there to make the patients think of happier times. There was a box of tissues on the low coffee table in front of them. Kleenex man-size. Clara didn't know they still existed and thought it was inappropriate to have sexist tissues in a room where women were at their most vulnerable. There was a window to the right which was ajar and a pleasant breeze wafted through the air, causing Caroline's notepad to flutter.

'Okay, and how are things with you and Christopher?'

'Good. I mean, well…not bad. Trying for a baby for so long takes its toll.'

Caroline nodded and waited for her to continue.

'Well, for example…' Clara chewed her lip, thinking. 'He doesn't like to talk about things so much and I sometimes take that to mean him not caring, when I know that's not actually the case.'

'And do you like to talk about things?'

'Yes. I guess that's partly why I'm here.'

More silence.

'I think maybe he thinks it's his fault. And it isn't. We both have issues. I just didn't expect to be that couple, you know?'

'What couple is that?'

'The one that can't have kids and each blames the other.'

'Do you think he blames you?'

'No.'

'Do you blame yourself?'

'No. Well, maybe. I mean, it should be easy enough to get pregnant. It is what's *supposed* to happen.' Caroline wrote something down. Clara tried to look discreetly at what she'd written, but the pad was angled away from her. 'Supposed to, as in I was supposed to go to uni, get my degree, get a good job, find a partner, get married. I did all that and then I was *supposed* to have children and I can't.'

Caroline nodded and tucked her pen into her thick hair.

Clara stayed quiet. Surely it was the counsellor's turn to speak now? To analyse what she'd said?

'And who says you're supposed to do all these things?'

'My parents? My friends? Society? Anyway, it doesn't matter, because they're the things I wanted to do, and usually I can get what I want, by focusing on it and working to achieve it.'

'I see. It's a common way of thinking. I suppose the question is, how do you feel when things are trickier than you'd anticipated?'

'I feel frustrated. And helpless. And guilty. And angry, sometimes.' Clara scratched her wrist.

'What makes you angry?'

'The fact that I can't do anything to change what's happening.'

'Is being in control important to you?'

Clara snorted, a half-laugh. She looked at the deckchair. 'Yes. I like to plan. A lot. And it kills me that I can't plan this.'

'So, maybe we can look at some techniques to help with that next time.' Caroline took her pen from her hair and pointed at the clock on the wall behind her. 'We're out of time for today.'

Clara looked at the needle the nurse was offering her. She'd practised on an orange and now the nurse wanted to see her use the empty needle on herself, before she handed over the massive cardboard box full of medication.

'So, I pinch some skin and push it in?'

She was buying time. She knew what she was supposed to do.

'Yes.' The nurse smiled, encouraging her. The needle was only an inch or so long and very fine, but still, it felt unnatural to stab herself with it. Christopher was looking at her nervously. He hated anything medical. Tough luck there, Clara thought. She sighed, took the needle and pinched an inch of flesh near her belly button. She hesitated a second or two then pushed it against her skin. It slid in easily and she couldn't feel much, apart from a slight sting at the entry point. She looked up at the nurse, who smiled, pleased with her.

'Great, now you can take it out again,' she said.

It slid back out just as easily and a tiny blob of blood appeared at the site.

'That's fine, nothing to worry about. Well done.'

Christopher was looking a bit pale. Clara put her hand on his thigh.

'Don't worry, I'm sure we'll get used to it,' she said, arranging her features into a smile.

At home, they moved aside the butter, olives and smoked salmon to make space for the medication in the fridge. It looked like a chemist's. There was also a big stash of empty needles which Clara put under the bed, along with a yellow sharps box with a skull and crossbones on to put the used needles in. Good job we don't have kids in the house, she thought, and rolled her eyes at her own vague attempt at a joke.

'Now all we have to do is wait for my period. Weird that for the first time in two years, I actually want it to come so we can get started.'

Christopher nodded in agreement.

Clara changed into her pyjamas and went downstairs. Christopher had poured her a glass of Malbec, opened a bar of dark chocolate and had Netflix paused at the start of the next episode of *Dexter*. She let go of a breath she didn't realise she'd been holding and felt herself relax a tiny bit. They were finally doing something and she would have a chance of getting pregnant. She wasn't going to think about the low odds right now, they were trying and that's what mattered.

She took a long sip of the wine. 'I won't be able to have this once I start the injections,' she said. 'Then hopefully not for nine months after that, either.'

She swung her legs onto Christopher's lap and he stroked the sole of her left foot.

'Hopefully,' he replied.

He hit the play button and they escaped into a world of likeable serial killers, where things were more straightforward.

'I want to do it,' Christopher said. A week had passed it and was time to start the injections.

'Are you sure? You don't like needles. I can do it myself.'

'I know you can, but I want to help, to be involved.'

'Fine. But we need to make sure we do it right. Let's watch the YouTube video again.'

She sensed his impatience as they hunched over her iPhone at the kitchen counter. They watched a slim dark-haired woman demonstrate: adding powder to a vial of liquid, gently swirling (not shaking) it until all the powder dissolved, then sucking the liquid up into the syringe. The woman held it up to the light and tapped it so any air bubbles came to the surface, then carefully squeezed the plunger a millimetre so the air escaped, and set it aside. Next, she 'prepared the site', which entailed wiping her lower stomach with an alcohol wipe. She pinched some skin, pushed the needle in and slowly pushed down the syringe. It was just as they'd been shown at the IVF clinic, and just as the video had shown them the first three times they watched it.

'Okay, I think we've got it,' Christopher said.

Clara had laid out the equipment in front on them, on the recently Dettol-ed kitchen island: vial of powder, syringe loaded with sterile water, alcohol wipe, sharps container and Lindt chocolate bunny (that was a treat for after).

'Ready?'

She nodded. 'Wait. Wash your hands.'

'I already did.'

'I know, but then you touched my phone.' Obediently, he walked over to the sink and washed his hands, lathering up and interlacing his fingers the way the posters at the doctor's showed you.

'Ready?'

'Yes.'

She watched him methodically perform the tasks they'd just watched on the video, satisfied he was doing it correctly. He got to the part where he had to squeeze out air bubbles, thumb and forefinger of one hand pinching the syringe, thumb from his other hand gently pushing at the plunger. He pushed too hard and an arc of liquid sprayed over the table, decorating the Lindt bunny's head.

'Christopher!' she yelped.

'Shit! Sorry.' He looked guiltily at the syringe, which was now half empty.

'For God's sake! You have to be more careful, it's very precise.'

'What do we do now?' He looked stricken.

She sighed, as though dealing with an errant toddler. 'Luckily for you, they give us a couple of spares, so we can start again. But don't mess it up this time, or we will run out and have to buy more and it might not come in time and…'

'Okay, okay, relax. I know what I'm doing now.' This time he made it through all the steps with no mishaps and was ready with the loaded needle.

'So, do you want to lay down, or…?' he asked, needle hovering uncertainly.

'What, on the kitchen island?'

'No, I mean, we could go upstairs.'

'I'll stand up, like she did in the video.' She stood up, unbuttoned her jeans, pulled her T-shirt up and used the alcohol wipe. He hesitated, then pinched some flesh like he'd seen in the video and slid the needle in. There was a faint sting.

'Okay?' he asked. She nodded and he gently pushed the plunger all the way in until the syringe was empty. He pulled it out and popped it into the sharps bin.

Clara sat down on the stool. 'Well, that wasn't so bad,' she said. 'Christopher? Are you okay?' His pallor was whitish-green.

'Erm, yes, I feel dizzy but nothing to worry about.'

Clara couldn't help but smile.

'Here, sit down.' She pulled out a seat for him. 'Do you want to share my chocolate?'

He nodded gratefully.

'Maybe you should do tomorrow's,' he said.

'Yes, maybe I should.' She unwrapped the gold foil and went to put the kettle on.

Chapter 13

March 2018

'I'm going to get blown away!' Clara steadied herself on a rock, hair flapping wildly in the wind.

'This is mad!' Deirdre half-shouted, trying to make herself heard as she hung on to a handrail on the rocky path. 'The beach will be sheltered. We need to get past this bit.' The foamy waves were pounding against the steel grey rocks which made up the jagged coastline. They were high above sea level, exposed to the elements. Clara's T-shirt pressed against her front and flapped behind her. She ducked her head so her hair blew over her instead of in her eyes.

'It's so... powerful,' she yelled into the wind.

Deirdre nodded and they pressed on.

They were on the coastal path, having set off from Coogee beach. Half a mile or so later the wind dropped and they were able to talk at a more comfortable decibel level. They rounded a corner and Bondi beach came into view. A vast expanse of white sand and blue sea, both littered with people, surfboards and lifeguards in blue tops. The first thing to get Clara's attention, though, was a swimming pool right next to the sea, waves crashing over the side as swimmers with goggles and swimming hats cut smoothly through the water, up and down, clocking up lengths. Next to the swimming pool, couples and families sat at tables outside a café, nonchalantly drinking coffee and eating paninis.

'Look at that! Looks like they could get swept over the edge,' Clara said.

'Yes, or something could get swept in. Like a shark.' Deirdre starting doing the theme music to *Jaws*.

'Don't, I saw a load of them on my skydive.'

'Ah, while you were strapped to sexy Sam.'

Clara snorted. 'Sexy Sam. Still can't believe I did that. It's starting to feel like my life at home happened to someone else and I'm different here.'

'That's a good thing?'

'Maybe. I don't know. What if I'm just running away and when I get back I'll be exactly as I was?'

'You think too much,'

'Yep. Guilty as charged. Can't help myself.'

'I don't think you'll be exactly as you were. Time has moved on and you'll have had lots of new experiences. But I don't think that's a magic fix, either.'

'No. I still keep imagining being here with Christopher.' She paused, then added, 'And our child.' She looked down at her feet. 'Not that I'm not having a great time with you.'

'Ha, I'm not offended, honestly. You're overthinking, again. You're stuck thinking about the past and about what might have been. Try to enjoy the here and now.'

Here and now, here and now, Clara repeated to herself.

'I know you're right,' she said.

It wasn't the first time she'd been told she thought too much. Christopher had regularly told her to 'get out of her head'. As if she could climb out of her thoughts and be something separate to them. Maybe she should go to some sort of retreat and learn how to clear her mind through meditation. She could eat organic food, get up at sunrise and sit with her legs crossed, making a humming noise. Could I squeeze that in before Singapore, she wondered? Become all Zen-like, immune to Facebook posts of my ex-husband and his woodland-walk loving new girlfriend? The thought of them together had less sting to it just now, though. Perhaps the wild wind was blowing it away. Either that or the rocks and sea rendered everything else insignificant.

They stopped to look at the crashing waves, the surfers and the blue sky. She could feel her skin tingling from the sun and wind and stopped to put on some more suncream.

The smell of coconut invoked nostalgia for summer holidays gone by: sipping cocktails with Christopher; sharing their pizzas at a seafront restaurant, so they each got to try the other's; walking along the beach hand in hand...

Dammit. Here and now, here and now.

'This is the best soup I've ever tasted,' Clara said. They were in Chinatown, still sticky and sandy from the afternoon at the beach, but the tempting smell had proved too much as they walked past.

'What is it again?'

'Beijing-style eggs, tomatoes and doughballs.'

'Different. But amazing,' Deirdre said between mouthfuls of char sui pork. 'Wanna taste?'

Clara dug her chopsticks in and offered up her soup. 'That's so good.' She wiped some sauce off her lower lip. 'I may be blowing my budget, but it's so worth it.'

'Yeah, I reckon travelling straight after uni is different. You're used to Pot Noodles and beans on toast.'

'You're right. I used to think chicken dippers were the best thing in the world after a night out.'

'Not so discerning as a drunk student.'

'No, I didn't know Beijing-style eggs were a thing. I was a novice foodie.' Clara took a sip of her wine. 'So, are you excited about starting your new job?'

'Sure. It'll be a shock to the system to have to get up and organised and off to work every day, though. But I am looking forward to having a more permanent place to live.'

'Ha, yes, with an iron and ironing board.'

'And a clean kitchen.'

'A wardrobe with enough hangers...A washing machine!'

'Now that does sound like bliss,' Deirdre conceded. 'How, about you? Are you ready for your course?'

Clara had had an email the day before saying she'd been accepted on the Teaching English as a Foreign

Language training course in Singapore. She was due to fly out next week.

'Honestly? I'm terrified. Feel like I'll be starting again. It's been great since I met you. The first month on my own was hard.'

'Ah, you'll be grand. You'll meet loads of people. Teaching English will be different. There'll be other teachers for a start, and the kids to keep you company.'

'Yeah, it'll be good,' Clara said, with more confidence than she felt.

'Hopefully you'll be able to put Christopher firmly behind you.'

'That's what I'm intending. I've de-friended him on Facebook. Just for my own sanity. I don't need to see photos of him and Sarah, but also I don't feel the need for him to see photos of me on my travels.'

'Well, my friend, I'm proud of you.' Deirdre pointed her chopstick at her across the table.

'Thanks. Hope I can stick to my guns.'

'I have every faith.'

'I'll miss you.'

'Me, too. We'll stay in touch.' Deirdre gave Clara's hand a friendly squeeze across the table. 'I want to hear all about your Singapore adventures. Though maybe stay away from skydiving instructors.'

Clara nudged her leg under the table. 'Yes, think I've had my fill of those.'

As she laid in bed that night, Clara could make out Deirdre's shape in the twin bed and hear her rhythmic breathing, signalling she was asleep. Tomorrow they'd part company and realistically might never see each other again. She wondered what would have happened if she hadn't met Deirdre on the Whitsundays tour. Would she have given in and gone home by now, or would she still be pretending to have a good time, posting photos on Facebook that told a lie? Her stomach clenched at the thought of starting again in Singapore, though she consoled herself again with the fact that she'd have some structure and she'd be bound to meet more like-minded people. She closed her eyes and fell into a deep sleep.

Chapter 14

July 2010

Jess had been in charge of organising Clara's hen do. Clara had made her take a solemn vow that there would be nothing tacky, no topless waiters and absolutely no strippers. Jess had listened when Clara said she'd prefer a party with the people she cared about to traipsing round a city centre, trying to keep track of everyone and shouting above music to have a conversation.

As they got close to their destination, Jess made Clara root around in the glove box for an eye mask so she couldn't see. Clara heard the tyres crunching on gravel, then the engine cutting out.

'We're here!' Jess announced. 'Don't move.' She jumped out and went round to the passenger side to open Clara's door, holding her hand as she climbed out, then turning her round. 'Okay, you can look!'

Clara pulled down the eye mask and blinked. 'What's this? A church?'

'It's a converted chapel. Look!' Jess grabbed her hand again and led her round the side of the building, to a large decked area with a barbecue, firepit, sun-loungers and hot tub.

'A hot tub!'

'Yep. And because I know how much you love a schedule, here you go.' She handed Clara an itinerary for the weekend.

'You laminated it?'

'We've got a new machine at work. Wanted to try it out, and now you can read it in the hot tub.'

Clara looked down at the laminated itinerary.

***Friday** 6pm onwards – arrival drinks, hot tub*

Saturday *– a special guest....* Clara looked up sharply and shot Jess a look.

'Don't worry, no strippers. I promised.'
...pub lunch, games, more hot tub
Sunday *– Hangover-cure English brekkie, hot tub.*

'I see the hot tub features a lot.'
'Yep.'
'I love it. Thank you.' She hugged her friend.
'Wait until you see inside.' Jess led Clara back round to the front door, where she followed instructions on her phone to access a giant key from a box on the wall. The huge door swung open and they were greeted with a room the full height of the chapel. The original pulpit and organ pipes were still there. The pews had been rearranged around a large central table and an open plan kitchen area sat behind the altar.

'Wow. This is different. It's great,' Clara said.

Jess's phone started ringing. 'It's Jo. Hi Jo, can you see the Golden Lion pub?...Yep, it's on your right. Good.... Keep going, then when you get to the roundabout turn left and there's a dirt track immediately to your right....See you soon!' She hung up the phone. 'Jo and Sarah are nearly here and Claire, Becky and Helen were setting off after work, together. They'll be here by seven. Shall we get our bags from the car and look round?'

Clara placed her holdall on the nearest side of the double bed and unzipped it, looking for her swimming costume. A white envelope lay on top of her neatly folded clothes. Puzzled, she took it out. Her name was written on the front, in Christopher's handwriting. She slipped her thumb under the flap and opened it to find a card inside, with a picture of a jelly ring on the front. Inside the card he'd written 'Told you you'd say yes, one day. Can't wait to make you Mrs

Davis. Have a fantastic hen do. Christopher xxx'. Clara smiled and held the card to her chest.

'Watcha got there?' Jess appeared from the bathroom in a navy blue polka dot bikini with a bow at the front.

'Nothing. Just a card. From Christopher.'

'Lemme see.'

She reluctantly handed it over.

'God, he's soppy.' Jess laughed. 'Come on, forget about him for the weekend. You've got the rest of your life to be married to him. Let's have some fun.'

'Let me get my costume on and I'll come down.'

'I'll pour you a prosecco,' Jess said as she left the room.

'Can I have a strawberry in it?' Clara called after her.

She located her black swimming costume quickly – she'd packed it near the top of the bag, for easy access, as Jess had told her three times to make sure she had it. Then she got out her pyjamas and laid them on the pillow and put her toothbrush and shampoo in the bathroom, before changing into her costume, grabbing the white robe from the back of the door and heading downstairs to find her friends.

The next morning they all gathered in the living room on the mezzanine level, awaiting the 'special guest'.

'I'll kill you if it's a stripper,' Clara said to Jess.

'I told you, it's not. Now drink your mimosa.' She was fiddling about with her phone, then it rang and she made her way to the doorway, giving the person on the other end directions. 'Yep, that's it. Keep going down the track and you're here.' She disappeared out of the door. Clara took a gulp of her drink and looked at her friends, but none of them were giving anything away. Jess reappeared, with a man of about thirty. He was good looking in a boy-next-door sort of way. Definitely not in a stripper way. He looked more like someone who would put on a suit and go to an office than someone who ripped off their trousers to reveal a leopard print thong.

'Hi, ladies, I'm Graham.' He brushed his dark brown hair off his forehead. He was carrying a large case that looked like the ones art students at university used to cart around. Clara raised a quizzical eyebrow at Jess. She smiled and said nothing.

'Which one is the bride-to-be?'

Jess pointed at Clara and she raised a reluctant hand.

'Don't look so worried,' he said. 'We're here to do some art.' He set his case down in the middle of the room and unzipped it to reveal large sheets of white paper, pencils and box of charcoal.

'It's a drawing class!' Jess blurted.

'Help yourself to a piece of paper and a pencil and I'll be back in a moment,' Graham said. 'Is there somewhere I can get changed?' he asked Jess.

Clara shook her head slowly at Jess as he left the room.

'What? He's not a stripper – it's art!'

'He's going to take his clothes off though, right?'

'Well, yes. It's life-drawing. But it's nudity, not stripping. It's tasteful and cultured.'

Pieces of paper and pencils were passed around and Graham reappeared wearing a navy blue dressing gown. 'Okay, ladies. Do we have any artists here?'

'Nope.' Everyone shook their heads.

'We'll start with looking at light and form. First, I want you to draw my hand and notice where the shadows are. Try to draw what you see, rather than what you expect to see.'

Clara moved her pencil across the page, trying to follow his advice. Claire snorted as she looked over her shoulder.

'What's that?'

'It's a vein.'

'Thought you'd given him six fingers.'

She looked at her drawing again, then turned the pencil round to rub out the vein/finger.

'Okay, ladies. Shall we have a look at your work?' They laid their drawings out on the floor and while he was commenting on the shading and texture, he removed his dressing gown. 'Next, you're going to draw me.' He stood up in the centre of the room and Clara's eyes went straight to his penis. It was the biggest one she'd ever seen in a flaccid state. No wonder he wanted to show it off. She forced herself to look back at his face, coughed and took another gulp of her drink. The room went quiet. There was that feeling of being in class at school, when you wanted to giggle, but knew you shouldn't. Once they got going, the mood relaxed and general chit-chat resumed. Clara found she enjoyed trying to recreate Graham's form on paper. The pencil on the paper was relaxing, though she wouldn't be giving up the day job.

'Was that okay?' Jess asked, after they'd had a go at drawing his bum with charcoals and he'd gone.

'Yeah, it was fun.'

'Oh, thank God. I was panicking this morning, wondering if I'd got it wrong.'

'No, it was brilliant. Thank you.'

'What time's lunch? I'm starving,' Helen said.

The pub was covered in ivy, and bright pink begonias decorated the windowsills. Inside was all wooden floors, open fireplaces and beams on the ceiling.

'Through here,' Jess said, and the others followed. She led them to a room at the back, a private dining area. The mahogany table was decorated with pieces of glitter, which Clara saw, on closer inspection, were in the shape of hens. The walls had been decorated with balloons and pink banners with 'Bride-to-Be' written in a swirly font. At the head of the table was a bottle of champagne in an ice bucket and a gift bag.

'That's your spot,' Jess said.

'This is beautiful. Thanks so much, everyone.'

Clara took her seat and opened the gift bag. Inside was a sash, tiara and veil and a giant inflatable penis. 'Have we not had enough penises for one day?!'

'Never! We can't have a hen do without some willies. Anyway, this one's for the game,' Jo said.

'What game?'

Jo nodded towards the wall where there was a life-size poster of a cartoon man with no clothes on, a smooth area where his genitals should be, and a cut-out of Christopher's face covering his. 'It's pin the penis on the hunk. Blow it up, it's Velcro.'

'Oh my God. It's Christopher!'

'You're a lucky girl,' Helen said, gesturing at the penis, which was taking shape as Clara blew it up.

'Don't make me laugh. I can't blow when I'm laughing.'

'Brilliant! That's got to be the quote of the hen do,' Jess said. 'Right, let's get this champagne open.'

They took it in turns to be blindfolded and to attempt to stick the blow-up penis in the right place on the poster. Helen came closest.

'That's because you're sober,' Becky said.

'Yep, I'm at a definite advantage,' Helen said, placing a hand on her swollen stomach. They sat down at the table and waited for their pre-ordered meals to arrive.

'When are you due?' Becky asked.

'November.'

'I can't believe you're having a baby already. Can I touch it? Your belly, I mean?'

'Of course.' Helen pulled up her top to reveal her spherical stomach. The stretched skin looked almost like plastic.

'Wow,' Becky said. 'Oh my God. It moved.'

'Yep. He's a little wriggler. Mark says his going to be a footballer.'

'They all say that!'

Clara was watching with interest. She couldn't imagine wanting to have a baby so soon. After that, life was changed forever and there were still things she wanted to do.

'How about you, Clara?' Helen asked. 'Are you and Christopher going to try, after the wedding?'

'No. Well, not straightaway, anyway,' she said. 'I want to be at least thirty before I'm a mum.'

'Well, don't leave it too long. You know your eggs don't last forever.'

'Oh, it'll be fine,' Clara said and topped up her champagne glass.

Chapter 15

April 2018

The humidity hit Clara as soon as she stepped out of the airport. It was hot in Australia, but this was something else. The air was thick and heavy; moisture clung to her skin and hair as though she'd been out in the rain. She wafted the front of her T-shirt to try get some fresh air circulating, but there was none to be had. Her back was slick under the weight of her backpack. She consulted her phone again and scanned the pickup point for someone holding up an 'International Academy' sign. Nothing to be seen. Clara swatted away a mosquito and bit her lip.

'Miss Ellison?' a voice from behind her asked. She turned to see a dark-haired, dark-eyed man about her age and height.

'Yes?'

'Welcome. My name is Jerome, I'm here from the International Academy to take you to your accommodation. How was your trip?'

'It was good, thank you.' It came out in a rush as relief loosened the knot in her stomach, then she dried up. Jerome was still looking at her expectantly. 'It's very hot here,' she added lamely, as nothing else sprang to mind.

'Yes. Let me take your bag.'

'Oh, no –' She started to protest, but he was already easing a strap off her shoulder. 'Well okay then, thank you.' She circled her shoulders in relief as he slung her bag over one shoulder.

'This way.' He led her through the throng of people and Clara tried not to lose sight of her retreating backpack as he weaved expertly through bodies. She scratched the nape of her neck. Her hair was damp and everywhere itched. When Jerome stopped abruptly at a white minivan, she nearly bumped into him. He threw her bag in the back and opened a sliding door at the side of the vehicle. Clara looked inside to see most of the seats were already taken. She jumped in and sat down next to a woman who looked equally hot and bothered. Unfortunately, it was no cooler on board the minivan. Jerome closed the door, then disappeared back into the throng.

'Where's he going now?' a voice from the back seat asked.

'Don't know, but hope he's quick,' Clara said.

'Me too, I'm sweating buckets over here.'

Clara turned at the sound of the Irish accent. Of course it wasn't Deirdre, but she smiled anyway. 'Tell me about it. I've come from Australia and I thought it was hot there.'

'We'll get used to it.' The voice from the back seat again. Clara swivelled to see a man fanning himself with his boarding pass. His forehead was shiny with sweat and she noticed dark hair curling over the top of his white T-shirt and smattering his toned forearms. That hair must make him extra hot, she mused.

'The training centre will have air-conditioning,' he continued. 'I'm sure of it.'

'I admire your optimism. I'm Clara by the way.'

'Jake.' He held out a clammy hand and Clara took it. She turned to look at the Irish girl.

'Hi, I'm Siobhan.'

Clara smiled. With her red hair, pale, freckled skin and easy smile, what else could she have been called?

'So, headed to the same place?' Siobhan asked.

'International TEFL Academy?'

'Yep.'

'Yep.'

'Oh, great, we're all in it together then.'

At that moment the front door of the van opened and the warm air stirred slightly as Jerome hopped back in. He donned his sunglasses and they were on their way. Clara could breathe more easily as the breeze from the open window eased the humidity. Jerome pointed out points of interest as he drove, and Jake kept up a conversation with him. She took the opportunity to rest her head and enjoy the breeze as the trees whipped by.

The minivan pulled up outside a bright white complex with a flat roof.

'Your accommodation,' Jerome announced proudly. Clara craned her neck to get a better look as she unfastened her seat belt. Her gut churned in that now familiar way. This was her home for the next four weeks. The side door slid open and Jerome took the bags out of the back. She made a move and stepped out into the soup-like air. Jake followed. He recommenced the fanning with the boarding pass he was still holding. Now he was standing, Clara noticed his impressive height. He must have been at least six foot four.

'Are you chewing gum?' Clara asked, stepping out behind him.

'Yeah, you want some?' He started rummaging in his rucksack.

'No. It's not allowed here.'

'What do you mean not allowed?' His rummaging slowed.

'As in it's illegal. You could be fined £1000, or sent to prison.'

'No.' He shook his head.

'It's true,' Clara said. 'It says so in my guidebook. Well, I'm not sure it said prison, but definitely a fine.'

Jake reluctantly took the gum from his mouth and folded it in his boarding pass, placing it in his back pocket in lieu of a bin. He looked like a guilty school boy. Clara felt bad.

'Don't worry, no one saw.' She winked at him, then wondered what on earth she was doing. Can I pull off a wink, she thought? I shouldn't be around people, especially attractive male people. He probably thinks of me as a kindly aunt now, anyway. The sort that gives advice and winks.

Perhaps I should have ruffled his hair just to complete the exchange.

He was smiling again when she chanced a look.

'Follow me!' Jerome, was heading off towards the building. The three of them picked up their bags and did as he said. He stopped and consulted a piece of paper on his clipboard as they entered a blissfully cool reception area. A marble floor squeaked under Clara's flip-flops and an impressive water feature reminded her she needed the loo.

'Jake Holloway, you're in room three-oh-one. Siobhan, one-two-nine and Clara three-oh-two.' He pronounced Siobhan's name Si-oh-ban. She corrected him. He consulted his paperwork again, squinting in confusion. 'Shee-vorn?' he asked tentatively. She nodded at him. 'Excellent, follow me.' He led them down a long corridor, arriving at room one-two-nine first.

'Sheevorn,' he said, enunciating carefully. 'This is your room.' Clara peeked inside and saw a neat twin room, containing beds with matching pink blankets over starched white sheets. She felt a pang for Deirdre and wished she was going to be her roommate. They bid Siobhan luck and followed Jerome around a corner and up a flight of stairs. Clara's shoulders were aching again under the weight of her backpack. Leaving her Australia guidebook in the hotel in Sydney hadn't made that much difference. She was relieved when he finally stopped and opened a door.

'Clara, this is your room, and Jake, this is yours.' He opened the door to the next room. Both rooms looked exactly the same as Siobhan's. 'Now, you have time to relax and unpack. Come to orientation at 4pm, in the conference room.' He indicated a plan of the building on the wall. 'Ground floor, back to reception, then take the door to the left.'

Jake gave Clara a thumbs up and disappeared into his room. She smiled back, deciding it was probably best not to attempt to speak to him like a normal person. She eased her backpack onto the nearest bed. Someone else's belongings were neatly organised on the other side of the room. A purple fluffy dressing gown hung on the peg on the back of the door, a laptop sat on the desk, slippers were stowed away under the bed and a copy of *The Handmade's Tale* was on the bedside table. *Who was my new roommate? And where was she?*

A door led to a compact and functional en suite. It was clean and smelt like lemons. The churning in Clara's gut eased. She could get on with a clean bathroom that smelt like lemons. The toilet had a strange hosepipe sticking up inside the bowl. She pressed a handle at the side and a jet of water shot up where your bum would be if you were sitting on it. They obviously valued cleanliness here. She grabbed her toiletries from her backpack and switched on the shower. A warm jet hit her tired skin and she started to relax as the water ran over her sweaty body. This was a new era. Phase two of 'The Big Trip' started here.

Chapter 16
April 2015

'How many did you get?' Clara was groggy from the sedative, her brain felt as though it'd been dipped in treacle and her thoughts were all clogged up and bumping into each other. This one was clear though. She needed to know how many eggs had been collected.

'The doctor will be through shortly to tell you.' The nurse patted her hand as she wheeled her bed into a recovery room. 'Get some rest.'

Christopher was waiting in the room, pacing up and down. He took the chair next the bed. 'Okay?' he asked.

She nodded and closed her eyes.

'Mrs Davis?' Her eyelids fluttered open again and she saw the doctor in his pale blue scrubs, holding a clipboard. He had the answer to the question written down, right there.

She nodded. 'Yes.'

'Please can you confirm your date of birth and first line of your address?' They did this at every stage. It was a measure against any mix ups, which Clara was grateful for, but her brain was still treacle and she ended up muddling up the numbers.

'First of the second... No, I mean second of the first... January...' The doctor was frowning at her.

'Her date of birth is 2nd January 1982 and the address is 49 Portland Way, M60 8UX.' Christopher supplied the information calmly and efficiently.

The doctor nodded. 'Thank you. The good news is we've collected ten eggs. That's an excellent result. More than we were expecting.' That cut straight through the fog in Clara's brain and she allowed herself to relax a tiny bit. 'The nurse will bring you a cup of tea and a biscuit and we recommend you stay for a least twenty minutes. Then you can go home as soon as you're ready. We will inject each of your eggs with Christopher's sperm and the embryologist will call you in the morning to let you know how many have fertilised. We'd expect to see about sixty percent, so six in your case. From then we'll update you daily with phone calls to let you know how your embryos are progressing and we'll cross our fingers for a day five blastocyst transfer.'

Clara looked at Christopher to check he was taking all this in.

'What time will they call tomorrow morning?' she asked.

'It's usually around 10am. Any other questions?'

They both shook their heads and thanked him and he went on his way to put the next patient out of their misery with the news of how many eggs had been collected.

'So far, so good,' Christopher said.

Clara closed her eyes again.

On the drive home, she leaned her head against the headrest, staring at a smudge on the windscreen, possibly made by a squashed fly. She considered asking Christopher to press the button to squirt water and wipe the window, but it was too much effort to speak.

Ten eggs. All with the potential to become a baby when injected with Christopher's sperm. How strange to think that if they picked one egg over another, they'd have a different child. Not to mention the choosing of the sperm. One out of millions, even with Christopher's low sperm count. Usually this would happen naturally, of course. Nature would decide which egg and which sperm came together, out of exponential possibilities. When you thought about it like that, the chances of any specific baby being born were so low, they were almost impossible. In that sense then, every baby was a miracle in its own way.

'You okay?' Christopher asked, breaking into her thoughts.

'There's a smudge on the windscreen.'

He turned on the wipers. She watched it disappear, then put her head back on the headrest and closed her eyes again.

'They collected ten eggs,' she said later, on the phone to her mum.

'That's great news.'

Clara said nothing.

'Isn't it?'

'Well, yes. But we won't know until tomorrow if any have fertilised. It's not guaranteed. We could have gone through all this for nothing.' At that, she burst into tears.

Clara's mum was out of her depth with this one. She was of a generation where a stiff upper lip was of the essence. When you hit hard times, you jolly well got on with it, and that was that. She'd nearly been married before she met Clara's dad. Her fiancé had got cold feet a week before the wedding. He was now living with a Scottish bloke with a ginger beard and a penchant for whiskey. Clara's mum had dutifully cancelled the church, the function room at the hotel and the flowers, and rung round her guests one by one. Then she'd got straight back to her teacher training course and qualified later that year. By the time she met Clara's dad she was an established primary school teacher, loved by her pupils and respected by her peers. She worked part-time while Clara was young but still managed to rise through the ranks and was now headteacher at the village primary school. The only time off she'd had in thirty years was when she had stage one breast cancer. A lumpectomy did the trick and she was back in the classroom within a couple of weeks, just in time for the Key Stage Two SATs. Clara sometimes thought her mum wondered what all the fuss was about.

'Love, you've come this far and all is well. Try not to get ahead of yourself. One day at a time.'

Chapter 17

April 2018

'Looks like it's going to be pretty full on,' Jake said, between mouthfuls of noodles.

'I'm looking forward to it,' Clara replied. 'It's a long time since I did any proper learning. It'll be like being back in school.'

Jake didn't look convinced that that was a good thing. 'I'm looking forward to the part where we work with kids.'

'Me too, but we need to know what we're doing first.'

'Ah, I'd happily wing it.' He flashed her a boyish grin as he wiped sauce from his chin.

Jake had knocked on her door and persuaded her to join him for dinner. They both needed to eat and didn't know anyone else yet. It would have been rude to say no. That's what she told herself, anyway.

'I know kids,' Jake went on now.

'Do you…you have kids?' Clara asked.

'Not my own.' He smiled easily. 'I worked with them at home. I volunteered at a youth theatre group.'

Clara let go of a breath she didn't know she'd been holding. 'That's great. What sort of things did they do?'

'You know, am dram, local pantos at Christmas. That sort of thing. They're great kids.' He paused while he concentrated on gathering up the last few noodles with his chopsticks. 'Some of them had a rough start in life, you know?'

Clara pressed her lips together and nodded. 'Where are you from, back home?'

'Liverpool.'

'Really? You don't sound like it.'

'You should hear me nan!' He affected a strong Scouse accent. 'We're a family of thespians. I can do any accent you like, dah-ling.' He drifted into plummy upper-middle-class.

'So, which one is the real you?' Clara asked.

'Just me, no fixed abode. I moved around a lot – uni in London and lived there for a while after. Then I've been a professional bum, travelling around, doing temp jobs inbetween to fund it. How about you? Whereabouts are you from?'

'The North.'

'The North. Is that a place?'

'Near Manchester.'

'You don't sound like you're from Manchester, either.'

'I lived in London for a while too and was at uni in Durham.'

'Fancy.'

She smiled at him, 'Not really.'

'What did you study?'

'Business Administration and Accounting.' She cringed at how dull that made her sound. Jake nodded solemnly, but his eyes were warm.'I know, it's boring!'

'Not at all. I love business administration. I have an annual subscription to *Business Administration Today*.'

Usually, a comment like this would have put Clara on the defensive, but his easy demeanour was disarming and she found herself laughing, in spite of herself.

'How about you? What did you do at uni?'

'Drama and Acting.' He stood up and did an over-the-top stage bow.

'Of course. That makes sense. So why are you teaching English and not Drama?'

'Ah well, TEFL combines my other two passions: travel and working with kids. Besides, there's more than one way to skin a cat. I'm sure I can work some drama into teaching English. The kids will love that.'

Clara raised her eyebrows. 'I guess. We'll have to see what they say in the training.'

He smiled and shook his head slightly. 'Fancy a drink?' He nodded towards the bar area in the training complex. Clara hesitated. It was an early start in the morning and the first day of the intensive training period. Plus, she hadn't met her roommate yet. She didn't want to come back late and tipsy and make a bad first impression. Then again, she was enjoying herself.

'Sure,' she found herself saying. 'But just the one.' He rolled his eyes in mock exasperation and led the way.

Clara learned over drinks that Jake had been nursing a broken heart when he'd set off on a round-the-world trip a year ago. Claire, his girlfriend of three years, was supposed to come with him, but she'd got cold feet the week before, when she'd been offered a permanent position at the law firm she was temping at. She was now a legal secretary with a promising career ahead. To rub salt into the wound, Claire had had a whirlwind romance with a trainee solicitor and moved in with him after three months. Jake had later found out via Facebook that they were engaged and planning a spring wedding in the Cotswolds, ostensibly because she'd been there on family holidays as a child. It was also a place she'd visited with Jake.

'So, you just set off by yourself?'

'Yeah. I thought about staying for Claire, when she first changed her mind. But the thought of it was stifling. We'd already booked the tickets, and she told me to go. She lost a lot of money.'

'That's a shame. Why do you think she changed her mind?'

'I don't think she really wanted to go in the first place. Too much of a home bird. Still hurt like a bastard, though.'

'I'm sorry,' Clara said.

'Don't be. I think we're both better off now. Besides, I soon got over it when I got to New Zealand.'

'Oh yes, why was that?'

He grinned into his drink. 'There may have been a few nice girls there.'

Clara shook her head in mock disapproval.

'Hey, I was newly single and heartbroken. What's a man to do?'

She smiled at him. He was cute, she decided. Good-looking in a boyish way, but after the Sam fiasco, she was definitely keeping her mind on the challenge ahead. She didn't need any distractions in her quest to find happiness.

Clara tiptoed into her new bedroom. One drink with Jake had turned into four, and despite her better judgment, she was tipsy. She didn't want to make a bad impression if her new roommate was sleeping. She edged round the door; the other bed was empty. Blanket still neatly tucked in, slippers still on the floor – she hadn't been back. Clara was relieved and disappointed at the same time. She changed into her pyjamas and went into the bathroom to brush her teeth. She was rinsing when she heard the bedroom door open and close. She wiped her mouth and peeped her head around the door. A girl with closely cropped hair, a tie-dyed T-shirt and a sparkly handbag was tiptoeing into the room in much the same manner as Clara had a few minutes earlier.

'Hi,' Clara said.

'Hello!' the girl said, in a stage whisper. 'Sorry, I've had a few drinks. I didn't want to wake you.'

Clara laughed, liking her immediately. 'You didn't wake me, it's okay. I've had a few drinks too and was worried about waking you!'

'Excellent, we'll be best of friends. I'm Anna.' She walked over and stuck out her hand. Clara stepped out of the bathroom and took it. 'I was hoping we'd meet earlier; shall we have another glass of wine and get acquainted? Or perhaps a cup of tea would be better, given we've both had a few already and we have an early start. I take it you're on the same TEFL course?' She paused for breath.

'A cup of tea sounds good.' Clara made a move towards the small kettle on the cabinet by the door. 'And yes, I'm doing the TEFL course.'

'Excellent, it's going to be wicked.' Anna pulled back her sheets and revealed a neatly folded nightie with She-Ra on the front. 'I'll get myself comfy as well, while we chat.' She turned away modestly as she swapped her clothes for her nightwear.

'Love your nightie.'

'Ah, yes. The Princess of Power. She was ahead of her time, flying the flag for powerful women in the '80s.'

'And that's the prettiest handbag I've ever seen.'

'It's fabulous, isn't it?' She held it up so it glittered in the light. 'I have a collection of glittery handbags and this one is my favourite.'

Clara poured the tea, handed a mug to Anna, then sat on her bed, cross-legged, her palms curled around her own. She felt warm inside. It was like being back at uni – drinks with an entertaining young man and now this friendly woman she was going to be sharing a room with.

Anna dug about in her glittery handbag and passed Clara a small card. 'I'll tell you up front, I have epilepsy,' she said.

'Okay.'

'It's no biggie, but I need to tell you as we're sharing a room, in case I have an episode.'

'Okay,' Clara said again.

'Don't be freaked out. It's not as scary as it looks. Basically, if it happens, make sure there's nothing hard close by that I could bang my head on. It usually passes quickly and I'll be ship-shape and shiny again.'

'Not freaked out. How often does it happen?' Clara studied the card she'd been handed, which gave basic instructions on what to do in case of a seizure.

'I haven't had an episode for about four months now. I've been having acupuncture and I swear it helps. Fuck knows how, but it does.'

'Well, it sounds like you have it all under control.'

'I don't let it stop me doing anything.'

'Well obviously, otherwise you wouldn't be in Singapore, all the way from....Where are you from?'

'Surrey.'

'Nice. I'm from 'oop north'. Near Manchester.'

'Yes, I could tell you're a northerner.'

Clara found out that Anna was a science teacher in a secondary school at home, but had got fed up with the increasing amount of paperwork involved. Her partner of five years, Netta, ran her own PR consultancy and could do it from anywhere. She had global clients and could conduct meetings on Skype. Netta was due to join Anna once the training course was done. Anna's face softened when she spoke about her partner, and Clara felt a pang – not for Christopher as such, but for the feeling of being in a loving and secure relationship.

An hour or so passed as they shared their stories of what led them here, Clara giving a canned version of what had happened with Christopher. Anna nodded sympathetically in all the right places and had been suitably outraged at Christopher's behaviour. So much so at one point that Clara almost found herself defending him. Eventually they decided they really must get some sleep before tomorrow.

Clara drifted off quickly. She already liked Anna. And Jake. As a friend. Absolutely, just as a friend. The relief of no more dormitories or gap year students or aimless travelling about soothed her anxious mind. She had a good feeling about what was to come.

Chapter 18

April 2015

The day after the egg collection, at 10am, Clara sat at the kitchen island with a cup of tea, waiting for her phone to ring. Christopher had gone into work, but he promised he'd have his phone on all morning. She pressed the button on her phone to make the screen light up. 10:01. She opened Instagram and posted about her egg collection and that she was waiting to see how many had fertilised. Then she worried that if the phone rang she might accidentally reject the call if she was fiddling with it. She put the phone down. Then she double-checked it was on loud. 10:04. She drummed her fingers on the counter and chewed her lip. *How long should I wait before I call them?*

She carried her phone and cup of tea to the living room and sat down on the settee, placed the phone carefully on the arm and picked up her Kindle. She looked at the time in the top right of the screen instead of reading the words. 10:06. *Okay, so I'll ring if it gets to half past.* The doctor had said 'around ten o'clock', not 10am on the dot.

Her phone rang. She jumped and sloshed tea on her jeans.

'Shit,' she muttered, grabbing at the phone. *Jess calling.* She cancelled the call quickly. It pinged almost instantly.

Jess: Any news? o

Clara: No, still waiting. I'll call you back as soon as I hear. x

Jess: Okay, as **soon** as you hear please! Love you. o

Clara put her phone back on the arm of the settee and adjusted the way she was sitting. She was sore from the egg collection. It had happened under sedation, so all she remembered was an anaesthetist with hairy knuckles asking her to count back from ten. She'd got to seven before the lights on the ceiling blurred, then the next thing she knew she was coming round in the recovery room. She knew from her research the procedure involved a needle going into her follicles via the vagina, and that without the sedation and painkillers it hurt. Her stomach had that dull ache she usually got when she had her period, combined with a general feeling of having been interfered with. Like things were strained inside. 10:11.

She flicked on the TV. The breakfast news was on. The FTSE 100 index was down by two percent, there'd been a five-car pile-up on the M25, and ice was melting in Greenland and Antarctica. 10:17. She turned the TV off and walked over to the window. An old man was passing by. He had a newspaper tucked under his arm and was carrying a Sainsbury's carrier bag. He glanced up and caught Clara's eye, as if he'd felt her watching. She looked away quickly. 10:18.

She sat back down and picked up her Kindle. She read the same sentence three times and still didn't know what it said. 10:21. Why weren't they ringing? Did they ring all the people who had good news first and put off the bad ones? Maybe none had fertilised and they didn't want to make the call to break it to her?

Clara needed a wee. She took her phone up to the bathroom and was buttoning up her jeans when it rang. She checked the screen: *Fertility Clinic calling.* She hadn't washed her hands. She hesitated a moment, then snatched it up.

'Hello?'

'Is this Clara Davis?'

'Yes.'

'Please can I ask you to confirm your date of birth and the first line of your address?'

Clara breathed through her impatience. '2nd January 1982, 49 Portland Way.'

'Okay, thank you. I'm ringing to let you know four of your eggs have fertilised.'

Clara let this sink in for a moment. *It wasn't none.* 'Four?'

'Yes, you have four embryos. This is good news.'

'The doctor said to expect six,' she said, sounding like a sulky teenager.

'On average we hope to get around sixty percent, but some of your eggs were lower quality. Don't be discouraged. We only need one.'

Four. She turned the number over in her mind and slowly allowed herself to feel excited. Four embryos was a whole lot closer than they'd been before.

'So, what happens next?' she asked, even though she knew.

'We'll keep an eye on them, and we'll call you back in two days. Hopefully we'll have at least one to transfer. We want to see the cells continue to divide, until they reach blastocyst stage.'

Clara knew that there was a chance, a very real chance, none of them would continue to divide and she wouldn't have one to transfer. She pushed the unhelpful thought down.

Two days later, Clara sat at her kitchen island. She pressed the home button on her phone to light up the screen. 9:59. It rang. She jumped and nearly threw the phone in the sink as she grappled to answer it.

After the rigmarole of checking her date of birth and address, the voice on the phone said, 'We have one strong-looking embryo. It's at the thirty-two cell stage.'

'One? What happened to the others?'

'Another one is also looking strong. It's at the sixteen cell stage. The other two haven't made it, I'm afraid. But don't be disheartened. It's what we'd expect to see. You only need one.'

That line again. You only need one.
'Okay.'

'So, we'll see you the day after tomorrow. We'll hopefully have a healthy blastocyst to transfer – maybe even one to freeze, as well.'

'Do you call me on the morning to confirm?'

'No. We'll only call if there's a problem.'

Clara rang Christopher at work to relay the information. Then she called her mum. Then Jess. Then she wondered how to fill her day and whether she'd done the right thing taking time off work for the treatment. She posted an update on Instagram and decided she needed to get out of the house. It was a warm day for the time of year, and there were lots of people about. Walking dogs, cycling, talking on phones. She wondered how the world kept going as normal, while she was suspended in a torturous limbo. She held her phone inside her pocket, just in case the clinic rang again to say something else.

She was going to need a plan, she realised, to get her through the next eleven days. Eleven days until she took a pregnancy test and found out definitively, yes or no. Unless of course her embryos stopped developing. Then she'd be put out of her misery in two days' time. Clara shook herself and decided she needed to take control and Do Something.

When she got home, she got out some A4 paper from the office. She Sellotaped four sheets together, making a large rectangle. Then she took some different coloured felt-tips, wrote down the days and planned an activity for each one.

Chapter 19

April 2018

Clara cringed at the words 'role play'. The mere mention at school had caused her to flush to her roots and consider faking a minor injury to get out of it. Jake was nodding along to the instructions enthusiastically, clearly in his element. Anna seemed, if not quite as enthusiastic, far from terrified.

Clara had a word with herself. *She was an infertility warrior, she'd travelled to the other side of the world on her own, she wasn't going to be intimidated by a bit of role-play.* She did a power stance in her head and gave her best impression of someone who was comfortable with this sort of activity.

'So, Clara,' the tutor was saying. 'I want you to be a disruptive child. And Jake, I want you to play the teacher. Try to engage the child and minimise disruption to the group.'

Jake practically rubbed his hands together with glee.

'Everyone happy?' the tutor continued.

Clara gave a firm nod. *Oh God.*

'Great, go ahead.'

Jake was up first.

'Okay, class,' he began, addressing Clara. 'Today we're going to do some maths.' He paused, to give her chance to be disruptive.

'I hate maths,' she blurted.

'Aha, but not the way I do maths,' he said, not breaking character. He gave her a winning smile. 'It's not boring old numbers in a text book. Wait and see.'

Clara found she did want to wait and see, but then remembered she was being a disruptive child.

'Maths is rubbish!' She panicked and didn't know what to say. She cringed at her attempts at acting. She could have sworn she saw Jake's lip twitch, but ever the pro, he continued seamlessly.

'I used to think so too, before I met...Mr Wizzy Numbers!' With a flourish, he pulled out a teddy and held it out triumphantly.

Clara let out a snort of laughter. 'Where on earth did that come from?' she asked.

'I bring him to all my maths lessons; you kids won't hate maths anymore.' He was still playing teacher and Clara was flailing.

'Well, I don't like teddies either,' she said in her best sulky voice.

'Don't worry, neither do I.' Jake leaned forward conspiratorially and to her dismay, Clara felt herself flushing. He turned his attention to Anna. 'Mr Wizzy is going to ask the questions and he wants you to shout out the answer as soon as you know it.'

'Okay.' Their tutor stepped in. 'Great work everyone. Jake, you did an excellent job of trying to engage the disruptive child without letting her dominate the group and take all the attention.'

Clara didn't think she'd ever dominated a group.

The tutor was a kind woman and didn't comment on Clara's lack of acting skills. She was like a friendly older relative to her students. She'd introduced herself on the first day as Karol with a 'K', as she'd perched her ample behind on the edge of the desk. She'd worn a purple silk blouse and the buttons gaped over her chest, revealing a glimpse of a functional, flesh-coloured bra. Clara had wanted to offer her a safety pin, but couldn't figure out a polite way to do it. Karol had told them all a personal story of how she was bullied at school and that she'd wanted to work with children ever since. She wanted to do her best to spot and put a stop to any unwanted behaviour. She'd taught in a secondary school for twenty years, before getting itchy feet and moving to do this job. She didn't mention a family of her own and she seemed young for any children to be fully grown, so naturally Clara wondered if she hadn't been able to have any. Of course, she'd never ask. Thankfully, today Karol was wearing a dress that didn't gape anywhere and her underwear was concealed.

Clara allowed herself to relax in the next session when it became apparent her acting skills wouldn't be required. They moved on to recognising and accommodating different learning styles. They'd be given suggested lesson plans, but they had the freedom to tailor them to their individual groups and use different techniques. Clara took copious notes in her new notebook. It had a purple paisley pattern on it, and she'd bought it especially for this course. Anna occasionally lent forward and tapped on her laptop keyboard, while Jake leant back in his chair, one foot resting on the other knee, nodding and offering a remark every now and again. He never once put pen to paper, or fingers to keyboard. *There's a confident learner,* Clara thought as she underlined 'Kinesthetic' in green to highlight it. She was enjoying herself, she realised. She was using her brain for something useful for a change. She thought of all those hours, days, years of thinking, obsessing about becoming pregnant, and how refreshing it was to put all that to one side and to have room in her head for something more useful and productive. Trying for a baby was no longer the thing that defined her.

They had a ten-minute break mid-morning and stepped outdoors, ostensibly for some fresh air. As soon as they were outside Clara realised there was no fresh air to be had. They went from the comfortable artificially controlled temperature inside the building into thick soup. Moisture hung in the hot air and Clara immediately felt her hair start to frizz. She attempted to smooth it with her hands and caught Jake watching her. She didn't know why he was looking at her. He could obviously have his fill of girls closer to his own age. He'd made that clear. She made a mental note not to do anything that could encourage him. She was here to do a job and get some distance from what had happened over the last few years. No further complications were necessary. She dropped her hands to her sides.

'Karol with a K is on form today,' Anna said. 'I don't think I could have handled another morning on morphology and syntax.'

'Really? I found that interesting,' Clara said. 'Numbers are my thing at work, or they were. I didn't realise how much there was to learn about language.'

'I'm not sure why we need to learn so much about language when we're going to be teaching eight-year-olds,' Jake said. 'Thought my eyes were going to bleed when she wrote down the hundredth example of a word with three or more morphemes.'

'There weren't a hundred,' Clara said.

'Well, it felt like it.'

Jake was perched on a low wall, his legs apart, one elbow resting on a ledge just behind him. Clara looked away from his forearm. It really was quite shapely.

'Today is shaping up to be more fun, anyway,' Anna said.

'I do love a bit of role-play,' Jake said.

'Enough about your personal life, thanks,' Clara said, then to her dismay, found herself flushing again. Where did that come from? She absolutely didn't mean to say that. It must be something to do with the heat here, she thought, and pulled at the neck of her shirt. Jake was smirking at her, eyebrows raised. She coughed. 'I think our ten minutes are up. Shall we go back in?'

Chapter 20

April 2015

'All done, lovey. You can get dressed now.'

Clara didn't want to stand up in case the embryo fell out. She wanted to put a pillow under her bum and stay put, but the doctor was expecting her to emerge, dressed and ready to go, so they could wrap up the paper blanket covering the bed and get ready for the next patient. Reluctantly, she took Christopher's hand and climbed off the bed. She moved slowly and carefully as she put her knickers and jeans back on. She'd spend the next ten days moving slowly and carefully, like she was balancing a full glass of water on her head and taking care not to spill it. It probably wouldn't make a blind bit of difference, but if the procedure didn't work, she needed to know it wouldn't be her fault.

An embryo was now safely tucked away in her womb. The other one hadn't made it to the freezer, but one was all they needed, as the nurses kept telling her. Now all it had to do was stay where it was, implant, and keep growing. It sounded so simple, put that like. The wait lay ahead, like a long winding path with hidden perils around every corner. But Clara had her plan – she was filling every day with something nice. She was having a pedicure, afternoon tea with Jess, going to the cinema, a matinee at the theatre – nothing too strenuous or active. She'd be balancing her glass of water everywhere she went. One social engagement she didn't want to think about yet was Jo's baby shower. She'd said she'd go but had an assortment of excuses ready if she decided she couldn't face it.

Jo was a friend from uni. She and her husband had got married four years after Clara and Christopher, and she'd got pregnant straightaway. Clara remembered a conversation at Jo's hen do. They were drinking prosecco in a hot tub and Jo had said how she was coming off the pill as soon as they got back from their honeymoon, and that she wanted a big family. Probably four kids. Clara had thought that seemed like an excessive number of children and she wondered what the big rush was. She'd been getting used to the idea that she was going to be married, never mind having babies.

One embaby on board, she posted on Instagram #embryotransfer #ivf #wishmeluck

She sent Jess a photo of the embryo.

Clara: Check out our embryo-baby x

Jess: That's weird. I mean, cool, but weird. How are you feeling? o

Clara: Right now, on top of the world. Anything is possible! I'm sort of pregnant – at least, the closest I've ever been. x

Jess: Amazing. I have a good feeling about this. ooo

Clara: For the moment, so do I. I can actually imagine it working. From what I've read, it's going to get tough over the next ten days though. Until I can test. It's the hardest part of the whole process. I'm going to need you.x

Jess: I'm here. o

Chapter 21

April 2018

'Wow, that view is awesome,' Anna said. Jake let out a low whistle. Clara said nothing as she took in the infinity pool to her left, where tourists languished on sun-loungers that looked as if they were floating on the water, and others rested their arms on the side of the pool, looking out to the glittering metropolis of skyscrapers. They were on the observation deck of the Marina Bay Sands Hotel, their first day off since the TEFL course had started, and their first proper day of sightseeing.

'This must be one of the richest places on earth,' Jake finally said, shielding his eyes as he scanned the horizon.

'It is,' Clara said. 'I think it was number three in 2017. It's the largest seller of microchips in the world.'

'Yes, it's one of the most business-friendly economies, as they don't have loads of strict regulations,' Anna said.

'How do you know this stuff?' Jake asked.

Clara raised the guidebook she was clutching, thumb marking her page.

'I watched a documentary,' Anna said.

Jake nodded, as if this explained everything. Anna crossed over to the other side of the observation deck and Clara followed. They looked down over the Gardens by the Bay. Two connected glass domes sat by the edge of the water, forming a huge greenhouse which reminded Clara of The Sage in Newcastle. To the right was a man-made forest with pink and green 'trees'. Clara consulted her guidebook.

'They are *supertrees*.' She gestured at them. 'They're fitted with solar photovoltaic systems that convert sunlight into energy…so they're basically like giant solar panels. They also act as temperature moderators, absorbing and dispersing heat…Not sure how that works. Oh, you can go up them and walk between them on skywalks.'

'That's got to be our next stop!' Jake had joined them. He was almost buzzing with excitement, now he had free reign to explore his surroundings. Their first week of training had been pretty intense. Karol was old-school in her approach and brought out Jake's rebellious side. He was itching to 'get stuck in' and kept insisting 'it'd all be okay', as if he deemed the training unnecessary. Clara was quite the opposite and was taking the training very seriously, writing copious notes and going over them in the evenings. She was getting nervous about being let loose in a classroom. A module on safeguarding had Clara close to tears, and the following day a crash course on grammar had her up late into the night, testing her knowledge of irregular and auxiliary verbs. Anna had happily joined in the extra-curricular work. Truth was, Clara was feeling pretty worn out and was glad of the day off too. Jake's excitable mood was infectious, and when they'd seen all they could see from the top of the Marina Bay Sands, they made their way down to the Gardens by the Bay.

After walking along the skywalks and discovering Jake had a mild fear of heights, they were all flagging and in need of a drink. Clara's guidebook told them Raffles was *the* place for cocktails, so an hour later they were seated around a small table in an opulent courtyard with colonial style pillars, with a famous 'Singapore Sling' each.

'Cheers.' Jake raised his glass. 'To the most expensive cocktail I've ever bought. And to TEFL. And new friendships.'

'Cheers!' Clara and Anna cut him off, keen to get to the part where they sipped their drinks, and they clinked glasses. It was delicious. Or it could have been their extravagant surroundings, the extortionate price and the fact that Clara was hot and thirsty that were distorting her opinion. Either way the cocktail slid down a little too easily and she felt herself relaxing. She stretched out her tired feet and tilted her face up to the sun. It was hot and sticky, but a gentle breeze from a fan in the corner was making it more comfortable. She could get used to this. She smiled as she observed her new friends. Jake, with his boyish good looks, still managed to look relaxed and content with damp patches at his armpits and sweat beading on his forehead. Anna looked like a fashion model with her oversized sunglasses and closely cropped hair. She wore a blue playsuit with hot pink dinosaurs. It wouldn't have looked out of place on a three-year-old, but somehow, she made it work. Clara would have felt plain in her denim shorts, white vest top and comfortable flip-flops, but the Singapore Sling was making her feel pleasantly fuzzy around the edges, and what she wore didn't seem to matter at all. She caught Jake glancing at her outstretched legs. It was an almost imperceptible look, as he shifted his gaze back to the courtyard quickly, but Clara clocked it. She looked at Anna to see if she'd noticed. Anna was busy examining a mosquito bite on her ankle. Clara was sure Anna would have been outraged, being a good feminist, but she was secretly pleased. She definitely didn't fancy Jake, despite the flushing that seemed to happen when she spoke to him, and she was sure he didn't fancy her, but it was nice he thought her legs were worth a quick glance. *Still got it.*

'So, where to next, dudes?' Anna asked. Her glass was almost empty.

Clara gave Jake a pointed look. 'You mean Jake's not getting another round in here?'

'You're joking, aren't you? I'll be on Super Noodles the rest of the week as it is.'

Clara reached into her shoulder bag. 'I'll have a look in my guidebook for a bar where we can get cheap drinks.'

'Don't bother, I know a place,' Anna said, draining her drink. 'It's not far from here. Follow me.' She actually winked at them.

Anna's 'not far' turned out to be a thirty-minute walk in the sticky sun, but they'd arrived in the heart of

Chinatown and the streets were milling with locals and tourists. She led them into a pub in a British-looking building. It was small and blissfully cool inside. Clara pushed her sunglasses onto her head and blinked as her eyes adjusted to the relative darkness. There was a simple bar along the wall to the right, with fairy lights along the edge and two giant disco balls hanging from the ceiling. Two women sat on tall stools at the table in the corner, heads bent together, deep in conversation, and a group of young Japanese women were playing cards next to the bar. Apart from that it was quiet.

Anna marched over to the bar, clearly feeling at home. 'Right, who wants what?'

'Gin and tonic, please.' Clara liked this Anna. 'Wait, do they have Fever-Tree tonic?' She peered into the fridges. 'Yes they do. I'll have a gin and tonic, please.'

'Sounds good to me. I'll have the same,' Jake said.

'Wicked.' Anna lent forward at the bar.

Several G&Ts later, Anna was chatting to a petite Asian girl wearing cut-off dungarees, and Clara and Jake were perched on bar stools.

'This is really good,' Jake said, as he took a sip of his drink. 'I always thought gin and tonic was an old lady's drink.'

'It's making a comeback,' Clara said. 'This is Hendricks. The cucumber brings out the flavour and it needs a good quality tonic.'

He nodded his head appreciatively.

'I think I've found my new tipple. It's better than JD and coke. So anyway, how does TEFL compare with Business Accounting and what was it?'

'Business Administration and Accounting.' Clara sensed she was being teased, but it was in a nice way. 'Totally different. It's nice to be using my brain again, though.' She swirled the ice cubes in her drink with her straw.

He nodded. 'Sure, I get that.'

'My mum's been a teacher all her life, so she's loving that I'm doing this. I'm just waiting for her to start giving me tips and emailing me suggested lesson plans.'

'Ha. I guess being organised runs in the family, then.'

'Probably. Still not sure how I'll be with actual children, though. Not had much experience.'

'Nothing to it.'

'Said with the confidence of someone who's spent a lot of time working with kids.'

'Yeah, well, they're just people. There's nothing special to know. You have experience of working with people, right?'

She rolled her eyes. 'Of course. I'm not a total moron.'

'Moron is not the word that springs to mind when I think of you.'

'Erm, thanks?' Clara sipped her drink and ignored the fact he'd just suggested he thought about her.

'So, I haven't asked you what made you pack in your job and travel across the world. You seem like the type to be all settled.'

Clara's hand stilled on her straw. *Here we go again,* she thought. But it was said with such easy-going innocence, she decided to answer truthfully.

'I was, but my marriage broke down. We couldn't have kids and, well, things didn't work out as I wanted.' She said it all in one breath, then looked at her flip-flops.

Jake looked at her thoughtfully. 'You know, sometimes when things don't work out as you wanted, all the best things happen.'

It was such an unexpected response that Clara looked up and found herself grinning at him. His care-free demeanour was contagious and she was more at ease than she had been for a long time.

'Maybe so. Let's see.'

'Let's see, indeed.' He winked at her.

Chapter 22

April 2015

Clara was sitting on the grass in the park reading her book. Or she had been, until her ears pricked up at the conversation going on between two old ladies sitting on the bench behind her.

'One of those test-tube babies.'

'IVF, they call it.'

'Tried for years. Don't know why they didn't just adopt. Plenty of kids need good homes. Selfish really. Don't agree with all this playing God.'

'You're right. If God wanted them to have kids they'd have had 'em. None of this IVF in my day.'

'My sister's next-door neighbour couldn't have 'em. They got a dog instead and were perfectly happy.'

'Well there you go. Dogs are very loving. Think I'd have preferred a couple of dogs to my lot some days.'

'I know what you mean. It's the sense of entitlement that gets me. They can't accept that sometimes they can't have everything they want.'

'Oh, you're right. My Suzie wanted one of those cats with no fur. Don't know what's wrong with your average moggie.'

'Thought it was her allergies. Did you bring the biccies?'

She turned around to look at them. They were sharing a flask of tea and putting the world to rights.

On 25 July 1978 Louise Brown, the world's first IVF baby, was born. In Oldham of all places, not that far from where Clara grew up. Patrick Steptoe, an obstetrician and gynaecologist, and Robert Edwards, a biologist and psychologist, along with nurse Jean Purdy, pioneered the fertility treatment and stayed up all night to watch the cells that became Louise Brown divide in a Petri dish. (Of course, technology has advanced significantly since then and the process is now monitored with a time-lapse camera called an embryoscope.) IVF was groundbreaking and big news at the time, dividing the nation. Some people were uncomfortable with science being part of making babies, some were horrified. It was reported in the press that Louise's parents received hate mail after she was born, including broken test tubes and menacing, blood-spattered notes. Others were hopeful. Couples who hadn't been able to have babies also wrote to them, sharing their tales of woe, of heartbreak, and offering their congratulations, telling them how they now had hope. A chink of light at the end of a long dark tunnel. It had worked for the Browns; perhaps these couples still had a chance of becoming parents.

There are always people with a fear of the unknown or of anything different to their own values and beliefs. Thankfully, forty-plus years and eight million IVF babies later, any taboo around the subject is mostly gone. How was it then, that Clara ended up sitting in front of that bench, at that time, on that day? If there was a God, it seemed he was laughing at her. She stood calmly and approached the ladies on the bench.

'Good morning,' she said. They looked up from their tuna fish sandwiches, shielding their eyes from the sun.

'Hello, love.' They both nodded at her and turned their attention back to their tea and sandwiches. Grey heads bowed, liver-spotted hands clutching Thermos cups.

'I couldn't help overhearing your conversation,' Clara continued.

They looked at each other, then back at her.

'Oh?' The larger of the two ladies raised her eyebrows in an innocent question, though a twinge of worry clouded her expression.

Clara took a deep breath. 'I'm afraid I'm one of the selfish people you were talking about.'

An awkward silence.

'I haven't been able to get pregnant for various medical reasons. And I've had IVF. I'm actually in the middle of it now and waiting to find out if it worked.'

More awkwardness. And then: 'I'm sorry, love. If we'd known, we'd never have...' the larger lady began, then looked at her friend for support. The friend remained resolutely silent and took a bite of her tuna sandwich. 'Well anyway, didn't mean to upset anyone,' she finished, realising she wasn't going to get any help.

Clara didn't trust herself to say anymore. She imagined saying something cutting and poignant and walking off head held high. What she actually did was mumble something about it being okay (even though it clearly wasn't) and head off.

'Well, I feel terrible now,' she heard the bigger woman say as she walked away.

'They said what?!' Jess asked, on the phone later.

'I know. I can almost understand the fear of the unknown and that they think our generation has it easy –'

'No! They need to be aware of who might be listening before they start spouting their poison.'

'Well, I'm not sure –'

'Wish I'd been there. I'd have properly laid into them.'

'Well, maybe it's as well you weren't, on this occasion.'

'Wow, okay.'

Clara sighed and pinched the bridge of her nose. 'Sorry.'

'No, it's okay. I get it. I'm focusing on the wrong part, aren't I? Are you okay?'

'Yeah. I'm not myself at the moment. It's just the whole, "why don't you just adopt?" thing, too.'

'That does suck.'

'It's not that I wouldn't consider it, I'm just nowhere near there yet. I'm still getting my head around the fact that our baby will have been made in a clinic, not through love.'

Jess laughed at this. 'Through love? What do you think it is that's making you and Christopher go through all this? I couldn't do it.'

'You got pregnant with Amelie on the first try, so you don't know what you'd do.'

'Ouch.'

'God, I'm sorry. Again. I think I should just go sit in a quiet room by myself.'

'Shall I come round? I could leave Amelie with Dave. Pick up some chocolate on the way?'

'No, it's okay.'

'Ice cream?'

'No. I'll be fine. Thanks, though.'

Clara hung up the phone, feeling worse than she had before. That was new. She considered going to speak to Christopher, but found him hunched over his laptop downstairs. She went back to the bedroom, flopped on the bed and opened up Instagram and typed:

'So this thing happened today…'

Chapter 23

May 2018

Clara sat at the front of the classroom looking at the sea of expectant little faces. She fidgeted with her hands in her lap as she mentally ran through how she was going to run the first session. She was well prepped, but doubt was creeping in now she was looking at actual children. *What if they didn't understand her? What if she was boring?*

The teacher, YongJae Lim, was speaking Malay. Her purple hijab complemented her skin tone beautifully. She gestured behind here at a smartscreen covered in squiggly writing and bright colours. Clara zoned out and imagined Jake in the classroom across the hall. He'd be all energetic and enthusiastic, making learning fun and having the kids eating out of the palm of his hand.

The teacher switched to English. 'I'd like to introduce Miss Ellison, all the way from England.'

Clara gulped and stood up. 'Hello,' she said, smoothing her skirt.

'Hello, Miss Ellison,' they sang back at her. Twenty-five sets of eager eyes were on her. You could have heard a pin drop. She didn't remember it being this quiet at her school.

'Hi, I'm going to be with you for a while, helping with your English. I'm looking forward to getting to know you all.' Silence followed, the little faces still watching her expectantly. Was she supposed to say more at this point?

'Erm, I'll meet you all properly soon…' She dried up.

'Thank you, Miss Ellison,' YongJae said. She addressed the class. 'Miss Ellison will be taking small groups of you throughout the day to help with reading and writing in English.'

It occurred to Clara that their English must be pretty good already. She might need to remember those irregular and auxiliary verbs after all.

The school building was impressive. Modern architecture, clean lines and lots of glass. Inside were light open spaces and bright colours. It was a place you wouldn't mind spending your days in. During the tour that morning, Clara had been open-mouthed at some of the facilities, including an on-site swimming pool and a climbing wall. It was a far cry from the crumbling comprehensive school she'd attended, with a dingy sports hall that doubled up as the canteen at lunch-time, so you dined with the odours of kids' sweat and rubber plimsoles.

Later that morning, Clara was sitting cross-legged in a circle with her first group of children. Her nerves had dissipated somewhat. In her group were twin Chinese girls with matching pigtails with pink ribbons. Their faces were identical: beautiful light brown complexions and big brown eyes you could get lost in. The only discernible difference was that one girl had a tiny scar above her lip. You'd miss it unless you looked closely. Clara guessed it was from a cleft palate. There were two Malayan boys and a girl who spoke English with an American accent, but was actually German. Her dad's work had brought her family to Singapore two years ago.

Clara asked the children to introduce themselves in English to get a feel for where they were at.

'I Chen, this my sister Lin,' the girl with the scar began. 'We eight years old. I ten minutes older as I born first.' She spoke proudly, in heavily accented English. Clara smiled and nodded at Lin, encouraging her to speak next. Lin looked at her sister and said nothing.

'She talk no much,' Chen said. 'But I help.'

'Okay, that's no problem,' Clara reassured them. She turned to one of the boys. 'What's your name?'

'Albertho.'

'Pleased to meet you,' Clara said, when he didn't elaborate further. She learned the other boy was called Johann and the German girl, Sofia.

'We're going to start with a story,' Clara said. The children watched her intently, arms and legs crossed, only speaking when she directly addressed them. Had she gone back to Victorian times, Clara wondered? Where children were taught to be seen and not heard? She thought back to her other interactions with young children and remembered them charging round, bouncing off the walls and demanding sweets. Maybe they were different at school? Or maybe things were different here. Either way, her audience was rapt as she opened *Alice in Wonderland* and began.

'Once upon a time…'

'I knew you'd be a hit,' Jake said.

'Well, I don't know about that,' Clara said. 'But I was expecting an element of crowd control. They were all so quiet and well-behaved.'

They were back at their new flat share, comparing notes about their first days. Jake, Clara, Anna and Netta – who'd now joined them – had found a three-bedroomed place together, making the rent much more manageable. Netta was supermodel pretty: high cheek bones, thick dark lashes and the longest legs Clara had ever seen. She'd had to stop herself staring when they'd been introduced. Netta was quick to smile, and Jake and Clara had warmed to her straight away. It was hard not to when they saw Anna light up when her girlfriend was around. They were at ease with each other, in that enviable way some couples had.

'Mine were well-behaved, too,' Jake said. 'I'll get them livened up when we start our drama sessions.'

'They were lovely children, but I'm worried about one of them,' Clara replied. 'Lin. She didn't speak at all.'

'Probably shy.'

'Maybe, but I think there was more to it than that. I mean, she literally didn't speak one word. Her twin sister did all the talking for her. I read the first chapter of *Alice in Wonderland* to gauge where their English is at. They're all actually pretty good. I asked them questions about what had happened and I couldn't get her to answer any.'

'Maybe try to get her on her own, without her sister there.' Anna joined the conversation; she'd been distracted looking at the cooking instructions on some instant noodles.

'That's what I was thinking,' Clara said. 'I really want to help her.'

Jake nodded at the packet Anna was holding. 'I think you just add hot water,' he said.

'Awesome. I'm starving and it's desperate times until we get our first pay packet.' Anna flicked on the kettle in their new kitchen. It was pretty basic, but they'd been incredibly lucky to find somewhere within budget, where they could all be together, and it was easy to get to the school on the MRT – Singapore's very efficient answer to London's underground.

As Jake and Anna debated the merits of chicken flavour noodles versus bacon flavour, Clara zoned out and found herself dwelling on Lin. She wondered how twins could be so different. They'd obviously had the same upbringing, so did that mean it was down to nature, rather than nurture? She imagined her parallel universe, where life had carried on the trajectory it was supposed to – the one where she and Christopher had had children – but this time, she imagined them with twins like Lin and Chen. They'd discuss over dinner what to do to help the one who wouldn't speak. They'd enlist help from teachers, their friends and their own parents. She'd join a support groups for parents of children with speech problems, make friends, start a campaign to raise awareness of the issue and maybe some sort of fundraising event. She'd do lots of research until she understood all there was to understand on the subject, then do her very best for her daughter, so she could lead a normal, happy life. In short, she was sure she'd fix it. She shook her head and brought herself back to the present. The noodle talk had dried up.

'So, how was your first day, Anna?'

'Pretty great, actually. The kids are awesome. Some kickass girls and the sweetest little boy. I think it's going to be a lot of fun.'

'We should go out and celebrate,' Jake said, getting up off his seat.

'Cash flow issue,' Anna replied, indicating her noodles. 'Plus, I said I'd be in when Netta gets home later.'

Jake turned his gaze to Clara, eyebrows raised.

'I could probably do with an early night, ready for day two – sorry!'

His shoulders sagged. 'Ah, well, I might go out for a wander, see what's going on.'

The next day Clara focused on Lin, without making it obvious. She asked them all what they liked to do at weekends: play football, roller-skate, play a game she'd never heard of on a games console, read – Clara was heartened to hear this one. But for every question directed at Lin, Chen would answer in the plural. 'We like to roller-skate in the park; we like to play with our cousins.'

'Can I ask you about Lin?' Clara asked YongJae in the staffroom at lunch.

'Of course. What about her?'

'Well, she doesn't speak much…or at all, actually.'

'No, she has selective mutism. Chats no end in front of her parents, apparently, but at school, and even in front of other family members, she never utters a word.'

'Gosh, but how does she manage?' Clara asked.

'She gets by because Chen does all the talking for her. She knows exactly what she wants all the time. They have – what's the word? Twin intuition.'

'Is it psychological? I mean, because she speaks in some situations?'

'It's psychological, as in there's nothing physically wrong with her. She can speak, as she speaks at home. But that doesn't mean it's not real to her. She was seeing a child psychologist last year, but her parents decided she'd grow out of it.'

'She seems engaged with what's going on. She was transfixed with *Alice in Wonderland*. I could tell she knew the answers to the questions I asked.'

'Yes, she's a bright girl,' YongJae said. 'Her written work is excellent.'

'Is there anything I can do to help?'

'You mean to get her talking? Nothing we haven't already tried. Just make sure she's included. It's something that will right itself in time.'

Clara made a mental note to do some Googling when she got home. She may not be in her parallel universe, where she was spearheading a one-woman campaign for better support for children with mutism, but she could still do her very best for Lin. And maybe, just maybe, she could help.

Chapter 24

April 2015

'We've got a new shade of pink in – Summer Rose. Or there's Berry Smoothie which is more lilac-toned.' The beautician held them both up. Clara tried to take the decision seriously. *Which colour would make it more likely that this embryo would stick?* She dismissed the ridiculous thought.

'Berry Smoothie.' She pointed to the bottle the beautician held in her left hand.

'Good choice. It's a lovely colour. I did my toenails in this shade before I went on my holiday to Alicante. It's nice and cheerful.' Clara could do with some cheer. 'We all went – my mum and dad and my sister…'

The beautician prattled on as she dried Clara's feet off and started massaging in a thick cream. Clara zoned out and enjoyed the sensation. She didn't want this bit to end. She should have booked a foot massage instead. Perhaps she could book one for closer to the test day. For now, she was doing okay.

'We went all inclusive. It's easier when you've got kids, isn't it?'

Clara retuned into what the beautician was saying. 'Erm, yes.'

'How old are yours?'

'What? Oh, I don't have kids.'

'But you're married, aren't you?' The woman nodded at the ring on Clara' left hand.

'Yes.' Clara willed her to shut up and get on with painting her toenails.

'Do you want them?'

Clara opened and closed her mouth like a goldfish. Should she lie and say no? Try to fob her off with a vague 'one day', or tell the truth?

'Yes, I want nothing more,' she found herself saying.

'Oh, are you trying then?'

'Yes, it's not straightforward though. I don't know if we can.'

'My sister-in-law had IVF. Now she's got twins. They're five. A boy and a girl.' Clara smiled tightly. 'And my friend's next-door neighbour tried for years, then as soon as they decided to give up trying and get the kitchen redone, she got pregnant. They just needed to relax and stop thinking about it so much.'

Clara gritted her teeth and said nothing. The beautician didn't seem to notice.

'So, are you going anywhere nice on holiday?'

'Nothing planned.'

'We go to Alicante every year. The kids love it and it's easy to get to.'

Clara gave her tight smile again, wishing she'd stop talking and finish Berry Smoothie-ing her toenails so she could leave. This was supposed to be her 'nice thing' to keep her busy. She might have to review her plans for the rest of the time and avoid anything that involved small talk with strangers.

Later that night, she admired her toenails in the bath. Christopher was in the bedroom doing something with his laptop. Probably working. She leaned her head back and closed her eyes, then sat up again and opened them. A nice gin and tonic would be good right now, but of course that was a no go. Same as running and going to the gym. She wondered again if she'd done the right thing by taking time off work. Trying your best not to be stressed was quite stressful in itself, as it turned out.

She padded into the bedroom in a fluffy towel. Christopher was engrossed in his laptop and didn't look up. It irked her. She cleared her throat. Still nothing.

'That was a nice long soak,' she said. He gave half a smile but kept his eyes fixed on the screen.

'Do you like my toenails?' she asked, lifting her foot up.

He finally looked up. 'Sorry, I need to get this finished.'

Clara nodded and changed wordlessly into her pyjamas. Then she went downstairs and flicked through TV channels. She picked up her phone and posted a photo of her feet up on the settee, making sure to get in her newly painted toenails. She captioned it: 'Two week wait treat #pedicure #infertilitysucks #sixdaystiltestday'

The replies started to come in.

Stay strong, your toenails look fab! x

Everything crossed for you hun *kissing face*

Hope it goes quickly for you! xx

She put her phone down and found she was smiling. The words of strangers had helped her feel just a little bit less alone and a little more like an acceptable human being.

Chapter 25

June 2018

'Why is it that Lin doesn't speak at school, do you think?'

It was playtime and the children were running around. Clara had no idea how they were doing it in the heat. She was hiding out in the shade at the side of the building, sitting on a bench, and she could feel the sweat beading on her upper lip. Chen had taken a shine to Clara and had brought her skipping rope over so she could play next to her. It was one of the rare occasions that Lin wasn't glued to her side.

Chen shrugged. 'Do you want skip with me?'

Clara laughed. 'It's too hot for me.'

'I skip fast,' she said, demonstrating.

'That's very impressive. I wish I could do that,' Clara said. 'Is…everything okay at home?' she asked, looking over her shoulder to check no one was in earshot, feeling she was crossing a boundary. She'd been Googling selective mutism and learned it could sometimes be triggered by abuse or a traumatic event.

'Yes,' Chen said. 'We had party. My cousin is six. He had cake with horse with spike.'

'A horse, with a spike?' Clara frowned. 'Oh, a unicorn!'

'Unicorn.' Chen smiled. 'Yes. He like unicorn. My uncle say unicorn for girls, my mum tell him to close mouth.'

Clara laughed. 'Quite right too. Boys can like unicorns just as much as girls.' She broached the subject again. 'So, where is Lin today?'

Chen had taken a break from skipping and was sitting on the bench next to Clara, swinging her legs. 'She sick.'

'Oh, dear, nothing serious I hope?'

'She eat too much unicorn cake at party and blerr.' She mimicked being sick. 'All the night.'

'Well, I hope she's feeling better soon. So, does she talk to your family at home? At the party?' Clara pressed.

'Yes, she talk.'

Clara tried again. 'So why do you think she doesn't talk at school?'

'She like me to talk at school.' The bell went and Clara was no further on. It occurred to her that perhaps Chen didn't know and her eight-year-old brain didn't think to question it.

The next day she got another opportunity. Chen was off ill and Lin was in school by herself. The vomiting obviously wasn't a case of too much unicorn cake, as it'd been passed on. Lin was silent as usual during her session with the group. With the permission of YaeJong, Clara asked her to hang back when the others had gone back to class. Clara got out her art supplies: A3 paper, crayons, stickers, ribbons, glue and glitter.

'We're going to get creative.' She smiled warmly at Lin. Lin looked blank. Clara tried again. 'Do some drawing?'

Lin gave a small, almost imperceptible smile. Clara started drawing herself, and pushed some paper and crayons towards Lin. The girl watched without moving for a while, then picked up a red felt-tip and started drawing a person. It had a big head and out-of-proportion body.

'I like your drawing,' Clara said encouragingly. 'Is it you?'

Lin shook her head.

'Chen?'

Lin smiled and nodded.

'It's very good. Can you draw yourself as well?'

Lin did nothing for a few minutes, then she picked up a green pen and drew a very similar mis-proportioned figure next to the first one, but much smaller. Clara was suddenly out of her depth. This child had been seeing a psychologist, who was qualified and experienced. She wasn't sure how she thought she could help, but Lin had got to her, with her big brown eyes and nervous smile. She hoped by spending one-to-one time with her, she might put her at ease and help her overcome her anxieties.

'I like it,' Clara said. 'Why are you smaller than Chen? You're the same size in real life.'

Lin paused and briefly made eye contact, then looked back down at her picture.

Clara waited a few moments and when it became clear she wasn't going to react to her questions, she said, 'Do you want to draw something else?'

Lin looked a little unsure, pen in hand.

'What do you like to draw?'

Something shifted in Lin's eyes as an idea came to her, and she bent her head and started drawing, sticking her tongue out in concentration. Clara smiled as a unicorn emerged on the page. They worked in companionable silence for ten minutes or so, then Clara had to take her back to her regular class. She thought there was a little something in Lin's demeanour as they headed down the corridor. She walked a little taller and was somehow less closed in on herself. Clara smiled warmly at her as she held the door to the classroom open and was rewarded with a second's eye contact and a tight smile.

She realised as she travelled home on the MRT that afternoon she hadn't thought about Christopher or her 'almost life' much at all over the past few weeks. Okay, she was thinking about it now, but only to note how she hadn't been thinking of it. She was settling into her new routine – the teaching job, her new friends. Life back at home and everything she'd left behind seemed unreal somehow. Even Australia and Deirdre (and Sam) felt like a lifetime ago. Was she doing it? Was she starting to shake off some of the misery and heartache of the past few years? Would she return home a new woman? Clara wasn't sure, but as she emerged from the train and saw the Marina Bay Sands in the distance and the sun setting over the water, she was calm and happy in the moment, and that was good enough for now.

Chapter 26

April 2015

Clara had five more days until test day. The night before the baby shower had arrived and she either needed to make a decision to go or send an excuse now. She weighed up the pros and cons.

Pros
- I have nothing else planned and need to keep busy.
- I want to see Jo and there'll be others there I haven't seen for ages and would like to catch up with.
- I could wear my new sandals and show off my Berry Smoothie toenails.
- There would probably be cake.
- I wouldn't have to make excuses for not drinking as it's unlikely anyone would be drinking at a baby shower.
- Perhaps the oxytocin from the pregnant lady would rub off on me and improve my chances of this working.

She frowned and crossed the last one out.

Cons
- There would undoubtedly be a lot of baby talk.
- I'd probably get asked when Christopher and I were going to have a baby.
- I'd have to look at Jo's bump and see how happy she is and pass a test called 'am I happy for her or am I a jealous bitch?'

She picked up her phone and wrote a new message to Jo.

Clara: Hiya hun, bet you're excited about tomorrow! I'm gutted to say, I think I'm coming down with a migraine so I'm going to go to bed now. Not sure if I'll be up to it tomorrow. x

Her thumb hovered over the 'send' button. She was ultimately putting off making the decision or tee-ing up an excuse. She pressed delete and put her phone down.

There were pink balloons everywhere. Looked like Jo was having a girl, then. Pink and white polka dot bunting had been hung across Jo's fireplace place, complementing the lavender Farrow and Ball paint on the chimney breast beautifully. A 'guess the baby's weight chart' was hanging on the wall, with a Waitrose fat-free yoghurt pot as a make-shift pen holder next to it. The kitchen island was adorned with cupcakes covered in pink icing and decorated with dummies and…Clara did a double take. Yes, those were nipples. *Nice.* Sandwiches cut into triangles, which Clara recognised as an M&S platter from meetings at work, humous and salad sticks, falafel balls and a Greek salad. A stack of paper cups with the words 'baby shower' on them in loopy script were stacked next to a selection of grown-up soft drinks. Tiny glittery storks made of different coloured foil decorated the surface in between. Jo will be sweeping those up off her kitchen floor for months, Clara thought.

'Thanks so much for coming,' Jo said, leaning over to give Clara a kiss on the cheek. She had to stretch over her bump to reach. Clara wondered how much she knew about her own situation. She hadn't spoken to her about her fertility problems and IVF directly, but Jess might have mentioned something.

'Of course. I'm glad I could come,' Clara said, extracting herself from the hug and straightening up. 'How are you feeling?' She nodded towards the perfectly rounded bump under her tasteful maternity dress.

'Oh, good, thanks. Well, more tired than I've ever been and I need a wee, like, every ten minutes. Also, I have varicose veins in my legs and...' She leaned in. 'Even one on my bits! And don't get me started on the stretch marks. But aside from that, all good.' She laughed. 'Not long to go now, anyway.'

Clara nodded and wondered if it was too early to grab a boob cupcake. Probably. What was it about pregnant women having zero filter? She couldn't think of any other scenario where it was socially acceptable to bring up your bits in response to a simple 'how are you?' question. She was at a loss for something else to say, but the doorbell rang and Jo excused herself to go and answer it, leaving Clara hovering by the buffet. She heard Jess at the door and relaxed a little. She perched on a bar stool and poured herself an elderflower pressé in a paper cup.

After the customary hug with Jo, telling her she looked radiant, blooming, Jess gave Clara a tight squeeze, not a pretend-hand-on-shoulder-air-kiss type of greeting. The squeeze said 'you're so brave for being here. I know it must be tough and I'm here for you.' Clara was relieved that any weirdness from their phone call the other day had dissipated. She couldn't cope with falling out with Jess on top of everything else.

'How are you?' Jess asked, releasing her. Her flame-red hair had been teased into a bun and a few escaping tendrils tickled Clara's cheek.

'I'm doing okay.' She nodded. 'Better, now you're here.'

Jess gave her hand a squeeze and winked. 'Great stuff.' She turned to Jo, 'Now, where's the prosecco?'

'I have some in the kitchen, I think. I didn't know if people would be drinking. Obviously I can't.' Jo stroked her swollen stomach lovingly. Clara averted her eyes and took a big gulp of elderflower pressé.

When did the steady stream of hen dos and weddings change into baby showers and christenings, she wondered? She'd been part of it up until a few years ago. She'd happily announced her engagement to Christopher on Facebook, complete with a photo of them toasting with champagne glasses, Clara holding her glass in her left hand to show off her solitaire diamond, set in a simple, but tasteful platinum band. She had plenty of 'likes' and all the right comments. Well done for being socially acceptable, for doing what's expected of you, for reaffirming others' life choices, for being part of something. She'd posted pictures of herself frolicking in the hot tub on her hen do, posing with prosecco glasses with willy straws in them. She liked being socially acceptable, but it was more than that. She liked knowing she was going to spend the rest of her life with someone she loved. She was fortunate and even excited. Back then, she'd already started to imagine what their children would be like at some unknown point in the future.

All their friends from uni had children now. Some were on their second or third. Clara and Christopher had become the couple people speculated about. 'Maybe they're happy as they are. They might not want children. They might be waiting for the right time. Best not leave it too long, though…'

'So basically, you have to look through the nappies, smell and *taste* if you dare. Then guess the chocolate bar,' Jo's sister was saying.

Jo was sitting next to a pile of nappies, wrinkling up her nose. Each had a melted chocolate bar inside, which understandably looked quite horrifying, given the context.

'Joshua's nappy looked like that first one yesterday,' said a blonde girl Clara recognised from Jo's work.

'Oh, God, we had an absolute poonami this morning. Always when you've got to be somewhere, isn't it? I was literally about to step out the door and I heard it come out. Then I saw a yellowy-brown patch on her Babgro. It was all up her back and all up her front. I threw the vest away. Took one look at it and was like – no.' Clara didn't know the woman speaking. The other mums in the room were nodding along and smiling sympathetically in the right places.

'Poppy did that in Sainsbury's!' The mums rolled their eyes, clapped hands over their mouths in understanding. 'I'm not kidding. I'd left the changing bag in the car. I literally had no nappies and no wipes or spare clothes. Lucky I was in Sainsbury's. I literally bought nappies and wipes and a whole new outfit! I had to keep the tags and explain what happened at the checkout.'

'Ha, amazing! Good job you were in a supermarket,' someone else said.

Clara arranged her features into the expression of someone who was interested and enjoying the conversation. Certainly not the expression of someone who was bemused, caught between thinking these women sounded a bit dull and babies sounded quite hard work, actually, and desperately wanting to be part of it.

'I know. I'd had literally no sleep the night before and I was just like – no! I can't cope with this.'

'Oh hun, have you tried sleep training? Jude is sleeping through now, after doing it for two weeks. You have to first sit next to their cot and shh them when they cry, but don't pick them up –'

'Oh, we co-sleep, it's so much easier for breastfeeding –'

'We switched to formula. Jude had tongue-tie when he was born and he couldn't latch properly. I tried, but my nipples were so sore and he wasn't getting enough milk and it was all so stressful –'

'You have to do what's best for everyone. Happy Mum equals happy baby. There's so much pressure to breastfeed and not everyone can –'

'I know. I went on Aptamil's website to order some formula and they make you read a government message about how breastfeeding is best for your baby, which you have to click to accept before you can even –'

'That's not on. That's going to make you feel really shitty.'

The mums pounced when there was the briefest of pauses, launching into their own tales of woe, or seeking reassurance. Was this a symptom of having limited interaction with other adults, Clara wondered? As soon they saw one, they felt the need to vomit up every thought they'd had since breakfast?

Jo sat next to her pile of nappies. She was examining the first one but hadn't gone as far as tasting it.

'Erm, I think this one is a Mars bar?' she said to no one in particular, as soon as there was a short lull in conversation.

'I'm just going to the loo,' Clara said. Then, realising no one was listening, she slipped away. She sat down on the lid of the toilet. She should cry or something, but she felt strangely removed from the situation, as though she was playing the role of an infertile woman at a baby shower, and not that this was actually her life. If this cycle worked and she got pregnant and stayed pregnant, would she be like these women, constantly talking about poo and breastfeeding? She wondered what the women talked about before they became mothers. She knew one of them was Head of Drama at a secondary school, one was a lawyer, one ran her own marketing consultancy. Surely they had more to say for themselves.

A knock at the door. 'Hey, you okay in there?'

It was Jess.

'Oh yes, fine.' Clara smoothed her skirt and opened the door. 'Just needed a minute.'

'I'm not surprised. Poor Jo looks like she needs a minute and it's her baby shower! Bit overwhelming, isn't it?'

'Yes, it is. You have a baby and don't talk about poo endlessly.'

'Well, my baby is three now, but no I don't, because it's not that interesting to anyone else. Dave got the poo stories, and his mum occasionally, but she loved to hear all about it.'

You mean you just don't tell me, then, Clara thought. She was getting all mixed up, not sure what to think about anything anymore.

'I might sneak off,' she said. 'Can you cover for me? Say I had a headache or something. They probably won't notice, anyway.'

'Of course. Run for cover! I'll call you later.' Jess gave her a quick hug. Not a long one that would set her off crying. She was thoughtful like that.

Clara walked home. It was only half an hour if she cut across the park and she needed to clear her head. Plus, it killed some time. She thought about Jo, looking bewildered and daunted at the baby talk. About her own inability to offer anything meaningful to the conversation. Her friendships were becoming strained. She was no longer conventional; the dots of her life couldn't be joined up with a socially acceptable narrative. Career – tick, house – tick, husband – tick. Well done, that's what you're *supposed* to do. But no baby? What was that about? She wasn't one of the single bunch, still going clubbing at weekends and sharing hilarious anecdotes about their latest Tinder dates, and she wasn't one of the mummies, meeting in coffee shops and talking endlessly about sleep training, weaning, and the different colours and textures of poo. She was a misfit.

Jo may be keeping up with what's expected and she may have what she wants, but that doesn't mean she's automatically happy, Clara thought. Same with all those mums with their poonami stories and sleepless nights. Maybe we're all just doing our best with the hand we've been dealt.

She promised herself then and there that whatever the outcome of this round of IVF and whatever the future held, she'd do her best to be happy. Even if the life she ended up with wasn't the one she'd have picked for herself.

Chapter 27

July 2018

Jake gripped his seat and closed his eyes.

'You're missing the view,' Clara said, exasperated. 'I forgot you were scared of heights.'

'I'm not.' He opened his eyes. 'Woah.' He shut them quickly again.

'You were okay at the top of Marina Bay Sands,' Clara said.

'That was different. It was stable – this is blowing in the wind and –' He broke off to tense his body as the cable car swayed in the breeze. Clara put a steadying hand on his arm, which he acknowledged with a quick twitch of the lip, eyes still closed. She didn't think about how putting her hand on his arm had come so naturally and how she could feel the muscles of his forearm. She let her hand linger a moment longer, then slipped it away discreetly and twisted round so she could see the skyline of Singapore shrinking into the distance. Ahead were the trees and bright colours of Sentosa Island, a giant playground for grown-ups. The cable-car started to descend, with a stomach-churning change of angle. Jake let out a low moan and Clara found herself touching his arm again. This time she patted it, in what she hoped was a reassuring and not at all patronising way.

'We're here – you can open your eyes!' she announced, as the cable car came into the turnstile.

'We're still moving,' Jake said, opening one eye a crack and peeping out. 'Oh, we're here.'

Clara stood and held out her hand, trying not to overanalyse the fact that it felt natural to hold out her hand for him. 'Come on, or you'll end up going straight back again.'

That got his attention. He jumped up and took her hand, letting her lead him over the gap and onto solid ground.

Clara rolled her eyes. 'You're going to be fun at a theme park.'

'I will! I love rides. Just not cable-cars.'

'You have a very specific fear of heights that's limited to cable-cars?'

'Yes. They wobble and it feels like you could fall down.'

'I did a skydive in Australia,' she said, pushing her chest out and shoulders back.

'You did not.'

'I did!' She felt a little smug. Jake had taken to teasing her about being sensible and strait-laced.

'In that case, let's find the scariest ride and go on that first.'

'Deal.' They shook on it.

They emerged from the cable car dock to be greeted by the smell of hot dogs and candyfloss, the sound of children squealing in delight, and the sight of trees, waterfalls and giant maps of the island on big signs. They stopped at the word SENTOSA in eight-foot brightly coloured letters and waited for their turn to pose for the obligatory photo inside in the 'O'.

Jake had been trying to persuade Clara to come to Sentosa Island with him for weeks. She'd been busy doing lesson prep and being a tourist, visiting galleries and buildings with noteworthy architecture, as recommended in her guidebook. She'd accused Jake of being a child, but had to admit, now she was here, she was excited. Memories of annual trips to Alton Towers as a teenager surfaced and she decided to bring her inner adrenaline junkie out to play.

A slow smile spread across her face as she spotted a red and white rollercoaster, looping and twisting high in the sky. The people riding it were sitting under the track, legs dangling then flying through the air as they went upside down round a loop.

She nudged Jake. 'We've got to go on that!'

He followed her gaze and swallowed audibly. 'Err, sure, yes we can go on that....I wonder if perhaps the queue is too big, though. Perhaps we should try something else first.' He gestured hopefully towards the log flume.

'We had a deal!' Clara said. They'd shaken on it, so it was binding.

'Right, of course... a deal's a deal.' He allowed himself to be led to the entrance to the queue, which was annoyingly long.

'It'll give you time to pluck up the courage,' Clara teased. They took up a place behind some Chinese teenagers, who were taking endless selfies through Snapchat filters and laughing hysterically at images of themselves with dog's ears and flower crowns.

'Would you like me to take one of all of you?' Clara offered. She was met by puzzled looks.

'It's okay, thanks,' one of them said.

She shrugged. Jake shook his head at her.

'What?' she asked.

'Teenagers don't want you to take a nice group photo of them. They only want to be in photos where they can control what they look like. Selfies all the way.'

'Really?' She suddenly felt old and out of touch. Christopher had a teenage niece they'd seen occasionally at family get-togethers. Aside from that, she knew nothing about teenagers today. She was assuming they were similar to her as a teenager, but she actually knew nothing of the world they inhabited. And she wouldn't ever get chance to know, she realised sadly. She shook her head, not wanting to go down that route.

'Hey, you okay?' Jake asked.

'Yes, fine. Just realising I must be getting old. We had to take the roll of film to Max Speilman and wait a week for photos to come back when I was a teenager. There were no filters to make your skin look clear or your bum look smaller.'

'They want their bums to look bigger now. I blame Kim Kardashian. It's all about the booty. Skinny's out.'

'Really? Big bums are fashionable? I really am out of touch.'

'Yep. Big bums, big eyebrows.'

'Eyebrows! Yes, I have seen those.'

'They're like two slugs. One of the girls in the theatre group at home has particularly striking ones. I find it hard to take her seriously.'

Clara laughed and felt the threat of her low mood passing. She wiggled her sensible make-up free eyebrows at him. 'What's wrong with actual eyebrows made of hair?'

'You got me. Glad we didn't do anything stupid when we were young.'

'You were young after me. Did you have curtains, or was that before your time?'

'Curtains, like, in our house?' He frowned.

Clara laughed. 'No! I meant your hair. Guess that was before your time, then.'

'Must have been. I was one of the cool kids, though.'

'I bet you were.'

'And I bet you were a goody-goody.'

Clara shoved him. 'I wasn't! I mean, I wasn't in the naughty group – the ones who stole Dewberry lip balms from the Body Shop at the weekend. But I wasn't a goody-goody. I skived a lesson once.'

'Ooh, you skived a lesson?'

'Yeah, but I did copy a friend's notes later so I didn't miss anything.'

Jake snorted. 'You rebel!'

The queue was moving forward and before they knew it, they were at the front. Jake was looking a little pale.

'You okay?' Clara asked. He nodded. They were being ushered forward by the staff. A teenager in a blue T-shirt waved them towards seats side-by-side. Clara climbed into hers and pulled the harness down over her body, enjoying the fizz of nervous anticipation in the pit of her stomach. Jake did the same, but looked less like he was enjoying it. The blue T-shirt boy walked between the seats, tugging on harnesses, checking everyone was fastened in. He gave a nod to a teenage girl, also dressed in a blue T-shirt, who pressed a switch. The metal floor beneath their feet started to lower, leaving their feet swinging.

'Ready?' Clara asked, trying to turn her head to look at Jake, but she couldn't quite make eye contact. Then they were off. Clara whooped as the wind rushed past her face. Her hair whipped into her eyes and she saw sky, ground, then sky again, never sure which way up she was. She wasn't usually a whooper, but rollercoasters had that effect. She found herself laughing as the ride finally slowed, adrenaline making her heart pound in her chest and her hands tremble. She was alive.

Jake was smiling at least as their harnesses lifted and the metal floor rose to meet their feet.

'Okay?' Clara asked.

'Yeah, that was ace. What's next?'

Clara grinned.

'I didn't have you down as a theme park sort of woman. How come I had to drag you away from art galleries to get you here?' They were lounging on the man-made beach, ice creams in hands.

She shrugged. 'I forgot how much fun they were.'

'So, are we going for a swim?'

'Sure.' Clara nodded. She had her swimming costume in her shoulder bag, just in case. She looked around for somewhere to get changed. 'Where are the changing rooms?'

'I don't think there are any.' Jake had already shed his T-shirt and was unbuttoning his shorts. Clara averted her eyes from his surprisingly hairy chest. He stood in his black Calvin Klein boxers.

'Come on. Why are you still sitting there?'

'Where are your swimming shorts?' Clara asked, looking around, embarrassed.

'I didn't bring them. No bother, these are same, same, but different.'

'Well, technically they're underwear, not beach-wear.'

'They cover more than that guy's "beach-wear".' Jake used his hands to do air quotes and pointed his gaze at a man standing in the surf. He was wearing a turquoise thong, hands on tanned leathery hips, looking out to sea and treating everyone on the beach to a view of his bare buttocks.

'Oh, God.' Clara looked away, then glanced back, unable to help herself.

'Come on, I'll cover you.' Jake was holding up his towel for Clara to hide behind to get changed. She hesitated. 'I promise not to look.' He turned his face away, still holding the towel up. Her vest top was quite long, so she could pull it down over her bum, then pull her costume all the way up before taking her top off. She was sweaty and sticky and the sea did look inviting.

'Oh, go on then.' She took out her black one-piece and executed her plan, trying not to think about Jake's proximity in the brief moment she had no pants on.

The water was delicious. She inched in until it was up to her waist. Jake ran straight in and dived under the water as soon as it was deep enough. He turned and floated on his back, head raised, looking back towards Clara.

'Come on!' he said. 'Now who's a wimp?'

'I didn't call you a wimp. I wouldn't say that,' she said.

'Pussy.'

'I definitely wouldn't say that!' She shook her head in mock disapproval, then took the plunge and started breast-stroking towards him. She gasped as her shoulders became submerged in the cool water, then relaxed as her body acclimatised, enjoying the feeling of stretching out her muscles, cutting through the water.

'Any progress with Lin?' Jake asked, as they floated on the waves.

'No, not really. I mean she interacts in her own way, but she doesn't speak.'

Jake looked thoughtful. 'I wonder if singing would be easier for her.'

'Singing? Surely that's more nerve-wracking than talking.'

'I don't know. It helps people with stutters, doesn't it? Or they can do it, anyway.'

'Oh, yes. Like Gareth Gates. A stutter is different to mutism though,' Clara said, feeling for the ground with her feet.

'My kids are doing a performance at the end of term. Maybe your group could join in. We could give them all parts.'

'Not actually a bad idea.' Clara might not know much about teenagers, but she could make a small difference to this group of young kids and one in particular. The thought steadied her. Jake was lying on his back in the water, hands gently sculling at his sides to keep him afloat. He actually was quite nice to look at.

'What are you looking at?'

'Nothing.' She looked away, back at the shore.

He smirked and changed position so he was upright in the water, head bobbing in the waves. 'Come on, I'll race you to that buoy. The winner has to buy the loser a drink.'

'Shouldn't that be the other way round?'

He paused. 'You're right, Miss Ellison, as usual. Okay, GO!' He set off towards the buoy. Clara front-crawled after him and, though he was stronger physically, their techniques were equally matched, and she reached the buoy just seconds after him.

'Drinks are on you! Mine's a double gin.'

He splashed her.

'Argh, I've got salt water in my eye!' She splashed him back, then tried to wipe at her eye with wet hands while treading water.

'Here.' He took hold of her elbow to steady her while she pressed the heel of her hand into her eye. 'Better?'

She nodded. Jake's face was inches from hers. Clara stopped treading for a moment and sank down a few inches. He still had hold of her arm and he pulled her upwards, just as a wave came and pushed her closer to him. Their bodies bumped together and her cheek brushed the side of his head.

'Sorry,' she said.

'Don't be. I enjoyed it.' His smile was relaxed, easy. She thought how straightforward it would be to lean in and kiss him. She inadvertently glanced at his mouth. It was amused, like his eyes.

'Erm, I've just remembered I have marking to do,' she said. 'We should head back to the cable-car.'

His mouth still smiled, but she saw something that looked a bit like disappointment in his eyes.

Chapter 28

April 2015

'I can't eat another cream cake, I'll be sick.' Clara pushed her plate away.

'You might be eating for two,' Jess said.

'Don't. I can't take it.'

'Sorry.' Jess looked down at her china teacup. 'Sometimes I don't know what to say. Ignore me if I get it wrong.'

'Don't be sorry. I don't think anyone could say the right thing at the moment. I'm wrung out and I'm exhausted.' She lifted the lid of the teapot to check how much was left. 'Yesterday I sat through a matinee performance of *Chicago* by myself at the theatre. It was the most depressing thing. Who goes to the theatre on a Wednesday afternoon? Old people. And me. The theatre was half-empty and I wished I'd stayed at home and hidden under the covers.'

'Aww, Clar.' Jess was still holding her hand.

'I sat there analysing whether I was having twinges of period pain, or whether my boobs felt more tender than usual. I gave them a squeeze without thinking and the boy selling ice cream nearly dropped his tray.'

Jess snorted.

Clara managed a weak smile. 'Do you think my stomach looks bloated?' She flattened her dress across her middle.

'Definitely,' Jess said. 'You're huge.'

'I think I am bloated. Here look at this photo.' She dug out her phone and showed Jess a photo she'd taken the night before in her underwear.

'You look pregnant there!' Jess said.

'It could be the progesterone hormones I'm taking, though; a side effect of that is bloating.'

Jess shrugged helplessly.

'Sorry. I'm doing your head in. I'm doing my own head in. I'm going to the toilet.' Clara was busting, but for the past couple of days, going for a wee was no longer the simple task it used to be. She was terrified she'd be bleeding. Yesterday, she'd gone every five minutes to check and now she'd got to the day before test day, she couldn't bear to look.

She closed the cubicle door and pulled down her tights. Then she sat down on the toilet and squeezed her eyes shut. She kept them shut while she did a wee, wiped, pulled her knickers and tights back up and flushed the toilet. *Okay, safe.* If she didn't know about it, it wasn't happening. She looked at her reflection as she washed her hands. Her face looked pale and pinched. She hadn't been sleeping well. Whatever the outcome tomorrow, she needed to get some rest.

Chapter 29

August 2018

The summer holiday was for six weeks for the kids. The TEFL staff had two weeks of 'consolidated training' before their holiday started. They went back over what they'd covered in their initial training at Easter, now they had the benefit of experience. Happily for Clara, no role-playing was required. This left them with four weeks free before the new school year started. Anna and Netta were heading back to the UK, splitting their time between London and Surrey, visiting family. Jake was also headed back to the UK for a few weeks to stay with his mum and dad and to see his friends. Clara had considered going home, but the truth was 'home' felt a million miles away and she wasn't sure she could face going back yet, much to her mum's disappointment. She did want to see her mum and dad though, so they'd settled on arranging a two-week trip to Thailand together.

They'd been naively optimistic with the arrangement to meet 'on Khao San Road', Clara realised now. She looked from left to right, jostled by tourists. A bright green 'Chang' sign buzzed over her head. Hawkers approached her, offering their wares: designer sunglasses, fake Rolexes, scarves, Tiffany earrings. Her 'no, thank yous' grew more terse with each approach as she craned her neck past them, scanning the crowds. The smell of street food thickened the air. Every sense was overloaded.

Her phone buzzed in her pocket. 'Mum? I can't hear you. You're where? I'm under a Chang sign. A CHANG SIGN. It's beer. Bright green. I can also see a stall selling sunglasses. SUNGLASSES. Mum?' She'd lost her. And then a gap in the crowds appeared and there were her parents, looking flustered and bewildered. Her dad was wearing a black leather bum-bag circa 1985 and clutching a fold-out map attached to his guidebook. Her mum had grown her hair and was wearing a pair of white sunglasses which looked suspiciously similar to those the street vendors were thrusting at anyone who stayed still for ten seconds.

Her mum flung her arms around her and squeezed her tight. 'It's good to see you, love,' she said, above the noise. 'Let me have a proper look at you.' She held her back at arm's length. 'You're all tanned. You look great.'

'Can I get a look in, June?' her dad said. Clara disentangled herself from her mum and embraced her dad. 'That was a long flight,' he said. 'But they had lots of films to choose from. I watched *The Wolf of Wall Street*. Bit racy in parts. Your mum wasn't keen.'

Clara laughed. 'I'm not surprised – not a film for the faint-hearted.'

'There were no peanuts either. Someone with an allergy on board. I thought you always got peanuts on flights. I had to eat two slices of the flapjack, your mum had made at home, before I could get on. They asked us all at the gate if we had anything that could contain nuts, or nut oil. I had them in my bum-bag and didn't want to throw them away. Then I had to wash my hands and promise not to breathe on anyone.'

Clara raised an eyebrow at her mum. This was quite a speech for her usually taciturn dad.

'He had a couple of beers on the plane,' she said. That explained it then. That, and the excitement of being somewhere new and seeing his only daughter after so long, had turned him into a verified chatterbox.

'They brought us cheese and crackers and orange juice in a tiny plastic container with a peely lid…' he was saying, as the trio made their way through the crowds in search of somewhere quieter to get a drink and some food before check-in at their hotel opened.

'So, how are you, love?' her mum said, as soon as they were seated in a café with more acceptable decibel levels.

'I'm actually pretty good,' Clara said. 'I love teaching. The kids are great.'

Her mum smiled in that knowing way she had.

'What?' Clara asked.

'Nothing. I'm glad. I always thought you'd like teaching.'

'Yes, there are two girls in particular I'm working with, Lin and Chen. They're twins and Lin doesn't speak at all outside of home. They call it selective mutism.'

Her mum was nodding and listening intently as Clara went over the details.

'Sounds like you're doing all the right things,' she said, when Clara paused and stirred her tea. 'I haven't come across it myself, but one of my teachers at school did her dissertation on mutism and anxiety-related disorders. I could ask her to send a copy?'

'Yes, that'd be great, thanks.' Clara sipped her tea. 'So, how's everything at home?'

'Fine, love. School's as busy as ever and your dad's been working long hours. Got a big case on.'

'Family dispute' he said. 'The usual custody battle, only not that usual as it's three-way between two gay dads and the woman they used as a surrogate.'

'Wow, bet that's a minefield,' Clara said.

'Yes, it was a lot simpler in my day. Probably time I retired.' He changed topics abruptly. 'Next door have got a new cat.'

Clara suspected he was worried he'd stepped too close to home, but she actually hadn't flinched at the mention of children and surrogates.

'Bloody tabby thing. It came in our kitchen and took a slice of ham from the counter that your mum had got out for a sandwich.'

'How did it get in?' Clara asked.

'Straight over the top of the stable door. Might have to start closing it, which would be a shame as I like the fresh air. Pesky thing.'

They continued their catching up over a lunch of pad Thai, green curry, chicken satay and coconut rice shaped like a teddy bear on the plate, much to Clara's dad's glee. (He'd taken several photos of it.)

When their hotel was open for check-in, they gratefully off-loaded suitcases, rested, showered, then changed clothes. Clara had her own room next door to her parents, which brought back memories of holidays when she was at that awkward age of being too young to go on holiday with friends, but thought herself too old to be away with her mum and dad. They'd visit quiet sides of Greek Islands with nice scenery and reasonably priced places to eat out, while she craved the excitement of the party town up the coast, where the kids from the year above at school had been.

She took the sundresses out of her now slightly battered backpack and hung them up in the wardrobe. She left her shorts and T-shirts folded up in the bag; they were only staying in Bangkok for two nights to do some sight-seeing before heading to the calmer Koh Samui for some relaxation.

'Your dad wasn't sure if we should say, but we bumped into Christopher the other week in Tesco,' Clara's mum said the next day, as they wandered around the Grand Palace.

'Oh?' Clara made an effort to sound indifferent.

'He was buying oranges,' her dad said.

'I hardly think that's relevant, Michael.'

Clara's dad went back to reading a sign about the Temple of the Emerald Buddha.

'He asked after you,' her mum said.

'And what did you tell him?'

'That you were doing well, seeming more like your old self.'

'Okay. Was he...was he with *her*?'

June looked down at her sandals and adjusted the shawl she had to wear to cover her shoulders, but which was uncomfortable in the sticky heat. She nodded once, then looked back up at her daughter's face.

Clara waited to feel a twist in her gut, a prickling sensation behind her eyes. Nothing came. 'Well, I'm not surprised; I knew they were together. To be honest mum, towards the end I think we were together more out of habit than anything else, and with everything that happened, well. I don't know...' She trailed off and shrugged.

June smiled at her daughter. 'You're made of strong stuff, love.'

'I do still miss him, or at least the life I thought I had. But coming here and doing this...well, I feel sort of...free.' She realised as she was saying the words that she'd stopped imagining Christopher at every turn. She'd left him somewhere between Sydney and Singapore and had become more focused on what she was doing day to day with the kids at school. Getting to know Anna and Netta, Jake....

They paused as a group of monks wearing orange robes walked by, stepping back to allow them to pass.

'Did you know, they wear orange-coloured robes because saffron was what was available to dye them, centuries ago?' Michael said.

'Did you read that in your guidebook, Dad?' Clara smiled at him and took his hand. Good old Dad, bringing them back to the present.

'Yes. I also read that this palace was built in 1782, after King Rama I ascended to the throne. Shall we take a look?'

The three of them wandered inside, leaving their shoes at the door, as was customary.

When they'd had their fill of the Grand Palace, they ate lunch from a street-food stall as they meandered around the streets of Bangkok, soaking up the atmosphere. Clara and

June decided to go for a massage and Michael opted for a coffee and his crossword book in a nearby café.

'Welcome,' said a petite Thai girl, who immediately made Clara feel like a giant. 'My name Jasmine. Come this way.' She led Clara and June down a corridor and to a small room at the back of the building with two changing rooms hung with blue velvet curtains. 'Take these.' She handed them each a folded bundle of silky red material. 'Leave clothes here.' She pulled back a curtain and indicated a hook on the wall of the changing room. Then she was gone. Clara shrugged at her mum and went into one of the cubicles. The silky material turned out to be a robe which just covered her bum. She wasn't sure what to leave on, so opted for just underwear. Her mum had done the same when she came out and was tugging at the robe to try and make it longer. They were obviously designed for petite Thai women.

Jasmine reappeared and led them to a room with a raised platform, where a row of yoga-style mats were laid out. To the right, a large Western man was being massaged by an elderly Thai lady. His stomach splodged out to the sides as he lay on his front and he flinched as she worked her elbow down one side of his spine.

'This is different to the spa day we had at Bannatyne's,' June whispered to Clara.

Clara nodded and pressed her lips together to keep from laughing.

'Here.' Jasmine gestured for them to lie down on the mats and her colleague joined them. Clara lay down on her stomach and tried not to think about the large sweaty man a few feet from her, or wonder whether they cleaned the mats in-between customers. Then Jasmine's hands were on her. Her thumbs pressed into the spaces between Clara's shoulder-blades. *Ooh that was good.* Then she took hold of both Clara's wrists and pulled them backwards so that her head and shoulders lifted off the mat and she was in a pose not dissimilar to the Swan in yoga. Jasmine pulled at one wrist so that Clara's spine twisted and she heard a loud popping between each vertebra. It was strangely satisfying and she found herself hoping for more. She turned her face to one side and could see her mum having a similar treatment.

Clara tried not to squirm as Jasmine reached her feet and started pulling at her toes one by one. She was reminded of watching Jess play 'This little piggy went to market' with Amelie. She'd start to pull her foot away in anticipation before Jess got to the little toe, then giggle with the sort of abandon only a child can have as her mum tickled her under the arms. What Jasmine was doing to Clara's toes, now, was more painful. The masseuse pulled each toe and twisted when she got to the end, like a mini Chinese burn. Clara kept her face turned away on the mat and winced, waited for it be over and hoped whatever she did next was more pleasant.

'Well, that was different,' June said afterwards, as they sat in the relaxation room sipping cups of herbal tea. 'I wasn't sure if she was trying to massage me, or torture me.'

'Thai massages are rougher. I feel good now though.' Clara rolled her shoulders and stretched her legs out. Her mother was watching her carefully.

'What?' she asked, relaxing her legs and crossing her ankles.

'Nothing, you just…seem like your old self. It's nice.'

Clara nodded thoughtfully. 'It's a long time since I've been "myself". I'm not sure who she is any more.'

'I know who she is,' June said, putting her cup down. She leaned forward a little. 'You know, I never told you this, but when things didn't work out with John –'

'John?'

'The man I nearly married.'

'Oh, I never knew he was called John.' Clara chewed her lip, wondered where her mum was going with this.

'Yes, John. So, when things didn't work out – those first few days when we should have been on our honeymoon in Filey –'

Clara smiled at this.

'– I didn't know who I was any more. John had been my future. We were supposed to spend our lives together. And we'd been together since we were teenagers, so I hadn't been my adult self without him.'

'But I thought you just carried on, took it all in your stride.'

'I did carry on. What else can you do? But it changed me, and I had to spend some time figuring out how to live the rest of my life.'

Clara looked at her mum, waiting for her to say more.

'I guess what I'm saying is, when I met your dad, I'd had the chance to think properly about what I wanted. I knew who I was and what was important to me.'

'Okay, and you're telling me this because...?'

'Because I think it might be the same for you. And I think you're going to be just fine, for the record.'

But I didn't just break up with someone – I couldn't have a baby, Clara thought. Out loud she said, 'I will be fine.'

June patted her hand. 'I know. Shall we go see what your dad's up to?'

The flight to Samui airport took half an hour and was uneventful: no time for a film and Michael enjoyed a packet of peanuts. They were checking into their beach bungalow, which would be home for the next ten days. June kept saying things like 'Oh, it's just like a postcard', 'Wait until I send a photo to your Aunty Pauline, Clara' and 'Can't wait for a paddle'. To be fair to her, it was pretty impressive. Even Clara, now a seasoned traveller, stopped to take in the relentless blue sky, powder white sand and gentle waves. She thought back to Whitehaven beach and Todd. She couldn't decide which was more beautiful but, in contrast to her teenage self, she was grateful she was here with her mum and dad.

They settled themselves in and Michael said he was going for a stroll along the beach. Clara and June sat on the terrace of their bungalow. looking out to sea and spritzing themselves with suncream. June was wearing her white sunglasses and had pulled the straps of her top down her shoulders to avoid tan lines. Clara sat further back so her top half was in the shade, the sun no longer a novelty.

'I could get used to this,' June said. 'Do you think I'm too old to go backpacking?'

'Yes,' Clara said. 'I think *I'm* too old to go backpacking.'

June turned to look at her. 'Don't be silly. Of course you're not.'

'Well, I felt it in Australia. They were all students on their gap year. Technically, I could have been their mum. Thank God I met Deirdre.'

'She sounded like a nice girl. Are you still in touch?'

'Yes, on Facebook and by text. She's settled in Sydney now, enjoying her job. I hope we'll be able to meet up again at some point, but not sure when. Depends if she goes back to Ireland.'

'And what about Jake?' June pushed her sunglasses to her head to get a better look at her daughter.

'Jake? He's great. We're having quite a lot of fun, actually. He's brilliant with the kids.'

'Shame he couldn't have come here with you. I'd have liked to meet him.'

'Come here? Why would he do that? We're not a couple, Mum! He's ten years younger than me, for a start.'

'Darling, I think if you're going to take anything from what you've been through, it should be to stop being so sensible and realise you can't plan everything.'

Clara didn't say anything for a minute or two, caught between being amused and insulted.

'My own mum telling me not to be sensible?' she said eventually.

'You know what I mean, love. Let yourself go. I think you deserve some fun.'

'Mum! Please don't tell me you're encouraging me to sleep with my friend Jake, who I happen to live with.'

Her mum didn't answer, as Michael chose that moment to arrive back from his stroll.

'Beautiful out there,' he said. 'Anyone fancy a dip?'

'I'll come, Dad.'

'You two go,' June said, adjusting her straps again to prevent tan lines on her arms. 'I want to soak up the sun.'

Clara and her dad walked down to the shore. The water was calm and shallow. They had to wade in considerably before it was deep enough to swim. They paused and faced the beach, bobbing next to each other.

'I think it's great what you're doing,' Michael said out of nowhere.

'Thank you.'

'Your mum worries about you. She's been so excited about this trip. Barbara from next door has been fed up of hearing about it.'

'I can imagine.' Clara smiled at the mental image of her mum shoving her Thailand Lonely Planet guide under Barbara's nose and asking her opinion on what clothes to pack.

'Between you and me, I caught Barbara leaving for her walk through the back way the other day. She jumped and spun me some yarn about not wanting the cat to escape through the front door. I think she didn't want your mum to see her and ask her in for a cup of tea and more travel talk.'

'Poor Mum.'

'Ah, she's fine. She just wants you to be happy, love.'

Clara nodded. 'I know.'

'And are you? Happy?'

The question caught her off guard and she stopped treading water for a moment. 'I'm getting there, I think.'

'Your mum mentioned something about a fella.'

'Did she?' Clara turned to face her dad.

'Jack someone?'

Clara sighed. 'Jake.'

'That's the one.'

'He's just a friend, Dad. He's younger than me and anyway, I'm not looking for a new man. I just want to get over what's happened and feel better.'

'I think you're right. These fellas are overrated.' He winked at her. 'Seriously though, love, it wouldn't do you any harm to let your hair down once in a while.'

What was it with her parents encouraging her to have a casual fling? Am I really that strait-laced and boring, she wondered?

'Thanks, Dad. I'll bear it in mind. It's Lin that's on my mind, more than Jake. The girl I told you about.'

'The one who doesn't speak?'

'Yes. I want to help her.'

'I'm sure you are helping her, love. This might not be the right thing to say and I'm sorry if it isn't, but I think you'd have made a great mum.'

'Dad, I –'

'No, I know. I don't want to upset you. What I meant was, I think you've got a lot to offer, even if you don't have your own kids.'

Clara said nothing. She watched the shore-line bobbing up and down as she floated on top of the waves. She could see her mum reading her book and sipping her drink. She was still a worry for her parents, she realised. She should have been married and have a couple of kids by now. She should have made them grandparents. The familiar swell of grief nudged at her ribcage.

'Are you okay?' Her dad was watching her.

'Yes,' she said. 'Shall we go back?'

They fell into a pattern of exploring the island in the mornings and relaxing on the beach in the afternoons. They tried out all the local restaurants and did a cooking course. June threatened to invite Barbara and Martin round for a Thai green curry as soon as they got home, and Michael shot Clara a secret eyeroll.

It was nice to have been looked after by her mum and dad for a while, and to see them enjoying themselves. It made Clara feel less guilty about the whole lack of grandkids thing. At least she could offer them a nice holiday.

By the time she arrived back in Singapore, she was rested in a way she hadn't been for a long time. She had a couple of weeks before Jake and the others arrived back, but she was looking forward to some day trips and having some alone time with her Kindle before the next school year started.

Chapter 30

April 2015

Clara took the test over to the window and held it up in the light. One line. She adjusted the angle back and forth and squinted. Still one line. She took a photo of it and increased the contrast, zoomed in. *One fucking line.* She threw the test in the bin and slammed the lid shut. Christopher was still asleep. She had been hoping to wake him up to the happy news that it had worked. Instead, she was going to have to be the bearer of bad news. She sank down until she was sitting on the bathroom tiles and rested her head on her knees. She'd made it to test day and her period hadn't arrived. She'd had such high hopes. She'd read other people's success stories, including those who'd had worse odds than them to start off with. She'd followed the advice, taken the right supplements, avoided stress, eaten the right foods, and it didn't make the slightest difference.

Four weeks of injections, ten eggs collected, four fertilised eggs, one embryo transferred, £5000 and an excruciating two-week wait had resulted in a big fat nothing.

She opened the bin and took the test out to check if a second line had appeared. Maybe I threw it away too quickly, she thought, while knowing she didn't. One line. She looked at the timer on her phone. Six minutes. The instructions said to discard any result read after five minutes. She held it up to the light again, anyway. Not the tiniest trace of a second line. She Googled 'faint positive pregnancy test' just to see the difference and so that she could actually look at a picture of a positive result. It didn't help.

She heard Christopher stirring, then the sound of him padding to the bathroom barefoot. He knocked gently and pushed open the door. She looked up at him from where she was sitting on the floor, still clutching the negative test and her phone. She wanted to delay the moment, for there still to be a chance, but it was over. She shook her head sadly. He gave an almost imperceptible nod and joined her on the floor. He put his arms around her and she allowed herself to succumb to her feelings of grief, bitter disappointment and frustration.

'Can you see one line?' She held out the test to him in case she'd missed something.

'Yes. It's negative,' he said, taking the test from her and putting it back in the bin.

Chapter 31

November 2018

Clara and Jake stood and applauded. Albertho had just finished his solo performance of 'I'd Do Anything' in the *X Factor*-style auditions.

'Amazing!' Jake said, beaming at him. 'A star in the making.'

'What a performance. Brilliant stuff!' Clara enthused.

Albertho looked from one to the other, eyes wide, cheeks flushed. He seemed to be waiting for more.

'Well done,' Clara said.

'So, I through to next round?' he asked.

'Absolutely!' Clara said.

He punched the air and actually jumped off the floor. 'Yessss!!!'

'Come here, buddy.' Jake raised his hands for a double high-five. Albertho complied enthusiastically, then made his way out of the audition studio.

'Are we doing a second round?' Clara asked Jake, after the boy was out of earshot.

'No. Everyone will get a part – it's just a case of which part.'

'He was very good.'

'He was fantastic. I've got him earmarked for Oliver.'

Johann was next up. He shuffled in, looking down at his black Adidas trainers.

'Okay, Johann, what have you got for us?' Jake tucked his pen behind his ear and leant back in his seat.

'I…um…I'm going to sing.'

'Excellent, anything in particular?'

Johann shook his head.

Clara got up from her seat and put her hand on his shoulder. 'Would you feel better doing a joint audition?' she asked.

He nodded.

A couple of minutes later, Clara returned with two kids from Jake's class. She knew they weren't looking forward to standing up there on their own, either. Jennah and Bruce joined Johann. His shoulders dropped a few inches from where they'd been hunched up around his ears and he looked up from his shoes.

'Off we go, then.' Jake signalled to Mrs Bakewell, the music teacher, at the piano and the trio mumbled their way through 'Food, Glorious Food' together.

'Excellent, guys. Thank you.'

'Chorus,' Jake and Clara said together as soon as they'd left the room.

Lin and Chen arrived next.

'Hi, Miss,' Chen said, a big smile on her face. Lin smiled too. 'I'm going to sing and Lin will stand next to me and we hold hands.'

'That's great, no problem.'

Chen sang confidently and, as promised, Lin stood by her side holding her hand. Clara was pleased she'd managed to do that and wanted to take part. They'd discussed it in their last art class. Or rather, Clara had talked about it and Lin had listened.

'You don't have to talk or sing, but I'd love you to take part in the play and be on stage with Chen. Does that sound okay?'

Lin had nodded and carried on with her drawing of a cat with a bow-tie, her tongue poking out in concentration.

'I think we have our cast,' Jake said, checking his list of parts and jotting down names next to them. 'Now the fun really starts.' It was said genuinely and Clara enjoyed watching him looking so contented and clearly involved in something he loved. It was contagious. She found she had a warm glow in her stomach as he enthused about how to structure the rehearsals to make sure each child was comfortable while being pushed to do something they could feel proud of.

A week later, rehearsals began in earnest.

'Excellent Albertho, good Sofia and Johann.' Clara praised the kids as they reached the high notes in their rendition of 'Got to Pick a Pocket or Two'. She watched Lin and Chen closely as the music teacher started from the top at the piano. Chen was singing along and Lin was sitting quietly, cross-legged, knee to knee with her sister. Her eyes were smiling and every now and again she tapped her fingers to the beat on her knees. She caught Clara watching and immediately stopped. Clara cursed herself – she shouldn't have drawn attention to it.

'Okay, everyone,' she said, as the song came to an end. 'Mr Holloway's class will be joining us shortly, so let's show them what we've got! Albertho, keep doing what you're doing. Everyone else, a little louder and big, big smiles.'

Clara was aware she actually sounded like a teacher these days. How did that happen? The kids' parents would be coming to the show and she was feeling strangely competitive, wanting her kids to be as good, or at least as enthusiastic, as Jake's. Most of all, of course, she was hoping to help Lin, who remained resolutely silent. She'd carried on seeing her one-to-one, with permission from her parents and YongJae. They had fifteen minutes, at the end of each lunch break, where they continued their arts and crafts, and Clara tried to find ways to engage with the little girl. She could tell Lin was becoming more comfortable; she'd respond by nodding or shaking her head to simple 'yes' or 'no' questions, but if Clara pushed further, she'd retreat into herself, dipping her head to avoid eye contact and becoming fascinated with what was on the paper in front of her.

'How are we doing, kids?'

'Good afternoon, Mr Holloway,' the kids chorused, trailing in after Jake as he held the door open for them.

'I'm Jake,' he said, pointing to his chest. 'No need for formalities.' He wasn't trying to be one of those cool teachers who are all 'down with the kids' – he was genuinely more comfortable being one of them than trying to be an authority figure. It was a slow battle, as the kids here were naturally deferential towards their teachers.

'Mr Jake, can I sit at the back?' a gangly kid with freckles asked as they filed in.

'How many times, Kristoff? It's just Jake. No *Mr* required.' Jake waved him in. 'And you can sit wherever you like. In you come, everyone. That's it, shuffle up, squeeze in.' He sidled up to Mrs Bakewell at the piano. 'Can we do "Consider Yourself" next?'

Clara's mouth turned upwards. She'd endured Jake singing this all the previous evening in their kitchen as he cooked spaghetti Bolognese, complete with actions and a wooden spoon doubling as a microphone. He was enjoying this more than the kids. They launched into the opening bars and Clara found herself sneaking glances at Lin again. Her shoulders were moving almost imperceptibly, a gentle sway to the rhythm.

At the end of the session, Chen and Lin approached Clara hand in hand, Chen pulling Lin along.

'Give to her,' Chen said. Lin looked down at her feet. 'Go on.' Chen nudged Lin's arm in Clara's direction. She was clutching a piece of paper.

'Is that for me?' Clara asked. Lin briefly made eye contact, looking furtive, then her gaze returned to her shoes. She held out the piece of paper, a small white sheet folded in half.

'*We thank you for the help with Lin and we would like to repay kindness. Please come to our house for eating. Thursday 6 o'clock.*
Mr and Mrs Wu'

'That's very kind of your parents,' Clara said.

'You come?' Chen was gazing up at her with such childish hopefulness that Clara found herself saying yes.

'So, you're going to their house for dinner?' Jake asked later.

'Yes. I didn't feel like I could say no. Anyway, I'm flattered.'

'You should be,' Jake said, in a rare moment of earnestness. 'You're doing a great job with the kids.' He held eye contact until Clara looked away.

'Thanks.' She smiled, feeling pleased and suddenly shy. 'I'm hoping she might speak, as she's at home, and then feel more comfortable in class.'

'Well, you're definitely making an impression. I haven't been invited anywhere for dinner.'

'What can I say? I'm instantly likeable.'

Anna came into the kitchen and started hunting through the cupboards for food. 'Get a room you two!'

Clara felt herself flushing and adjusted her posture so she was turning away from Jake, who stayed relaxed and open, immune to Anna's teasing.

Clara knocked tentatively on the red door and waited. There was shuffling inside, and the jangle of keys. The door opened and she was greeted by a narrow-shouldered woman wearing a flowery apron.

'Mrs Wu?' Clara asked. The woman was older than the other parents she saw dropping their kids off at school. The twins had been a surprise later in life. Their older daughter was twenty-five and living with her fiancé.

'Zhang,' she said, holding out her hand. 'Miss Clara.' She pointed at Clara's chest.

'Just Clara.' She smiled at her.

'Just Clara.' Zhang nodded, look of concentration on her face.

'Oh, sorry, I meant you can call me Clara. No need for the "Miss".'

Zhang looked at her blankly. 'Miss Clara?'

She nodded. That'd do. Zhang's husband appeared at her shoulder. He was not much taller than his wife, with neatly parted black hair and thick-rimmed glasses. The look, back in the UK, would be called 'geek chic', but somehow his brown corduroy trouser and bottle green tank top combo didn't lend themselves to chic, so that just left geek.

'Welcome, welcome!' he said, pumping Clara's hand enthusiastically. 'Come, come.'

Mr and Mrs Wu led her down the corridor and into a pleasant-looking front room with worn leather sofas, a dark green rug and Chinese lanterns hanging from the ceiling. There was a delicious smell coming from the kitchen: a mixture of soy, grilled meat and honey. Clara's stomach rumbled in anticipation.

'Tea,' Mr Wu said. It was a statement rather than a question and he scurried off to the kitchen.

'Sit.' Zhang pointed to the brown leather sofa. It occurred to Clara that this would be trickier than she thought, with the language barrier. She took her seat as instructed.

'You have a beautiful home,' she said gesturing around her. Zhang smiled, but it wasn't clear if she'd understood.

'Your house. It's lovely.' Clara tried again.

'Lovely,' Zhang repeated.

Clara heard clattering on the stairs and she breathed a sigh of relief as the girls bounded in.

'Miss!' Chen cried. She careered around the corner then slowed, unsure of herself. Lin hovered behind her.

'Girls!' Clara held her arms out. She wasn't sure of protocol, but a hug in this situation seemed appropriate. Chen made her way over and Lin followed more cautiously. She put an arm around each of the girl's shoulders.

'How are my star pupils doing?' she asked.

'You want see our bedroom?' Chen asked.

'Maybe after dinner.' Clara tried to fob her off. She couldn't very well take herself off upstairs with the girls without their parents giving the go ahead, and their mum didn't understand what she was saying. She was already planning on turning this experience into an amusing anecdote to tell Jake later. Chen sat down on the settee next to her and Lin sat next to her sister.

Mr Wu returned, carrying a tea set on a tray. A blue-and-white patterned tea-pot and three cups with no handles. There was a matching sugar-bowl with brown sugar-cubes, but no milk, she noted.

'Tea,' he stated again. He placed the tray on a low coffee table and poured. 'Sugar.' He placed a cube in each cup, stirred once briskly, and handed a cup to Clara. She took it, taking care not to burn her fingers. It was delicious and she was glad he'd added the sugar without asking.

'Thank you for the tea. And for inviting me into your home.'

Mr and Mrs Wu looked at her, their heads ducked in deference. 'You must be very proud of your girls,' she continued.

'Ah, yes. Lin tell us how you do art class for her. Very special.' His eyes crinkled behind his glasses.

'Oh, it's a pleasure.' She couldn't get her head around Lin telling them anything, when she'd never heard her utter a single word.

'She bring pictures home. We put on fridge. She look forward to your classes. Very much.'

Lin was examining a loose thread on her skirt, head bent low.

'I love teaching both the girls. Their English is fantastic.'

Zhang said something in Mandarin.

'She say, she very happy for our girls to speak English. They able to do more things. Be great,' Mr Wu translated.

'They already are great,' Clara said. 'I'd like to help and I'd like to help Lin in particular. I mean, if I can.' She didn't want to interfere.

'Lin, she speak when she comfortable. At home, no problem.'

'Chen would like to show me their room,' Clara said slowly. 'Is it okay if I go up with them?' Both girls turned eager eyes towards their father, silently pleading.

'Please,' he said. 'Is fine.'

Chen jumped up immediately 'Yes!' She took Clara's hand. Lin stood up, smiling too and the trio headed upstairs.

'This my bed. This Lin's bed. This our fish. This our favourite teddy. He speak.' Chen demonstrated by squeezing the bear's paw. 'Pleased to meet you,' the bear said.

'Wow, so he does!'

Lin was sitting on her bed watching.

'Which is your favourite toy, Lin?'

Lin looked at her sister.

'It's this unicorn.' Chen picked the toy up from where it lay on the floor.

'That's beautiful. Now Chen, I know you're such a big help to your sister, but can we see if Lin would like to answer herself?' Chen nodded and sat down next to her sister.

'What is the unicorn's name?'

Chen opened her mouth to speak.

Clara held her hand up. 'Let's give her a minute.' Then to Lin, 'No rush, just tell me when you're ready.'

The girl's brown eyes were huge. She briefly made eye contact, then looked down at her lap. Her lip twitched and she scratched her neck.

When nobody said anything for a good few minutes, Clara said, 'Shall I guess?'

Lin nodded.

'George?' They both laughed and shook their heads.

'Henry?'

'It girl!' Chen said, unable to contain herself. 'See, eyelashes, mean it girl.' She gestured at the unicorn's long eyelashes made of lace. So that's how they determined a toy's gender.

'Oh, silly me. Julia?' More laughter and shaking of heads.

'Karen?'

'No!' Chen said.

Lin cupped her hand and whispered in Chen's ear. Clara could just about hear her hushed tones. Did this count, she wondered?

'She want me to tell you,' Chen said 'Elsa.'

'Elsa! Of course.' Clara smiled. 'She has white fur and a sparkly blue mane. What else would she be called?'

Chen was showing Clara where the fish food was and telling her how they took it in turns to feed the fish, when Mr Wu called up the stairs that dinner was ready.

'This is delicious.' Clara swallowed a bite of spring roll which was like no spring roll she'd ever tasted before. The vegetables were crunchy and fragrant and the pastry thin and delicate.

Zhang said something in Mandarin.

'She give you some to take home,' Mr Wu said.

'Oh no, there's no need.'

'Yes, she give. You freeze, then deep fry.'

'Oh, well thank you very much,' Clara said.

Mr Wu nodded, satisfied. 'Freeze, deep fry,' he said again.

The girls were daintily eating noodles, faces close to the small bowls they held in one hand, chopsticks in the other. The big round table was adorned with a bright red table cloth and many plates with different types of food. Dim sum, fried rice, beef in a sticky sauce, something that looked like...chicken feet. Clara did a double take. She claimed she was full when that particular dish was offered. She looked away when Zhang picked up a foot and gnawed on the toes, deftly avoiding the claws. She bet Jake would have been game for trying one if he'd been here. She thought about asking them to throw a couple in with the spring rolls, but didn't want to seem cheeky.

It was pleasantly cool in the Wu household. A ceiling fan was creating a welcome breeze. Clara enjoyed being in a family home. It had been a long time. She felt a pang for her own home. Her childhood home with her mum and dad. It'd been nearly a year since she'd set off on her travels and Christmas was approaching. A huge Christmas tree made entirely of lights had appeared at the shopping centre and the Gardens by the Bay had been transformed into a Christmas Wonderland. It seemed Singapore went big on Christmas. It'd be Clara's first one not at home and while she didn't want to be back there being reminded of the family she didn't have, she wasn't quite sure how she felt about spending it here, either.

The family she was sitting with now had slipped into a comfortable silence. She observed the ease with which they passed dishes back and forth. Mr Wu occasionally praised his wife on her cooking skills. She would smile and bow her head, almost shy. When appetites were sated and chopsticks abandoned in bowls, more tea appeared. Pu-erh tea, Mr Wu informed her, was good for digestion. It had an unusual taste – sweet, but somehow bitter at the same time. Lin and Chen were tucking into a pink pudding the colour of blancmange and the consistency of jelly. Clara was offered some but couldn't squeeze in another bite. She'd had to undo the button on her shorts when she visited the loo and was self-consciously pulling her T-shirt down and hoping no one noticed.

All too soon it was time for her to leave. She thanked the Wus for their food and hospitality.

'You must come again,' Mr Wu said, shaking her hand.

Zhang enveloped her in a hug with surprising strength, given her petite frame. 'Miss Clara,' she said, pressing a Tupperware box into her hands.

'Freeze, deep fry,' Mr Wu reminded her.

'Yes, I'll look forward to them. Thanks again. Bye, Chen. Bye, Lin.' She bent to kiss them both on the cheek.

'See you at school!' Chen said.

Lin waved and smiled. Clara's hand was still on the door handle pulling it closed as she heard Lin's voice for the first time. 'Bye.'

'So, she actually spoke?' Jake asked later.

'Well, she whispered to Chen and she spoke when I was halfway out of the door, so I don't know if that counts. I mean, she already spoke at home and I was pretty much gone –'

'But she was saying bye to *you*.'

'Well, yes. I suppose she was,' Clara admitted.

'So, that's progress.' Jake was grinning at her. 'We should celebrate.'

'Not more drinking,' Clara said. 'We have work tomorrow.'

'No, I have these.' Jake held up two tickets to a basketball game.

'Basketball?'

'Yep, you ever been?'

'No.'

'Well, then. I know you're up for new experiences, so we'll go. It'll be fun.'

Clara shrugged. 'Well okay, I suppose. Why not?'

Jake's enthusiasm was infectious and she hadn't fancied an evening in, anyway.

An hour later, they were sitting near the top of the stadium watching some very tall men bounce a ball, trying to get it through a hoop. Jake was leaning forward, his hands on his knees, a strand of his dark hair stuck to his forehead.

Clara took a sip of her Coke and watched the action unfold. They were quite nifty with the ball, bouncing it through their legs and around the opposition.

'So, who do we want to win?' she asked.

'Doesn't matter. I just enjoy watching.'

Clara thought of Dave and his football and how Jess would have to put up with sulking if his team lost, or worse, got relegated. When that happened they didn't have sex for weeks (apparently a long time by their usual standards). She'd always been secretly glad that Christopher had no interest in football. It freed up a lot of Saturdays and she never had to sit in the pub, bored, while he cheered occasionally and swore more often. Somehow, she couldn't imagine Christopher cheering over the footie. Just not his bag.

Watching Jake now was different. He was enjoying the skill of the players, the atmosphere and the shared experience. She had to admit, it was hard not to get swept up in it: the determined looks on the players' faces as they totally lost themselves in the game; the families in the crowd; small kids sitting on their dads' shoulders; groups of young women cheering their team on. It was nice to be part of it. It was wholesome. The players shook hands during the break and the spectators joined a queue for ice cream. There was no tribalism, no bravado, no lager and fighting – just people having a nice time.

'Enjoying yourself?' Jake asked. He dug his small wooden spoon into a tub of rocky road the size of a Petits Filous; portion control was carefully observed here.

'Do you know what? I actually am,' Clara said.

'No need to sound so surprised.'

'Well, no. It's just sport isn't really my thing. But this is fun.' And it was. Then it dawned on her that she'd observed the families without that gut-wrenching longing. There was a pang, yes, but it was rather like a bee sting once the vinegar has been applied; it was still there, but more of a nagging itch than a sharp pain.

Chapter 32

January 2013

Clara looked at the smiley face on the ovulation test and felt a surge of excitement. She was ovulating. It was their sixth month of trying. This had to be it. It usually took around six to twelve months to conceive, so they were on schedule. It must be their turn. Christopher was on his way out of the door downstairs. That's okay – they should have a good twenty-four-hour window. She'd make sure they had sex that night. After dinner perhaps. That way she could make sure she laid on her back with her legs in the air for a good half a hour after, too. She went downstairs and threw together ingredients for a chicken casserole in the slow cooker, then headed out to work.

'That was good.' Christopher said, using his crusty bread to mop up the last of the sauce.
'Glad you enjoyed it. So, shall we go upstairs?' Clara brushed his leg with her foot under the table.
'Now? I've just finished eating. I'm stuffed.'
'Okay, let's wait an hour or so then.'
'I'm not really in the mood, to be honest. I've got some more work to do.'
'I'm not in the mood either, but we have to. I'm ovulating.'
He let out a breath. 'Okay, give me half an hour or so.' He started gathering up the plates to load up the dishwasher, then sat down with his laptop at the kitchen island to respond to emails, or whatever he was doing.
Clara went upstairs to get ready. Her legs were a bit prickly, so she gave them a quick shave. She checked the underwear she was wearing. Comfy blue knickers and a white T-shirt bra. She rummaged in her top drawer for a matching set and put them on. Dark red and lacy, that was better. The bra gave her an extra lift and was on the tasteful

side of see-through, showing just a hint of nipple. She arranged herself on the bed to wait. Ten minutes later, she was getting cold, so she put her dressing gown on and picked up her Kindle to read while she waited.

'Ah, finally', she said, when he came into the room forty minutes later.

'What? I haven't finished, just came to get this.' He picked up the laptop charger.

Clara sighed noisily. 'Can we just have sex now, then you can finish your work?' She took off her dressing gown. 'Look, I put my nice underwear on.'

He looked from her to the door and back again. 'Okay.' He put down the charger and unbuttoned his shirt.

'We should use this fertility lubricant,' she said. 'It helps the sperm get to the egg.'

'You really know how to get a man going, don't you?'

She unfastened his belt and trousers and kissed him. 'Is this better?'

Clara tucked her legs underneath her on Jess's settee and rested her glass of Pinot Grigio on one knee.

'Trying for a baby is hard work, as it turns out. I've never wanted sex less.'

'I bet Christopher is enjoying it!'

'No, not especially. It's weird. All those years having sex for fun and trying not to get pregnant, then as soon as you have to do it for the reason nature intended, it stops being fun.'

Jess took a gulp of her wine. 'We're going to try too,' she said.

'Really? I thought you wanted to get married first.'

'I've given up waiting on that one. Thought we may as well go for it. I've stopped taking the pill.' She made her eyes go big and wide.

'Wow. Is Dave on board with this?'

'Of course, he is. Well, he knows I've stopped taking the pill. I told him it'll probably take a year or so, anyway. So he's okay with it.'

'You should hurry up. I have a good feeling about this month. Imagine if we get pregnant at the same time. We could be on maternity leave together and our kids would be best friends.'

'I know, I thought of that. We should try to synchronise. I'll text you when we're going to have sex, so you can get on it too.'

'It doesn't work like that – you have to do it when you're ovulating.'

'Really? I was just going to jump on him a few times a week and see what happens.'

'It's all about the timing. There's only a couple of days a month you can actually get pregnant.'

'What? They didn't tell us that in sex education at school.'

'I know. I thought if you had sex without a condom once, bam, you'd be pregnant.'

'Hmm.' Jess took a drink of her wine.

'Hey, Clara.' Dave appeared from the kitchen, wearing his jogging bottoms and carrying an axe. 'Pregnant yet?'

'Dave!' Jess scolded.

'What?'

'It's okay. No, not yet. We're working on it.'

'If Christopher needs some help with the task, I'm up for it.'

'*Dave*!' Jess threw a cushion at him. 'Go chop your wood.'

'Sorry about him,' she said to Clara as he left the room.

'He's fine. I might not tell Christopher he said that though! What's he doing chopping wood?'

'It's for the new log burner we're getting. Haven't I told you?' Jess reached for her phone to show Clara a photo of it.

Clara lay in bed with a hand on her stomach. She was trying not to get her hopes up, but they'd had sex three times while she was ovulating and she had a feeling this was going to be their time. She imagined the cells dividing inside her womb, attaching to the lining and growing, becoming a new life that was part her and part Christopher. She hoped Jess followed her advice about pinpointing when she was ovulating so that she'd get pregnant soon too. They could do the stuff pregnant people did, together. Go to antenatal classes and do yoga. She imagined the four of them in a class learning about breathing and panting and crowning. Christopher sitting behind her on the floor, and Dave behind Jess, while they all laughed at some stupid joke Dave had made. They could go to Pizza Express after and she and Jess would have to make sure they didn't order the Fiorentina as it had a runny egg on it, or anything with prosciutto as the meat was cured, not cooked. They'd drink sparkling water instead of wine and chit-chat with the waiter about the fact that they were best friends and pregnant together. Yes, wasn't it lovely? They'd been friends in school and their kids would be too. They'd go on family holidays together. Camping trips, where the grown-ups could sit around a camp-fire and drink red wine, while the kids frolicked in a stream nearby. Or maybe they could hire a villa. She imagined them all lounging on sun-loungers, while the kids took it in turns to splash in the pool.

The bed sagged as Christopher climbed in beside her. She turned on to her side, away from him and he put his arm around her waist. She pressed his hand lightly into her stomach.

'I have a good feeling about this month,' she said.

'Hmm.' He kissed the back of her head and they drifted off to sleep.

Chapter 33

November 2018

Anna turned on her side on the settee where she'd been dozing. She was wearing her She-Ra nightie.

'You and Jake seem to be getting on well.'

'Yes.' Clara looked up from the dissertation on mutism she'd been reading and smiled in spite of herself.

'Dude, he likes you,' Anna said.

'I like him too.'

'….And?' Anna raised herself up on her elbow to get a better view of Clara so she could scrutinise her response.

'And nothing. We're two friends who like each other.'

Anna laid back down, head flopping on the cushion. 'I was hoping for some salacious gossip.'

Clara shrugged, but a smile played on her lips.

'You do like him.'

'Maybe, but I'm not looking to get into anything. I don't want any complications just now.'

'Shame. I can see you two together.'

'Sorry to disappoint. You and Netta seem happy?'

'Oh, yeah. We're polar opposites in a lot of ways, but it works.' She shrugged as if she couldn't fathom it.

'And she's managing to keep her business going from over here?' Clara asked.

'Yeah, it's going pretty well. The world's a smaller place nowadays. She's flying back to London for a few weeks on Tuesday, though. Some things still need to be done face-to-face.'

'Sure.'

'So, how are you getting on as an independent woman?'

Clara took a sip of her tea and thought for a minute. 'Better than I thought, to be honest. But my bed does feel empty sometimes. Not that that means I'm going to invite

Jake into it,' she added quickly when Anna raised an eyebrow. 'Although, if I'm totally honest, I'm not sure I miss Christopher as much as what our relationship stood for.' She shifted in her seat and tucked a leg underneath her.

'How do you mean?'

'I liked being married and knowing where things were going, or at least thinking I knew where things were going. But it wasn't right for a long time. I miss how we used to be, but towards the end, well…' She trailed off. 'I think by coming here and doing something different, you meet people who are similar to yourself. I don't feel like a social outcast because I'm separated from my husband and don't have kids.'

'I don't think too many TEFL teachers have husbands and kids,' Anna conceded.

'Right, so I fit right in.'

'Is that important to you, to fit in?'

'You sound like the counsellor I stopped seeing,' Clara said. At that moment, Jake appeared in the doorway, saving her from answering. Anna's question had lodged a seed in her mind, though, that she'd revisit later. Right now, Jake was carrying the biggest pizza box she'd ever seen. Her stomach grumbled as the scent of garlic and tomato wafted across the room.

'Who's hungry?' he asked.

'I think I love you,' Clara replied, without thinking. Jake grinned and Anna gave her a pointed look. She tried to hide her embarrassment by shuffling the pages of the dissertation she was reading into a neat pile, then standing up and busying herself gathering plates and glasses.

'Did Clara tell you she got Lin to speak?'

'What? No! That's huge!' Anna said.

'Well, not quite. I mean she whispered to Chen in front of me and she said 'bye' as I was leaving. But I was on my way out and she already spoke at home, so –'

'That's amazing, dude! Definitely sounds like progress to me. Awesome. Hope you're pleased with yourself.'

'I am, rather.' Clara smiled as she helped herself to a slice of pizza.

It was five weeks to Christmas and where Clara would usually have been stressing about how long to cook the turkey for and how many types of pigs-in-blankets to do, and whether Christopher's dad would comment if she didn't put pancetta in with the sprouts and chestnuts, now her biggest concern was working out the best time to Skype her mum and dad, given the time difference. There would be a Christmas lunch at the training centre for current trainees and those who'd recently attended. Clara, Jake, Anna and Netta were all going. There were twenty-five of them in total and they were doing a secret Santa, so Clara only had to buy one present. A far cry from all her friend's kids she usually had to consider, though she'd probably have to make it up to them all when she did return home.

Clara's phone pinged.

Jess: Who's the hottie from the theme park? o

It took her a minute to work out what Jess was talking about. Jake had posted photos from Sentosa Island on Facebook and tagged her. She glanced up at him. He was absorbed in his pizza and couldn't read what was on her phone from where he was.

Clara: That's Jake x

Jess: You didn't mention he was a stone-cold fox o

Clara: *laughing face* Didn't notice x

Jess: Yeah, right o

'What's so funny?' Jake asked.

'Oh, it's just my friend, Jess.'

He adopted teacher mode. 'Anything you want to share with the class?'

'Erm, she thinks you're a fox.'

'Is she single?' He sat up straighter on the settee. 'And is she a fox?'

'She's long term-engaged and has two kids,' Clara said, ignoring the way her stomach clenched at his enthusiasm.

'What's long-term engaged?'

'She's as good as married. Definitely not single, anyway.'

'Too bad.'

There was something in Jake's eyes Clara couldn't quite decipher. Anna was watching the exchange with interest.

'So, shall we watch a film?' Clara asked, keen to steer the conversation to more comfortable territory.

'Sure.' Anna picked up the remote control and staring scrolling through options. They settled on *Four Weddings and a Funeral* for nostalgia's sake, and Jake didn't even try to hide his tears when John Hannah read the Auden poem.

Chapter 34

January 2016

'You could try again, but I'd suggest you give some real consideration to using an egg donor.' The consultant produced a leaflet called *Creating Your Family Using Donor Eggs*. It showed an illustration of a man and woman sitting on a settee, a baby nestled between them in a Moses basket.

They were back in the consultant's office, six month's after their second failed attempt. Same neat bob, same bright overhead lights and vase of flowers, only this time it had tulips in it.

'As predicted, you didn't respond well to the stimulation,' she said. 'Particularly on your most recent cycle.'

Clara took the leaflet mutely and turned it over in her hands.

Christopher spoke up. 'Could we try a different type of stimulation?'

Clara sat up straighter in her chair.

'Yes, that is an option, but there are no guarantees. The odds are still against you and I wouldn't want to give false hope.'

'But there would be a chance of it working?' Clara asked. She couldn't help sounding hopeful, despite the consultant's words.

'A small chance, yes.'

'If we wanted to use an egg donor, how would we get one?' Christopher asked. Clara gave him a sharp look; she wasn't ready for this.

'We have a list of donors and we'd match you on physical characteristics. Then you'd have the chance to read more about the person and make a final decision.'

Clara said nothing.

'Some of our donors are altruistic, which means they do it for no other reason than to help people. They're not paid, as such, though we do compensate them financially to cover potential loss of earnings. They don't get anything other than the satisfaction of having helped. Some donors are women who are having IVF treatment themselves and are willing to share the eggs they've collected.'

'Some women get enough to share out? Why do they need IVF then?' Clara asked, aware her tone sounded petulant.

'People need IVF for all sorts of reasons.'

'And are these women doing it out of the goodness of their hearts as well?'

'They want to help, yes, and they get their own treatment at a reduced cost.'

'Right.'

'I think we need some time to think it all through.' Christopher was taking control again. This wasn't like him.

'Of course,' the consultant said. 'Give us a call when you're ready.'

'It's up to you,' Christopher said, later, as they ate fish and chips.

'It's not just up to me. Don't put it all on me.'

'No, I mean I'll support you, whatever you decide is best.'

'I want to have a baby that's mine and yours. That's sort of the point.' She put her chips down and sighed.

'So, you want to start again with your own eggs? A new fresh cycle?' After the failed first cycle, Clara had powered through to the next attempt, barely pausing for breath. Encouraged by having a healthy embryo to transfer, she'd convinced herself she could do it again and it might just work. The results were worse than the first time. Three eggs collected, none made it to blastocyst stage. One was transferred, with a warning it was of low quality. She had repeated her routine of doing something nice every day for her second two-week wait and was ready to go and sit in a quiet room by herself for a few days by the end of it.

It was in the toilets of a restaurant when she saw it. They were out for Christopher's friend's birthday. Dark red blood. Her hands had trembled as she'd hastily wedged a wad of tissue into her knickers. She hadn't even got to test day. It had all ended in that moment, alone in the toilets. Biggest fail so far. Her chest constricted, her breath coming in snatched bursts. Surely this couldn't be happening, again.

She'd thought she'd fall to pieces, but that had come later. Right then, she'd calmly washed her hands, gone back to the table, ordered dessert along with the others and made polite conversation with Christopher's friends, as her womb contracted and cramped and her heart ached.

In the follow-up appointment the consultant had advised against another round with Clara's eggs, given the low chance of success and obvious emotional toll it was taking. They'd decided to have a break. And now, here they were. 'Yes. No…I don't know,' she said.

'No rush to decide.' Christopher put his arm around her shoulders.

'No, but I'll feel better once I know what the plan is.' Clara got the leaflet out of her bag and flipped through the pages. There was an image of a woman reading a book to a small child, with the caption 'We encourage openness and honesty between parents and children born through donated eggs.'. She showed it to Christopher. 'So, we'd have to tell the child that he or she wasn't biologically mine.'

He took the leaflet from her. 'We don't have to do anything, but it looks like that's what they recommend. It also says any child born from a donor egg has the right to find out who their donor is when they turn eighteen.'

'What? Let me see that.' She took the leaflet back. 'So, I could get rejected by my child when they're eighteen and they decide they want to meet their "real" mum.'

'I don't think it'd be like that. It says it's just to satisfy curiosity and not for them to build a relationship.'

'Hmm.'

'It's a big thing and if you're not comfortable with it, we won't do it,' Christopher said simply.

'What if it's our only chance to have a baby?' *What then?*

A few weeks later, Clara agreed to see the profile of an available egg donor the clinic had on their books, on the understanding she wasn't committing to anything.

'She's got brown hair,' Clara said.

'So do you,' Christopher said.

'Mine is light brown.'

'Maybe hers is light brown too.'

'It doesn't say that.'

'It doesn't say it's dark either.'

'Is dark hair a problem? I have dark hair. The baby could get that from me anyway,' Christopher said.

Clara said nothing.

'The only real question is whether you're comfortable with this. If you're not, then hair colour is irrelevant.'

'I want to be.'

'She's got brown hair,' Clara said, again. This time to her mum, over a cup of tea at her mum and dad's kitchen table. Clara's mum nodded and held her hand out for the print-out of the profile of her donor egg match.

'She's got a maths degree. You're both good at numbers. And she's a similar height and build to you.'

'I know. She's sporty too. Look, it says she plays netball.'

June studied the print-out. 'And she gives to charity.'

'She's an all round excellent human being, judging by this profile. But she's not me. I mean, what if the baby didn't feel like mine? Even after I've carried it and given birth to it?'

'Darling, you have so many options these days. I'm not sure it's always helpful.'

'Okay, but using donor eggs is an option, and maybe our only option.'

'You could adopt a baby.'

Clara sighed loudly. 'Do you know how difficult it is to adopt? It's not like the old days, where you'd go pick a baby from the orphanage who had a teenage mum. It takes eighteen months to be approved. They interview everyone who knows you and dig around in your past. Even then, it's not straightforward. You can wait years and not be matched, and if you are, you're much more likely to get an older child, not a baby. One with problems. They don't take kids away from parents lightly. They have to have been through some serious stuff and I'm not sure I'm strong enough to deal with all that.'

Clara's mum nodded as she dunked a ginger biscuit into her tea.

'At least this baby would be Christopher's and I'd get to be pregnant.'

'Darling, you know I'll support you whatever you decide, and it wouldn't be any less my grandbaby if you go ahead.'

Clara studied her fingernails against the marble surface. Her pink nail varnish contrasted pleasingly against the grey. 'I want a baby, Mum. I don't know what to do.'

'What does Christopher think?'

'He says he'll go with whatever I want.'

'Well, there you go.'

'I know, but that puts all the pressure on me to decide. What if every time the baby does something, and I think – well she didn't get that from me, must have been her egg donor?'

'I don't think it's that simple love. Every child is unique and special; they're not just a mish-mash of their parents' characteristics.'

'I suppose…'

'Anyway, this lady is kind enough to donate her eggs to help someone else create a family. If you want your child to inherit any characteristics, that'd be pretty incredible, and more important than hair colour.'

Clara smiled. 'Maybe she's a better option than me, anyway.'

Clara's mum took her hand. 'Never.' She winked. 'You'd be her mum and bring her up and you'd be the best mum ever.'

'How do you know it'd be a girl?'

'Oh, I imagine you with a girl,' she said, in that all-knowing Mum-like way she had.

And so the following week Clara found herself calling the clinic and saying she wanted to go ahead with the donor eggs. A very in-depth series of forms filled out later, they were all set. The clinic gave her the pill to take to synchronise her cycle to her donor's. It would feel perverse to take the contraceptive pill when she so desperately wanted to be pregnant, but she'd dutifully do as she was told. At least there wouldn't be any needles this time and no egg collection – for her, anyway. That was for her brown-haired superwoman with the power to grant wishes.

Chapter 35

November 2018

Clara opened her eyes and pressed her phone to check the time. 8:03. She stretched and rolled onto her back, allowing herself to feel lazy pleasure that today was Saturday and she didn't have to rush to get up. Her Kindle was on the bedside table where she'd put it down at a cliffhanger last night. The protagonist had to decide whether to confess to a crime she didn't commit in order to save her daughter. She picked it up and propped herself up on the pillows. After reading a page or so, she heard movement. Jake was up. Anna – or perhaps Netta – was up. Someone turned on the shower, then she heard voices.

'…I didn't…She's not interested anyway, not in that way…..' Jake said.

'….thinks you're after her best friend….saw her face…likes you…' Anna said.

Clara put down her Kindle and strained to hear. She cursed Netta as she started to sing in the shower. All she made out then were a few words and snippets of phrases. 'Sentosa…flirted…got changed under a towel…basketball' from Jake and 'vulnerable…talk to her…you'd make a…give it chance.'

Then the shower stopped and they both walked away until they were out of earshot. Clara sank further down in bed and tried to re-engage with her book. It was no good. She allowed herself to consider what she'd just heard. Another fling wasn't something she wanted and neither was a serious relationship. She'd probably be going home in the summer. So logically, she should steer clear. But she enjoyed being with Jake and he was, as Jess put it, a stone-cold fox. They had a week of intensive rehearsals for *Oliver!* coming up, before the show on Friday, so she'd put it out of her mind for now. There was plenty to keep them occupied. She gave up on her book. It sounded like the woman was going to confess, but she'd find out later. She swung her legs over the side of the bed and headed for the bathroom.

The three of them were in the kitchen eating toast and cereal when Clara came down.

'Morning,' Jake said. 'What you up to today?'

'I was thinking of heading out for a walk this morning, then I want to go over the plans for the rehearsals this week and make sure we're all set.'

'Cool. Fancy some company on your walk? Where you headed?'

She hesitated. *Should I try keeping my distance? But we live together and work together anyway, so…what's the difference?*

'Sure, why not? I thought I might check out that bird place. Jurong.'

Anna and Netta exchanged a look, which Clara pretended not to notice.

'There are only 23,000 African penguins left in the world. They're endangered,' Jake read from the sign.

'You can adopt one. Or two. Ben and Bella, the penguin couple.'

'Don't. I'd adopt them all. I'd open a zoo, like in *We Bought a Zoo*.'

'What about your dreams of making a living from acting?'

'Maybe I'd combine the two. We could put on performances for the visitors. Me, Ben and Bella, we could do *Oliver!*'

'Yes, I'm sure there'd be no problems whatsoever with that idea.' Clara laughed as they left the penguins and headed towards the aviary. They looked up at a huge waterfall. The sound of the water, the birds and the heat made it feel as though they were in a jungle. There were bridges up high, close to the ceiling, to allow visitors to enjoy panoramic views of the landscape and spot the more reticent birds.

Clara nodded at the bridges. 'Can we go up there, or will you freak out?'

'I will not freak out. Come on.' He put his hand on her upper arm to steer her along and she tried to ignore the feeling of his fingers on her bare skin. Since half-overhearing the conversation between him and Anna that morning, she was overanalysing everything, even more than usual. What Jake said. What Jake did. How she felt about it. His hand dropped away from her arm and her skin felt hot where he'd touched it.

'Think it's this way,' he said.

She followed and noticed the way his T-shirt fitted snugly over the muscles in his back. It was quite a pleasing shape to look at. She shook her head and told herself she must stop objectifying him. They were friends and she didn't want to make things weird. A stand of leaflets showing pictures of the different birds in the aviary caught her attention and she stopped to pick one up. This was safer territory.

'That's a purple glossy starling.' She pointed at a stunning-looking creature with shiny purple, green and blue feathers. It was perched on a low tree-branch and was perfectly still, head cocked to one side as though listening out for something. They stood quietly to watch it, until it took flight and soared over their heads.

'What's that one?' Jake, asked pointing to her leaflet.

'Err, it's a "helmeted guinea fowl",' Clara read.

'It looks like a –'

'Unicorn?'

'We'll go with that.' Jake's eyes were crinkling at the edges.

'Ooh, look at that one!' Clara pointed again. 'It's a red-crested turaco. It's so pretty.'

'That is pretty. I'd get some of those for my zoo. I wonder what they'd be like at performing.'

As he spoke a bird poo slopped out of the air and landed on his chest, leaving a grey smear on his T-shirt. He didn't notice.

'Err, think you may have a problem using birds in your performance.'

'What's that?'

Clara nodded at his T-shirt, lips pressed together in quiet amusement.

'Oh, shit.'

'Yep. Literally.'

He held the material away from his skin and looked around helplessly.

'Hang on. I think I have some Wet Ones in my bag.' Clara rummaged around and produced the goods. 'Here.' She dabbed at the mess, while he held his T-shirt away from his skin, and then folded it on itself to scrub at the stain when the worst of it was off. His skin was warm through the thin fabric, and the heat began to feel stifling. She avoided his eyes while she wiped, only looking up to meet his gaze when she'd stepped back.

'Thanks,' he said. There was something in his eyes that she didn't want to see.

She held up the Wet One. 'I need a bin.'

'A bin, yes. Err, over there.'

After more bird-spotting from the bridges and, thankfully, no more poo incidents, they made their way to the café. Clara sat across the table from Jake, a safe distance away. If she didn't touch him and didn't look at him too much, all would be okay. It was fine to be friends with an attractive man. She wasn't some hormonal teenager. She was a grown-up with a fully functioning brain, which was telling her it wasn't a good idea to get involved.

The café had a marble floor and pillars reminiscent of a Greek temple. It was blissfully cool inside and had those huge menus you needed two hands to hold. Quite handy, as Clara could use it to hide behind with the ruse of choosing what to eat. She'd already decided she'd have tomato and mozzarella salad, maybe some bread on the side, but she held onto the menu a while longer.

'You okay behind there?'

'Yeah, just deciding.'

'I'm going for the tuna Niçoise salad. I'd like some bread with it, though.'

Clara put down her menu and smiled. 'I was thinking about bread, too. Let's share some.'

'I'll go order.' Jake headed up to the counter and Clara sat back in her chair and looked around. A brown-skinned woman was feeding a baby under a cloth covering. The cloth was patterned with leaves and complemented the green dress the woman was wearing. Clara wondered whether she had one for every outfit. It had a sort of peephole at the top so she could see her baby. A toddler sat to her right, clutching a thick crayon in chubby fingers and scribbling on the picture provided by the café. A black-and-white picture of birds was turning into a riot of colour, with no regard for the lines. Clara thought of Lin and her careful attention to colouring-in during their art sessions. She'd spend a lot of time concentrating, getting the shading just right, and then look up proudly when she'd done, looking for praise, which of course, Clara gave in abundance.

'Got you a lime and soda,' Jake said, putting down a glass with beads of condensation on the outside.

'Brilliant, thanks.' She took a long refreshing gulp.

'Can we go to the birds of prey after this?' Jake asked.

'Yeah. I want to see the flamingos, too.'

'Birds of prey, flamingos. It's a plan.'

The food came and they passed half an hour chatting and eating, talking about birds, teaching and the upcoming concert at school.

Later that afternoon, back from their day out, Clara sat on the balcony and called her mum. It was hot, but she'd found a spot of shade by moving her chair right to one edge and turning it sideways.

'I'm so glad you like teaching,' June said. 'I knew you would.'

'Yeah, I do. I keep thinking about Lin. I think the concert will be really good for her.'

'Sounds like you're doing a great job with her, love. And how's Jake?'

'He's fine. We went out together today, actually. To Jurong bird park.'

She could hear her mum's smile. 'Sounds nice.'

'We're just friends, mum.'

'I didn't say a word!'

'I can hear what you're thinking.'

'Don't know what you mean.'

'Okay. I'm sure you don't. How's everything at home, anyway?'

'All good, love. Your dad's been busy at work and he's decided to do up the shed so he can use it to make his model boats. Think he just wants to get out of the way when Barbara pops round. He spent an inordinate amount of time in the downstairs loo when she was over yesterday. Thought there must have been something wrong with the prawn sandwich he had for lunch, but he just wanted some peace…'

As June talked, Clara sank down in her chair and stretched her legs out so her feet were in the sun.

Jake poked his head out of the door. He was holding two beers. He raised one towards her in a question. She smiled and took it. He sat down next to her while she finished her conversation.

'When you open your zoo, can I bring the kids from school on a trip?' Clara said once she'd hung up the phone

'Sure. Maybe bring umbrellas or raincoats for the aviary, though. It'll have an aviary, of course.'

'Of course. I think Lin and Chen would love to see a helmeted guinea fowl.'

'Just the name sounds wrong, never mind what it looks like.'

'That's because your mind is in the sewer. It looks like a unicorn.'

'If you say so.' He raised an eyebrow. 'Anyway, after this,' he raised his bottle of beer, 'I'm gonna have to love you and leave you. Meeting up with some of the lads from training. It's one of their birthdays.'

'Oh, okay.' Clara tried to hide her disappointment. Firstly, from herself, and when she failed at that, from Jake. 'I still need to go over the plans for the rehearsals and I want to finish my book tonight, anyway.' It sounded lame, even to her.

Chapter 36

March 2016

Clara picked a bit of fluff off her skirt and tried to focus on what the woman in her office was saying.

'I tried to contact HMRC myself, but had to wait on the phone for forty minutes, then the person who answered passed me through to someone else and I was cut off...' The woman, Rachel, stopped to tap on the screen of her phone with a manicured nail. 'So, anyway. I wasn't sure whether I need to set up as a sole trader or a limited company.'

Clara forced her brain onto the topic in hand. 'What do you expect your annual turnover to be?'

'Hang on, I have my business plan with me.' She bent forward to pick up her laptop bag from the floor. Her hair fell forward and she tucked it behind her ear before she sat back up. Clara looked more closely at the colour of her hair. It was brown. Rachel had driven from Cheshire for this meeting. The clinic said they don't match egg donors and recipients from the same geographical location, to limit the chances of them running in to each other. Was Cheshire far enough away, she wondered?

'Do you make any charitable donations?'

'Yes, I have a standing order to Cancer Research each month. Why, can I offset that?'

'Possibly.' Clara's heart was beating faster than it should be.

'How old are you?' she blurted.

'I'm thirty-nine. Is that relevant?'

'No.'

Rachel looked confused.

'Sorry, never mind. You were getting your business plan.'

Thirty-nine was probably too old. Egg donors tended to be under thirty-five.

'Yes, here it is. So, my projected annual turnover in the first year is –'

This woman is not my egg donor, stop being a crazy person. Although...

'Sorry, did you say you played sports?'

'Sports? I grow and sell cacti. That's the business I'm setting up.' Rachel stopped tapping at her laptop keyboard and looked at Clara. She had lovely blue eyes, and a very straight nose. They wouldn't be bad genes for her child to inherit.

'I know, "Prickly Plants". Great name for a business, by the way. I just like to build a complete picture of my clients when we start working together. That's why I'm asking.'

'Okay.' She still looked a little wary. 'No, I don't play sports. I did a 10K run last summer though.'

'Oh, that's great. Perfect!'

Rachel's lovely blue eyes clouded in confusion. 'Erm, thank you. Okay, so we were talking about my annual turnover and whether I need to set up as a limited company.'

'Yes, of course. I'll talk you through the pros and cons, and then it's your decision. Don't worry about HMRC. I can manage that side of things for you.'

Clara managed to stay relatively professional for the remainder of the meeting and Rachel said she'd be back in touch, so at least she hadn't lost the company a client. She got back to her desk and pinged Jess an email.

Clara: Are you free for lunch? x

The reply pinged back within minutes.

Jess: Yes! I need to get out of here. Got a big pitch tomorrow and Giles is verging on another meltdown. 1pm? Pizza Express? o

Clara: See you there! x

'So, you just randomly asked this woman if she played netball because she had brown hair and was around the same height and build as you?'

Clara shrugged. 'Well, yeah.'

'Clar.' Jess shook her head.

'What?'

'I love you, you know that. That's why I'm going to ask you something now that you might not like.'

Clara put down her lime and soda.

'Go on.'

'Are you sure you're comfortable with the whole egg donor thing? Because you don't have to go ahead with it, you know. You could still back out.'

'I…' Clara swirled her straw and watched the bubbles rise to the top of the glass. 'She's had her cycle synched to mine. It's all arranged for next week.'

'That doesn't mean you have to do it. Clar, this is huge. You need to be a hundred percent sure.'

'I am. It was just a wobble.'

'You sure?'

'Yes.' She stretched her lips into a smile. 'No, really. I mean of course I'd rather be using my own eggs, but we've tried that and it hasn't worked. This way, I just might get to be pregnant and then we'd have a baby.'

Jess waited in a way that invited her to say more.

'I have to try. I just have to.'

'Okay, I won't ask again. Now, are you getting the pollo ad astra because I want the American hot, and we could share a few slices?'

Clara smiled in relief. 'Yes, I'll get the pollo ad astra. Shall we spilt some dough balls, too?'

'Now you're talking. So, Giles, he said last week he wants me to do the presentation, but now he's in a major stress because comms are saying we need to use a new PowerPoint template and he's not sure his animations will work. I was like, dude, chill. I can sort the slides. Honestly, he's such a stresshead.'

Jess had worked for marketing agencies since she graduated and she loved the thrill of chasing new clients. The pitches were her forte.

'Who are you pitching to?'

'A government organisation. Public Health something or other. The campaign is about reducing teenage pregnancy rates in the North of England. Sounds really cool, actually…Oh my God. I'm sorry! Totally didn't think.'

'What? Oh! Don't worry, I won't combust on the spot because you said "pregnancy".'

'American hot?' The waiter appeared.

'Put them anywhere, we're sharing,' Jess said.

'How's Christopher?' she asked, once they were done switching slices and had each gobbled down a few dough balls.

'He's fine. He just gets on with things. He's busy at work.'

'He's always busy at work.'

'I know, but I get the feeling he's throwing himself into it on purpose so he doesn't have to think about all the IVF stuff.'

'He's there for you though, right?'

'Yeah, well. I mean, yeah.'

Jess narrowed her eyes. 'Do I need to come have a word with him?'

'No!' Clara grimaced at the thought. She could just imagine how that would go down. Christopher was private, he didn't like it that she discussed 'their business' with friends, though he accepted it was her way of dealing with things.

When they'd cleared their plates, they both had to dash back to work.

'Call me anytime,' Jess said. She blew Clara a kiss and headed in the opposite direction. Clara felt lighter as she walked back to the office. The events of that morning seemed ridiculous. Amusing even. She imagined turning the story into a funny anecdote once she and Christopher had a couple of kids and all this was behind them.

Chapter 37

December 2018

The day of the concert had come around and their shared house was a hive of activity. Netta was back in London and would have to miss the performance; Anna was pretending not to be disappointed. She was making last-minute adjustments to the costumes. Clara was checking through her detailed running order;

18.00 sound and lighting check

18.15 parents start to arrive – offer drinks

18.30 all children backstage in costume

18.45 play starts

Jake was sitting at the kitchen table eating scrambled eggs, as relaxed as ever.

'Where the fuck is the gold cotton?' Anna said to no one in particular as she rushed around the kitchen, picking up items and replacing them, opening and closing cupboard doors as if it might appear among the packets of noodles and tins of baked beans.

'Do you think we've allowed enough time to get the kids in their costumes? What if they're late?'

'Will you two chill out? You're ruining my breakfast vibe. It'll all be okay. We've rehearsed and the kids know what they're doing.'

'Got it!' Anna held the gold thread aloft.

'Great. Now sit down, please.'

'I think we're okay,' Clara said, running her finger down the timetable.

'Yes, *of course* we're okay,' Jake said.

The head of the year group had stuck her neck out in allowing the three of them to organise the Christmas concert (Jake's powers of persuasion had won her over) and Clara was determined not to let her down. They'd spent their sessions practising the songs, with some acting thrown in, for their condensed version of *Oliver!*. Jake was playing Fagin and was very impressive. Some of the kids looked frightened when he was in character, with his sneaky eyes and hunched-over posture. Anna was on costumes and Clara, naturally, was on logistics and communications – a letter to parents and a poster on the staff notice-board that she'd knocked up herself.

Clara had kept a watchful eye on Lin during the rehearsals. Generally the little girl sat quietly next to Chen, who belted the songs out with enough volume and enthusiasm for the both of them. Yet, every now and again, Clara could have sworn she'd seen Lin mouthing the odd word. As soon as Lin noticed her watching, she'd stop and bow her head, so Clara was forced to look away.

The school day whizzed by and, before they knew it, it was time to set out the chairs in the school's impressive hall. The mahogany parquet floor gave way to red-carpeted steps leading up to the stage at the front. The burgundy velvet curtains, usually tied back out of view, gave the room a theatrical feel, perfect for tonight's performance. The windows at the top of the high walls minimised the natural light coming in, and with the air-conditioning you'd forget you were in Singapore. It could just as easily have been an upmarket town hall or concert venue in the UK. An impressive grand piano was positioned on the left-hand side of the stage, which Mrs Bakewell would play. The set had been a project for the drama and art students and the stage looked impressive, with its backdrop of grimy nineteenth-century London.

Clara felt her stomach fizz with nerves and excitement. It could have been a Broadway show she was involved in, for all the time and energy she'd invested in it. She'd never got this sort of kick from accountancy.

'Twenty-five.' She counted out loud as she put down the last chair in a row. 'I think we're all set.' She checked her watch. 5:30pm.

Jake nodded at her. He was already dressed as Fagin, in a long, scruffy, dark green overcoat, a red silk scarf, an impressive stick-on beard, and long hair with a bandit hat perched on top. He kept slipping in and out of character, which Clara had found funny, but now it was starting to grate as she tried to get things organised.

Right now, Jake was pursing his lips and rubbing his chin thoughtfully. 'All set, me darlin',' he said, in a schmaltzy cockney accent, and performed a theatrical bow.

Mrs Bakewell arrived and started testing notes on the piano, and the school's technician came to check the lights on stage. Clara checked her schedule and allowed herself to relax. Everything was running to plan. The costumes were in a neat pile backstage, ready for the children arriving.

The rest of the preparations went smoothly and a sense of anticipation hung in the air. The audience took their seats and the children fidgeted backstage, adjusting their costumes, shuffling and whispering to each other.

'Five minutes to go, kids.' Clara gave them a thumbs up.

'Mate, you're more nervous than them,' Anna said, as Clara returned to her seat backstage. They'd found a spot where they could sit hidden from the audience, but with a good view of the children. Clara peeked out from behind the curtain at the sea of faces now sitting on the chairs they'd laid out. She gulped, glad she didn't have to go out there.

'I'll be okay once it gets going. It's all the build-up. Makes me nervous. Anyway,' Clara nudged her with her knee, 'you're a fine one to talk.'

'I don't know what you mean. I'm as cool as a cucumber.' Anna winked at her, but Clara wasn't convinced. The way she kept wringing her hands and jiggling her legs up and down gave her away. They were all invested in this.

Mrs Bakewell started the opening bars and the kids arranged themselves as they had in rehearsals. The curtains came back and they were away. They were starting with 'I'd Do Anything' as a crowd-pleaser and to get warmed up. Clara felt herself relaxing as the first song went without a hitch, and Anna stopped her hand-wringing and started tapping her foot to the music. Clara had a clear view of Lin, who was on the far end, purposely positioned at the other side of the stage to Chen. She was smiling but quiet as the other children sang. Jake came on and received uproarious applause from the audience after his rendition of 'Got to Pick a Pocket or Two'. Clara could feel his energy. The audience sat up straighter. Whispered conversations halted and packets of sweets were set down on laps. The parents may have been there to see their children, but there was something about Jake that gave him great stage presence.

Albertho came on as Oliver. He suited the role well, with his dark-blond wavy hair and pale skin. He could have been a London boy. Clara could see his parents in the front row. His dad, a large man in an expensive suit, had his fingertips pressed together. He was mouthing the words, as though trying telepathically to help his son remember his lines. His mum was more relaxed, basking in her son's success. As he delivered the famous line perfectly, asking for 'more', she clapped her hands together and grinned. Clara wouldn't have been surprised to see her leap out of her seat into a standing ovation, but she managed to contain herself as Mrs Bakewell played the opening chords to 'Food, Glorious Food'. Albertho had obviously flourished with Jake's mentoring.

Clara looked at Lin again. She was sure she just sang 'hot sausage and mustard'. She swung her gaze round to Anna to see if she'd noticed. Anna was staring straight ahead.

'Anna,' she whispered. 'I think Lin just *sang*, did you see?'

She continued staring.

'Anna?' It was like she was in a trance.

Clara nudged her knee with her own. Nothing. She had a sinking feeling in the pit of her stomach and a flash back to Anna handing her a small card when they'd first met, all those months ago. *Oh God, now*? Almost as soon as she'd had the thought, Anna's body convulsed and she fell off her seat, hitting her head on the floor. Even with the loud music Clara could tell it was a whack. She was still convulsing. Clara shrugged off her cardigan and put it under Anna's head to prevent her doing any more damage and signalled for Mrs Bakewell to cut the music.

'We need an ambulance!' She'd left her own phone in her locker, not wanting to be disturbed during the show. Someone called for one. The kids stopped their singing but stayed where they were, uncertain. The audience shifted in their seats, craning their necks to try to see what was going on.

Jake had appeared, he'd taken his bandit hat off, but was still wearing his long greasy wig. 'She's coming around.'

A breath escaped Clara.

'Huh?' Anna blinked, looking at the concerned faces leaning over her. 'Oh, for fuck's sake. Not here,' she said, as she started to piece together what had happened. She sat up quickly. 'Oww.' She put a hand to head.

'Don't try to move yet,' Clara said. 'You banged your head. Here, lie down.' She patted her cardigan pillow and encouraged her into the recovery position.

Anna did as she was told, but then said, 'They need to carry on with the concert.'

'Don't worry about that,' Clara soothed.

'No, seriously, they've all worked so hard. The show must go on.'

Jake looked at Clara, seeking her opinion. Clara, in turn, looked around at the kids on stage, hovering about in their positions.

She nodded decisively. 'She's right. I'll stay with her. You get back on stage, Fagin.'

She heard him apologising for the interruption and reassuring the audience all was okay, and Mrs Bakewell restarted.

What Clara didn't see as she held Anna's hand, waiting for the ambulance to come, was Lin joining in for the chorus.

'Mild concussion. She needs to rest,' Clara said placing her keys on the coffee table. Jake turned the TV off and roused himself from his semi-snooze.

He nodded. 'Good news, then.'

'I feel awful,' Anna said.

'Get yourself to bed,' Jake said.

'No, I mean I feel awful that I was a big, fat show-stealer.'

'You didn't steal anything. We hardly noticed.' Jake winked at her. 'Seriously, though, the kids smashed it. The applause at the end brought the house down.'

'Really?' Anna's embarrassment eased.

'Yes, it was great. We'll tell you more about it tomorrow. Get some rest.'

'I am pretty knackered, as it goes.'

'I'll be in to check on you every hour,' Clara said.

Anna rolled her eyes. 'Please don't. It was a tiny bump. I'm fine.'

After Anna had left the room, Clara sank down on the settee next to Jake. 'I feel so guilty,' she said.

'Not you as well. Why?'

'Because she was just staring and I should have realised. I could have stopped her falling. Netta will kill me.'

'She's fine. Don't beat yourself up.' He touched her hand lightly. 'I imagine you were watching the show rather than her. And Netta will be grateful you looked after her.'

'I was, I – Oh my God, did Lin *sing*?' she asked, suddenly remembering.

Jake grinned at her and nodded his head 'Yep! "Hot sausage and custard".'

'Amazing. In front of all those people as well.'

Jake held his hand up for a high five. Clara shifted position to high five him back.

'It's "mustard", by the way.'

'What is?'

'"Hot sausage and mustard." The song.'

'No.'

'Of course, it is. Why would you have custard with sausages?'

'They don't have to be together. They're just naming all the foods. Like –'

'"Cold jelly and mustard?"' she asked, teasing him.

'Maybe you're right, come to think of it.'

'I usually am.' She nodded sagely.

'You actually are,' he said. Then he kissed her.

Clara found herself kissing him back for about three seconds.

She broke away. 'What are we doing?'

He shrugged. 'Kissing.'

'We don't do that.'

'We could do that.'

'I don't know.'

'Come on, what is it? You need a spreadsheet to figure it out? I like you and I'm pretty sure you like me.' He kissed her again. This time she didn't argue. His mouth was warm and his skin surprisingly soft against her face. She remembered he'd had a close shave earlier that afternoon, so his Fagin beard would stick on. She pulled away again and could see traces of eyeliner around his eyes that he hadn't washed off properly.

'You still have make-up on.'

'Well, it's obviously doing it for you'. He leaned in again and she laughed into his mouth.

She stopped laughing as he put his hand in her hair and gently pulled, and at the same time, his tongue found hers. She adjusted herself on the settee so she could get closer and her hand found its way inside his shirt. She'd wondered what it would be like to run her fingers through his chest hair, and now she was. The hair was soft and the skin underneath was hot.

But wait…

'What if Anna comes back in?'

'She won't. She's out for the count.'

'She might get up for a drink or something.'

Jake groaned and stood up. Clara looked away when she saw the bulge in his trousers, then looked back. He'd seen her looking and a smile played on his lips. He held his hand out to her.

'Come on.'

She took it and followed him into his bedroom. She'd been there before, seen the books on the shelves and the navy duvet cover. She looked at the shelf more closely now. *Improvisation for the Theatre*, *The Golden Rules of Acting* and, more surprisingly, *Socrates in Love*.

'Have you read this?' she asked, pointing to it.

'Sure.' He shrugged. 'There's philosophy in acting. In everything, actually.'

'You continue to surprise me, Jake Holloway.'

She sat down on the navy duvet. It had been neatly made and smelt like washing powder and men. He sat next to her, his thigh touching hers.

'I like you,' she said. 'But I need to say upfront: I'm not sure what I want. I mean, you know I've only just come out of a marriage. I'm not sure I want anything serious and I don't want to lead you on.'

'You think too much. Don't worry about me. I'm a big boy.'

She inadvertently glanced at his crotch and they both laughed. Then they were kissing again and all the worries went out of Clara's mind. She undid his shirt and slid it down over his shoulders, then put her lips to the base of his neck and breathed in his male scent. He fumbled with her dress.

'How does this thing come off?'

Clara sat back and undid the side zip, then pulled it over her head. She silently thanked God she'd put on matching underwear before the concert. Her black bra accentuated her cleavage and Jake leaned in to kiss her chest and the top of her breasts. He deftly undid the strap and took her left nipple in his mouth.

'Oh,' she groaned, looping her fingers into his hair. He pushed her gently backwards until she was lying on the bed, and his mouth traced kisses downwards. By the time he reached her stomach she was moaning softly and arching her back. She closed her eyes and gripped the sheets as his tongue travelled further south.

'Well, Miss Ellison, I was right.'

Clara turned on her shoulder. 'About what?'

'I thought you'd be a saucy minx, once you let yourself go.'

'A saucy minx? What are you, an erotic fiction writer?' She pulled a face.

He nudged her leg with his. 'I could be. I could write about heaving bosoms and throbbing members.'

'Throbbing members!' She put her face to his chest and kissed him. 'You're funny.' She lay back on the pillow, then said, 'Do you think Anna heard us?'

'No.'

'I should go check on her.'

'Yes. You might want to put something on first, though. Here, take this.' He picked up his shirt from the floor.

'I'm not putting that on. She might be awake and then she'd know!'

'So what?'

'No. I'll go get my dressing gown.'

'She's fine,' Clara said later, going back into Jake's room. 'Fast asleep.' She hovered awkwardly in the door, not sure whether to climb into the navy bed beside him to go to sleep, or go back to her own room.

'Get over here.' Jake pulled the duvet back and made the decision for her.

Chapter 38

April 2016

Clara lay awake listening to Christopher snoring softly beside her. It was test day. Again. 6:30am. She needed a wee but couldn't face taking the test. After a further twenty minutes tossing and turning, she went downstairs and searched for a container to wee into. The jam was two-thirds empty. She spooned the remainder into a Tupperware tub, then washed out the jar. She headed for the bathroom, clutching the clean jar, but hesitated on the stairs. *What if the washing up liquid interfered with the test results?* She dithered, bladder protesting, then went back to the kitchen and boiled the kettle to sterilise it and make sure it was fully clean. She hopped about from foot to foot, waiting for the water to boil, then swilled it around. Satisfied, she jogged up the stairs and into the bathroom. She weed in the jar, splashing her hand, which was inevitable, then she set it down next to an unopened pregnancy test on the bathroom shelf and went back to the bedroom.

Christopher was awake. 'Have you done it?'

'No. I'm not doing it this time. It's your turn.'

'I don't think it works like that.'

'I've weed in a jar. Go dip the test in for ten seconds and wait for the result. Then it's your turn to tell me.' He looked doubtful, but dutifully headed off for the bathroom. Clara hid her head under the covers, heart thumping in her chest. She heard him pee loudly, then the sound of the toilet flushing and the tap going on. She squeezed her eyes shut and tried to think about nothing.

The door opened and Christopher padded in. Clara slowly pulled the cover back and peeked at him with one eye. He was holding the test in his right hand and his expression gave nothing away. Clara stayed quiet, wanting to delay the inevitable.

'I think there's another line,' he said. *That's not fair – there's never another line when I take a test.* How bizarre that this was Clara's first thought. She sat up and shook her head to clear it.

'Show me.' She held her hand out and he passed it over. There was one very definite control line and… the faintest hint of another. *But was it a smudge on the plastic casing?* She licked her finger and rubbed at it. It stayed there. She turned on the torch on her phone and shone it at the little window. Yes, there was a line and another faint line. Her hands started to tremble.

'Is it really there? Are you sure you used my wee?'

'Yes. Unless someone else peed in a jam jar in our bathroom.' Christopher was grinning now and Clara gave a tentative smile back. She pressed her hand to her flat stomach.

'Is there really something in there? Am I actually pregnant?'

'Yes.' He put his arms around her and she hugged him back and sobbed, her somersaulting stomach calmed as the news began to sink in. This was really it. Four years, two IVF fails, hundreds of injections, thousands of pounds, countless arguments and emotional turmoil and they were here. She was holding a positive pregnancy test in her hand for the first time in her life. She didn't think it was possible for them to turn positive in her hands. Technically, this had turned positive in Christopher's hand, but still.

'Will you get me a drink of water?' she asked suddenly.

'Of course.' Christopher took the empty glass from her bedside table and refilled it. She gulped it straight down.

'I need some more.'

He looked at her quizzically. 'What's this? An early pregnancy craving?'

'No, I need to do another test.'

'Oh.' He gave a good-natured eyeroll.

Half an hour later she unwrapped a Clear Blue digital test and peed on the stick. The egg-timer turned on the digital display for at least an hour – well, really about three minutes – and then 'Pregnant 1–2 weeks' flashed up on the screen. There was no debating that.

'Christopher!' Clara shouted through her laughter. 'Look.' She held out the test and he grinned at her with an enthusiasm she'd almost forgotten he was capable of.

'I'm so happy for you.'

'For us, you mean.'

'Yes, of course, for us.'

'That was a weird thing to say.'

'I meant us. I'm happy for us. Let's go out for breakfast to celebrate.'

'Good idea. Let me get ready and we'll go.' She kissed him on the lips.

As soon as Christopher was out of the room, Clara picked up her phone and opened up her Instagram account. She needed to share the news with her support network. The women she'd never met in real life had become her friends, her salvation. She posted photos of the positive tests and included a 'sensitive post' warning to respect those for whom the sight of a positive test would trigger all sorts of negative emotions. She captioned it, Finally our turn. Still in shock #bigfatpositive #pregnant #ivfsuccess #allthefeels

She put her phone down while she got dressed, then eagerly picked it up again and opened Instagram. Twenty likes and ten comments. She scrolled through them.

AMAZING!! So, so happy for you xxx

Enjoy the magic *kissing face*

Welcome to the best club in town xxx

She 'liked' and responded to each comment, then hugged her phone to her chest and sat for a minute, basking in the joy that came with living a moment she hadn't been sure she'd ever get the chance to.

Next, she called her mum.

'Hello, love.'

'Mum, where are you? You sound like you're in a washing machine.'

'I'm at the swimming pool. Tell me. Is it good news?'

'Yes! It's good news, Mum. I'm pregnant. I'm finally pregnant.'

'Oh, love. Oh, my goodness. That's…oh, love.'

Clara closed her eyes. 'I know, I can't believe it.' Then 'How do you have your phone in the swimming pool?'

'I left it on the edge under my towel on the loudest setting. I was next to it finishing a length when it rang.'

'Seriously?'

'Well, I wasn't sure what time you were testing and I didn't want to miss your call.'

'Oh, Mum.' Clara smiled down the phone. 'We're getting ready to go out and celebrate. I'll come see you later and we can talk properly. I'll let you finish your swim.'

'Okay, love. Congratulations. I'm absolutely delighted.'

Next up was Jess.

'Oh my fucking God,' she said by way of greeting. 'You're preggers, aren't you?'

'How did you know?' Clara laughed.

'You'd have texted me and told me not to ring if it was a "no".'

'That's true, I would have.'

'So you are? You really are?'

'Yes.'

'Aaarrrgh! Dave, DAVE, Clara's pregnant!' she shouted.

Clara heard Dave say 'Congratulations!' in the background.

'Yes, you can have a biscuit Amelie,' Jess said. 'Ask Daddy to get it. I'm on the phone. I can't believe it!'

'I know, me neither. I'm sending you the photos of the tests now.'

'I've got them. Yep, that's pretty conclusive. Oh, I'm so happy! We have to celebrate. Shall we do lunch?'

'Well, I'm actually going out with Christopher in a minute, for breakfast, so I'm not sure.'

'What? Well, I suppose that's fair. Maybe a coffee later, then. I'll get Dave to stay in with Amelie. I hope you have a girl. I've still got all Amelie's baby clothes. Kept them just in case. Argh, I'M SO EXCITED!'

Jess was getting louder and louder.

Clara's face was starting to ache from grinning. 'I know, me too. Listen, I'm going to have to go, Christopher is waiting.'

'Okay, call me later. There's so much more to discuss.'

'Will do.'

'CONGRATULATIONS! Love you.'

'Love you too.' Clara hung up the phone. After putting on make-up and running a brush through her hair, she was good to go. Soon she and Christopher were seated opposite each other for a slap-up brunch at their favourite restaurant.

'The baby is the size of a poppy seed.'

'A poppy seed? That's tiny.'

'I know. This is what it looks like.' Clara held up her phone.

Christopher squinted at it. 'It looks like a blob.'

'I know. It'll start to look like a tadpole soon, before it looks like a baby. I think I'm still in a state of shock.'

'Me too. Maybe we should go away, to celebrate.'

'Go away?'

'Yes, on holiday.'

'Like a babymoon?'

'Babymoon?' Christopher raised an eyebrow as he reached for his coffee.

'Yes, you know. Last holiday as a couple, but celebrating our baby coming soon.'

'Right.' He smiled. 'Let's book something. I can take a week off work in a couple of weeks. It'd be nice to have some relaxation after all the stress we've been under.'

Clara poked at her egg yolk and watched the golden liquid pool across the plate, then remembered she wasn't supposed to eat runny eggs now she was pregnant. She pushed the yolk to the side with her knife and wondered if it was okay to eat the muffin that had touched it.

'I don't know, though,' she said. 'Would flying be okay? It'd be so early in the pregnancy.'

'You could check with the clinic, but surely a week on a beach would be good for the baby, as you'd be relaxed.'

'I suppose –'

Christopher whipped his phone out and began scrolling through deals. 'Cape Verde, half-board, seven nights; Portugal, self-catering. This one looks good – the Amalfi Coast, Sorrento.' He turned his phone around to show her a photo of a blue sea and white buildings nestled into cliffs.

'That does look lovely and I do have some leave to take at work…I suppose it would be nice to have a last holiday, just the two of us, before we're a family. A family.' She grinned at him across the table and he reached out to squeeze her hand.

'We did it.' Christopher raised his coffee cup. 'To us, finally becoming a family.'

Clara clinked her orange juice against it. 'Finally.'

Chapter 39

December 2018

The bride wore red: a beautifully made floor-length gown embroidered with gold thread. She walked around tables with her new husband, greeting guests and watching him do shots.

'This is different,' Jake whispered to Clara. 'Why is he getting smashed? And when's the actual ceremony?'

'Oh, the ceremony has already happened,' Clara said. 'This is more of a party with friends and family. It mainly involves lots of eating. And drinking, by the look of it.' She nodded towards the shots circulating.

'How do you know all this stuff?' Jake asked.

'I researched it all, when Lin and Chen gave me the invitation.'

'Of course, you did.'

'Well, I didn't want to make a faux pas at their big sister's wedding, as an ignorant Westerner.'

'I can't imagine you doing that, somehow.'

Since the school concert, Clara and Jake had become sort of an item – in that they went places together and had sex. Clara was trying not to question what this meant too much. Jake was fun to be around; he made her feel light, as though serious, real-life issues – such as the fact he was ten years younger than she was and may want children one day – were irrelevant. She marvelled at how they actually did seem irrelevant to Jake, who was a master of living in the moment. Clara was trying to adopt this attitude, but found it much easier to live in the moment once she'd planned what was going to happen next. Right now, what happened next was anyone's guess.

The bride and groom were approaching their table. 'Welcome and thank you for coming.'

The groom pulled out a chair for his bride, then sat down. He wore a black suit with a red bow-tie, perfectly matched to his wife's dress. His dark hair was beautifully coifed; with his flawless complexion, he looked as though he'd been airbrushed. Only he had a slight flush to his cheeks – probably on account of the shots he'd been downing. He set down an ornate navy-blue-and-gold ceramic bottle and a tray of shot glasses and began pouring, one for himself and one for each of the guests. His wife was excused, it seemed.

'What is it?' Jake asked, sniffing his glass.

'Baijiu. It's tradition.'

'Ah, well, in that case, bottoms up!' Jake raised his glass and the others followed suit.

'Down in one!' the young groom said. Clara did as she was told, then tried her best not to gag as the overwhelming taste of rotting fruit hit her palate. The shot's only redeeming factor was that the alcohol content quickly killed the flavour, but it left her with a burning throat and watering eyes. Jake coughed once, then proudly raised his empty glass.

Clara sipped her water. 'You look beautiful,' she said to the bride.

'Thank you.' She smiled demurely. 'I'm so glad you came. My mum and dad told me lots about you. You've really helped Lin.'

'She's a lovely girl, and so is Chen. It was very good of you to invite me, and my guest.' She indicated Jake. The bride smiled and touched Clara's hand kindly. They stood and made their way to the next table to repeat the ritual.

'How is he not sloshed?' Jake asked, when they were out of earshot.

'Ah, well, I read that smart grooms replace some of their shots with water, otherwise they'd be on the floor.'

'How come the bride is excused?'

'Tradition, I guess. That's one equal right I wouldn't necessarily fight for. Don't tell Anna I said that,' she added quickly.

'Your secret's safe with me. Anyway, didn't you say the groom has to pay for the bride?'

'I didn't quite say that. It's a tradition that the groom collects the bride on the morning of the wedding, and that the bridesmaids make it difficult for him, so sometimes he bribes them with money or presents.'

'Make it difficult for him, how?' He raised an eyebrow.

'Things like hiding her shoes, or hiding the bride –'

'Hiding the *bride*? Like in a basement or something?'

'What? No, of course not in a basement. What's wrong with you? I mean she'd be upstairs and they'd make him do challenges first, like press-ups, or a quiz on the bride's family, before she'd be allowed to come down. Sounds like a fair balance of power to me.'

'I'm sure Anna would be okay with that tradition.' Jake's laugh revealed a row of straight white teeth, not a filling in sight. And then he said, 'Do you think you'd get married again?'

Clara swallowed her water the wrong way and started coughing and spluttering.

'Are you okay?'

She held a hand up as a fresh bout of coughing started. 'What made you ask that?' she asked, when she'd recovered.

He shrugged. 'Dunno. Just being at a wedding. I wondered.'

Clara looked at him; his eyes were clear, innocent. He seemed oblivious to the loaded question he'd asked.

'I don't know,' she said honestly. 'I never thought I'd get divorced. Or that I'd be living in Singapore in my late thirties. So never say never, I suppose.' Was it her imagination, or did he look satisfied?

'What about you?' she asked.

'Oh sure, someday.'

She decided not to let the conversation follow the logical path – not to ask the obvious next question that came after asking someone if they wanted to get married. Instead, she took another sip of water (carefully) and said, 'I'm still flattered the Wus invited me to their daughter's wedding.'

'Are you kidding? They love you.'

Clara didn't say anything. She was remembering another wedding a lifetime ago, when she'd been sure she knew which path her life would take. How was it that ten years later she was halfway across the world, at a completely different wedding, with a man who wasn't Christopher? She felt a pang for Jess and imagined her being here with her. They'd have downed a few more baijius and would be on the dance floor. Except in real life, as they lived now, they wouldn't. Jess would be on 'mum duties' and leaving early so as not to mess up the bedtime routine. Not for the first time, Clara wondered whether to go 'home' at the end of the school year. What would be waiting for her there? She'd hoped for a fresh start with a new perspective but feared a lonely existence as an outsider. She'd been away from home a year now and it made sense to stay for the rest of the school year. After that, she wasn't sure what to do.

'Food.' Jake sat up straighter as a waiter approached, carrying a tray of steamed dumplings, chicken skewers and pancake rolls. He set the food down in the middle of the table and Clara's mouth watered. She tucked in and as she laughed and joked with Jake and enjoyed the food and atmosphere, thoughts of 'what next?' were pushed aside.

When the wedding came to an end, it was still light outside, and still warm, so they decided to walk back. Clara was pleasantly light-headed from the drinks she'd had. When her hand brushed Jake's and he took it in his, she didn't object. They walked down the street like any other couple. Clara enjoyed the simplicity of it; they liked each other and were having a good time together. She dismissed the fact that they effectively already lived together as being irrelevant, as it was purely incidental, and they did still have their own rooms, even if they spent most of their time in hers.

'Hey,' Jake said, as they reached a fork in the path. 'Shall we go this way and grab another drink?'

Clara hesitated. She'd been ready to go home, but she didn't want to disappoint. 'Sure,' she said, 'but I don't want to be too long. I have some marking to do in the morning.'

God, I sound like my mother, she thought. Jake rolled his eyes at her and led the way to a bar overlooking the water in the Marina.

'G&T?' he asked, as they claimed a table outside.

She nodded. 'It'll have to be just one, at these prices.'

He winced as he looked at the menu, then headed inside to the bar.

Paying for the view, Clara thought, taking in the sight of the Marina Bay Sands Hotel, which they'd explored when they first arrived. She hadn't tired of the view of the three skyscrapers with a boat on top. It really was quite unlike anything else. The lights from the buildings twinkled on the water and the smell of cut flowers wafted up from the vase on the table. They were in the heart of the financial district, and between where she was sitting and the water was a busy walkway – a main route from the skyscrapers to the quieter residential areas. Clara sat back and enjoyed some people-watching. It was busy for the hour. There were couples hand in hand, even some families still out. The men and women dressed in suits and walking back from a late-shift at the office reminded her of Christopher. In fact, that man in the distance looked just like him. He even had his walk.

Hang on. What? Unless he had a doppelgänger, Christopher was in front of her wearing his work suit, and he was heading straight towards where she was sitting.

Clara stood up, then sat back down. He'd be in front of her in a matter of minutes. She looked around frantically. Jake was still at the bar, giving his order. Then she sat perfectly still, eyes fixed on Christopher's approaching form. When he was a couple of metres away, without thinking about what she was doing, she shouted, 'Christopher!'

He turned his head. 'Clara!' He came over and she stood up, glancing back towards the bar, where Jake was paying for the drinks. 'Wow! It's so good to see you.'

'What are you doing? Are you actually here? Why are you here?'

'I'm working. They needed someone to fly out and visit J.P. Morgan over here.' He nodded over his shoulder towards the building he'd apparently just come from. 'I can't believe I've bumped into you like this.' He bent to kiss her cheek and at that moment Jake arrived with the drinks.

'Hello,' he said, placing the drinks on the table and holding out a hand. 'I'm Jake.'

'Christopher.' He took the hand. 'Clara's husband.'

'Ex-husband!' Clara cut in.

'Technically, yes.'

The smile on Jake's face froze. It became plastered on, instead of looking like it belonged there. 'I didn't know we were expecting you.'

'We weren't,' Clara said, through clenched teeth. Christopher bristled at the 'we'.

'Okay, look. I'm gonna give you guys some space,' Jake said. 'Clara, will you be okay?'

'Yes, I'll be fine.'

'Call me if you need me. I'll wait up.' He hovered, unsure whether to go in for a kiss. He decided against it and backed away.

'I'm sorry,' she mouthed, as he set off in the direction of their flat.

'Is that your new boyfriend?' Christopher asked, as soon as Jake was out of earshot.

'No. Maybe. It's none of your business, anyway. Christopher, what you are *doing* here?' She was suddenly angry.

'I told you. Working.'

'Right, and you didn't think to mention it? You knew I was here.'

He sighed and held his hands up. 'Okay, look. I may have volunteered to come. They needed someone to meet with the client and I said I'd do it. I didn't know if you were coming back for Christmas or when I'd next see you and it seemed like a good opportunity.'

'A good opportunity for what? Why do you need to see me at all? What about Sarah?'

'Sarah…' he started and trailed off.

'She does know you're here, right?'

'Yes, of course. She's…she's actually here too.'

'Oh, it just gets better, doesn't it? Christopher, what the fuck?' Clara was shaking now. She picked her up gin and tonic and took a big gulp.

'Look, it's late and you're obviously getting upset. I'm so sorry. I didn't plan it to be like this. I didn't want to come mess with your life. Can I walk you home? I would like to talk to you, but maybe on your own terms? We could have a coffee tomorrow?'

'I…' She was at a loss for words. 'I am going to go home, but I don't need you to walk me.' She took another gulp of the expensive drink, then stalked off after Jake.

Chapter 40

April 2016

'You should definitely get this one.' Jess held up a hot-pink, triangle-style bikini.

'Really?' Clara touched the flimsy fabric of the top. 'Doesn't look like it'd give much support.'

'Your boobs are in the best condition they'll ever be in. After pregnancy and breastfeeding, well, you owe it to them to show them off now.'

Clara laughed. 'I guess I could try it on.'

She placed it in her basket along with a sundress, a pair of shorts and a floral sarong. She'd spent the last week, since the positive test, mainly grinning, often laughing and basically finding enjoyment in everything she did. The night before, she and Christopher had gone out to dinner, and the waiter had asked if they were newlyweds. Must have been something to do with the fact that they were holding hands over the table and smiling at each other. They'd laughed and told him they were just happy. Their mood seemed to be contagious and he'd brought them extra sides on the house and shaken both their hands when they left, in an oddly formal move.

Jess held up a short halter-neck leopard print dress. 'Do you reckon I could pull off this?'

Clara pulled a face. 'In Manchester?'

'Oh, sorry, we're not all jetting off to Sorrento for a week of mooning around.'

Clara grinned at her friend.

'I've never seen the two of you like this. Well, not since you were at uni.'

Clara's smile stretched further. 'I know. It's like when we just met.' She lowered her voice. 'The sex has been *amazing*.'

'La la la.' Jess stuck her fingers in her ears. 'I don't want to think about Christopher having sex. I know him too well. It'd be like my brother having sex or something. Urgh.' She shook her head. 'Good for you, though,'

They made their way to the changing rooms which brought them through the baby section. This would usually have Clara staring resolutely ahead and marching through. Now, she paused. She looked.

Jess watched her carefully. 'You could get something, you know.'

'I don't know. It's very early. I have to believe everything will be okay, as the alternative just doesn't bear thinking about, but still. You know, I don't want to tempt fate.' She picked up a denim pinafore dress with a big love heart on the front. 'This is cute, though.'

'It might be a boy.'

'I just have a feeling it's a girl. I know that's silly, but I do.'

She put the dress down and reached for a cream Babygro with grey rabbits on it.

'This is gorgeous. Feel how soft it is.'

'It's lovely.' Jess raised her eyebrows in a way Clara understood to mean: *I won't encourage you to buy it. I know you think you should wait, but also, I won't judge you if you do.*

She put it back.

After a lengthy trying-on session (dress – yes, shorts – no (wouldn't fasten), pink bikini – *oh, go on then*) they were ready for a cup of tea and a nice sit down. They agreed to stop at Costa for a rest and a review of what they still had to buy. Jess waited outside the shop while Clara went to pay. When she came out, clutching a bag, she didn't tell her that the cream Babygro with the grey rabbits had found its way into her basket and was now nestled in-between a pink bikini and a sundress.

Later that afternoon, Clara took it out and looked at it. It was hard to believe a human being could be that small. She lay down on the bed and placed the Babygro on her stomach, stroking the soft material.

'I'll take this to the hospital to be the first thing you wear,' she said to her stomach. Then she shook her head, feeling silly, and stood up to put her new clothes straight into her suitcase, along with her beach towel, pyjamas and Christopher's swimming shorts. She jumped as she heard the front door open.

'Hello?' Christopher.

'Up here. Down in a sec.'

She found a pink box that had had some fancy toiletries in – a gift for her birthday – and carefully folded the Babygro and put it inside. She tied up the ribbon and placed it on the top shelf of her wardrobe.

She skipped downstairs and greeted Christopher with a kiss on the lips.

'You look happy,' he said.

'I am happy.'

Chapter 41

December 2018

By the time Clara got back to the flat, her anger had morphed into confusion, and then an overwhelming tiredness. She managed to convince Jake she hadn't known Christopher was coming and that she didn't know why he was here, and that, no, she definitely wasn't going to get back with him. They had eventually fallen asleep, Clara with her head on Jake's chest.

The next morning she woke to a text message.

Christopher: I'm so sorry about last night. It was shitty of me to arrive unannounced. The last thing I want to do is cause you more upset. I'd very much like to see you, though. Give me chance to explain. I fly home in two days. How about a coffee this afternoon? x

Clara was back to being furious with him for turning up and intruding on the new life she was starting to build. It wasn't fair. Jake was still sleeping next to her. Feeling restless, she slipped out of bed and padded downstairs to put the coffee machine on. Anna was in the kitchen, dressed in her running gear.

'Morning, you're up early,' she said. Then she caught Clara's expression. 'Everything okay?'

'Not really, no. Christopher is here.'

'Christopher? Here?' She looked over Clara's shoulder.

'Well, not *here* here. But here in Singapore.'

'What's he doing here?'

'He's working, but he says he wants to see me.' Clara took a mug out of the cupboard and went to the fridge for the milk.

'And you're going to?'

'No.'

Anna said nothing while she filled her water-bottle.

'I don't want to deal with it.' As Clara said the words out loud, she realised that perhaps not dealing with it wouldn't help her in the long run. She couldn't run away and pretend it wasn't happening; that had never been her style. But, also, there was something else gnawing at her. *What could he possibly want?*

'It might help. It does sound like you left in quite a rush when you set off for Australia.'

Clara sank down onto a dining chair with her coffee. She looked at his message again, then hastily typed a reply.

Clara: Meet me at the Wired Monkey in Little India. 2pm.

She hit send before she could change her mind.

Later, when she was deciding what to wear, she again wondered if she was doing the right thing. The heat didn't allow for her preferred option of jeans and a T-shirt, and her shorts were all stained with suncream and had grown tatty from months of being squashed in a backpack. She eventually put on a dress she wore for work. The cut showed off her figure and the royal blue set off her tan nicely. Satisfied, she picked up her bag and left the flat.

She arrived first. She chose a seat where she could see the door and ordered a latte. Christopher arrived right on time. Of course he did. He used a handkerchief to mop his brow. He was wearing a suit with no jacket. He'd obviously come straight from work – must have been in-between meetings. Clara tried not to think about how this had never been an option when she'd wanted – no, *needed* to see him during work time when they were together.

He spotted Clara and raised a hand, and made his way over.

'Hello,' he said.

'Hello.' She stood up and he leaned over to give her peck on the cheek. She smelt his aftershave: musky and earthy. It caused a physical ache in her chest, quickly followed by a twist in the gut, which resparked her annoyance at him being here.

They both spoke at once.

'You look good.' he said.

'Why are you here?'

'I told you. Work.'

She glared at him.

'Okay, look. I wanted to see you. Sorry, can we get some coffees first?'

She sighed as he stood up to go to the counter.

'Can I get you anything?'

'I've ordered. Sit down, it's table service.'

He fiddled with his shirtsleeves, trying to pull them up higher, then sat down. He was nervous, she realised. She saw it in the way he clasped his hands on top of the table, then unclasped them and laid his palms flat. His face looked a little thinner. There were a few more fine lines around his eyes and a touch more grey at his temples, but he looked well.

'So, how's teaching going?' he asked.

'Christopher. I'm going to ask you again and then I'm leaving.' She picked up her bag to illustrate her point. 'What are you doing here?'

'I had a breakdown,' he blurted.

She put the bag down. 'Go on.'

He took a breath and wiped his fingers over his forehead. 'After you left, I sort of fell apart.'

Clara looked down at the table

'Not having a child, it was…well…you know how it was, then you went too. I know I wasn't good at talking about things, but I always thought we'd get there in the end. That we'd be a family.'

'I thought so too.'

'One day, not long after you'd gone, I was at my mum and dad's for dinner and she mentioned James. I just lost it. I was crying and everything, they didn't know what to do with me. I took some time off work and they strongly recommended I see a therapist. It was basically a condition of having time off work.'

'I can't believe you took time off work.'

'You're not the only one who was affected by all this, you know.'

She looked down, chastised. 'I know that. Of course I know that. But I still don't know why that would mean you had to come here and see me.'

'I wanted to apologise and I guess I wanted some "closure". That's my therapist's word by the way, not mine.'

'Apologise for having an affair?'

He smarted. 'You know nothing happened. I mean, not until after –'

'Nothing happened? So you didn't close off from me and talk to her about our problems?'

'Well, I….' He trailed off, clearly thrown. 'I mean, we didn't –'

'You didn't sleep with her?'

'No! I didn't, not when we were together.'

'But you did after.'

'Well –'

'I knew that already. That you didn't sleep with her, when we were together.'

'You did? Then why did you –?'

'Why did I what? Leave?'

He nodded.

'It wasn't a marriage any more. There was nothing left. You wouldn't speak to me and the fact that I knew you spoke to her hurt more than if you'd just had sex with her.'

He looked as if he'd been slapped. 'I didn't cheat on you.'

'You disengaged.'

He steepled his fingers together, blew out a breath. 'I didn't know how to help you. You were so…broken.'

'I know.'

The waiter arrived and interrupted them. Christopher ordered a black Americano and a glass of water.

'If you knew about Sarah, why didn't you say anything?'

Clara sighed and looked down at her coffee. 'Honestly? Because getting pregnant was more important than whether you were having an affair.'

Christopher let out a breath. Clara wasn't sure if it was understanding in his eyes, or pity. She didn't want his pity.

'It was the only thing that mattered. I thought if I could just achieve that one thing, I'd worry about the rest later. I can see now, I'd lost all sense of perspective. I feel more like myself again and I want you to know, I don't blame you. I did, for a long time, but what we went through…it broke us both in different ways.'

She was surprised to see he had tears in his eyes. He was looking down at the table again, fingertips brushing over the grain of the wood.

'I found it hard to talk about things with you. But I know that didn't help you.'

'It didn't.' She took a sip of her latte. 'But I suppose –'

'You suppose what?'

'Well, I mean, this way, we can each have a fresh start. Start to put what happened behind us. Not that I would have chosen that.'

Christopher nodded, then shook his head. 'I'm sorry.'

'I'm sorry too.'

They both sat back in their seats, the tension dissipated.

'It's strange seeing you.'

'Strange,' he mused. 'Not sure that's a compliment.'

'It is what it is. It's strange to see you after so much has happened. I spent the first few months away missing you and imagining you here with me, and now you are here, but everything is different.'

'Yes. Are things serious with that bloke then? Jake?'

'No, we're just having fun.'

He bristled at the word 'fun', but said nothing.

'So, how's Sarah?'

'She okay. She's been pretty understanding, you know?'

'Well, Christopher, I didn't think I'd ever say this, but I wish you both well.'

'Thank you.' His eyes showed he meant it. 'And thank you for meeting up with me.'

Clara went for a walk through the botanical gardens afterwards. It was busy with tourists and locals enjoying the views, but somehow it still felt peaceful. She sat down on a bench next to a waterfall and did nothing except listen to the sounds of the birds and the water and appreciate the contrast between the lush green trees and the fuchsia of the flowers. By the time she got back to the flat she felt calm. Content, even.

'How did it go?' Jake asked, as soon as she was through the door. He was sitting at the kitchen table flicking through a book in a manner that suggested it was a prop.

'It went well. Thanks.'

'So, what did he say?'

Clara sighed. 'He just wanted to say sorry, really and I guess clear the air.'

'Hmm.'

'What does that mean?'

Jake turned a page and said nothing.

She came and sat down beside him. 'Are you okay?'

'Well, I wasn't sure if…'

'If what?'

'I know you said you wouldn't go back, but I didn't know if you'd change your mind once you saw him. I mean, you are married.'

'Were.'

'Huh.' He looked back at his book.

'Jake, I'm not getting back with Christopher. It's been over between us a long time. Long before I even set off on this trip. The only thing keeping us together in the last few years was the hope of having a baby. We weren't making each other happy.'

'Really?' Relief flooded his face and something about his response put Clara on edge.

'Yes. Now, do you want to eat out or grab something here? I'm hungry.'

Chapter 42

May 2016

'Do you think I'm showing? The baby is the size of a lentil now.' Clara was wearing her bright pink bikini in their hotel room in Sorrento.

Christopher glanced at her stomach. 'No.'

'Well, I can tell. Although it could be pizza and ice cream.'

'Quite possibly. Come on, get your towel in your bag, I want to hit the beach.' He swatted her backside.

'Nearly ready. If it's a girl can we call her Sophie?'

'It's early to talk about names, isn't it?'

'I've wanted the name Sophie since I was little.' She shrugged into her sundress, shoved her towel and Kindle in her bag and perched her sunglasses on top of her head. 'Okay, I'm ready. Let's go.'

They walked hand in hand down the rocky path towards the beach. Christopher caught Clara's elbow when she tripped in her flip-flops.

'I'm fine,' she said, pulling her elbow away, though she secretly enjoyed the attention. It made her feel special. She put a protective hand on her stomach and paid more attention to where she was treading on the uneven surface.

Later she lay on a yellow sun-lounger and wondered if it was okay for her stomach to get hot. Would the baby be too hot? She adjusted the parasol so her top half was in the shade, just in case. Christopher had his headphones in and his eyes were shut. She rested her head against the lounger and watched a family frolicking in the waves on the shore. She smiled. That will be us soon, she thought.

Her mum had had her reservations when Clara told her they were going to book a last-minute holiday.

'Is that a good idea?' she'd said. 'After everything you've been through to get where you are, wouldn't it be better to rest at home?'

'I can't rest for nine months, Mum. I spoke to the clinic and they said there's no reason not to carry on as normal. And I think a holiday will be good for us. Got to be better than being at work, anyway.'

'Well, if you're sure –'

'I'm pregnant! The hard bit is done.'

June had frowned into her cup of tea, but said nothing further.

The family Clara was watching had settled down at the shore and were building a sandcastle. A blonde-haired toddler wearing a costume that covered her arms and legs was tapping at an upturned bucket with a bright blue spade. Her mum eased the bucket off the sand to reveal an imperfect castle. One side crumbled and sagged. The little girl clapped her hands together anyway, then she planted a chubby foot in the middle of it. Her mum laughed and brought her in for a cuddle. Clara smiled. Finally, all was well in her world.

'We've got to have a trip to Pompeii while we're here,' Christopher said. He'd taken out his headphones and was reading his guidebook.

Clara hesitated, thinking about the crowds and the heat. She shuffled up her sun-lounger, so more of her body was in the shade.

'I don't know. Won't it be packed?'

'It says here it's quieter in the mornings. We could get up early. It's only half an hour on the train.'

'Hmm.'

'Come on, let's go tomorrow. Then you can spend the day after on the beach with your Kindle. "The archaeological site covers a vast 150 acres," it says here.' He tapped the page of his guidebook.

He looked so hopeful and happy sitting there in the sun, his skin already a shade darker. It had been such a long time since they'd felt carefree and contented and Clara found herself wanting to indulge him.

'Okay, we'll go tomorrow. It sounds good.'

The next morning Clara awoke early with an upset stomach. She thought back to what she'd eaten the night before. Freshly made ham and mushroom pizza at a trattoria near their hotel. That shouldn't have set her off. She made her way to the bathroom swiftly and hunched forward on the toilet, against the stomach pains. She felt better after a few minutes. Probably the heat or the water here, she thought, and mentally shrugged it off. She did a wee, then, as she wiped, she noticed a brownish smear on the tissue. She paused, toilet-paper mid-way to the toilet bowl. She examined it more carefully. It was only a smear. Probably nothing to worry about.

Christopher was stirring as she climbed back into bed. He put an arm around her waist and snuggled into her. She put her hand on top of his and tried to say something about what had happened, but the words caught in her throat. She couldn't think how to say it lightly. Without making it into a 'thing'. She closed her eyes, but no more sleep came. She listened to Christopher's rhythmic breathing and laid there reassuring herself. She told herself that spotting during early pregnancy was normal and, anyway, it wasn't fresh blood. It was probably fine. Her stomach was fine now.

There was more when she got up properly an hour or so later, but again it wasn't a lot, and it was dark brown.

'Christopher?'

'Uh?' He answered with his mouth open, dental floss wedged between his incisors.

'I don't think it's anything to worry about, but…' She forced the words out 'I'm bleeding a little bit.'

He paused, a piece of floss dangling out of his mouth. 'Oh.'

'Yes, but it's only a tiny bit. I'm sure it's fine. I know lots of people who have bled early on and it's been nothing.'

'Okay.' He resumed his flossing, reassured.

'I'm seven weeks pregnant and I'm spotting.' Clara had left Christopher in the bathroom and was on the phone to the clinic back home.

'Okay, it's quite common and most likely nothing to worry about, but just to be sure you can come in for a scan and we'll hopefully be able to put your mind at rest.'

'I'm in Italy on holiday.'

'Ah! Well in that case don't worry about it. Spotting is common, especially if it's brown. It'll be old blood clearing out from your cervix. If it gets worse, or you get any fresh red blood, I'd recommend seeing a doctor where you are, but don't panic. That still doesn't necessarily mean you're losing the pregnancy.'

'Ok, thank you.' Clara hung up the phone and relayed the message to Christopher.

'It's probably fine. I wish I could go in for a scan to double-check, though,' she said.

'We can go for a scan when we get home.'

'Yes.' Clara nodded with more confidence than she felt.

'Are we still going to Pompeii?'

'Yes, we may as well. It'll take our minds off it.'

Christopher got out the timetable he'd picked up in reception. 'There's a train at 8:32, or 8:56, or 9:12.'

'Okay, let's wander up there and get the next one.'

The train rattled along the the coastline and Clara watched a pair of Italian teenagers. They were listening to music, swapping headphones back and forth and jigging to some unheard beat. One of them was clutching a skateboard and the other had a small metal scooter by his side. Christopher was engrossed in reading about Mount

Vesuvius and looked up every now and again to spout off some fact or other. Clara nodded and tried to focus on what he was telling her, not on what may or may not be happening inside her. Soon they were disembarking and joining a queue for the attraction. The station was right outside and the guidebook had been right: it wasn't so busy at this time.

They wandered round the ruins, posed for photographs and ate overpriced ham and cheese sandwiches at a café, and Clara was managing to recapture the mood of yesterday. They were on holiday together, having a nice time. She didn't want to spoil it with unnecessary worrying. They agreed to explore for another hour or so, then catch the train back and spend a few hours by the pool at the hotel, before heading out to dinner.

Christopher circled a man frozen in time for nearly two thousand years, arms raised over his head in defence.

'That's incredible,' he said, squatting down to get a better look.

Clara looked away. It gave her the creeps, incredible or not. She wandered off towards some statues on pillars and stopped by a statue with wings. A fly tickled her thigh, she bent down to brush it away absent-mindedly. Her fingers were wet. She glanced at them and was confused to see red. *Was that blood?* She looked down at her leg and saw a line of red blood running down the inside of her thigh, smudged where she'd scratched. It hadn't been a fly tickling her leg. Her stomach dropped to her knees. *No, no, no.* She looked around frantically. Christopher was still examining the frozen-in-time man. There was a sign for the toilets in the other direction. She followed it quickly and locked herself in a cubicle. The stale heat and smell of urine caused her to heave. She steeled herself as she eased down her shorts and tried to avoid sitting all the way down. Her knickers were soaked through. Her thighs gave way and she dropped to the toilet seat and flopped her head forward over her knees. She steadied herself with a deep breath. Okay, so she was definitely bleeding rather than spotting, but it might still be okay. The nurse's words popped into her head: 'Doesn't necessarily mean you're losing the pregnancy'. She reached for the toilet roll and wiped. Bright red blood soaked through the tissue. She twisted round and looked in the toilet bowl and saw a stream of red against the metal bowl. *It was not okay.* A sob rose up in her throat and her shoulders shuddered. A noise escaped her lips, somewhere between a moan and a wail. Someone knocked on the door. An American accent.

'Everything okay in there?'

'Erm, yes thanks.' She cleaned herself up, put a wad of toilet roll in her knickers and unlocked the door. The knocker looked concerned. 'I'm okay, thank you. I need to find my husband.'

The lady smiled at her uncertainly and Clara bade a hasty retreat. Christopher had moved on to the statues and didn't seem to have noticed she'd gone. She went to stand next to him.

'Did you know Pompeii wasn't discovered until 1748, by a surveying engineer? Nobody knew it was all here for well over a thousand years.'

'Christopher.'

'The people would have been killed by the heat alone. Then they were preserved by the falling ash from the volcano.'

'Christopher.'

He looked at her for the first time. 'Yes?'

'The bleeding is worse.'

'What does that mean?'

Clara couldn't trust herself to speak. She shook her head.

Christopher looked down at his feet. 'Should we call the clinic again?'

'There's no point. I know what's happening.'

'Are you sure?'

'There's a lot of blood. I can't...I just...can we go back to the hotel?'

'Of course.' He went to hug her and she turned away. She couldn't break down here. That would come later.

She'd only known she was pregnant for three weeks. But it was long enough. Long enough to talk about whether it'd be a girl or boy. Long enough to apply cocoa butter to her tummy, morning and night. To take folic acid. To consider baby names. To start a Pinterest board for the nursery. To talk to her tummy.

To plan.
To imagine.
To dream.
Long enough.

Chapter 43

December 2018

Clara stirred and rolled onto her back. As she slowly started to wake, she became aware of a feeling that something exciting was happening today. A certain lightness in her chest, a tingling in her fingers. She opened her eyes and saw Jake's dark hair on the pillow next to her. His chest was rising and falling gently. He was making a little 'pffft' noise on every out breath. She thought it was cute, but at the same time was aware it had the potential to become annoying after a while. She propped herself up on her elbow to get a better look at him. The navy duvet covered half his torso, his tanned skin disappearing under it at the waist. He could have been a model on an aftershave advert if they'd added some dramatic music and got him to do some brooding looks at the camera.

She was taken back briefly to a time she'd visited Venice with Christopher and they'd happened upon a photoshoot for Calvin Klein next to the Rialto Bridge. The model – with rippled abs, and buttocks like cantaloupe melons, and wearing nothing but a pair of tight white CK briefs – had caused an old lady to bump into her husband, who'd also paused for a gawk. Christopher had joked that he could look like that if he had a spray tan and swapped running for weight-lifting.

'Of course, you could,' Clara had lied, and had taken his hand as they carried on inching through the crowds to the tourist hot spot.

Now she put her hand on Jake's chest and wove her fingers through the coarse hairs. His eyelashes fluttered, then he opened his eyes and put his hand on top of hers.

'Merry Christmas, gorgeous,' he said.

'Merry Christmas.' She rested her head on his chest and he put his arm around her. They stayed like that a little while, enjoying the feeling of not having to rush about. Clara heard Anna or Netta padding down the hall to the bathroom and pushed herself up into a sitting position.

'Do you want your present?' Jake asked, leaning over the side of the bed.

'Are we doing presents now, or should we wait until after dinner?'

'After dinner? Are you kidding? My presents were all open long before breakfast when I was a kid.'

'That doesn't surprise me. We used to do presents from family after Christmas dinner at home.'

'What, no ripping off wrapping paper as soon as you woke up?'

'No, I have some self control. Ever heard of delayed gratification?' Clara patted his bum as he continued to root around down the side of the bed.

'Got it!' He held up a small box. 'Well, I'd like you to open it now.'

'Okay.' She propped herself up against the pillows. Her heart started to race as she took in the size and shape of the package. *Surely not?* She peeled back the paper to reveal a blue velvet box. *He wouldn't, he couldn't.* She had a flashback to him asking her if she'd get married again at the wedding and her stomach clenched with panic. With shaky fingers she eased the box open to reveal a pair of vintage earrings. She let out a long breath and her body relaxed as she carefully lifted one out for a closer look.

'Oh, thank you! I wasn't expecting anything like this. You could have got me a box of chocolates. I'd have been happy.'

'I saw you looking at them in that shop window.' He was beaming like a child.

'Well, that's very thoughtful of you. Do you want yours?'

He nodded and put his hands behind his head as he waited. She headed over to the wardrobe and took a moment to steady her breathing without him noticing as she pretended to search. It seemed absurd, now. No way he'd have been thinking about proposing, but it gave her the jitters all the same. She'd pull at that thread later. Not one for Christmas day. She returned to the bed with three beautifully wrapped packages, in dark blue shiny paper, complete with silver bows. He picked up a long, thin, sausage-shaped one.

'What the –? Did you get me a dildo?'

She swatted his arm. 'No. Open it.'

He tugged off the silver bow and tried to tear at the paper, but it was the foil type that doesn't rip.

'Here.' She eased back a section of Sellotape.

'A cucumber?' He looked bemused.

'Open this one. It'll make more sense.'

He opened a bottle of Hendricks gin and a six-pack of Fever-Tree tonic.

'Excellent! Thanks. I was getting worried.' He pecked her on the lips. 'So, who did you get for secret Santa?'

'I can't tell you that or it's not secret,' she said.

He shook his head, as if he should have known better than to ask. 'I'm going to jump in the shower.' Clara watched him leave then picked up her phone.

Jess: Merry Christmas!! Bet you're still in bed with that gorgeous man of yours. I've been up since 5am and Dave has already been at the sherry I got for his mum *eye roll emoji* o

Clara smiled and leaned back against the pillows to type.

Clara: Merry Christmas! I am still in bed. A small gathering of 25 for lunch, but thank God I'm not doing the cooking. Miss you x

After a breakfast of bacon, eggs and Bucks Fizz with Anna and Netta, and respective Skype calls to families, they headed to the training centre for the Christmas do. Mariah

Carey's 'All I Want for Christmas' was playing and the room had been decked with fairy lights, strung from the ceiling. A real Christmas tree stood in the corner, tastefully decorated in red and gold. Despite the lack of snow and the fact Clara was wearing a sundress and had her shades perched on her head, it looked and smelt like Christmas. A long trestle-table had been set up in the centre of the canteen. It was adorned with wine glasses, Christmas crackers and name cards for the place settings. Clara and Jake were seated next to each other, with Anna and Netta opposite. They'd all chipped in fifty Singapore dollars for the food and drink, and the catering staff from the centre were preparing and serving. The budget seemed to have stretched a long way, judging by the quantity of prosecco bottles on a separate table, next to a hand-written sign saying 'Secret Santa presents here'. Clara tucked hers behind a larger box, so no one would see which one she bought.

Netta made a beeline for the table and grabbed an already open bottle. 'Who's up for a glass of fizz?'

'Please, yep, hit me,' came the responses. Glasses were filled, raised and clinked.

'I'm going to mingle,' Anna said, and headed off to say hi to a tall man with a weak chin who Clara vaguely recognised from the training course. She spotted Siobhan, whom she'd met when they first arrived, deep in conversation with a man wearing a T-shirt with a reindeer on the front. Netta took a gulp of her prosecco and perched her bottom on the edge of the table, leaning back to cross her long legs at the ankle.

'What would you usually do on Christmas day?' Clara asked her.

'We'd usually be at my sister's. She has a big house and kids and likes to play hostess.'

Clara nodded. 'Sounds good. It's a treat for me to not have to do the cooking, or be left with a mess.'

After an hour or so of chit-chat about Christmases at home and the pros and cons of spending the holiday season away from families, the group took their seats at the table. Crackers were pulled, jokes were read and heads were decorated with paper hats.

'Top up?' Jake asked, reaching for the nearest bottle of red. It shot up in the air as he lifted it, as if he'd expected it to be heavier. 'Jeez, that went down fast,' he said.

Netta pushed her glass forward. 'I'll have some.'

Jake poured the remnants in her glass. 'Don't worry, plenty more where that came from.' He reached for a full bottle. It had already been opened and had the cork pushed lightly into the neck.

Clara put her hand over her half-full glass. 'Not just yet. I need to eat something first.'

'I'm okay for now, too,' Anna said.

'You're both so *sensible*. Come on it's Christmas!' Netta had a slight slur to her voice. Clara clocked Anna giving her a pointed look.

Jake topped up his own glass, oblivious to the nuances of the exchange happening in front of him. 'This is nice wine,' he said, reading the bottle in the manner of a connoisseur. 'Hints of cherries, blackberries and a floral bouquet.'

Clara nudged him with her foot under the table.

He looked at her blankly. 'What?'

She changed the subject. 'So, do you reckon we should invite some people over on New Year's Eve? Or maybe go out for dinner?'

'I'm easy,' Jake said.

'Dudes! We have to go out,' Anna said. 'How many New Year's Eves are we going to spend in Singapore?'

'Good point, well made. Out it is,' Jake said.

'Anna can take us to her favourite bar in Chinatown,' Netta said, too loudly.

'Sure, we can go there,' Clara said. 'We should check if we need tickets, though. Are they doing anything special for New Year's?'

There were vague nods and shrugs as their soup starters arrived. Netta picked up the bottle to top up her glass again and Anna gave her a sharp look.

'What?' Netta asked, looking directly at her.

'Nothing…Just, should you be drinking so much?'

'I find "should" is a rather unhelpful word,' Netta said. 'Excuse me.' She rose and headed off in the direction of the toilets.

'Is everything okay?' Clara asked Anna.

'Yes, yes. She just likes to drink too much sometimes,' Anna said. 'It's not a problem,' she added, quickly enough to make it sound like there was a problem. Clara and Jake exchanged a look.

'Honestly, it's fine,' Anna continued. 'Christmas is hard for her as her dad died around Christmastime.'

'Oh, I had no idea. She never mentioned it.' Clara said.

'She wouldn't. She doesn't really like to talk about it. Prefers to drink herself into oblivion.'

Clara widened her eyes at her to indicate Netta was on her way back. Anna busied herself buttering her bread roll as Netta reclaimed her seat, but it was too quiet.

'Talking about me where you?' she asked, as she settled herself.

'No, babe. We were talking about the soup.' Anna put a hand on her knee, clearly looking to smooth things over and salvage the meal. It seemed to work as Netta's body language softened and she picked up her own spoon.

The rest of the meal passed by pleasantly, and after they were all stuffed with turkey and all the trimmings, it was time for a lively game of charades.

A middle-aged woman with a functional hair-do and a smock-style dress waved her arms about.

'Tree?'

'Clouds?'

'Sky?'

She shook her head and started moving, gesturing at her head.

'Hat?'

'Head?'

'Top?'

She shook her head again and changed tack, dropping on all fours and putting one hand over her bum to indicate a tail.

'Dog?'

'Cat?'

'Squirrel?'

'SQUIRREL?' she said.

'Hey, you're not allowed to talk,' someone replied.

She raised herself up on her fingertips to make herself bigger and did a silent roar.

'Lion!' Jake shouted.

'*The Lion King*,' Netta said.

The woman pointed at her. 'Got it,' she said. 'Your turn.' She held out a bag full of slips of paper, for Netta to choose her challenge.

Netta picked out a slip 'Oh, for fuck's sake,' she said as she read it. 'Right.' She put her wine glass on a nearby table and stretched out her arms and legs, as if limbering up. She bent her knees and walked around with her hand over her eyes as if shielding them from the sun. There was silence for a moment.

'Erm, searching?' someone said.

Netta shook her head and reached for a sip of her wine, before trying again. She darted about the room as if looking for something. She stumbled, then caught herself and raised her hands in a 'I'm okay' gesture.

'Looking? Finding? *Finding Nemo*!'

She shook her head and after a bigger gulp of wine, raised both her hands at her sides in a shrug. It wasn't clear if this was part of the charade, or whether she'd given up.

'Confused?' Clara said.

'It's mission impossible,' Netta said, shrugging again and slopping some wine onto the floor.

'Maybe try "sounds like",' Clara suggested, touching her ear.

'No, it's *Mission Impossible*. The film. Someone else should have a go.' Netta sat down in a chair, clutching her wine. Someone else got up to do a charade and the day continued, but Anna and Netta slipped away early.

'I've never seen Netta like that,' Clara said to Jake, later. 'Hope she's okay.'

'Guess she likes a drink,' he said.

'Who'd have thought? She always seems so together. I thought they were the perfect couple.'

'No such thing.'

'No? I thought you were a big romantic softie.'

'Softie? I do like a bit of romance, but I know things don't have to be perfect for you to be happy.'

Clara was quiet as she considered this. He was so light-hearted and happy-go-lucky most of the time, but every now and again he had the ability to surprise her.

The week in-between Christmas and New Year passed with lazy days and lots of eating and drinking. Not that different to being at home. They headed out on New Year's Eve.

Clara sloshed some of her Pinot Grigio down the back of her hand as the crowd jostled her. She wiped it on the back of her dress and hoped it wouldn't leave a smear.

'Okay?' Jake yelled over the music.

She nodded. Netta and Anna were dancing in an area that had been cleared of chairs and tables and was serving as a dance floor. Some indie song was playing that Clara hadn't heard of.

'Wanna dance?' Jake said into her ear.

'Sure.'

The wine was sliding down easily and it was good to be out on New Year's Eve. The previous year, Clara had been staying with her mum and dad, finalising the plans for 'The Big Trip'. She'd sat up with her parents watching Jools Holland, and at midnight had opened a bottle of prosecco and done the obligatory awkward dance to 'Auld Lang Syne'. At ten past midnight, she'd gone to bed in her childhood room, reflected on how she'd got to where she was, and fretted about her plans to set off to Australia in a couple of weeks.

Jake was leading her to the dance floor. She held his hand and moved between bodies, turning sideways to avoid bumping into people. As they approached Anna and Netta the music changed, and 'Billie Jean' started playing. Clara smiled to herself as she began moving to the rhythm. Jake was a good dancer, which didn't surprise her. Christopher had always been a bit stiff on the dance floor, preferring to watch from the sidelines. The four of them danced together, mouthing the lyrics and raising their arms above their heads, sloshing more of their drinks down their arms.

A large screen above the dance area showed the time and Clara was surprised to see it was already close to midnight. The countdown began, and a tray of champagne glasses appeared, as if by magic. Clara helped herself to two and passed one to Jake. She noticed Netta decline as Anna took hers. She'd been drinking something Clara had assumed was a gin and tonic, but actually could have been lemonade, or water. Either way, no one drew attention to it as party poppers were pulled and kisses exchanged. They made their way up to a roof garden and watched fireworks explode over the marina. In that moment, Clara was proud. Proud of what she'd achieved in the last year and, while she wouldn't have chosen the path her life was taking, she was grateful that at this precise moment in time, she was happy. She leaned back into Jake. He put his arm around her waist and kissed the top of her head.

Chapter 44

May 2016

'I'm so sorry, love.'

Clara stared forlornly into her mug. Her mum was a firm believer that all could be solved, if not at least helped, with a good cup of tea. 'I feel stupid.'

'Why on earth would you feel stupid?'

'For being so happy. For thinking we'd done it and it was all going to work out.'

'That's not stupid, that's normal, love.'

'Maybe if we hadn't gone on holiday, if we'd just stayed here –'

'It wouldn't have made a blind bit of difference. The clinic told you that.'

'You didn't think we should go. I should have listened to you, not Christopher.'

'Love, you didn't lose the baby because you went on holiday.'

'Maybe not, but it must be my fault. My body wasted the embryo. I couldn't keep it safe.'

'It doesn't work like that, you know it doesn't.' June's voice was stern and Clara held up her hands in defeat.

'Okay, I know it's probably not my fault, realistically, but it's just so cruel. I thought that two lines equalled a baby, and now if I ever get a positive test again, I won't feel happy and excited, I'll be worried and anxious.'

'One step at a time, darling. You need time to grieve and heal, before you think about anything else.'

'We have to try again; we have two embryos in the freezer. I can't let our egg donor have donated for nothing.'

'Don't think about that now. Just concentrate on looking after yourself.'

Clara sipped her tea and said nothing.

'How's Christopher doing?'

She shrugged. The truth was he had hardly spoken about it since they got back from Italy. He'd dutifully accompanied her to the clinic, where they'd given her a scan and confirmed that, unfortunately, she was no longer pregnant, but she shouldn't be discouraged as the good news was, she *got* pregnant, and she should call them when she was ready to try again. Then he'd gone back to work and, in his own Christopher-like way, had just got on with it, leaving Clara wondering if she'd imagined the whole thing.

'He'll be hurting too,' said her mum.

'I don't know. It's like he doesn't want to acknowledge it.'

'I'm sure he's sad, but perhaps it wasn't real for him in the same way.'

Clara looked up sharply. 'It was his baby too, and it's as real as it got for us. I was pregnant.'

'I know you were, love. People deal with things differently is all.'

'It feels like because it was early, people think it's no big deal and I...it...was...we lost our baby.' Clara felt a fresh bout of tears rising. She thought she'd cried out over the past few days. 'You know, I rang work and said I wouldn't be in for a couple of days and it was like they wondered why. They asked if I was okay physically.'

'But they're okay with you taking time off?'

'Well, they have to be, don't they? They have a policy and they follow it, but I still felt like they wondered what all the fuss was about.' It was as if her employers didn't want to acknowledge it. A broken leg would have been much easier to understand.

People who had enthusiastically congratulated her on her pregnancy had said nothing when they'd learned she'd miscarried. Logically, she knew they didn't know what to say, but on a more visceral level, she'd slipped deeper into the abyss of infertility. She'd glimpsed being part of the world she so wanted to belong to, but she didn't fit. People didn't want to hear of baby loss, as it made it too real. Something happening close to them meant it could happen to them. Clara made people uncomfortable. She wasn't the same as those women discussing sleep patterns and potty training – she never would be – and society didn't know what to do with her. She didn't know what to do with herself.

'In my day, you probably wouldn't have known you were pregnant,' her mum was saying now.

'In your day I wouldn't have been, as there was no IVF!' Clara snapped, putting her tea down and causing it to slop over the side of the cup. 'So, do you wonder what all the fuss is about as well?' Her tears were flowing now.

'Of course not, darling.' June moved some marking, she'd been doing, aside and sat down next to her daughter. 'Come here.' She enveloped Clara in a big hug until her sobs eased.

'I don't know what to do now, Mum.'

'Shh, shh. Don't worry about that now.'

'But I need to know what's next. Then I can get my head around it.'

'What's next is, I'm going to make a fresh pot of tea and see if I have any chocolate biscuits in the cupboard.'

'You're going to work?' Clara asked Christopher the next morning, as he started putting his suit trousers on.

'Yes.'

'I thought you might stay off too.'

'I've got a meeting with a new client.'

'Okay, never mind then.'

'Don't be like that. Not going to work won't achieve anything.'

It will achieve something, she thought. It'll stop me feeling I'm going through this alone. Stop me feeling I'm the only one who is hurting or the only one who remembers our baby died.

Out loud she said, 'Okay, fine. I'll get some steaks for dinner. What time will you be home?'

'Six, hopefully. Sounds great.' He pecked her on the lips and was out of the door.

Clara went down to put the kettle on and stared at the steam rising. She wondered whether she was coping as well as she should. She guessed that for Christopher, it might be making him think of his brother. Not that he'd ever say. He probably thought this was small fry in comparison.

The kettle had clicked off a few minutes ago, but Clara's mug sat empty. She resolved to speak to Christopher properly over dinner that night. Not about his brother – she knew better than that – but about the miscarriage and about what they'd do next.

She took a tea-bag out of the cupboard and started shuffling things about, looking for biscuits. She was turning into her mother. It wasn't even 9am. She stopped looking, made the tea and took it through to the living room to drink biscuit-less. She scrolled idly through her Instagram feed, then started Googling 'chances of recurrent miscarriage', 'causes of miscarriage' and 'chances of success IVF donor eggs'. Of course, she didn't learn anything new and didn't feel any better for it. After an hour or so had passed, she flicked on the TV and started watching a travel programme and imagined herself somewhere else.

'The steaks are good,' Christopher said, later that night. He'd been late home from work, but Clara had waited, determined that they'd eat together and have a proper conversation, even though she'd been starving and they hadn't sat down until 9pm.

'I got them from the butcher's. How was work?'

'Ugh.' He shook his head. 'Manic. How was your day?'

'Fine.'

Silence ensued as they ate.

'I…I think we should talk,' Clara said after a while.

Christopher's chewing slowed. She could almost feel him tensing up. She knew him too well.

'Okay, what about?'

'Oh, I don't know – the weather? What do you think?' She couldn't stop herself snapping.

'Okay, okay. What do you want to say?'

'I don't know.' This wasn't really going to plan. 'Just that I'm struggling and I want to know how you feel.'

He nodded but didn't speak.

'Well?' she pressed.

'I feel sad, of course I do. But I do think it's encouraging that you got pregnant.'

Clara shook her head, then nodded. 'It is, but I feel so bereft, emptied out inside. I spent most of today crying.'

'Perhaps you should go back to work, keep yourself busy.'

'So, pretend it didn't happen, you mean?'

'No, of course not, that's not what I meant…'

'Because that's what you do, isn't it? Pretend it didn't happen and it's like it never did.'

His eyes hardened. She'd gone too far.

'Sorry, I didn't mean that, I'm just upset.'

He got up from his seat and came and put his arms around her, but she wasn't comforted. It was a gesture, rather than a natural reaction. He was doing what he thought he should and she didn't feel like doing what she thought she should. She shrugged him off and went up to the bedroom, lay down on the bed and closed her eyes.

Later, Clara was crossing the landing on her way to the bathroom and overheard Christopher on the phone downstairs.

'I tried but she walked off. I don't know how to make her feel better.'

She paused and listened to what came next.

'It's not just her who's struggling though. I'm pretty gutted too.'

She made her way downstairs, treading lightly.

'So, anyway I'll send you what I've got. It'll help with the meeting.'

'Yep, you too. Bye.' Christopher hung up the phone as Clara entered the kitchen.

'Who was that?' she asked.

'Just Sarah from work. Are you feeling better?'

'You got in from work at 8 o'clock and you're still working?'

'No, it was a quick phone call. How are you feeling?'

She shrugged. 'Okay.'

But she wasn't. An uneasy feeling was taking hold.

Chapter 45

January 2019

'That looks ace. Do we get to have a go?' Jake was looking up at the climbing wall as the children picked up harnesses and tried them on for size.

'Sure you wouldn't be scared?' Clara teased. 'It's quite high.'

'I think I could cope.'

Mr Symonds, the PE teacher, looked up from adjusting a harness on one of the children. 'You're welcome to try after the kids have had a go,' he said.

'Really?' Jake sounded less sure of himself now, as though he'd been expecting the answer to be 'no'.

Things were settling back into a normal rhythm after the excitement of the concert, Christopher's surprise visit and Christmas. Clara and Jake had been invited to observe a PE lesson taught in English, to 'broaden their experience and to see the kids they taught in a different environment'. Clara had been worried it'd bring back memories of PE at school: forgotten kits and borrowed gym knickers that were a size too small, black plimsolls and dusty gym equipment, changing rooms full of hormones, girls self-conscious about their changing bodies, and clouds of Impulse body spray masking the smell of sweat. Strange to think she'd spent more time and energy trying to get out of PE than actually doing it, and yet now she paid for aerobics classes and gym memberships, doing many of the things she'd been so keen to avoid.

But this purpose built 'leisure area' brought back no such memories. Not a speck of dust or pair of gym knickers in sight. The ceiling was double-height, with a mezzanine level at one side for spectators. The climbing wall took up the whole of the other side, with its rubber hand and foot holds colour coded in bright shades to indicate difficulty levels. At the bottom were bright blue mats as thick as mattresses, ready to provide a soft landing for any child who abseiled down with too much enthusiasm.

Mr Symonds had the children lined up on a bench in their harnesses and was giving a safety talk in a range of languages, to make sure everyone understood the important stuff. No more than two climbers at a time. Start with the green; if you're comfortable with that, progress to the blue. No one was going to try red today. No, not even you, Johann. Maybe next time. Let's see how we all get on first.

'Who wants to go first?' he asked, once the preliminaries were over.

Chen's hand shot up, but Lin put her hand on her sister's arm to pull it back down. Johann's right arm was firmly in the air and he was using his left arm to try and push it up higher. His body strained with the effort of trying to be noticed. Albertho's hand was more tentative, hovering near his shoulder. No one else volunteered.

'Johann, Albertho, you're up.' Johann jumped out of his seat and Albertho followed, more slowly.

'So, we're going to start with green, and remember, if you lose your footing and slip, the safety-harness will catch you.' Mr Symonds attached their harnesses to the safety-ropes.

Jake was standing back to get a good view, his face tilted upwards. Clara watched the way his shirt stretched over his chest as he put his hands on his hips – a gesture that had become familiar to her over a relatively short space of time. The Christmas break had intensified things between them: lazy mornings lying in bed together, long lunches in Singapore's food courts, sampling specialties on offer at food stalls, evenings spent walking hand in hand or sitting on their balcony drinking beer and talking about the kids at school. Jake had gotten over Christopher turning up and was now relaxed about it, as he was pretty relaxed about everything. It was as though someone had pressed fast forward on their relationship; their closeness was progressing at the speed of a holiday romance. But this was a long holiday. For now, Clara ignored any niggling thoughts about what it all meant and what might happen next. She had a sudden urge to go and stand next to him and wrap her arms around his waist, but, remembering where they were, she shifted her focus back to the kids, who were now a few feet from the ground on the wall. Albertho was finding his stride and climbing with deliberate movements – a foot here, a hand there – his brow furrowed in concentration. Johann was more gung-ho, scrambling for footholds, valuing speed over precision. He was initially ahead of Albertho, but slipped and sailed the few feet back to the mats in his harness. Albertho carried on, slow and steady.

'Okay, it's not a race, Johann', Mr Symonds said. 'Take your time.' Of course telling an eight-year-old boy it wasn't a race had the opposite effect, and Johann hit the wall again using a similar technique. Frustration seeped out of him as Albertho got further ahead. He slipped again, then said he'd had enough, and stared resolutely at the floor.

Next up were Lin and Chen. They each approached the task in much the same way – careful, thought-out moves, climbing beside each other in an almost synchronised fashion. They reached the top together and held hands as they pushed off the wall to sail down to the mats.

'That was amazing, girls,' Clara said, as they returned to their seats on the bench. She was rewarded with broad smiles from them both.

As the other kids took their turns, Clara found herself itching to have a go. She wanted to find out if it was as easy as it looked and also whether she could beat Jake to the top.

'Can we really have a go?' she asked Mr Symonds once the kids were done.

'Sure, it's the end of the school day. I'll get you set up. I have some adult-size harnesses in the store room.'

Clara met Jake's eye, imploring him to agree. He held her gaze. 'Fine. If you really want to, let's give it a go.'

'Are we going for green first?' Clara asked him, once the kids were gone and they'd had a summary of the safety talk again from Mr Symonds. Jake nodded and took hold of a green handle, hoisting himself up of the mat. Clara did the same. She looked ahead for the next hold and tried to emulate what Albertho had done. It was, in fact, harder than it looked. Her arms ached already and her right calf was cramping as she held her foot in an awkward position. She ploughed on. As she got higher, her palms grew slick with sweat, making it more difficult to grip. Jake was ahead of her, the muscles in his calves bulging as he secured his hold. She couldn't see his face, but he was doing a good impression of a seasoned climber for whom heights were not a concern. She held her abs tight as she moved her left hand to a hold higher up, and then her right foot. Her foot slipped off the surface and she scrambled to get another hold, but managed it and kept going. Jake had slowed ahead and was looking as if he'd had enough.

'Keep going!' Clara encouraged him from behind. The muscles in her shoulders were aching and her legs were like jelly, but she kept on. A hand here, a foot there, until she reached the top. She leant back slightly to be sure the harness had her weight, then kicked off the wall to float back down. Jake had stopped short of the top.

'You're nearly there,' Clara said, standing firmly on the ground, arms and legs aching.

'I'm done,' he said. 'I'm coming down.'

'Okay, come on then.'

'I...can't,' Jake said.

'The way down is easy. Look at the wall in front of you. Don't look at me.'

He didn't move.

'Okay, you can keep your feet on the wall. Sit back slightly and let the harness take your weight.'

He did as he was told and inched his way back down, moving his feet one at a time.

'I can't believe you made me do that,' he said, as soon as his feet hit the mat.

'I thought you wanted to!'

Now the kids and Mr Symonds had gone, she put her arms around him. His heart was pounding against her body. 'Perhaps we should stay away from heights from now on,' she said to his chest.

He pushed her away, gently but firmly.

'What's wrong?' Her gut twisted with anxiety. She hadn't seen him like this before.

'Nothing. I need some space' He started walking towards the door. Clara sank down on the bench, bereft. What had she done? It wasn't like him to be stroppy.

'I'll be back. Just give me a few minutes.'

She watched the door close behind him and wondered what to do with herself. Someone walked along the landing on the mezzanine level and glanced at her sitting on the bench by herself. She willed them to keep moving, to not stop and ask what she was doing there. They carried on their way and were soon out of sight. She examined her nails, scraped some coral nail polish from the cuticle on her thumb, then tapped her fingers on her knees. The door opened and Jake reappeared.

'I'm sorry.' He crossed the room and made his way over to her.

She stood up. 'No, I'm sorry. I shouldn't have pressured you into doing something you didn't want to.'

'Thing is, I'm sort of scared of heights.'

Clara smiled. 'Really?'

'I used to have nightmares when I was a kid about being on top of a tall building, or at the edge of a cliff, and I was always about to fall. One time, when I was about five, my brother dared me to climb to the top of the climbing-frame in the playground. He was seven and could make it up there easily. I got about two-thirds of the way up and froze.'

Clara nodded, waiting for him to go on.

'I couldn't function. My mum was calling to me but it was like she was miles away. Everything got clouded and distorted. She had my baby sister in the pram. In the end she had to leave my brother with her and climb up herself to coax me down. He ripped the piss out of me for it.'

'Kids can be cruel,' Clara said, shaking her head.

'Yeah, well, he saw it as an opportunity to wind me up. But don't worry I gave as good as I got. Anyway, I've sort of been in denial, I guess. Sometimes it doesn't bother me, like at the top of the Marina Bay Sands, and even the Supertrees weren't too bad. Something about it being solid underfoot. But with the cable-car to Sentosa, and that climbing wall just then, it was like I was right back on the climbing-frame.'

'I'm sorry,' Clara said, again. 'If I'd realised, I never would have suggested –'

'Shh, it's okay.' He took her in his arms. Relieved, she relaxed into him and breathed his scent of Hugo Boss mixed with something altogether more earthy and inherently male.

'How about we order Thai food and watch a film tonight?' He checked no one was around then slid his hands down to cup her behind.

'Sounds perfect,' she said, and allowed him to pull her close.

Later, as they laid out cardboard takeaway containers on the coffee table, she had a strange detached-from-reality feeling. They were getting too close. The events of the afternoon felt like a milestone in a new relationship; he'd shown her a new side of himself. She imagined a conversation between herself and Jess.

We had our first fight.
That means it's getting serious.
He told me about his childhood.

He loves you.

No! We're just having fun. He definitely doesn't love me.

Imaginary Jess raised an eyebrow and smirked.

'Are you okay?' Jake made her jump.

'Yes, fine. Sorry. I was just thinking.'

'You don't want to do too much of that.'

'No, you're probably right.'

'Do you want the last spring roll?'

Clara took it and pushed her worries to the back of her mind.

Chapter 46

December 2016

'I can't think of a worse time to tell you this.' Jess looked down at her hands. She was pushing a packet of sugar back and forth between her forefinger and thumb.

'You're pregnant,' Clara said.

Her friend looked up sharply. 'You know?'

'I guessed.'

Jess nodded. 'Because I didn't have a glass of wine at Martin's birthday meal?'

'Well, there's that, and also your boobs are massive.'

Jess looked almost guilty and pulled her wrap-dress higher over her cleavage.

Clara immediately felt bad. 'Congratulations,' she said.

'I'm sorry.'

She was going to have to try harder. She took a deep breath. 'Don't be sorry. You're having a baby. That's brilliant! I don't want you to be worried about talking to me about it. I'm happy for you'

'Then why are you crying?'

Clara dabbed her wet cheek with a paper napkin. 'I can be happy for you and sad for me at the same time.'

'Of course, you can.' Jess looked nervous, unsure of herself. Clara hated that. They'd been friends since they were eleven. They'd been there for each other when they started their periods a few months apart. They'd compared notes when they kissed boys behind the youth club during afternoon break. They'd helped each other through numerous break-ups. Been on holidays together, talked about how their kids would play together. Now Jess was pregnant with her second and Clara was… left behind. But the worst of it was, it was making her best friend feel awkward around her.

'I'm so sorry,' Clara suddenly said. She stood up and embraced her friend.

'You have nothing to be sorry for,' Jess said.

'I'm sorry you couldn't tell me straightaway. When you were pregnant the first time, you sent me a photo of the test before you'd even told Dave! And now you're sitting there all nervous, because of my problems. Well, fuck it. Fuck infertility. You're pregnant and that's great. Let's order another slice of carrot cake to celebrate.'

'Wow. That even rhymed!' Jess looked bemused by Clara's outburst, but she didn't need telling twice about the cake.

'Fuck infertility,' she said, holding up her fork for Clara to tap hers against. They munched their way through the cake and Clara asked all the questions you ask your friend when they tell you they're pregnant; When was she due? (July.) Would they find out what they were having? (Yes.) What did she want? (A boy would be nice, so that they had one of each, but another girl would be lovely as well, so they could grow up close, but most of all, happy and healthy, of course, of course.) How did Amelie feel about becoming a big sister? (Excited. Not sure she really understands.)

Clara dutifully played the role and tried her hardest to sound natural and like the friend Jess knew and loved. More tea was ordered and they moved onto other topics: was Christopher's mum still doing that annoying thing where she rang to see if it was okay to call in when she was already outside the door? Had Clara decided whether to go ahead with the extension? And wasn't it sad that Fidel Castro had died, though he did have a good innings? Clara went through the motions, laughing in the right places, asking questions, giving thoughtful responses.

She cried herself to sleep that night.

'So, your best friend is pregnant,' Caroline said at their next appointment. 'And how does that make you feel?'

Clara didn't even flinch at the clichéd counsellor question, as she was desperate to tell her how it made her feel. 'Like I'm a failure. Like something that is seemingly beyond my capabilities is so easy for other people. It should be easy and yet it doesn't work for me. I'm broken. And then I feel guilty, because instead of being happy for my best friend, who I *love*, I'm thinking about myself and my own problems.'

'Okay.' Caroline noted something on her pad.

'I don't think it's going to happen for me. When it happens to others all around me, it brings home the fact that it isn't going to happen for me, and I feel stupid for hoping it might.' Clara blinked her eyes a few times and considered reaching for a tissue from the new, plain grey, gender-neutral square box on the table, but brought herself under control. She looked at the deckchair picture. It was wonky; she wanted to straighten it.

Caroline nodded. 'And what do you think it is, specifically, that makes you feel that way?'

'When I allow myself to hope. I'm setting myself up for more disappointment and heartache. I shouldn't allow myself to think it's going to be any different. But if I don't allow myself that, then why am I even bothering with the treatment?'

'Why are you?'

'Because it *might* work. And if it doesn't, I have to know I did everything I could.'

Caroline nodded. 'You mentioned control in an earlier session. Is feeling in control important to you?'

'Yes. I am a control freak.'

Caroline gave a tight smile. Clara guessed she didn't approve of her calling herself a freak.

'And how do you think that helps or hinders your situation now?'

'It hinders because I *can't* control it. And there's the rub.'

'So, you don't like being out of control, and yet you're in a situation that is impossible to control.'

Clara knew this was the part where she was supposed to come up with her own answer. She could say something deep about accepting what she couldn't control. Instead she said, 'Sorry, do you mind if I straighten that picture? It's bugging me.'

'Be my guest.' Caroline actually laughed. Clara didn't think counsellors did that.

She stood up and straightened it, then resettled herself in her seat.

Caroline changed tack. 'What about Christopher? Do you think he'd like to attend a session with you?'

Clara shook her head. He'd looked alarmed when she suggested it. 'You keep going, if it helps' he'd said. 'I don't feel the need to talk about it to a stranger.' She hadn't brought it up again. 'It's not really his thing.'

'Let me know if he changes his mind,' Caroline said. 'We could book a longer slot.'

'I will, but I don't think it's likely.'

Caroline was looking at the clock again. Time up. She thanked her and said she'd see her next week.

On the way home, Clara gave some thought as to how she could feel okay with not being in control. Perhaps she could start small and, say, let Christopher do the food shop and not do a menu plan. The thought left her feeling twitchy, but maybe if she did that and it was okay, it could help. He was a dab hand at rustling up a spag bol and as long as they could still get a Thai takeaway this Friday, she was pretty sure she could manage it.

Chapter 47

March 2019

'Are you coming for a run with us?' Netta asked, her perfect body clad in baby blue Lycra. Anna was bouncing on her toes next to her, wearing hot pink running shorts, a yellow vest and a baseball cap with a glittery peak.

'I don't know how you can in this heat,' Clara said. 'I could do with doing something, though. I'm feeling out of shape.'

'Come on,' Anna said, as she fiddled with her Garmin. 'Woman up and come with us.'

Clara hesitated. Jake was doing an extra drama class with the kids and wouldn't be back for a while. She had nothing else to do and she'd noticed an extra wobble to her bum when she jogged up the stairs the other night that didn't used to be there.

'Oh, go on then. As long as you're not going too far.'

'We'll go easy on you.' Netta winked at her.

Five minutes later they were outside and Anna was leading the way. It was good to be moving, but it was like running through soup. The air was thick and heavy and Clara was coated in a sheen of sweat within minutes. She took a healthy glug from her water bottle and kept up, not wanting to slow them down. They jogged along quietly for a while, the Singapore skyline glittering in the distance. They entered the botanical gardens where the trees, festooned with a light pink blossom, provided some welcome shade. Though they didn't do much to ease the temperature. They ran through a tunnel made of plants and past a lake, which Clara was tempted to jump into.

'Guys,' she said after a while. 'I need a rest.' Sweat was dripping down her forehead and had made her mascara run and sting her eyes. Her breath was coming in short bursts. 'It's too hot for me.'

Anna jogged on the spot and nodded. She had a big wet patch down the front of her yellow T-shirt, but it didn't seem to bother her.

'Have a seat under this tree. We'll do another lap then come back for you. We can take it easy on the way back.'

'No worries,' Clara said gratefully. She sank down on the grass in the shade of the tree and sipped what was left of her water. Her muscles felt pleasantly tired, but she longed for some cooler weather. She liked going for runs when her cheeks tingled with the cold and her breath clouded in front of her. It made her feel alive. This made her feel sluggish and itchy. She scratched her wrist as a mosquito landed on her. As they edged towards summer, she knew she had to make a decision about whether to stay on for the next school year, or go home. Home was a funny thought, as she no longer actually had one. Christopher had bought her out of the house after the split. Of course she had means; she wouldn't be homeless and she could always stay with Jess or her parents in the short term. Maybe with Jess – Clara wasn't sure living with her parents as an adult would empower her to make a fresh start. Alternatively, she could stay here. Anna and Netta were mulling it over. Netta had to make regular trips back to the UK, but her business was doing well enough that the cost wasn't an issue, and Anna was enjoying the work at the school. Clara was making headway with Lin, and it'd be nice to have another year with her and the other kids. Jake – well, then there was Jake. He didn't strictly have a plan, in true Jake style. He might stay here another year, or he might try TEFL in South East Asia. Over the summer he planned to travel to Laos and meet up with some old friends from back home, and he'd asked Clara to go with him. She felt the need for a spreadsheet coming on. She'd have her options colour-coded with a list of pros and cons for each. She'd give each pro and con a numerical weighting so she could put in a formula and it'd tell her the answer. Of course, she was free to ignore the answer, but it would help figure it out.

'Whew.' Netta reappeared and sat down on the grass beside her. Her face was pink with the heat and exertion and she glowed with sweat. But she still looked beautiful, like an advert for running clothes: 'You too can be fit and beautiful if you buy this blue Lycra outfit.'

'Where's Anna?' Clara asked.

Netta nodded to a figure in hot pink shorts and a yellow T-shirt jog-walking towards them.

Clara laughed. 'Oh, how did I miss her?'

'Whew.' Anna echoed Netta's words as she approached, mopping her brow with the back of her wrist. 'How you doing, Clara?'

'Okay. Though I think I'll stick to walking next time. I'll run when I get home and it's cold.'

'Have you decided you're going, then?' Netta asked

'No, not decided either way. I was just thinking about it, actually.'

'What's waiting for you at home?' she asked.

'Not a whole lot. I'll need to start afresh and think about what my life could look like.'

'That's sort of liberating though, isn't it? Empowering,' Anna said, as she stretched her hamstring.

'Liberating, yes. But also, scary, bewildering.' Clara scratched her wrist again. *That damn mosquito.* 'I don't think I've ever properly stopped and thought about it before, you know? I've gone along and done what was expected, without overly thinking about whether it was what I wanted.'

Anna and Netta looked at her, waiting for her to go on.

'That's not to say I've done things I didn't want to. It's only when something doesn't work out the way you wanted, you start to question everything.'

'Sadly, a woman's success is still judged by whether she's reproduced, and everything else comes second,' Anna said. 'If a woman successfully sets up her own company, as Netta has, one of the first questions she'll be asked when meeting new people is whether she has kids. When the answer is "no", you can see them thinking, "ah, well, you have to make sacrifices if you want a successful career." It's a double standard. No one would ask a man the same question; it's assumed he can do both.'

'I did want children and I did want a husband, and not because that's what's expected, but because, I just did. Do.'

Anna nodded and sat down on the grass. 'And what about Jake?'

'What about him?'

'Are you two serious about each other?'

'We're having fun, seeing what happens.'

Anna raised an eyebrow. 'Mate, come on. I know you better than that already. Clara doesn't "see what happens".'

Clara laughed. 'I'm trying it on for size.'

'Oh yeah, and how's that working out for you?' Netta asked.

Clara just smiled in response.

'Look at her, all loved up! It's sweet,' Anna said.

'I'm not loved up. I do like him, though.'

Anna shook her head, smiling. 'Come on, we should get back. Let's walk.'

'Thank God you said that. I can't face any more running.'

Later that afternoon, Clara started making notes in her notebook; she would input it into a spreadsheet, later.

Travelling with Jake
1. It would be fun.
2. Get to spend more time with Jake.
3. Would be nice to see more places.
BUT
1. I might feel old when I meet his friends.

2. I didn't actually like backpacking.
3. Is it fair to allow us to carry on getting closer, when I'm not sure what I want?

She underlined the last point twice. Then wrote:

Staying in Singapore to teach for another year
1. Would enjoy the teaching.
2. Would see Lin and Chen and might be able to help Lin more.
3. Could delay facing reality for another year.
   BUT
1. Not sure Anna, Netta or Jake would even be here. Might have to start making friends all over again.
2. Might have to find somewhere else to live, or get new flatmates from somewhere.
3. Would I just be delaying figuring out what do with the rest of my life?

She paused and realised the third points under each heading were basically saying the same thing. A knock at the door made her jump and close the notebook.

'Hey.' Jake poked his head round. 'What you up to?'

'Nothing,' she said, sliding the notebook under the pillow.

'I've run a bath and no one else is around. Fancy joining me?'

'It's okay, I had a shower after my run.'

'I didn't mean to get clean.' He winked at her and started doing a mock sexy dance as he pulled his T-shirt over his head and threw it at her. She laughed and threw it back.

'Okay,' she said. She could return to the list later.

Chapter 48

December 2016

It smelt like pine. Pine mixed with the mustiness of the decorations, which had been in the attic all year. It used to be a happy smell. Christopher was wedging the Norway Spruce into a red bucket, using stones from the garden in an attempt to keep it upright. It leant to one side, on the verge of toppling.

'Why don't you put some Christmas music on?' he asked.

'You hate Christmas music.'

'Yes, but you like it. Come on, it might get you in the Christmas mood.'

She bristled at his words, and said nothing.

'Is this straight?' he asked, from between the branches. He was kneeling on the floor, trying to keep the bucket still and hoist the tree into position, simultaneously.

'No.' With a sigh, she got up off the settee to help.

'There. It looks good,' he said, half an hour later, when they'd secured the tree and finished decorating it.

Clara nodded, but stayed quiet as she retook her place on the settee.

'Come on, cheer up, will you? It's nearly Christmas.'

'Exactly. It's nearly the end of the year, and we still don't know what our next move is.'

'Don't think of the end of the year as a deadline. We said we'd try to take the focus off trying for a baby, then rethink our options in the New Year. That's all.'

Clara put her face in her hands. She was tired of this conversation. 'I hoped we wouldn't need to. I stupidly thought if we tried hard enough not to focus on it, it might just still happen. Naturally, I mean. Even though that's ridiculous after everything we've been through.'

'It's not ridiculous. I hoped for that too. But, well, it didn't. So, can we just enjoy Christmas and worry about that later?'

Clara stared at him. In that moment he was a stranger. 'You enjoy Christmas. I'm going upstairs.'

She heard him swear under his breath as she left the room and all its fake joy.

She couldn't even call Jess right now. Things felt weird since she'd told her she was pregnant again, and she didn't want to make her feel more guilty about being pregnant by calling her to complain about the fact she was not.

Clara always got a bit reflective and introspective at this time of year. Her birthday, right at the start of New Year, intensified the feeling that it was a fresh start. This time she'd be turning thirty-five. That watershed age that is known to mark the slow decline of your fertility. Though it seemed hers had been on the decline for a long time already. In the bedroom, she took out some Post-Its and some A3 paper. It was time to make a plan. 2017 had to be the year that something happened.

Christmas day itself was a low-key affair at Clara's parents. Barbara and Martin from next door came for dinner, as their son was with his wife's family, and they were at a loose end. They'd obviously been warned off the topic of children, or grandchildren, as the subject was neatly avoided during the turkey and Clara's dad's pigs-in-blankets with a twist. (The twist was two pigs per blanket, much to Martin's glee.) They pulled their crackers, read the jokes and interesting facts – as these were Waitrose crackers, they aimed to educate as well as entertain. Clara learnt that Scotland has 421 words for 'snow', and that the letter 'Q' is the only letter not to appear in a name of a U.S. state. Christopher was on good form, entertaining Barbara and Martin with a tale about how he'd set up a sponsored run at work and motivated the whole of the finance team to go for a run at lunchtimes. He left out the more important part: that he'd raised £500 for a charity that supported bereaved parents and families.

'Are you okay, love?' Clara's mum asked while they were tidying up in the kitchen.

'Yes. No. Who knows? Jess is pregnant. Again.'

June's hand stilled on the pan she was scrubbing. 'Oh, love. When did you find out?'

'Few weeks ago. She told me when we went for coffee.'

'Well, that's lovely news. For her.'

Clara made a sound that was somewhere between a snort and a laugh. 'It is. *Of course*, it is. But I feel so horrible because she's my best friend and I love her, but I'm jealous.'

'Come here.' June shook the excess water off her Marigolds and gave her daughter a hug. 'Next year has got to be your year.'

'I don't know if I can face it again, Mum. I mean, I got pregnant. Then it went away. I'm not sure I could go through that again.'

'You don't have to decide anything right now.'

Clara pulled at a loose thread on the tea-towel.

'What does Christopher think?'

'Who knows what he thinks? Apart from Sarah, maybe.'

June's eyes narrowed in confusion. 'Who's Sarah?'

'Just someone at work. He's always working and I know he talks to her.'

June frowned, but didn't say anything further. A pointed silence.

'Forget it. Don't know why I said that. I just want to know what we're doing next.'

'Well, you don't have to make a decision right now. You have plenty of options and there's every chance things will work out for you. Shall we just try to enjoy Christmas, for now?'

Clara snorted. 'You sound like Christopher.'

'Maybe Christopher has a point.'

Clara glared at her mum. 'He's just pretending everything is fine. Everything is not fine.'

'I know, love, but it doesn't help to dwell on it all the time.' She passed her a baking tray.

'This is still greasy, Mum.'

June sighed and took it back. 'Your dad's overdone the oil on the roast potatoes. Likes them extra crispy.'

Clara put down the tea-towel and stared out of the window. A pigeon was pecking at the frozen ground. She tried to give herself a mental kick up the backside; she didn't want to be a killjoy at Christmas. She took the re-cleaned baking tray and forced herself to be upbeat.

'Are we opening presents after this?'

'Of course, love.'

'Good. Hope dad likes his Bart Simpson socks.'

'Are you ready?' Christopher asked. It was Boxing Day and they were due at his parents' house for a leftovers Christmas lunch. His mum's sister was visiting from France, where she now lived, along with her daughter and family, who were going for the day, too.

Clara gave her lashes a final coat of mascara and stepped back to see the overall look. Perfectly respectable. The concealer had worked wonders on the dark circles under her eyes and the foundation covered her blotchy skin. No one would guess she'd spent a lot of the night crying.

'Yep,' she called, shoving her make-up bag in the wardrobe and picking up her handbag.

'Christopher! Clara! Merry Christmas. Do we still say that on Boxing Day? I think we do. It's a bit early for Happy New Year, anyway.' Christopher's mum embraced them both in turn, giving Clara an extra tight squeeze.

'Yes, I think we do, Mum. Merry Christmas.'

'Merry Christmas, Christine,' Clara said, easing herself out of her embrace.

'Come in, come in. Don't stand in the doorway.' Christopher's dad appeared from the kitchen. Tea-towel slung over one shoulder, red cheeks suggesting he'd already been at the sherry. 'Hope you're both hungry.' They were ushered through to the living room, where a huge tree dominated one corner of the room. It was tastefully decorated in silver and pink baubles of different sizes, with a golden star on top. If you didn't look closely, you'd miss the two 'Baby's First Christmas' baubles, one for James and one for Christopher, tucked away to one side, near the bottom. It was as though they were too painful to have in plain sight, but keeping one of them in its box wouldn't be right, either. Clara imagined Christine decorating the tree, deliberating over where to put them. She felt momentarily guilty about her sulkiness when they were decorating their own tree. She was grieving for a baby she hadn't yet had, whereas Christopher's parents had loved their son for the first ten years of his life, and then lost him. That was a pain no one should have to endure.

They'd just sat down and been offered a Bucks Fizz when the doorbell rang.

'That'll be Linda,' Christine said. Clara had met Linda a few times over the years. A small woman with a big personality. She'd had a mid-life crisis a few years back and died her hair pink, much to Christine's chagrin. It was back to its usual shade of mid-brown when she came into the room. She was wearing a bright red dress, nipped in at the waist to show off her slim figure. Her husband Geoff was almost a head taller than his wife, and his belly protruded over the leather belt on his jeans. In followed their daughter, Jen, her husband, Paul, and an assortment of kids. The room was suddenly a cacophony of noise and jollity as hands were shaken, drinks were offered and the kids started talking at once, telling their great-aunt and uncle what Santa had brought them.

Christopher and Paul struck up a conversation about the route they'd taken to get here and whether the temporary traffic lights were still in force on the high street. Jen made a beeline for Clara.

'Did you have a good day yesterday?' she asked.

'Yes, thanks. Quiet. Spent it with my mum and dad and their next-door neighbours. How about you?'

'Definitely not quiet.' She looked at her kids. A girl of about five was pulling a plastic truck out of her brother's hands. 'Ava, that's Caleb's! Caleb share with your sister. Let her have a turn. Thank you.' Jen rolled her eyes at Clara. 'Can't get a minute's peace. Your quiet day sounds like bliss.'

Clara gave a tight smile.

She put her hand on Clara's upper arm as though she were imparting some worldly wisdom. 'I mean I love them, course I do, but right now, a few days on a remote island by myself would be heaven. Actually, forget that, I'd take five minutes to go to the toilet in peace.'

'I can imagine,' Clara said. 'Excuse me a moment, I'm just going to get a drink.'

Jen looked at the full glass of Bucks Fizz in Clara's hand.

'I mean another drink. A cup of tea. Would you like one?'

'I'm okay at the moment, thanks.'

In the kitchen, Clara got her phone out to text Jess. She got halfway through a message, then deleted it and put her phone away. What if she didn't understand? Jess might be longing for some peace and quiet as well. She put the kettle on. Might as well keep up the pretence. She was reaching for a teabag when her phone pinged.

Jess: How's it going with the in-laws? Hope you're having more fun than me. I'm currently hiding in the loo as

Dave's sister is trying to get me to join in her embroidery class. I'd rather stick the embroidery pins in my eyes. o

Clara snorted and typed a reply.

Clara: My day not much better. Christopher's cousin has just more or less said I'm lucky I don't have kids, as it must be nice and peaceful. x

Jess: Okay, you win. That woman is officially evil. Go back in there tell her to fuck off. o

'What are you laughing at?' Christopher said.

Clara turned and pocketed her phone.

'Oh, nothing.' She shouldn't have doubted Jess. She was still smiling as she poured hot water on her teabag. 'Do you want a cup of tea?'

'No, thanks. Are you coming back? My mum's asking if you're okay.'

Clara followed him back into the living room and had a perfectly reasonable conversation with Jen about the merits of cats versus dogs as pets.

Chapter 49

May 2019

Clara watched Lin sketching out two rudimentary people. One was tall, and she used a brown crayon to scribble some hair on its head, then very carefully drew some small dots on the chin for stubble. On the slightly smaller figure she used a light brown crayon for the hair and a red crayon to do a big smile.

After a brief interlude for the concert rehearsals, Clara's one-to-one art lessons with Lin had become a weekly full-length session. YongJae had seen the progress made and agreed that Lin could be excused from class.

Lin carefully drew fingers for each figure, making them intertwine so they were holding hands.

'Who is that?' Clara asked, pointing at the smaller figure.

Lin pointed at her.

'Me?'

A nod.

'And who's this?'

'Jake,' Lin said confidently. No hesitation.

Clara resisted the urge to stand up and do a dance and instead calmly carried on with the conversation. 'We're holding hands?'

Lin nodded and, with her red crayon, drew a big love heart between the two figures. Clara laughed.

'You love each other,' Lin said. Her voice was almost identical to Chen's but ever so slightly softer – a more timid version of her sister. Clara fought her instinct to react to the fact that Lin was acting as though it was completely normal to speak to her.

'We're good friends,' Clara said.

'It for you.' Lin handed over the finished drawing.

'Thank you so much. Can I put it on my fridge at home?'

Lin nodded. It was time for them to make their way back to class. Clara was bursting to tell YongJae what had happened, but the lesson was in full flow as she escorted Lin to her desk next to Chen, and back to her silent bubble in the main classroom.

'She actually had a conversation with you?' Jake said, as they rode the MRT home at the end of the school day.

'Yes! As though it was nothing.'

'That's brilliant. She obviously feels comfortable around you.' He had to crane his neck to speak to her, hanging onto the steel pole so he didn't fall into the crowd of fellow commuters.

'I know. She still won't speak in class, though. I wonder if it's that she sees me as a friend now.' Clara was clutching the same steel pole, lower down.

'That's no bad thing. You're helping her. This is a massive deal.'

She nodded, but still had a feeling that she needed to do more.

'Let's have a G&T when we get back to celebrate. I think there's a cucumber in the fridge.' His eyes had that mischievous look in them that she'd grown to love, or at least, like quite a bit.

All was quiet when they got home. Anna and Netta must have gone out. They took their gin and tonics onto the small balcony to enjoy the last of the sunshine. Clara found herself having a strange out-of-body experience. On the surface everything was perfect. She had a job she loved – something she now realised she hadn't had before. She had this attractive, funny man she cared about a great deal and who seemed to be pretty keen on her. She was living in a great city, where there was always something new to do or see. And yet. There was still an 'and yet'.

'Are you any closer to making a decision?' Jake asked the next day.

Clara examined a loose piece of skin at the edge of her thumbnail. It'd been several weeks since he'd finalised his plans to meet up with his friends in South East Asia for the summer and asked Clara if she'd like to go with him. She was also getting close to the deadline for letting the school know if she wanted to renew her contract for the following academic year. They'd be happy to have her; they'd been clear about that.

The formula she devised in her spreadsheet had been inconclusive. There were equal pros and cons both for going with Jake and for staying on in Singapore for another year. In short: it hadn't helped.

'I'm not sure I can come.'

Jake said nothing for a few beats, and then, 'You can. You mean you're not sure you want to.'

'It's not that simple,' she said.

'It is, if you want it to be.'

She looked at him. His eyes were hopeful. He really believed it was that simple. 'Give me a few more days,' she said.

He shook his head slightly. 'Fine, but I'm booking flights this weekend.'

'I know. I will make a decision.'

Jess: So, this gorgeous bloke wants you to go have a summer of fun with him. What's the problem? I'd be in like Flynn. o

Clara: I don't know. I really want to feel excited about it, but somehow, I just don't. x

Jess: You're crazy. o

Clara: Jake is great, but he is ten years younger than me. Not sure I'd fit in with all his mates. What if it was a repeat of backpacking in Australia and meeting people like Todd? x

Jess: You won't know if you don't try, but it sounds like you've made up your mind anyway. o

Clara: I think I have. x

Chapter 50

March 2017

Clara and Christopher were out for lunch at their new-found favourite Indian, which happened to be a ten-minute drive from the clinic.

'So, I'm officially PUPO,' Clara said, breaking a poppadom.

'Poo - what?' Christopher asked.

'P-U-P-O. Pregnant Until Proven Otherwise.'

'I see. PUPO. Well, one day at a time.'

Clara nodded and sipped her water.

'Thing is, even if I get a positive test in two weeks, I won't be able to relax and be happy like last time. I'll be worried it could get snatched away again.'

'One day at a time,' he said again.

Clara sighed, irritated. He was right, but it wasn't that easy. Being pregnant once and losing it had changed things. It was no longer about seeing two lines on a stick. Even if she got that far, it didn't necessarily mean you got a baby at the end of it. It meant more worry and anxiety. Every trip to the toilet had the potential to end in disaster. She'd be on edge until the first scan at the clinic at seven weeks confirmed a heartbeat, then again until the twelve-week scan, when the chance of miscarriage rapidly reduces – if she got there. Perhaps she'd be able to relax after that?

It was ten months since the miscarriage. It had taken Clara that long to feel able to have another attempt. In January, with Christmas out of the way, they'd decided they'd had enough of waiting and seeing and made the decision to call the clinic and book in for a frozen transfer. They had one more embryo in the freezer from their donor. If this time didn't work, they had the option of one more try, and then, who knew? Clara consciously adjusted her posture as she dipped her poppadom in the mango chutney. She was aware her shoulders were bunched up around her ears and she needed to stay relaxed. She took some deep breaths, like she did at yoga, and felt her muscles slowly start to unknot and her posture ease into a more natural position.

'I think I might try the tarka daal,' Christopher was saying. 'Or the murgh saag. Are we sharing or having our own?'

'Whatever you like.' Clara picked up her menu and tried to focus on the words in front of her. 'You know, if it works this time, the baby would be due at Christmas.'

Christopher put down his menu. 'I thought we weren't going to get ahead of ourselves.'

'We're not, I just…never mind, it probably won't work anyway. I don't know why I'm getting my hopes up. I'll have the palak paneer, but I want pilau rice,' she added.

'You get rice, but I don't want any.'

'But I want some of your garlic naan.'

'Fine.'

'I might just get my own.'

'That's fine.'

Clara moved her glass of water to the centre of the metal coaster and used the red fabric napkin to mop up a few splashes from the table before placing it back on her lap. She surreptitiously placed her hand on her stomach and said a silent prayer to the little embryo in there. The waiter had appeared and Christopher relayed their order, complete with two naan breads and pilau rice.

'I'm going to the loo,' Clara said, pushing her chair back from the table. When she came back Christopher put his phone back in his pocket.

'Who were you texting?'

'No one.'

Clara held his gaze.

'Just Sarah from work. She was asking how it went.'

'Why does Sarah from work know anything about this? It's weird.'

'It's not weird. We work together, I see her everyday – we're bound to talk.'

'You talk to her more than you talk to me.'

'Don't be ridiculous.'

'You need to be careful.'

'Careful? Look, come on, let's enjoy our lunch and the fact that you might soon be pregnant again.'

'I thought we weren't getting ahead of ourselves.' At that moment their meals arrived and they descended into a prickly silence as they dished out their food. Christopher pushed the rice towards Clara in a passive-aggressive manner and claimed one of the naans as his own, placing the whole thing on his plate.

Clara relented on the way home. 'Let's not be like this.' Her belly was full of curry and she worried about whether it was the best thing for the embryo. What if it gave her diarrhoea and that dislodged it? 'We should be sticking together, not niggling at each other over stupid things.'

'You're right,' he said, placing his hand on her thigh. She put her hand on top of his.

'Okay, let's be nice to each other now.'

'Agreed.' Christopher's phone pinged and she instinctively glanced at the screen. **Sarah – work.** She withdrew her hand from Christopher's and looked out of the window, silent. She couldn't let her mind go there now; she had her embryo to think of. She placed a hand on her stomach and did her yoga breathing again.

Chapter 51

June 2019

'What the actual fuck?' Anna put down her glass of wine and sat up straight to get a better look.

'What?' Jake did a twirl. He was wearing fish-net stockings, suspenders and a red-and-black basque. His hairy chest was on show above the lace and he'd borrowed some of Clara's make-up to complete the look.

'He wanted to go as Rocky,' Clara said. 'This is the more modest outfit, believe it or not.'

Netta nodded appreciatively. 'Well, if anyone can pull off a pair of gold pants, it's you. Although I think you made the right call here. You make an excellent Frank N Furter.' She took in Clara's outfit. 'Clara, you're Janet, right?'

Clara pulled at the white petticoat and adjusted her crop top. 'Yes, I'm the *before* Janet.'

Jake smacked her bum. 'Before her sexual corruption.'

'Okay, you two, keep a lid on it,' Anna said, picking up her wine. 'Whose idea was this?'

'His.'

'Hers.'

They both spoke at the same time.

'You said you wanted to go to the theatre,' Clara said.

'Yeah, then you turned up with tickets to *The Rocky Horror Show.*'

'They were half price! And anyway, didn't hear you complaining. Think you're enjoying those suspenders.'

'Remind me to put my earplugs in when you get back tonight,' Anna said.

'Too right. I plan to steal Janet's innocence.'

Clara laughed and shook her head. 'Come on, we'll be late.'

'Not sure whether to have an ice cream or a glass of wine,' Clara said.

'What's wrong with both?'

They were standing at the queue for the bar area, at ease in their outfits among many other men and women in suspenders and basques. People gave each other appreciative glances, commented on the more outlandish outfits and asked each other to take photos as they posed, bending knees, dropping shoulders and pouting.

A man in a blonde wig, shiny gold pants, gold boots and nothing else, brushed past them to get to the bar. His chest and legs were completely hairless and orange-tinted with fake tan. Clara wondered if he'd waxed and tanned especially for this. Probably.

Jake nodded towards him. 'I think I made the right call.'

'Yes, the fishnets definitely work on you. You should make them part of your every day wardrobe.' They reached the bar. 'I'll have a glass of wine. Might have an ice cream at the interval.'

They got their drinks and found a table to sit at before the show started. Clara pulled her petticoat straight so it wouldn't get creased and crossed her legs. Jake sat down and crossed his legs too.

'Why are you sitting like that?'

'I feel a bit *on show.*' He gestured at his crotch area.

'I wouldn't worry about that here.' She glanced around the room. 'I think *on show* is sort of the point.'

'I bet some of these people are strait-laced as hell normally. I bet that Rocky goes to work in a suit and spends his Saturdays playing golf.'

'Rocky' was flexing his mediocre biceps and lunging to show off his legs, while the other members of his party egged him on and snapped photos on their phones.

'He's probably an investment banker.' Clara wasn't sure where that came from. There's no way Christopher would have come to *The Rocky Horror Show* with her. He'd once spent a whole evening with pursed lips during one of her work Christmas dos, when the office temp had booked a burlesque show, and the women wore nothing but nipple tassels. Jake would have been in his element. She smiled at the thought.

'What?'

'Oh, nothing. I just think we're going to have a good time tonight.'

He leant forward and kissed her. His stubble was rough against her chin.

'Oops, better stop that.' He crossed his legs the other way and adjusted his shiny black pants.

Clara shook her head and smiled as she picked up her wine glass.

The Tannoy told them the show would begin in five minutes, so they made their way to their seats.

Clara was rapt during the overture. Her shoulders started to sway to the music. The majority of the audience obviously knew the drill, shouting out and heckling the actors in the right places. By the time they got to 'The Time Warp', she and Jake were out of their seats, doing the moves with the rest of the audience, joining one homogeneous mass. Clara was sandwiched between Jake and a Riff Raff who could have actually been Richard O'Brien. He performed all the moves with an extra flourish. She edged closer to Jake to avoid getting elbowed during the 'really drives you insane' part of the song.

Jake leaned in to talk in her ear when the song was over. 'That's quite a pelvic thrust you have, Miss Ellison.'

She batted him away, smiling as they retook their seats. Riff Raff to her left was leaning forward, elbows on knees, letting out a random whoop every now and again.

After the show they collected their jackets from the cloakroom to cover up their outfits for the journey home. Walking through the streets of Singapore wearing basically underwear was probably not advisable. The weather gods were on their side; the usual humidity had eased fractionally and there was a slight breeze in the air. They decided to walk through the park.

'So, you've lost your virginity. How was it for you?' Jake asked.

She looked at him quizzically.

'You were a *Rocky Horror* virgin.'

'Oh! Wondered what you were talking about. Loved it. So much fun.'

'Still one of my favourites. We did a version with the youth group I volunteered with last year.'

'Really? How old were they?'

'Fifteen to eighteen. We made some adaptations so we didn't get complaints from parents. The kids had a ball.'

'I bet.'

They rounded a corner in the park and a sports ground came into view. Some teenagers were kicking a ball around, yelling at each other and charging about.

'I like how the kids seem to do wholesome activities here,' Clara said. 'You don't see them on street corners with bottles of cider, do you?'

'No. Might be a good place to raise kids. I'd consider living here in the future.'

Clara tensed, but as they were walking side-by-side and Jake was watching the game of football, he didn't notice.

'Do you see yourself with kids?' She forced it out, trying to sound as neutral as possible.

'Sure, some day. I want to travel more first, though. Not ready to settle in one place. Not sure I ever will be, to be honest. My dad calls me a hobo, but I prefer to think of myself as a free spirit.'

'It's good that you know what you want. I think you should do what makes you happy.'

He stopped walking and looked at her, sensing something had shifted in her tone. 'Hey, you okay?

'Yes, I'm fine.' She took his hand. She actually was fine.

They didn't have sex that night; Jake fell asleep quickly, sprawled on his back. Clara opened her laptop and her spreadsheet and started quietly tapping away. An hour later, she knew what she had to do.

Chapter 52

March 2017

'Thanks June, this looks excellent,' Christopher said, placing a paper serviette in his lap.

'I can't take the credit. I've been at yoga with Sue. Yoga nidra. We basically had a nice lie down. Nearly fell asleep. This is all Michael.' She gestured at the roast chicken, Yorkshire puddings and various pots containing different varieties of veg.

'There's two types of stuffing: sage and onion, and sausage meat and rosemary. I made the apple sauce as well, with the apples from next-door's tree.'

'Impressive.'

'They have too many of them. Barbara's made apple pies, apple strudel and apple jam. That's just in the last week. Said we're doing her a favour, taking some off her hands.'

'Well, it's delicious,' Christopher said, going back for an extra dollop.

'You're quiet, love,' June said to Clara.

Clara shrugged and pushed a piece of chicken through her gravy. She sensed her mum and dad exchanging a glance. She should really make more of an effort.

'I'm okay. I just find this the hardest time. There's nothing to do but wait.'

'Can you try to keep busy again? Do lots of nice things?' June asked.

'I went to the cinema with Jess yesterday.'

'Anything good?' Michael asked, at the same time as June said, 'What else have you got lined up?'

'Work's busy and I'm meeting Jo for lunch tomorrow, but not sure it's the best idea. She'll want to talk about her baby and she'll feel awkward about it.'

'Well, it'll be nice to get out, anyway.'

'I'm worn out, Mum. I can't sleep and I can't eat.' Clara pushed her plate away, as though to illustrate her point. 'I wish I could just hibernate for two weeks.'

Christopher shuffled uncomfortably. 'Perhaps we should talk about something else. I –'

'Thing is, it's even worse this time, because it worked last time with the donor, so there's reasonable chance it will again.'

'That's a good thing, surely,' Christopher said.

Clara glared at him and he put his head down and went back to spearing carrots. She felt a twinge in her lower abdomen. Something akin to period pain. There were four days to go until test day, meaning it could be period pain. Or it could be implantation pain. If she were pregnant, the embryo would be burrowing into the lining of her womb, right about now. She put a hand to her stomach.

June noticed. 'Are you okay, love?'

Clara nodded. 'I'm going to the toilet.'

In her parent's bathroom, among the five different types of talc and bottles of Old Spice, she tensed as she pulled down her knickers. Realistically, it was too early for her period to start, but she knew only too well anything could happen. She glanced down. Nothing. She was safe for now. The cramping in her stomach eased and she wondered if she'd really felt it at all.

'Everything okay?' June asked, as she sat back down at the table.

'Yes. *The Last Word*, Dad.'

'Sorry?'

'You asked what film we saw. It was called *The Last Word*. A comedy. It had Amanda Seyfried in it.'

'Who?'

'You know, the girl from *Mamma Mia*.'

'I do know her – very pretty. Can really carry off a one-piece swimming costume.'

'Michael!' June scolded. But it made Clara smile for the first time in a week.

Christopher scraped his plate clean and sat back in his chair. 'That was excellent, thank you.'

'Hope you saved room for pudding. Can you guess what it is?'

'Something with apples?'

'Yes!' Michael rapped a hand on the table. 'Apple turnovers. It's a Nigella recipe. We've got some cream as well. But only for people who eat all their dinner.' He nodded at Clara's plate.

'Dad, I'm thirty-five, not five,' Clara said, but she was smiling. She took another bite of Yorkshire pudding to show willing. 'You know I usually love your Sunday dinners.'

'I know, love. I'm not offended.'

'Can I take it home in a doggy bag? I might be able to squeeze in some apple turnover.'

'Course you can.'

'Sit down,' Christopher said as June started to clear the plates. 'I'll do it.' He took the plates into the kitchen and left the three of them sitting there.

'I know it's really tough, love. I'll be in this week if you want to come round after work. Or if you want to go get some tea one night.'

Clara looked at her mum's eager face and saw the worry in her eyes. Guilt gnawed at her insides.

'Thanks, Mum. I'll see how I get on.' She forced a watery smile.

'My nipples are tingling,' Clara said on the drive home.

'What does that mean?'

'It could be a pregnancy symptom.'

'Has it happened before?'

She shrugged and looked out of the window. It had happened before. It had happened during the other two-week waits, both when the result was negative and when it was positive. So basically, it meant nothing at all. She put a hand to her stomach again to see if she could feel any bloating, which, again, would mean nothing. It could be a sign of early pregnancy; it could be that her period was coming, or it could be down to apple turnover and cream. They'd decided to go into the clinic to have a blood test to get the results this time. Clara had sworn off pregnancy tests a few months after the miscarriage, as she'd developed an unhealthy relationship with them. She'd read that your body wants to get pregnant again after a miscarriage and you're at your most fertile. Even though she'd become pregnant through using an egg donor, and they'd already tried for years naturally with nothing happening, she'd grabbed hold of a piece of hope and not let go. She'd thought she'd be one of those stories everyone hears about: 'she had fertility treatment and everything, then when she least expected it, she got pregnant naturally!' No. Christopher had had to stop her going back to the bin for the fifth time to check a negative test. He'd taken it outside and put it in the dustbin. Clara hadn't told him she'd gone back to check again – dug under the potato peelings and scraped some leftover porridge off the stick just to make sure she hadn't missed a faint line. She knew then something had to give. She made a vow never to purchase another pregnancy test again. Hence the blood test on Thursday. Somehow, she thought, if she found out a different way, the result might be different. It made no sense, but rational thought had no place in the mind of a person struggling with infertility.

'Well, we'll just have to wait and see.'

Clara didn't even register that Christopher had spoken, lost in her own circling thoughts.

'I think I'm a bit bloated,' she said, pushing at her stomach.

'Like I said, let's just wait and see. Not long now.'

She didn't know in whose world four days was not long. She looked at him like he was an unsolvable mathematical equation, while he kept his eyes fixed firmly on the road.

'I think it's good that you're at work this time. It'll help keep your mind off things.'

'Yeah, because I'm so engaged with my work, I can't think of anything else while I'm there.' As soon as she finished speaking, she realised how she sounded. 'Sorry.'

He lifted his hand off the wheel in an 'It's okay' sort of gesture.

'I'm struggling this time. If we don't have a baby at the end of this, I'm not sure I can do it again.'

'One day at a time.'

'Will you STOP fucking saying that!'

He flinched and his knuckles went white on the steering wheel. He said nothing, his jaw clenched.

Clara's anger quickly morphed into despondency and then she was crying, great big heaving messy sobs.

'Oh, Christ,' he muttered under his breath. 'I'll pull over.'

They stopped in a pub car park and he hugged her and stroked her back while she sobbed herself dry. When she was hiccupping and blowing her nose, he said, 'Whatever happens, we'll figure it out.'

She nodded, though she wasn't sure they would.

'Maybe we should go on holiday again.'

She nodded again, though she wasn't sure they'd do that, either.

When they got home, she crawled into bed, even though it was only 8:30pm. Christopher stayed downstairs and watched a documentary about the Roman Empire. She slept solidly for about four hours, exhausted by the emotional outpouring. Then she woke hungry and cursed herself for not eating her roast dinner. After half an hour of tossing and turning, she padded downstairs to make some porridge. She sat at the kitchen island in semi-darkness, spooning in mouthfuls of oats and honey, without really tasting it.

Chapter 53

July 2019

YongJae handed Clara a huge bouquet of flowers. The class clapped and Clara did a curtsey to distract from the fact her eyes were brimming. It was the last day of term and Clara had finally made the decision not to renew her contract and to return home. Her flight was in a week.

'A token of our appreciation. What can we say? You know how great I think you are, but more important is what the children think.' YongJae was beaming ear to ear. 'They wanted to do something special. Meet us on the front lawn after class.'

'That sounds ominous,' Clara said 'Should I be nervous?'

'Not at all. Is there anything you'd like to say on your last day?'

'Yes.' Clara placed the flowers on the table behind her. 'I'd like to say thank you. The last year has been, quite honestly, probably the best of my life.' The sea of faces looked at her eagerly, waiting for more. She was reminded of her first day when she'd been so nervous and unsure of herself. 'I won't go into details, but I'd been through a rough time before I got here.' She chewed her bottom lip. 'I was lost, to be honest, and well…now I'm probably a little less lost. Though not necessarily any better at speeches.'

YongJae gave a small laugh.

'The best part has been getting to know each of you,' Clara went on, 'and watching you grow as individuals. You're some of the brightest kids I've ever known and, truly, it's been an absolute pleasure to teach you.' She paused there to swallow a lump in her throat. She looked at Lin, who was sitting next to Chen. She was leaning back in her chair, her forearms resting lightly on the table in front, her expression relaxed. 'Anyway, I can't wait to see what the surprise is!'

Half an hour later, Clara stepped out onto the front lawn. A huge red-and-white-checked blanket had been thrown across the grass. Trestle-tables from the classrooms had been set up under the shade of the tree and they were covered in cucumber sandwiches cut into tiny triangles, scones with jam and cream, an oversized tea-pot and a jug of what looked like Pimms.

'It's an English picnic.' Lin was by her side. No one else was in earshot, apart from Chen, but when Clara looked up, she saw YongJae had seen her speak. She was beaming at Clara.

'Wow. This is brilliant, thank you so much,' Clara said to Lin and Chen.

'There are sandwiches and all English things. We Googled what English people eat,' Chen babbled. 'Do you like jam? And cucumbers? My dad said cucumber sandwiches sound rubbish and no good like Mum's dim sum, but we wanted to get you ready for going home.'

'It's perfect,' Clara said. 'I'm so flattered that you've done all this for me.'

'There are games too,' Chen continued. 'English ones. Croakey.'

'Croakey?'

'Yes, you hit ball through a tiny tunnel, with stick. It was in *Alice in Wonderland* that you read us. The Queen of Hearts played with flamingos.'

'Croquet! I'm surprised you remember that.'

'Yes, croakey. You can teach us how to play.'

'I haven't actually ever played it, I don't think…' Clara said. 'We can learn together though, can't we?'

Chen smiled and nodded, then the girls took hold of one of her hands each and led her over to the picnic table to start loading up her plate. Jake appeared from the building. His white, short-sleeved shirt was open at the neck, revealing a few dark hairs. His tailored knee-length khaki shorts sat pleasingly on his hips, the way they did on those brochures for TM Lewin or Charles Tyrwritt that used to arrive through the door. His work look varied considerably from his casual clobber; Clara knew which she preferred. Was she crazy for leaving all this and going home to somewhere she didn't actually have a home anymore? She'd agonised over the decision and although she wasn't lying when she said the past year had probably been the happiest of her life, she also had a nagging feeling she was in limbo. This wasn't her real life. It was a welcome interlude from it, but at some point she was always going to have to return and make some big decisions. The longer she put it off, the more the nagging feeling grew.

'So, do you like your surprise?' Jake asked.

'You knew?'

He winked at her. 'Might have.'

'I like it very much. Thank you.'

'Don't thank me – the kids did it all. And anyway, it is a joint send-off.'

'Of course.'

It was Jake's last day too, and he had a couple more weeks here before flying to Laos to meet his friends from home. Then he planned to take up a new TEFL post in Chang Mai in Thailand in September.

'Chen's right, you know. These cucumber sandwiches are not as good as Mrs Wu's dim sum.' She frowned as she chewed and swallowed. 'Never did see what the fuss was about. The scones with jam and cream look amazing though, and this Pimms is going down a treat.'

Jake tapped his plastic against hers.

When the parents arrived to pick up their kids, and Clara knew in all likelihood she'd never see them again, she had to bite the edges of her tongue and swallow hard to stop the tears coming.

'Thank you. You a very special person,' Mr Wu said, taking her hand in both of his.

'It's been an absolute pleasure,' Clara said, again.

'If you ever visit, please look us up. Come for dinner.'

'I will, I promise.' Clara said. Mr Wu stepped back a few paces to give her chance to say bye to the girls. She bent down and Chen threw her arms around her neck.

'Bye, Miss. We will miss you. We got something for you.' She rummaged in her bag. 'It's Elsa.' She pulled the unicorn out and thrust is towards Clara.

'Oh no, that's your favourite. I want you to keep it.' Clara pushed the toy unicorn back. Chen looked relieved and put it back in her bag, then stepped over to her father and took his hand.

Clara turned to Lin. 'Well, I'm going to miss our art classes,' she said.

'Me, too,' Lin said. Chen and her dad were grinning at her with pride.

Clara squeezed her in a tight hug. 'You look after yourself. Remember you're a very clever girl and you can do anything you want.'

'I know,' she said, in the simple way only a child could. Then she joined her dad and sister and Clara waved them off as they got in their car and drove away.

'You could still come with me, you know,' Jake said later, when they were lying in bed. 'Change your flight.'

Clara shook her head as she traced her fingers down his chest.

'It's too late. Anyway, I'd cramp your style. Enjoy yourself with your friends.'

'Cramp my style? Are you crazy? Hatters would love you, and Jobby would too.'

'Wait, you have a friend called *Jobby*?' She raised her head to look at him.

'Yeah, Paul Jobson. Why?'

'You know "Jobby" means poo, right?'

'No, it doesn't!'

'Well, it did at my school.'

'Ha, I'll tell him you said that. Anyway, I was trying to get you to change your mind.' He lifted her hand from his chest and kissed her fingertips.

'I can't,' she said again. 'The flights are all booked. I have to go home.'

'I don't see why you have to.'

She sighed. 'We've been through this. I know you don't understand, but I don't know how else to explain. I need to go live the rest of my life.'

'And what do you think you're doing now?'

'I'm figuring out what I need to do.'

'So, I've been a convenient little hobby before you go back to your "real life".' He raised his hands to do air quotes. She sat up, perturbed by the change in mood. This wasn't like him.

'No, of course not. I like you a lot. It's not been an easy decision to make.'

'Right, not easy, but solvable with a spreadsheet. Did you use a formula to decide if you should sleep with me in the first place? A column for yes and a column for no?'

Clara reached for her cotton dressing-gown, which was draped over the bed-post, and pulled it round her shoulders. 'That's not fair.'

He paused a moment to think. 'Shit, sorry.' He rubbed a hand over his face. 'I didn't mean it. I'm just gutted you're going home.'

'I'm gutted too. But I do have to.'

He nodded, resigned. 'Okay, well let's not waste time fighting.' He kissed her on the lips this time and gently eased the dressing-gown from her shoulders.

Chapter 54

April 2017

'What do you mean it's inconclusive?' Clara dug her fingernails into her palm as she tried to process what the nurse was saying. Were they just dreaming up new ways to torture her?

'The blood test picked up some HCG, but much lower levels than we'd expect to see at this stage in a pregnancy.'

'What does that mean exactly?'

'We'll repeat the test in two days and we'll have a clearer idea then.'

'No, what? *Two days*? I can't wait two days. Today is the day we find out. Am I pregnant or not?'

'As I said, it's inconclusive.'

'But if there's some HCG, I must be pregnant?'

'It's an indication, yes, but we'd expect your levels to be higher. I know it's difficult, but we should know for sure in a couple of days.'

She knows it's difficult? I don't think she does, otherwise she wouldn't be saying 'a couple of days' so lightly, like it was nothing. Like the last two weeks hadn't felt like a thousand years. Clara didn't have any careful plans for the next two days; today was the day she found out – yes or no.

'We'll know soon,' Christopher said, taking her hand. Clara glared at him. He should know better; he should understand the agony, which was now being prolonged. He was siding with the nurse, or at least, putting social niceties ahead of her need to know what the hell was going on. Of course, her vow never to buy another test went out of the window. Thankfully, she hadn't told Christopher, so he didn't flinch when she said they needed to stop at Asda on the way back. The first thing she did when she got home was wee on the stick. The very thing she'd insisted she couldn't face doing. There was the faintest of faintest second lines, if you squinted and held it in the right light. Christopher saw it too, but didn't approve of her 'obsessing'.

Clara shut herself in the bedroom, alone with her phone. She took a photo of the test and posted it on Instagram. Faint second line – BFP?? (She'd become au fait with the lingo. BFP = Big Fat Positive). Responses started to pour in.

I see the line! Congratulations *smiley face*
It's faint, but it's defo there! *three pink love hearts*
Looks like it to me, yay!!!

She should have been reassured, but she'd purposefully left out key information so she'd get the response she wanted. She was eleven days post-transfer, which put her at sixteen days post-conception, given the frozen embryo was five days old. Any infertility warrior would know that you'd expect to see a much darker line on a pregnancy test at this point. So, it was as the nurse said – inconclusive. Clara knew, without the clinic or any anonymous online buddies telling her, it was most likely a chemical pregnancy, or very early miscarriage. She turned her phone off, crawled under the covers and fell asleep, exhausted.

She woke only to force down some soup that Christopher had brought her, then fell back into a fitful sleep, sheets twisted between sweaty legs, eyes crusty from crying. She dreamt of lines on tests and swollen bellies, her dreams making her wake with a jolt and place her hand on her stomach, then reach for the test on her bedside table and shine the light from her phone on it to see the faint line again. At 6am, exhausted from her torment, she swung her legs over the side of the bed and walked to the bathroom. She took out a new test and closed the door. One line. Then after five minutes, the tiniest trace of a second line that you really could only see if you held it at the right angle and blurred your eyes a little. This wasn't right. She was supposed to wait forty-eight hours, as the HCG levels would have doubled in a healthy pregnancy, but she knew. If this was a healthy pregnancy she'd be seeing dark lines. She took the new test and yesterday's test downstairs with her and placed them on the kitchen island as she made strong coffee. She drank the coffee, then put her head in her arms and wept. The loud, snotty, no-holds-barred kind, tears streaming and dropping onto the shiny marble surface.

'There you are,' Christopher said, padding into the kitchen in his dressing-gown a few hours later. Clara had been consoling herself with messages from her online friends after posting a photo of the two tests side-by-side, with the times and dates written on them – the full story this time.

Some weren't letting her give up hope.

Maybe your wee was more diluted for the second test? (It wasn't, she'd done it first thing in the morning.)

You're not out until Aunt Flo shows! (online talk for period)

Remember PUPO!

Others were more realistic and accepting of the situation.

So sorry hun, lots of love xxx #infertilitysucks

Oh, that's so unfair, so sorry xxx #fuckinfertility

Crying face sending hugs xxxxx

Christopher stood next to her and put an awkward hand on her shoulder. 'How did you sleep?'

Clara looked at him, eyes smudged with yesterday's mascara, dried tears on her cheeks, hair a bird's nest from the constant tossing and turning. 'Great,' she said.

'We might get good news tomorrow.'

She almost envied his naivety. 'We won't get good news.' She showed him the two tests.

'Why are you doing more tests? Let's see what they say at the clinic tomorrow.'

She laughed bitterly. 'You can see what they say. I *know* what they'll say – "Sorry, you're not pregnant, but hey, you nearly were, so why not try again?"'

'We'll wait and see, then deal with it when we have more answers.' He moved away from her to put the kettle on and rummaged in the cupboard for the porridge. 'You want some?' He held it up. In that moment, she detested him. How could he be asking if she wanted porridge like it was any other morning? She left the room without answering. She needed to get away from him and his well-rested face and his fucking porridge.

'I'm sorry, Clara – your HCG levels have fallen. Your level is now four and it was twenty-five. We'd expect to see numbers in the thousands in a healthy pregnancy.'

She nodded stiffly. The nurse wasn't telling her anything she didn't already know. The third and indisputably negative test she'd done that morning had dispelled any last shred of hope she'd had. Christopher's face fell and Clara pitied him. He hadn't believed her. He'd only believe the nurse. 'You have one more frozen embryo. It's encouraging. You got pregnant once and very nearly a second time. It's most likely the embryo attached briefly, but then came away. That's why you had low levels of the pregnancy hormone in your system.'

Nobody said anything.

'It's a lot to take in,' the nurse continued into the heavy silence. 'I suggest you take some time, then get in touch and let us know what you want to do next.' Just like that, they were cast out onto the cold pavement, bereft. Empty arms, empty womb, empty heart. Empty.

Chapter 55

July 2019

Clara sat on her backpack to inch the two halves of the zip closer together. She'd ditched her guidebooks and several pairs of worn-out shorts along the way, but somehow it was still a struggle to squeeze all of her belongings into the bag. She shifted her weight and managed to align the zip so it fastened. Relieved, she lent the backpack against the wall and looked around the room that'd been home for the past year.

She felt almost the same sense of trepidation at going home as she'd felt about setting off almost eighteen months ago. Was she going home a different person? Had she come to terms with the events that led her here? She wasn't sure, but a seed of an idea had been germinating in her mind for the last few weeks. She hadn't talked to anyone about it, but it had helped swing the decision to go home.

There was a gentle tap at the door. Anna poked her head in 'Good to go, dude?' She opened the door and looked at the empty room.

Clara nodded.

'The taxi is here.' Anna held her arms open to Clara. 'Mate, it's been an absolute blast,' she said, as she squeezed her. 'Don't forget me.'

'Never,' Clara said. 'You'll be back in the UK soon enough and we'll meet up.' Anna and Netta were going home too, but taking the scenic route back with a trekking trip in Nepal, then Interrailing through Europe, before getting back in time for the start of the new academic year, so Anna could go back to teaching at her old school.

'Get a room, you two.' Jake grinned as he came in and hoisted Clara's bag onto his shoulder. 'Jesus, what have you got in here?'

Clara didn't respond. She let go of Anna, giving her hand a last squeeze, and followed Jake out to the taxi. 'Say bye to Netta again for me,' she said over her shoulder as they left. They climbed into the taxi and Anna stood and waved at the door until she couldn't see them any more.

Clara was quiet as she watched the scenery roll by. Jake had his hand on her knee. It was making her leg sweaty, but she didn't ask him to move it. He was making idle chit-chat with the driver about a recent basketball match and Clara was grateful she didn't need to join in. She rested her head against the headrest and put her hand on top of Jake's.

The hustle-bustle of the departures terminal was a welcome relief after the quiet of the empty room she'd left behind. People were moving about with purpose: bags to check in, queues to join, boards to check. Clara's own flight, direct to Manchester, was happily on time. They followed the hordes of people towards the queues for the check-in gates. Clara felt something tapping at her leg. She looked down and saw a young girl with dark hair. For a moment she thought it was Lin, but this girl was younger, probably about five or six.

'I'm lost,' she said, brown eyes clouded with worry. 'I don't know where Mummy and Daddy are.'

'Okay, don't worry. We'll help you find them,' Clara said, bending down to her level. The girl nodded.

'Over there,' Jake said. 'Customer services. They should be able to do an announcement.'

'What's your name?' Clara asked the girl.

'Sophie.'

Clara smiled to herself. 'Okay, Sophie. We're going to find your mummy and daddy.' She held out her hand and the little girl took it.

Two Tannoy announcements, ten minutes and four rounds of spot the difference in Sophie's activity book later, her grateful parents arrived at the customer services desk.

'Thank you so much,' the girl's mum said, after she'd finished kissing, cuddling and berating Sophie for wandering off. 'I turn my back for one minute...!'

'Oh, don't worry,' Clara said. 'I know what they're like. I'm glad we could help.'

Jake was watching her with an expression she couldn't quite figure out as the reunited family disappeared back into the throng.

'What?' she asked.

'Nothing. I just...I know you wanted kids. If it's any consolation, I think you'd be a natural.'

Clara was taken aback. They hadn't discussed it since that time in the bar in Chinatown, when they'd first been getting to know each other. It had become a sort of unspoken agreement that it was a no-go area. She didn't say anything now.

'Come on, let's get you checked in.'

They walked together to the check-in gates and Jake hung back as she went up to the counter and heaved her backpack onto the belt. As she watched it disappear, she thought back to another airport, eighteen months ago, when she'd dithered with her coffee cup and struggled to get the bag on her back. She'd been full of nerves, excitement and disbelief at how her life was panning out. The disbelief had gone, but she still had the nerves and maybe even a touch of excitement about what could come next.

'Shall we get a coffee before you go through security and I have to leave you?'

Clara checked her watch. 'Yes. We have time.'

They sat opposite each other at an overpriced Starbucks. They were wedged between a Chinese a family of four and an elderly couple. The parents in the family both had books open on their laps and the two kids stared at screens and slurped milkshakes through straws. The elderly couple were engrossed in a conversation about the best type of raised planter to get for their decking.

'I'm going to miss you,' he said.

Clara felt self-conscious that there were so many people around who could easily listen in.

'You'll have a great time with your friends.'

'Yeah, I will. But I'll still miss you.'

To her dismay, she felt her eyes brim with tears.

'Come here,' he said, and led her off to a quieter area.

'I'm sorry,' she said. 'Sorry for not coming with you. It's just not the right thing for me. But I have loved spending this time with you. If I were ten years younger, or you were ten years older, maybe things would have been different –' She stopped and wiped at her eyes.

'Hey, it's going to be okay, you know.' He kissed a tear off her cheek.

'I know,' she said, and for the first time, she actually believed it might be.

Chapter 56

May 2017

The counsellor's hair was looking even more unruly than usual. She had the top section pulled back from her face with a bright blue scrunchie; the rest fell about her shoulders in a cloud of wiry brown and grey. Clara wondered if she should recommend a good hair-smoothing serum to her. She was wearing a beige jumper which did nothing for her skin tone.

'How are you feeling about it?' she was saying.

Clara zoned back in. 'Pretty bad, to be honest.'

Caroline pushed the box of tissues towards her. It was another new box. Nothing offensive – it had a picture of a boat on it. Clara wasn't crying, so she didn't take one.

When it became clear Caroline wasn't going to say anything else, she said, 'I feel empty, drained of all emotion.'

Caroline nodded and wrote something on her pad.

'I don't have the energy to try again. I'm done.'

'That's a brave decision to make and one I can help you with. But I would say, give yourself time to grieve and to heal before making any big decisions.'

It was the most Clara had ever heard her say in one go. She looked towards the window. It was closed today. She could see into an office block opposite – people sitting at their desks, drinking coffee and getting on with their lives. It struck her as odd that things just went on. People carried on doing what they do, the sun rose and set, and all the while her life was in tatters.

'How is Christopher?'

Clara snorted.

Caroline did her best neutral look.

'Things are not great between us,' Clara admitted. But then found she didn't want to go into this any further. She couldn't say, 'We're hardly speaking. He spends most of his time confiding in another woman and I've never felt more alone'. Despite everything, and depsite the fact that Caroline was a professional, she still had some pride, and she couldn't bear to be pitied. Instead, she moved the conversation away from the topic.

'I'm not sure I'm ready to talk about everything yet. I think I need some time by myself to process everything and decide what's next.' She smoothed out a wrinkle in her skirt. 'Do you mind if I…if we…call it a day for now? I'll make another appointment for a few weeks.'

Caroline smiled but Clara thought she caught disappointment in her eyes. 'Of course. Call reception when you're ready and they'll book you back in. Take good care, Clara.'

That was the last time Clara saw her.

The day after Clara's session with Caroline, she and Christopher visited Jess and Dave.

'Tea?' Jess shouted from her kitchen.

'Please,' Christopher said, moving a giant stuffed elephant from the settee so Clara could sit down. Amelie was laying on her tummy on the floor doing some colouring in. Christopher sat on the floor next to her.

'Do you want a hand?' Clara called through to Jess.

'No, no, make yourselves comfy,' she called back. Clara settled herself on the settee as Dave appeared in his boxers, towel around his neck.

'Mr and Mrs Davis, hello!' he said, unfazed.

Jess appeared with two steaming mugs. 'Dave! Put some clothes on.' She looked around for somewhere to put the tea, expertly clearing the coffee table of toys with her foot. She placed the mugs down, seemingly oblivious to the new mess on the carpet. 'Clara and Christopher don't need to see you naked.'

'Why, are you threatened by my manly prowess?' He winked at Christopher and puffed out his man boobs. He'd obviously got comfortable since becoming a dad.

Jess threw her slipper at him. 'Go! Get dressed!' she said. Then muttered, 'For God's sake,' as he left the room. 'Sorry about that.' She eased herself down next to Clara, one hand supporting her swollen belly. She dislodged a piece of Duplo from under her thigh and tossed it onto the pile of toys on the floor. 'How are you doing?'

'Oh, fine. Well, not so good, actually.' Christopher glanced up at her from his position on the floor. He wasn't comfortable talking about what he considered 'private matters'.

Jess nodded sympathetically.

'What are you drawing?' Christopher asked Amelie. It was a series of scribbles in different colours as far as Clara could see.

'A mermaid.' She looked at him as if to say 'duh, can't you tell?'

'Of course it is,' Christopher said. 'Is this her tail?'

'No, that's her hair.'

'So, any ideas what you want to do next?' Jess asked Clara.

'Mummy!' Amelie jumped up from the floor. 'Where is my blue crayon?'

'I don't know, darling. Is it in the bucket?' Jess nodded towards a large blue bucket for building sandcastles at the beach, which was overflowing with crayons, pieces of paper covered in scribbles and various plastic figures.

'Noooo!' she wailed. Christopher looked alarmed at the sudden change in mood.

'Ugh, let me have a look.' Jess placed a hand on the side of the settee, ready to wrench herself from her seated position and waddle over to the bucket.

'Let me help,' Christopher said, gesturing for her to sit. He started searching through. 'Here it is!' He held up a blue crayon triumphantly.

'Noooo!' Amelie wailed again, decibel levels increasing. 'I meant the light blue one!'

'Amelie, do you want to go to your room?' Jess said in a warning tone.

The girl shrieked and Clara winced. She had to stop herself covering her ears.

Amelie stamped her foot. 'I *need* the blue crayon.'

'Well, that's not how we get what we want, is it?' Jess said. 'And we don't stamp our feet. I'll help you look if you stop shouting.'

Amelie stuck out her bottom lip and started crying. 'Sorry, Mummy.' She threw herself at Jess with such force she was thrown back against the settee.

'Okay, darling.' She shushed her and stroked her hair.

Dave reappeared, thankfully fully dressed in jogging bottoms and a hoody. 'What's going on in here?' he said.

'A drama about a crayon,' Jess replied. 'Why don't you play with Daddy for a bit?'

'Wanna ride a horse?' Dave said, and dropped to all fours. Amelie jumped on his back and he crawled around the room making neighing noises, while she giggled with delight.

'So, you were saying?' Jess prompted, trying to pick up the threads of their conversation.

Clara was aware of Christopher listening and had a pang for the days when it'd be her and Jess in a bar, glasses of wine in their hands, no interruptions from rambunctious children, and no feeling judged by your husband.

'Oh, you know. I'm okay, getting on with things.'

Jess nodded, as if waiting for her to say more.

'Mummy!' Amelie wailed again. 'I banged my leg. Owwwwww!' She climbed back onto Jess's lap, tears and snot streaming down her face. Clara felt like a creature from another planet as she watched Jess soothe her child. Not for the first time, she wondered why she wanted what Jess had so badly, but a bigger part of her ached. Ached to be needed, to have her own child interrupt her conversations with friends, to be part of this club.

'Do you feel better for seeing Jess?' Christopher asked on the way home.

'Are you serious? I hardly talked to her. Between Amelie and you, it was impossible.'

'Bit of a handful, isn't she? Wait, what do you mean me?' he said.

'I don't feel like I can talk freely. I feel like you don't want me to tell her anything.'

'You can tell her anything you need to, to feel better.'

'I can't be better, just like that,' she snapped.

'I know, I know. Maybe you should go for a drink together.'

'She's seven months pregnant!'

'Well, a coffee then, I don't know.' Christopher stopped at a red light. He sighed and looked down at the steering wheel. Clara noticed some fine lines around his mouth. He looked older. She probably did too.

'It's good to have you back.' Clara's manager stood up from his desk, signalling the conversation was over.

'Thanks. I'm glad to be back.' It wasn't exactly a lie. Clara was sick of moping around the house. She left his office and sat down at her desk. Her plant had died. She'd water it later and see if it could be revived. She picked up the photo of her and Christopher on their wedding day – big smiles and shining eyes, they had everything in front of them then. If she'd known exactly what was in front of them, she wouldn't have been smiling so much.

'Hey, Clara! Welcome back.' It was her colleague, Janet, the office busybody.

'Thanks.'

'Are you feeling better now?'

'Yes, thanks.'

Janet hovered, no doubt waiting for more information on what had ailed her. When she realised none was forthcoming, she said, 'Well, you look well,' and carried on the direction of the kitchen, mug in hand.

Clara connected up her laptop and sighed as she saw her overflowing inbox. A message dropped in at the top from Christopher. She clicked on it.

Christopher: Hope your first day back goes well. I'll probably be late home tonight, don't wait to eat dinner. x

Great.

Another one from Jess.

Jess: Hope today isn't too painful! Fancy lunch? o

Clara brightened at that one.

She typed a reply.

Clara: Yes! Wagamama at 1pm?

Only four hours to go. She reluctantly started on her work emails, making her way from the top down.

'So, how are you really?' Jess asked at lunch time, dipping her chicken into her katsu curry sauce.

'I'm lost,' Clara said truthfully. 'I don't know who I am any more.'

Jess paused, fork halfway to her mouth. 'But you're going to try again?'

'I don't know. What's the point? I'd be trying again for a baby that's half some woman's I've never met and half a husband's I don't even know if I like any more.'

'Wow, okay. Is it too early for wine?'

Clara shrugged.

'We'll have a large glass of Pinot Grigio over here.' Jess said, signalling the waitress. She smoothed her napkin on her lap. 'Just sorry I can't join you. So, tell me everything.'

'You already know everything. I'm just wrung out, I'm…done.' As Clara spoke the words out loud, she knew it was true.

'Done with IVF?'

'With everything.' She took a grateful sip of her wine.

'Everything?'

'IVF, my marriage.'

Jess's eyebrows shot up. 'Woah….Really?'

'He's having an affair.'

'Christopher?! No way.'

'Well, I don't know, but he's always with Sarah from work. He's seeing her tonight.'

'He's told you that?'

'No. He said he'll be late home, but he'll be going out with her.'

'How do you know?'

'She's always texting him and ringing him. He says it's about work, but I've heard him talking to her about the baby stuff. He talks to her more than he talks to me.'

'Oh, Clar.'

'I know, everything's gone to shit.' Clara shuffled the noodles around her plate forlornly, then reached for another sip of wine. She looked at her oldest friend. Her cheeks were fuller than they once were and she looked tired, but she also looked vibrant. Her belly strained against her pink wrap-dress; she was absent-mindedly resting a hand on it as she ate her lunch. Everything was right in her world. Clara felt grey and two-dimensional next to her. Those two young girls who'd grown up together had ended up in different worlds. Physically they were sitting opposite each other, but there was an invisible barrier between them. They could look into each other's world and think 'that looks nice', or 'I'm glad that's not happening to me', but they couldn't understand any more. Not really. And despite everything else Clara had been through, it was that, that was the undoing of her.

'I'm sorry, I've got to go,' she said, pushing her chair back and putting some money on the table.

'What? Where are you going?' Jess was trying to get up from the bench, but Clara was already halfway to the door. She saw her sit back down and rest her chin on her hand, defeated.

She didn't go back to work, she went home. Then she did something. Something she'd never done before and never thought she would. She logged into Christopher's Facebook account. She knew his password; they'd never had anything to hide from each other. There was a string of messages between him and Sarah.

Christopher: It didn't work, she's not pregnant.

Sarah: I'm sorry, do you want to come round again after work? xxx

Christopher: Yes.

Sarah: I'll get a bottle of wine.

Christopher: We might need two.

Christopher: I'll bring them. And I'll cook.

Clara felt sick. She kept reading.

Sarah: What will you tell Clara?

Christopher: Just that I'm working late again. She never speaks to me anyway.

Sarah: *sad face*

Christopher: Don't be sad. I have enough of that at home.

Clara ran to the sink and vomited. She turned on the tap and rinsed out her mouth, then stood there until her breathing slowed. She logged out of Facebook and closed the laptop. She didn't need to see anymore. She rang her mum and told her she was coming round. Twenty minutes later, she was sitting on the settee at her mum and dad's, cup of tea in hand.

'I'll get the biscuits,' her mum said.

'This is going to take more than biscuits to sort out.' Clara was almost laughing at the absurdity of it. 'I'm not pregnant, my husband would rather spend his time with another woman and I couldn't care less about my job. What else is there?'

'You have us, love.' Her mum patted her hand.

'I know, but what about my own life? I'm thirty-six. It wasn't supposed to be like this.' Clara was strangely calm, as though she'd used up her allocation of emotions for the year – for a lifetime, probably.

'I don't think "supposed to be" is always that helpful.'

'You're right, Mum. Fuck it. I'm going to do something drastic.' She picked up a biscuit. 'Sorry for swearing,' she added.

'I'll let you off this time.' Her mum smiled, as though she knew something Clara didn't.

Chapter 57

July 2019

As soon as Clara left the airport, she was aware that the air was different. It was much colder, yes, but it also smelt different: a familiar combination of trees and leaves, exhaust fumes, wet tarmac and – well, cold. It was a welcoming smell and she relished the freshness of the breeze as she shivered. She was home.

'Clar! Over here,' a familiar voice shouted.

'Jess!' Clara jogged as much as she could with her backpack on and flung her arms around her friend.

'Ah, it's so good to see you!' Jess said, breathing in as she held her.

'Wait, did you just smell my hair? Weirdo!' Clara laughed.

'I totally didn't just smell your hair, but it wouldn't be that weird if I did. I missed you.'

'I missed you too. Where are the kids?'

'Dave's mum's. For *two nights*!' Jess grinned like a Cheshire Cat. 'So, I was thinking, we dump your bags at mine, go for drinks and an early dinner, then more drinks and –' She slowed seeing Clara's expression.

'I'm kind of knackered after the long-haul flight,' Clara said. 'Where's Dave?'

'He's out with the football lads. Maybe we could get a pizza and have a bottle of wine? Get our PJs on early?'

'That sounds amazing.' Clara smiled and breathed a sigh of relief.

'Great. We can catch up on the last eighteen months. I want to know all about Jake.'

'We're not together any more,' Clara said.

'I know, but he's gorgeous and *young* and I've only had sex with Dave for the last twenty years. I want to live vicariously.'

Clara laughed. 'Oh, please don't ever change. It's so good to see you.'

They made their way back to Jess's car and, before long, Clara was safely installed in Jess and Dave's spare room. She'd unpacked just enough of her stuff to find clean pyjamas and she'd borrowed some of Jess's slippers and a dressing-gown.

'Wine,' Jess said, handing her a glass of red. 'You look amazing, by the way. All chilled out. And where did those boobs come from?'

'Oh yeah, I've put on a bit of weight.'

'It suits you.'

'Thanks. Ooh, that's good,' Clara said, taking a sip of Malbec. 'I've missed being cosy. The rain is actually nice.'

Jess pulled a face. 'I'm sure, after all that horrible sunshine. That tan is outrageous, by the way.'

Clara laughed. 'You mentioned pizza?'

'Right, right.' Jess picked up her phone. 'Double pepperoni? Garlic dip?'

Clara nodded. 'Perfect.'

They settled on Jess's settee while they waited for the delivery. Her living room had been tidied up and the toys were all stacked away in a corner. Clara sat cross-legged, glass of wine resting on one of her knees as she faced Jess.

'So, tell me everything,' Jess said. 'Start with Jake. No, wait. Start with Christopher. I can't believe he flew out just to see you!'

'Well, he flew out for work, but yes, he did admit it was partly to see me.'

'Were you pissed off?'

'I was at first, but when he explained himself, I felt sad for him and I understood.'

'Really?' Jess looked dubious.

'Yes. He said he wanted "closure".' Clara put her glass down so she could air quote.

Jess pulled a face. 'I think he closed things off all by himself.'

'Maybe. But now I've had a bit of perspective, I don't actually think it was all his fault.'

'Of course it was his fault. He had an affair.'

'Yes, but before that. I didn't speak to him about anything. It was like it was all happening to me, when actually it was happening to him too.'

'Hmm.'

'He's been seeing a therapist.'

'You're kidding! Christopher? Who'd have thunked it.'

'I know, weird. He said he had some sort of breakdown after I'd gone. He never really dealt with losing James, you know. Having your brother die so young doesn't really leave you. And then when he couldn't be a dad…'

'Shit, yeah.'

'You're not going back to him, though?'

'No, of course not. He's with Sarah, anyway. And just, no.'

Jess did her satisfied nod.

The doorbell rang. Pizza.

'So, what's your big plan, now you're back?' Jess asked, wiping garlic mayonnaise from her lip.

'I don't have one. Not a fully thought out one, anyway.'

'You don't have one? You've changed.' Jess narrowed her eyes at her. 'What have you done with the old Clara, lover of spreadsheets and five and ten-year plans?'

Clara smiled. 'I've realised planning doesn't always work and sometimes the best things happen when they're not part of a plan.'

'That's deep.'

'There's always a place for a spreadsheet, though, and one thing I do need to plan is where to live.'

'You know you're welcome here as long as you like,' Jess said.

'I know, but come on. Me, you, Dave and two kids – I'd be getting under your feet in days.'

'Never.'

'I'll start looking at places to rent, while I figure out what I'm doing.'

'You're okay for money though, aren't you?'

'Oh, yes. I've still got the money from my half of the house when Christopher bought me out. I'll buy somewhere, but not yet.'

Jess nodded thoughtfully as she helped herself to another slice of pepperoni. 'I'll help you look. It'll be fun. Now, tell me all about Jake.'

The next morning Clara went out to the estate agent's and arranged to view three flats to rent. Then she went to Paperchase to buy some new stationery, while conceding she hadn't completely abandoned her love of planning. If a new notebook with a swirly blue-and-purple pattern on the front couldn't help her sort out the rest of her life, nothing could. Next she went to the supermarket to get supplies to cook dinner for Jess, as a thank you for letting her stay.

***

Three weeks later

Clara hung up the last of her clothes in her new wardrobe and tucked the empty suitcase at the back of it, out of sight. Next to it was a pink box tied with a ribbon. She hesitated, then lifted it out and sat down on the bed. She eased the top off and pulled out a tiny cream Babygro with grey rabbits. The fabric was soft against her cheek and it absorbed her tears into its fibres.

'Goodbye, Sophie,' she whispered. 'I won't forget you.'

She carefully placed the Babygro back in the wardrobe on the top shelf, where it wouldn't get crushed. After she'd dried her eyes, the word *acceptance* sprung to mind.

Perhaps that's what it had all been about. The break-up, 'The Big Trip', Jake, coming home. A journey to acceptance.

She padded downstairs and flicked the kettle on. There was a letter on the doormat between the leaflets for takeaway pizzas and a flyer about God's Kingdom from the Jehovah's Witnesses. It was in a white envelope and had been forwarded on from her parents' address. Clara sat down at her kitchen table and opened it. Two folded up pieces of paper were inside. She opened the first.

Dear Clara
We trust you have good trip home to England. We write to thank you from the bottom of our hearts for the work you did with our girl. Lin is different person since you. She never stop talking about you and has named one of her dolls, Clara. Most important, she is able to speak a little outside of the home. She continues to get help, but has turned corner, and we believe this is down to you. You have a precious gift, we hope you continue to use for good.
Mrs Wu wanted me to enclose spring rolls, but I told her they would go bad. I am enclosing a letter from Lin instead.
Yours,
Mr and Mrs Wu

Dear Clara
Thank you for being my favourite teacher. I love our lessons the most. I used to not like speaking when not in my home, but now it's not so scary all the time. I miss you. Our new teacher visited at summer school and she smells funny but is okay. I hope you are happy in England.
Lin xxx

Tucked behind the letter was a photo of Lin and Chen, heads together, grinning at the camera. Lin had lost her front teeth and had a gappy grin. Clara smiled and held the letter to her chest, then went to stick it on the fridge next to the picture Lin had drawn of her and Jake.

She took the out milk and went back to the counter to pour it into the tea. Her new flat had a view down to the river, which she could see while standing at the kitchen sink. There was a family walking along the riverbank. Two kids wearing wellies were carrying fishing nets, dipping them in the river, then holding them up expectantly. From what she could see, the nets were coming up empty. It wasn't long before the older girl splashed the boy by accident and he started crying. The mum crouched to give them both a cuddle and they carried on with their walk.

Clara carried her mug of tea and a stack of biscuits through to the living room. The sun was streaming in through the window and there were dust particles floating in the air. The sunlight had made a warm patch on the settee. She sat down in the warmth and tucked her legs underneath her, then turned on her laptop, opened a new search tab, and typed:

Teacher-training qualification

She spent a good hour reading course descriptions, entry requirements and fee information. She made notes in the new notebook with the swirly pattern.

Then she made a fresh cup of tea, turned to a clean page in her notebook, took a deep breath and typed:

Adopting as a single parent.

Thanks and acknowledgements

There are many people I'd like to thank for helping me to write this book, some helped in big ways, some in small. All greatly appreciated.

Here goes.

Thanks to my husband for being supportive of my writing. For helping me to take myself seriously and do things I never thought I could. And on a practical level, for recognising writing is something I need to do and for looking after the children to give me time to get on with it. You're not bad, as husband's go.

To my good friend and fellow author, Rebecca Ryan for being a constant source of support. For sharing the highs and lows and reading and critiquing early drafts. And later drafts. And blurbs. And synopses. And general musings. I honestly don't think I'd still be churning out books without you as my writing buddy. Thanks just doesn't cover it.

To Mark Connors for the early edit and for helping me make the leap from essentially publishing my personal diary, to fiction writing. This book wouldn't exist without your encouragement, constructive feedback and many Saturday mornings and Monday nights at novel class. It's been a blast. My sincere thanks.

To all the friends who've been along for the ride on Mark's novel class; Gill Lambert, Debi Lyons, Phil Batman, Amy Garbett, Jackie Taylor, Jane Cameron, Faye Kenny-Broom and Debi Lewis. And Rebecca Ryan, who totally deserves the double mention. Thank you for listening to early drafts, for giving me a confidence boost when I needed it and for your honesty and ideas.

My editor, Helena Fairfax for your endless wisdom in all things writing. For pushing me to make my work better even when it means some painful changes and for polishing this manuscript until it shone.

My Aunty Lesley for the very comprehensive proof read complete with colour coded post its. And Laura Stewart and Debi Lyons for subsequent proof reads. If there are any typos still loitering in the pages of this edition, it's on all of you ;-)

To Kerry Jordan, my cover designer for your exceptional design skills and for understanding my books as well as I do. I did a little dance when I first saw the cover. Thank you.

To Fertility Network UK, not only for your ongoing support with my books, but for the work you do every day, making life just a little less lonely for those struggling with infertility.

My sister for listening to my endless writing chatter, for reading several drafts without complaint. Thanks for your quiet wisdom, shrewd observations and for always noticing those pesky missing commas. You really are the best sister.

My mum for reading all my drafts and telling me my work was as good as the 'actual book' you were reading. And for trying to hold a conversation about plot twists and character development with my two small kids jumping on you. Thank you.

My dad, who sadly passed away last year. Thank you for being you and for always telling me things would turn out okay in the end. They did. And Dad, if they have books wherever you are, maybe skip the chapter with the sex scene.

Finally, thanks to my children, big and the smalls for brightening my days and for constantly throwing obstacles in the way of my writing, but without whom I'd struggle to find the drive to do it anyway. Love you all infinitely.

If you enjoyed this book, I'd be ever so grateful if you'd give me an honest star rating and review on Amazon.

I love to hear from readers. You can email me at toriday@mail-me.com, find me on Instagram @ToriDayWarrior, Twitter @ToriDayWrites or visit my blog www.toridayblog.wordpress.com.

Check out my first book, Warrior. This one is very personal to me, as it documents my own personal infertility journey.

Warrior

Ever had to leave the room when someone announces their pregnancy?

Ever felt like weeing on sticks is your only hobby?

Wondered if you're losing your mind?

Then this book is for you.

Tori takes us with her on her roller coaster journey to conceive. She documents the highs and lows with complete candour, striking self-awareness and a sense of humour. Hope prevails throughout the crushing monthly disappointment, the medical appointments, the setbacks and the waiting. Oh, the waiting.

Full of tears, laughter and told with love.

Thanks for reading

Love Tori x

Printed in Great Britain
by Amazon